ORACLE LAKE

Also by Paul Adam

Unholy Trinity

Shadow Chasers

Genesis II

The Rainaldi Quartet

ORACLE LAKE

Paul Adam

Thomas Dunne Books
St. Martin's Minotaur New York

THOMAS DUNNE BOOKS.
An imprint of St. Martin's Press.

ORACLE LAKE. Copyright © 2003 by Paul Adam. All rights reserved. Printed in the United States of America. No part of this book may be used or reproduced in any manner whatsoever without written permission except in the case of brief quotations embodied in critical articles or reviews. For information, address St. Martin's Press, 175 Fifth Avenue, New York, N.Y. 10010.

www.thomasdunnebooks.com
www.minotaurbooks.com

Library of Congress Cataloging-in-Publication Data

Adam, Paul, 1958–
    [Flash point]
    Oracle lake / Paul Adam.—1st U.S. ed.
        p. cm.
    ISBN-13: 978-0-312-37025-1
    ISBN-10: 0-312-37025-3
    1. Reincarnate lamas—China—Tibet—Fiction.   2. Dalai lamas—Fiction.
3. Tibet (China)—Fiction.   I. Title.

PR6051.D3156 F57 2007
823'.92—dc22

                                                              2007011057

First published in Great Britain under the title *Flash Point* by
Little, Brown, an imprint of Time Warner Books UK

First U.S. Edition: July 2007

10 9 8 7 6 5 4 3 2 1

The Dalai Lama is an individual, and even the institution of the Dalai Lama came into being at a certain stage of Tibet's history. In the future it may disappear, but the Tibetan nation will always remain.

The Dalai Lama, 1985

You see, a nation is dying. My strength comes from the justice of my cause, and I think from my compassion, but I need help. Not just with a few nice words, but with some kind of action.

The Dalai Lama, 1996

PROLOGUE

McLeod Ganj, India

There was a scent of death in the air. Not a tangible odour, but something more subtle, more insistently pervasive. Tsering could sense it all around him, seeping in through his nostrils, his eyes and ears, even his skin. The atmosphere, despite the brilliant sunshine bathing the slopes of the mountains, was heavy with gloom. The breeze which gusted up incessantly from the valley was, for once, strangely absent. No birds sang, the scraps of bread left out on the table in the garden were untouched. The only sign of life was a distant speck in the sky, a white-bellied vulture circling ominously over the high peaks. A stillness of despair enfolded the shabby collection of buildings clinging precariously to the hillside, stifling everyone in the vicinity with its desolate embrace.

Tsering made his way slowly up the path from the monastery. At his side, struggling against the steep incline, was the stooped, elderly figure of Pasang Rinpoche. Every few paces they paused for the Rinpoche to draw breath, his laboured wheezing marking time like the rhythmic chanting of the monks they could still hear below them in the courtyard of the *gompa*. Then they walked on, Tsering holding the Rinpoche's arm, almost dragging him up the steps to the terrace outside the green-roofed bungalow.

The uniformed security guard, a sub-machine-gun slung casually across his chest, nodded them through the entrance without a word. Inside it was quiet. Abnormally quiet. Footsteps sounded down the hallway, a door opened releasing a brief snatch of muffled conversation before clicking gently shut again. There was no one about. The chatter, the hectic bustle of activity that normally filled the building were gone, replaced by an anxious, unnerving silence. Above all, one man's presence was missing. One man's voice, his distinctive throaty laugh that infected all it touched with a joyous warmth. It had been missing for two days now. With a sense of foreboding that turned him cold, Tsering realised it would never return.

A middle-aged man in the maroon and yellow robes of a monk came out of a room and waited for them. Tsering followed Pasang Rinpoche down the hall, no longer holding his arm but walking a few paces behind him, showing the respect due to an incarnate lama.

Pasang Rinpoche stopped outside the room.

'How is he?' he asked softly.

'There has been no change,' the monk replied. 'Go in, the doctor is just finishing.'

The monk pushed open the door to allow Pasang Rinpoche to enter. Tsering caught a glimpse of the unconscious figure in the bed before the door closed again, shutting him out. He felt a stab of sorrow. He was a Buddhist. He knew that death was an inescapable reality of *samsara*, the relentless cycle of life and death and rebirth from which only enlightenment could bring release. He meditated on death every day. Knowing he could not avoid it, he did not worry about it. He knew with absolute certainty that he would be reborn and looked on death simply as changing bodies, much as one might change clothes when they became old and worn out. But that acceptance of death did not mean he was immune from grief. He was human. His faith could not erase the emotions that made him human. When the figure in the bed slipped from the world, Tsering would feel happiness for the passing of his spirit but sadness for the loss of the man.

Retracing his footsteps down the hall, he went out into the garden. He wanted to escape the oppressive clutch of the bungalow, feel the heat of the sun on his face. The lawn had been recently mowed. Tsering slipped off his sandals and stepped on to the turf. It was cool, soft beneath his feet. He dug in his toes, pressing himself down into the lush grass, imagining his body taking root in the earth, drawing strength from it.

He tried to clear his mind, stripping away the coarser layers of consciousness to find the pure emptiness underneath. It was something he'd trained for years to perfect, but today he could not do it. Today, the serenity of the void was to be denied him.

Gazing out over the garden, beyond the flowers and the shrubs to the wooded hillside that descended to the valley floor, he became aware that his vision was distorted by tears. The world was out of focus, just a blur of light and moving shadows. He felt as if he were in limbo, all time and sensation arrested as he waited for His Holiness the Fourteenth Dalai Lama of Tibet to die.

San Vicente Province, Southern Colombia

The village was below them in a shallow valley. It was a small settlement, no more than ten or twelve wooden huts clustered around a central square. Smoke trickled from a few chimneys, drifting lazily in the hot still air before dispersing over the rooftops. On the near side, the jungle smothered the hillside, thinning out a little as it reached the bottom of the slope, but beyond the village the land was cultivated. A small lake of uniform green vegetation stretched into the distance, lapping the edges of the valley: coca bushes.

The patrol moved off down the track, the *commandante*, Pablo, leading the way. As they reached the base of the hill, the village less than a hundred metres away, the *commandante* stopped and held up a hand. Something was wrong; Maggie sensed it too. The village was too quiet, no sounds of voices, of dogs barking, of children playing. Pablo gave a signal and the guerrillas spread out, approaching the huts from different directions. Maggie had her camera on her shoulder, the 'record' button on, the lens focused on Pablo and his second-in-command, Mercedes, as they moved cautiously across the open ground that surrounded the village.

At the first of the huts, Pablo paused, his AK-47 levelled, and pushed open the door with his foot. There was no one inside. Hanging back a few paces, Maggie caught a whiff of woodsmoke, of tortillas baking. Her hands were sticky on the camera, her heart beating so hard she wondered if she could keep the picture steady. Pablo nodded at Mercedes and they split up, taking opposite sides of the track as it made a dogleg around another hut. This time Mercedes pushed open the door. Again the hut was deserted. Mercedes glanced at Pablo, her face taut, her eyes flickering nervously along the track. Pablo gestured discreetly with a finger. Mercedes stepped behind the hut, circling round to the other side. Maggie stayed with Pablo, following him around the corner.

In the central square they found the bodies.

They lay in the dust where they'd fallen. Men, women and children, sprawled on their backs, on their sides, their clothes and faces spattered with blood.

Pablo saw them first. He stopped abruptly, ducking back instinctively into the shelter of a hut. He waved urgently at Maggie but she'd already taken cover behind him. The *commandante* looked out, scanning the square, the huts on the other side and the jungle-clad slopes that curved around behind the village. He waited a few moments, then crept slowly out, the AK-47 at shoulder level now, sweeping in an arc as he moved across the square. The other guerrillas were emerging into the open. Maggie edged out, filming the group from a distance as they converged on the centre of the square. She zoomed the lens in, close enough to make out the faces of the dead, to see their eyes and mouths gaping wide. She felt sick, felt the bile rising in her throat. She'd seen bodies before, too many bodies, but she'd never lost the sensation of horror, the gut-churning nausea the sight always brought. And she'd never lost the sense of personal repugnance, of sordid voyeurism she felt as she recorded the images for the benefit of a distant audience who couldn't have cared less about the victims.

Pablo crouched down beside one of the bodies, a man whose face had been almost blown away by the exit wound of a gunshot to the back of the head. He touched the man's arm. The skin was still warm. *Madre de Dios*. Pablo glanced up in alarm, raising his rifle and straightening up at the same time. He shouted a warning, but too late. The hail of bullets caught him across the chest. Mercedes, standing next to him, was cut down in the same salvo, her body reeling and crumpling to the ground. The other guerrillas opened fire, shooting blindly at their hidden assailants. Then they ran for cover. But they were mown down before they reached the edge of the square.

Lying in the dirt where she'd thrown herself after the first murderous onslaught, Maggie scrambled to her feet and scuttled away, diving behind the nearest hut and pressing herself to the wall, her body heaving with panic. The door to the hut was next to her. She pushed it open and went inside. One of the windows overlooked the square. Maggie crawled across and cocked an eye over the wooden sill. The guerrillas were all down. Maggie counted them. Eight bodies.

She pulled away and leaned back against the wall, her legs stretched out on the floor in front of her. She took a few deep breaths, wondering if she was going to throw up. Her stomach was turning over, her chest so constricted each gasp for air was painful. Had the gunmen, whoever they were, seen her? She'd kept back near the edge of the square. Maybe they hadn't. She knew she should get out; get away from the village and into the jungle. But she didn't know exactly where the gunmen were. Perhaps she'd be safer staying put.

She knelt up again and risked another look out of the window. A group of armed men was emerging into the square. They were wearing uniform but Maggie couldn't make out the insignia. She picked up her camera and held it so the lens was just poking over the windowsill. Pressing the 'record' button, she crouched out of sight, watching the men in the tiny monitor on the side of the camera. They were walking across to the bodies of the guerrillas, prodding them with their boots. One of the bodies twitched. The gunman in the lead – a tall man with a face like a stripped skull – took out his pistol and administered a *coup de grâce*, then calmly lit up a cigarette.

Maggie zoomed in, getting a closer look at the men. They weren't Colombian Army, she was sure of that. Shit! That made them paramilitaries, one of the right-wing death squads that roamed this part of the country, swooping in to hit the FARC guerrillas on their home territory before retreating to the Government-controlled areas to the north and east. She was in trouble. She ejected the tape from her camera, sealed it hurriedly in a protective plastic wrapper and stuffed it down the front of her trousers. She inserted a fresh cassette into the camera and walked across to the door. Easing it open, she peered out. The track seemed clear. She didn't hesitate, flitting across to the next hut and concealing herself behind it. She could no longer see the square, but she could hear the para-militaries talking and laughing. Another hundred metres and she'd be in the jungle. She moved back on to the track, taking the corner at a fast jog.

She ran straight into him. A paramilitary coming in from the other side of the village. He was as surprised as she was. For a second he just stared at her, then his sub-machine-gun jerked up. Maggie cradled her camera under her left arm and threw her right arm in the air.

'*Periodista*,' she cried. '*Periodista americana.*'

She was sure he was going to shoot her.

'Journalist,' she repeated in Spanish. 'American journalist.'

The paramilitary gaped at her uncertainly. He licked his lips, frowning. Maggie held his eyes, trying to stop herself shaking. Her legs felt as if they were going to give way underneath her. Then the barrel of the sub-machine-gun dropped an inch or two. She exhaled with relief. The paramilitary gestured with his head. *Move!* Maggie turned and walked back down the track.

They confiscated her camera and put her in one of the huts

by the square. The tall man with the skull face, who seemed to be in charge, strolled in behind her, sub-machine-gun dangling barrel-down from his shoulder, a smouldering cigarette in his hand. He sat down in a chair and looked her over with hard, pitiless eyes, lingering a while on her damp T-shirt tight over her breasts. Maggie knew what he was thinking. Her brain was racing, running over her options. She'd been in difficult situations before. There was always a way to handle them.

'What the hell do you think you're doing?' she said indignantly in English.

Try to get them on the defensive. Put doubts in their minds. Above all, never let yourself be a victim.

'You speak English?' Maggie demanded. 'I'm a journalist. *Periodista*. I want my camera back.'

Skull Face inclined his head, sucking on his cigarette.

'You're American?' he said in accented English.

'Yes.'

'You came with those FARC scum out there?'

'Yes.'

'You're not American, you're a Brit.'

Another voice this time, coming from behind her. Maggie turned her head. A figure came forward out of the shadows. He was wearing military fatigues but not carrying a weapon. His blond hair was cropped short, the skin of his face and neck turning pink in the sun. Unmistakably American.

'Does it matter?' Maggie said.

'Maybe. Who're you working for?'

'CBS,' Maggie lied.

'On your own?'

'No, the reporter, my producer are back over the hill. They couldn't keep pace with the patrol.'

'But you could?'

The American perched himself on the edge of the table and looked at her directly.

'Yes,' Maggie said without flinching.

He looked at her a while longer, then turned to the camera on the table next to him. He picked it up and examined it.

'A nice piece,' he said appreciatively.

He studied the controls and ejected the tape cassette, then slipped the cassette into the pocket of his tunic.

'You got any more tapes?' he asked.

'Some spares in the bag.'

'You doing a story on FARC?'

'For the evening news.'

'Giving them the oxygen of publicity. You know those people are terrorists, drug dealers, kidnappers?'

'It's a legitimate story.'

'The fuck it is.'

'There's a civil war going on down here.'

'Oh yeah, and whose side are you on?'

'I don't take sides, I take pictures.'

The American rested a hand on his knee, his leg swinging gently over the edge of the table. Maggie tried to recall how many of these crew-cutted 'advisers' she'd encountered around the world. Almost every troublespot she'd been in, there was one somewhere in the background. Quiet, unobtrusive men who'd left their morality behind with Uncle Sam when they packed their kitbags.

'Is that right?' he said reflectively. 'You know how many people FARC have killed? Not just here, but in the US. I mean the kids in Cleveland and LA they kill with the cocaine they traffic. You've seen the bushes out there. These people are making big money.'

'The way I hear it, the Colombian Government and your friends here are making even more.'

'Bullshit! They're trying to clean this country up, free it from the scourge of drugs.'

'You get that out of some manual they gave you at the Pentagon?'

The American pushed himself off the table and took a step towards her, his finger jabbing in her face like a gun.

'Let's get something straight. We're the good guys here. I'm sick of media people like you distorting the truth.'

'You want to go on camera?' Maggie said. 'Go on the record

and give me an interview. I'm sure the American public would love to know exactly what you're doing down here.'

'No one in the US gives a fuck about what's happening down here.'

'Maybe that's the problem.'

'No, maybe people like you are the problem. Are you a pinko, or just another tight-assed anti-American Brit?'

'I love the Americans. It's self-righteous hypocrites I can't stand.'

It was a rash thing to say. The American glared at her, his eyes bulging with anger. Maggie regretted the comment immediately. In her present position the American was probably her only hope. Skull Face certainly didn't look like a man who would worry too much about the US media.

'Look, just give me my camera and I'll get back to the rest of my crew,' Maggie said.

'Ah yes, your crew.'

The American studied her closely. Maggie could sense he didn't believe her.

'Yeah, and I'll have that tape back too.'

She was pushing it. But she had to act as if she didn't know what they were going to do to her.

'Like you said, this is a war zone,' the American replied. 'I'll have to have the tape checked by the military censor. We wouldn't want anyone to get the wrong idea, now would we?'

'No, of course not.'

'What happened here today, well, it happened. In a war you get skirmishes, people die.'

Maggie didn't say anything. What was he trying to do, convince her, or just himself? She knew what had happened was no skirmish. The FARC guerrillas could look after themselves, but the villagers had been herded into the square and executed in cold blood.

The American glanced at Skull Face and gave a slight nod.

'We'll escort you back up the hill.'

Maggie followed them out into the square, trying to guess how they'd do it. She was too dangerous to let go.

The peasants and guerrillas they could leave to rot, but they'd be careful with her. She was a Western journalist. They'd take no chances. The Americans were their paymasters, they wouldn't want anyone finding her body.

Here in the square? she wondered. Probably not. The jungle was better. Make her walk. It would save them having to carry her afterwards.

Skull Face called over two of his men and said something inaudible in Spanish. Maggie looked around the square. The sun was high in the sky, burning the air and the dust on the ground. Flies crawled over the bodies of the peasants and the guerrillas, huge black clumps of insects throbbing and buzzing across the exposed flesh. She wiped the moisture off her forehead with the back of her hand. She could smell her own sweat, feel her heart pounding. But she was quite calm, her senses alert, watching for the right opportunity.

They gave her back her camera and the two paramilitaries accompanied her up the track, one in front, one behind. Maggie attempted to talk to them in her halting Spanish, a delaying tactic to distract them from their orders, but they just grunted and ignored her. She'd already sized them up. They were peasant boys in uniform, none too bright. She wondered how long she had, how far away from the village they deemed it necessary to take her. As the path neared the brow of the low hill, she made her move. Doubling over suddenly, she gripped her stomach and began to moan softly. The paramilitary in the lead glanced round. Maggie winced and stumbled to a halt.

'*Qué pasa*?' the paramilitary asked sharply.

Maggie groaned. 'It hurts here. I need the toilet,' she replied in Spanish.

Giving him no time to object, she handed him her camera – to get rid of the burden and to reassure him she was coming back – and pushed past him, fumbling with the belt of her trousers.

'*Cinco minutos*,' she said, parting the undergrowth and disappearing into the jungle.

The ground sloped up over the crest of the hill, then dropped away steeply on the other side. Maggie pushed aside the bushes, picking her way through the thick vegetation. Within moments the two paramilitaries were out of sight. She increased her speed, trying to make as little sound as possible. Fifty metres in, she started to run, ripping aside the fronds and branches, plunging recklessly down the hillside. She heard a shout, knew they were coming after her.

Suddenly, she lost her footing. Her legs slid away beneath her and she tumbled down the slope, crashing through the undergrowth. Thirty, forty metres she rolled before, clawing at the ground with her hands, she managed to slow her descent. She clambered to her feet, winded and bruised but no worse, and staggered on. There was a burst of automatic gunfire in the distance, but they were shooting indiscriminately. The bullets came nowhere near her. Maggie estimated how far behind her the paramilitaries were. One, maybe two hundred metres. Not far, but perhaps enough in a dark, impenetrable wilderness like this.

She maintained her rash pace; she couldn't afford not to. The earth was loose, covered in a thin layer of leaves and debris that was as slippery as ice. Three or four times more she overbalanced and careered wildly down the hill. Her arms and face were striated with scratches, the deeper wounds oozing blood. She heard the sound of rushing water ahead and burst out through a thick wall of shrubs to find herself on the top of a low cliff. Below her, a narrow river foamed and surged through a tight gorge, boiling over submerged rocks before rushing away down a series of cascades. Maggie paused, whooping for air. The drop to the river wasn't far. Twelve, fifteen feet at most. But the torrent was hazardous, threatening. She looked around hurriedly for an alternative. Downstream the terrain was impassable, a sheer wall of rock dripping with moss and trailing creepers. Upstream was easier but it was the wrong direction. She didn't have much choice. Taking a deep breath, she jumped.

ONE

Maggie spent half her life in the distant outposts of the globe, but only when she returned to London did she really feel as if she were in the Third World.

Her connecting flight from New York touched down at Heathrow at 7.30 am. By 8.15 she'd collected her baggage, passed through Customs and was waiting on the platform of the Piccadilly Line for a train into central London. At 8.45 she was still waiting. At nine o'clock, after yet another garbled, incomprehensible apology over the PA system, a train finally arrived and sat in the station for another ten minutes before – crammed to bursting point – it pulled out.

An hour and a half later, the stench of closely packed, perspiring human flesh still clinging to her nostrils, Maggie emerged into the dull light of day. It was overcast, a slow, intermittent drizzle dripping from the leaden sky: typical English weather, too gutless to make up its mind what to do. She waited twenty minutes for her bus, shivering in the damp, penetrating cold, then sat for a further hour as the double-decker negotiated the congested streets at a pace that would have shamed a Calcutta rickshaw.

By the time she reached her home it was the early afternoon. It had taken her almost as long to get from Heathrow to south London as it had from America to England. And she didn't even get to watch a film. There were holes in the pavement outside her flat and inside, sandwiched between the brown envelopes and junk mail, a card from Thames Water saying her water would be cut off for the day for 'essential work on the mains'. The thought of a hot, lingering bath and a pot of tea was all that had kept her going through the travails of the morning. Now she could have neither.

'Sod it!' Maggie said with feeling, dumping her bags in the hall and going through into the kitchen.

She poured herself a shot of Laphroaig, sipping the whisky slowly, the rough, peaty flavour erasing the taste of travel in her mouth. Then she sorted through her mail: electricity, gas and phone bills which always seemed to be lying in wait for her when she came home; the usual offers of loans and credit cards from organisations she'd never heard of; a statement from her bank that made depressing reading and a letter from her branch manager, Mr J.S. Campbell, explaining why he found it even more depressing than she did, and how he was going to have to charge her an exorbitant sum to alleviate his distress. Maggie kept up a regular, if a touch hostile, correspondence with Mr Campbell. It was a comforting thought while she was enduring some distant hell-hole that one of his cheery missives would inevitably be there, lurking on the doormat, when she finally made it back to London.

She checked her answering service next. She'd already called from New York before she left, but there was one new message that had come in just that morning. She listened to it playing back and stiffened.

It was a man's voice, a foreign voice imbued with the timbre of the Indian sub-continent.

'This is Kapil. The ocean is draining away fast. Only days to go. Get here before it is too late,' it said.

Maggie listened to the message a second time to make sure she'd heard it correctly. Then she finished her glass of whisky, slipped her wet coat back on and went out. She didn't bother with the bus this time. The hell with the expense, she took a taxi into central London.

David Ackland was in a meeting when she got to the offices of WNSA, near Covent Garden. Maggie scrounged a cup of tea off his secretary and made herself comfortable in a leather armchair in his office. She'd waited in worse places. The chair was deep and soft, the lighting subdued, the tea – a rather subtle Darjeeling, she noted – hot and wet which was all she asked. The room had the clean, state-of-the-art, high-tech, cutting-edge bullshit feel favoured by television companies: lots of tinted glass and stainless steel, a huge desk devoid of anything except computer and mouse, and a thick cream carpet which looked as if it needed mowing twice a week. It was strange, she reflected, how the poverty WNSA always pleaded in relation to its freelance fees seemed to evaporate when it came to its office furnishings.

'Maggie, good to see you again. You been waiting long?'

David Ackland breezed in and tossed a pile of papers down on to his desk. He was a slim, well-groomed man in his early forties, his appearance assiduously nurtured by an hour in the gym every morning before work and regular visits to the fleshpots of Gstaad and Tuscany. He took off his linen jacket and draped it carefully over the back of his chair before sitting down.

'You look awful, Maggie.'

'Thanks. That's just what a girl likes to hear.'

'You know what I mean. I didn't expect you back in so soon. I thought you'd take some time off. Maybe have a holiday.'

Maggie tried to remember when she'd last had a break of any length. Five, six years ago, maybe. She'd spent three weeks in a Russian army detention cell, picked up as she tried to get out of Groszny, but most people wouldn't count that as a holiday.

'You went through a bloody tough time out there in Colombia,' Ackland said. 'I wouldn't have wanted to be in your shoes. No *waaay*.'

Maggie took that as a compliment even though Ackland's idea of hardship was probably missing his morning *latte* at the espresso bar across the street.

'I'm okay,' she said.

She still had the scratches and the bruises, but she was used to that. After escaping from the jungle she'd gone back to Bogota and filed her story. Her tape had been syndicated across the world. She'd even done a couple of pieces on camera for WNSA and the American networks – her fifteen minutes of fame. The media had run with the story for a couple of days, then lost interest and moved on, seeking new sensations to satisfy their voracious, but fickle, appetites. As the crew-cutted 'adviser' had commented, no one in America – or any other developed country for that matter – gave a damn what happened in South America. Dead Colombians, like the truth, were simply more unmourned casualties in yet another dirty, irrelevant little war. It made Maggie angry, but she'd learned to live with her anger. The only way to cope with a job like hers was to care, but not care too much.

'We haven't heard any more from the agencies in Colombia,' Ackland said. 'No one's found the bodies.'

'The paramilitaries will have made sure they were disposed of,' Maggie replied. 'They don't want to leave that kind of evidence lying around. But it will happen again. That war is going to run and run.'

'You think so? Even with the Americans getting involved?'

'The Americans will make it worse. They're getting themselves into another Vietnam down there.'

'What if they hit the guerrillas hard?'

Maggie shook her head. 'The civil war's been going on for nearly forty years. FARC are one of the best-equipped guerrilla armies I've ever seen, and I've seen a few. They're not going to throw down their weapons just because Washington sends a few advisers to Bogota.'

'What about the billions of dollars for the fight against drugs?'

Maggie gave a cynical snort. 'Come on, David. You know the Colombian Government has no interest in stopping the cocaine trade. It's far too lucrative. The guys at the top will take the Americans' money, build themselves a new swimming pool, buy their mistresses a country house and carry on as usual. The Americans are naïve to think otherwise.'

Ackland leaned back in his chair and looked at her. 'So

what do you want to do next? You interested in going back to Afghanistan? You know the country, the politics. We could use you there.'

'I had more than enough of Afghanistan last time. But there's something else. I want to go to India.'

'Oh yeah?'

She waited until she had his full attention. 'The Dalai Lama is dying.'

Ackland took a moment to respond. 'We haven't heard anything. Nothing on the wires. Are you sure?'

'I was in McLeod Ganj a few years back. For Channel 4. A colour piece on the Dalai Lama's sixty-fifth birthday, getting his pension, his bus pass, all that kind of crap. I cultivated a contact close to the Tibetan Government in exile. You never know when these things will pay off. Well, I got a phone message from him this morning.'

Maggie repeated Kapil's words.

Ackland gazed at her sceptically. '"The ocean is draining away fast." Is that some kind of code?'

'Dalai Lama means "Ocean of Wisdom". I thought you knew that.'

'Sure, I'm an expert on Tibetan etymology.'

'It was a title bestowed by Altan Khan back in the sixteenth century. Dalai is a corruption of the Mongolian *ta-le*, meaning ocean.'

'Fascinating,' Ackland said. Then he pursed his lips as if he were assessing an indifferent claret. 'You trust this contact?'

'He's reliable.'

'Can you call him back and get more information?'

'This is India. He's not on the phone. He probably made the call from a post office or a hotel, somewhere like that. It's a big story, David. We could be first with it. The only agency with a camera on the spot when it happens.'

Ackland sucked on a knuckle, staring pensively into space for a time. Maggie knew he was calculating the syndication revenues, doing the rough arithmetic in his head.

'What do you plan to do?' he asked.

'Get over there and wait. If Kapil's right, it'll only be a few days.'

'Okay. We'll take what you get.'

'I'll need a new camera.'

'Camera?'

'Yeah. Mine's somewhere in the middle of the Colombian jungle.'

'It was insured, wasn't it?'

'Of course. But I won't get the money back for months. I'll need to hire one.'

'How much do you need?'

'Five grand should cover it.'

'That's on the high side.'

'Come on, David. You must have made a killing with my Colombian tape.'

'I'll give you three thousand for equipment hire. I want receipts. All offset against your fee. The usual terms.'

Maggie grimaced. These commissioning editors, it was amazing how they could screw you without even leaving their desks.

'Okay,' she said. 'But I want cash. I'll get a better deal that way.'

And hang on to more of it, she thought. A cheque would simply disappear into the bottomless pit of her overdraft.

'I can't get cash before the morning,' Ackland said.

'That's fine. I'll pick it up tomorrow.'

Maggie had always found it apposite that the traditional heart of the British film industry should be in Soho, that seedy, unprepossessing enclave of peep-shows and 'erotic' revues where brassy whores and grasping pimps plied their sordid trade – one or two of them not even producers.

She'd been in similar districts all over the world, but there was something particularly drab and furtive about Soho: the blacked-out sex shop windows promising more than they could ever deliver, the pushy touts outside the porn theatres, the pathetic pasty-faced middle-aged men drifting around the litter-strewn streets. It was all so tame and repressed and utterly joyless.

Turning on to Berwick Street, Maggie almost bumped into a swaying tramp, one hand clutching what looked like a bottle of Scrumpy, who was urinating on the pavement whilst a group of Japanese tourists watched open-mouthed. She sidestepped the scene, skirting a pile of black bin liners dumped in the gutter spewing rubbish, and kept walking. The air was ripe with the smell of the street market – squashed fruit, fish heads, cabbage leaves and mouldy cardboard boxes rotting by the kerb. The walls of the surrounding buildings were smeared with graffiti and a palimpsest of cheap fly posters while up above on ledges and windowsills scrawny pigeons sat motionless like window cleaners' dirty rags.

Maggie turned down a side street and stopped outside a shop with a heavy steel grid bolted over the front window. Beyond the glass was a haphazard display of film and video equipment. Maggie went through the door. The inside was brightly lit, the walls papered with glossy posters for Sony, JVC, Kodak, Fuji, Aaton, Panavision. A pimply youth in a black T-shirt glanced up from the boxes he was unpacking.

'Hi.'

'Is Mac in?' Maggie asked.

'I'll get him. Can I give a name?'

'Maggie Walsh.'

The youth disappeared through a door at the back of the shop. Maggie drifted across to one of the glass display cabinets and studied the camcorders inside it. They were getting smaller, more sophisticated by the month. Soon every home video enthusiast could be a Kubrick or a Spielberg.

'Maggie, how're you doing?'

Maggie turned. Chris MacIntyre was framed in the doorway, tie undone, shirt sleeves rolled up.

'Come on through. You want a drink?'

'No, thanks.'

Maggie followed MacIntyre into the office.

'What happened to Kenny?' she asked, jerking her head towards the pimply youth out in the shop.

'Got a job in a post-production house. Barry's been with me a few months now. But then it's been a while since you were in.'

'I've been away.'

MacIntyre smiled at her. Maggie saw the affection in his eyes and hoped it was nothing more. All that was over long ago as far as she was concerned.

'You know how it is,' she said.

'Yes, I know how it is.' MacIntyre's expression was wry, maybe a little regretful. 'So what can I do for you?'

'I need a camera.'

'I thought you already had a camera.'

'I lost it in Colombia.'

'Careless. You were still making payments, weren't you?'

Maggie nodded. 'About ten grand outstanding, I think.'

'Nearer fifteen.'

'Is it? Well, what's a few thousand between friends? You'll get the money, Mac. In full. Just as soon as the insurance pays out. Trust me.'

'Now where have I heard that before?' MacIntyre said ruefully. 'You looking to buy, or hire?'

'I'd been thinking of hiring, but on reflection I might be better off with something small and light. Not too obtrusive. I was looking at the camcorders outside.'

'You doing a long piece, documentary, or just a few clips for the news?'

'Probably just a short news item.'

'I've got just the thing. New Sony mini-DV. Broadcast quality, Zeiss lens, optical zoom, XLR audio inputs, menu-selectable 16:9 aspect ratio framing guide, variable electronic shutter, the works. I'll show you.'

He led her out into the shop, unlocked the display cabinet and took out a small silvery camcorder.

'Feel the weight,' he said, passing it to Maggie.

She studied the camcorder. She'd used one before on

several occasions. They were useful if you wanted to look like a tourist, film secretly where professional photography would have been either forbidden or too dangerous.

'How much?' she said.

'Three-seven-fifty, but I can let you have it for . . . say, three-two-fifty.'

'That's too much.'

'How much do you want to spend? Yeah, I know, as little as possible.'

'What else have you got?'

'For less? They're not as good. That's not just sales talk. That's straight up.'

'Show me anyway.'

He took out more camcorders and talked her through the specifications of each. Maggie let him go on, though the technical details of a camera had never interested her much. She just wanted to know if it could do the job.

'You want to think about it?' MacIntyre said when he'd finished.

'The Sony,' Maggie said. 'I'll give you two-five. Half in cash.'

'Two-five? You realise what that does to my margin?'

'You'll still make a profit. You think I don't know the mark-up on these things?'

'Two in cash, the rest cheque.'

'Okay, if you throw in a couple of spare batteries and a battery charger. Oh, and did I mention a portable, battery-powered lamp?'

MacIntyre sighed and shook his head wearily. 'Jesus, Maggie, have you got Sicilian blood, or what? Okay, you've got a deal. You want to do the paperwork now? Come back in the office.'

Maggie watched him as he filled in the sales sheet at his desk. She wasn't sure what she'd seen in him, when was it? Three years ago? She couldn't remember. Just before East Timor, she thought. That was the only way she kept track of time, gauging her whereabouts, the messy details of her private life, by whatever conflict she happened to be covering. Mac was a nice guy. Good-looking, okay body, a bit thin but then she didn't go for overmuscled men. Not the greatest conversationalist in the world. He liked facts, was a real bore when it came to anything mechanical – cameras, cars, computers, he knew how they were all put together and liked to tell you. But he was sweet, dependable, pretty good in bed. He just wasn't her type. She didn't know what her type was. Maybe she didn't have one. Maybe no one really did, they just learned to compromise.

MacIntyre passed the sheet across for Maggie to check.

'Can you give me a second receipt?' Maggie asked. 'For the full list price. Just to keep Ackland happy.'

'You still ducking and diving?' MacIntyre said. 'Aren't you tired of all this yet? Why don't you get a staff job somewhere? Get an easier life.'

'Can you see me at the BBC or ITN, sitting around on my backside all day, running up a drinks' bill? I know those guys. The reporters don't want to go more than an hour's ride from the nearest five-star hotel. The first sign of trouble they're on the first plane out.'

MacIntyre scribbled out another receipt.

'Put the batteries and charger on at list. And a box of spare tapes as well, will you?' Maggie said.

MacIntyre shook his head, a mixture of disapproval and admiration. 'Anything else?'

'That'll do. I'll bring the money in tomorrow. Pick up the gear.'

'Whenever.' He was looking at her. 'We're closing up soon. You want to go for a drink?'

'I'm not sure that's a good idea, Mac.'

'I'm over it, you know.'

'You got someone?'

He nodded. 'Works for Kodak, just down the road.'

'Serious?'

'I don't know. Maybe.'

'That's nice, Mac. I'm glad for you. Yeah, I'd like a drink.'

They went to a pub near Leicester Square. Walking down through Soho, dodging the traffic, the crowds on the streets, was an ordeal for Maggie. The noise, the stink of exhaust fumes, the frenetic activity disturbed her equilibrium. Less than a week ago she'd been in the Colombian jungle, on her own, struggling to survive. Now she was back in civilisation, on familiar territory, she should have felt at ease, but it all seemed strangely unreal. Every time she came back she felt the same way.

A few drinks and a couple of cigarettes relaxed her. MacIntyre was easy company. He didn't force himself on you, he was content to let things take their course, peacefully sipping his pint of bitter, talking if you wanted to, remaining quiet if you didn't. That was one of the things Maggie liked about him. He wasn't scared of silence.

It always took her a while to adjust to people. To people leading normal, comfortable lives. So much of her time was spent in places where comfort was unknown and normality was fear and violence and deprivation. In her early, naïve days she'd believed the pockets of bloodshed and suffering around the world were isolated, exceptional instances, but now she knew it was life in Britain, in the West, that was the aberration. She came back, tried to adapt, and for a short while returned to her old life. Seeing friends – those few with whom she still kept in contact – going to the cinema, the pub. But each time it got harder. The parochial, self-satisfied indulgence of the developed world disgusted her. The greed, the complacency, the smug superiority. She found it more and more difficult to fit in, to cope with the closed eyes and minds around her and with the guilt she felt at being able to come back to affluence and security – to walk away and forget what she'd seen – when the people she'd left behind had no such opportunity.

'You want to go for dinner?' MacIntyre asked as the pub started to get more crowded, the noise level rising so that it was hard to make themselves heard. 'You look as if you could do with a decent meal.'

Why were men always passing comment on her appearance? Maggie wondered irritably. First Ackland, now MacIntyre. But there was some truth in the remark. She knew she'd lost weight, was starting to look gaunt. Eating was never one of her priorities when she was working. She lived on coffee and cigarettes. The thought of a proper meal, a bottle of wine, was appealing.

'You have somewhere in mind?'

'What about Vinnie's?'

Maggie wasn't sure. They'd gone there regularly when they were together. The place aroused associations, memories she didn't think it wise to revive. But the food was good, and it was quiet; well away from the rowdy tourist havens of central London.

'Why not?' she said.

They took a cab to the restaurant and had pasta and chicken and zabaglioni and too much Chianti. Then they walked back through the dark streets to MacIntyre's flat, Maggie knowing what was going to happen, sober enough to make the decision, drunk enough not to care about the consequences.

MacIntyre made coffee and they made a pretence at small talk, impatient to move on.

'You want me to call you a cab?' MacIntyre asked eventually, going through the motions.

Maggie shook her head. She couldn't face going back to the cold solitude of her flat. She'd been away, on and off, for months. There were pressures that built up, that needed a release before they exploded.

She kissed him, tasting the wine, the garlic. His hands slid over her body. Warm, familiar, urgent.

Maggie broke away for a moment. She didn't want to mislead him.

'I'm leaving for India tomorrow,' she said.

MacIntyre held her gaze. 'You'll always be leaving for somewhere, Maggie.'

TWO

For more than forty years, McLeod Ganj had been the home of the Tibetan community in exile. This small settlement, perched on a ridge high above the Kangra Valley, had been built as a hill garrison by the British in the 1860s. Vestiges of their presence could still be seen in the curious bungalows scattered over the steep slopes and in the Anglican church of St John's in the Wilderness whose quaint, rustic belfry emerged shyly from the treetops, a tiny bit of rural England transposed to the foothills of the Himalayas.

The Dalai Lama had arrived here in 1960, almost a century after the British, to find a dilapidated ghost town rotting away in the damp, overgrown forest. Pandit Nehru had chosen it on the commendable grounds that it was virtually uninhabited, remote and mountainous like the Dalai Lama's homeland, and on the more devious grounds that it was a long way from Delhi – an isolated backwater with poor transport and communication links where the Tibetan exiles could be dumped and quietly forgotten. That the Indian premier's cynical calculations had backfired was due in part to the Tibetan refugees' determination and resilience and part to the awesome, inspiring personality of their leader. Over four decades, the Dalai Lama had established himself as a world figure of unique standing: a statesman untainted by politics, a religious leader untouched by bigotry or intolerance who had a moral authority afforded to few others on the global stage. Struggling against huge problems of poverty and the logistics of resettlement in an alien land, not to mention an almost universal indifference to his people's plight, he had succeeded in keeping his exiled community together and been a constant, nagging thorn in the side of the Chinese, refusing doggedly to allow their occupation and campaign of genocide in Tibet to be forgotten.

Since the first tiny handful of refugees arrived destitute and shivering, McLeod Ganj had grown into a thriving town of 8,000 people. There were exile communities in other parts of India, in Nepal and Bhutan, but the heart of the Tibetan diaspora was still here. Houses had been built on the hillsides around the town, cultural institutes, a library and various Government organisations had been created and sustained, and hotels and restaurants had sprung up to cater for the pilgrims and young travellers who came to the town seeking spiritual enlightenment.

Maggie had been here several times before and always found it uplifting, yet also depressing. The home the Tibetans had made for themselves was impressive considering what they'd started with. They'd established businesses, created jobs, even founded new monasteries for the study of the Buddhist faith that was such an integral part of their culture. But poverty and hardship were still very much in evidence. Many of the new homes were little more than shanties. And there was something pathetic about the offices of the administration in exile, a tiny collection of buildings that wouldn't have come close to accommodating the smallest borough council in Britain. And yet they were fighting against 1.3 billion Chinese. It was a demoralising realisation and Maggie often thought that somewhere in McLeod Ganj, among the *chortens* and prayer wheels and fluttering prayer flags, there should have been a shrine to Saint Jude, the patron saint of lost causes.

She met her contact, Kapil, in a café in the centre of the town, a Tibetan-run hostelry which served tea and *momos* – stuffed Tibetan dumplings – but also pizza and macaroni cheese and a selection of cakes including Black Forest gateau for the Western backpackers who needed occasional reminders of home on their arduous treks around the world.

They sat at a table near the window, looking out at the gold-topped *chorten* dedicated to the memory of those suffering under the Chinese occupation of Tibet. A continuous stream of pilgrims was circumambulating the monument, spinning the prayer wheels around its base and murmuring the ubiquitous mantra, *Om mani padme hum* – Hail to the Jewel in the Lotus.

'So what's the latest?' Maggie asked.

Kapil glanced around the café and kept his voice low. 'It's very hard to find out. The Tibetans, particularly the ones at the top, are very close-knit. They don't talk, they don't gossip. Many of them are monks. You know how monks are. Very tight.' He clenched both hands into fists to emphasise the point.

Maggie nodded patiently, aware that this complaint was simply a tactical opening in the trading game they were playing. The harder it was for him to come by the information, the more she would have to pay him for it.

'Is he still ill?' Maggie said.

'Oh, yes.'

'You've seen him?'

'Only his doctor and his ministers can see him. He's cancelled all his audiences and official business for the forseeable future. They're saying he has flu but it's much more serious than that.'

'What do you think it is?'

'Cancer, maybe. Or a stroke.'

Maggie sipped her coffee, thinking out loud. 'Not cancer. If he had cancer he'd be in hospital somewhere. Probably in Switzerland or the US. Having chemotherapy or radio-therapy.'

'Whatever it is, it's terminal,' Kapil said.

'How do you know?'

'Things I've picked up. You can sense things over there.'

'You've been inside his residence?'

Kapil shook his head. 'They don't allow people like me inside the residence. I'm just a servant.'

There was a hint of rancour in his voice. Kapil was Indian, not Tibetan. He was a delivery driver for the wholesale merchant in Dharamsala, a few kilometres down the hill, who supplied the Tibetan Government in exile with everything from soap and toilet paper to cooking oil and rice. There was friction between the Tibetans and the local Indian population, many of whom resented the preferential treatment the Tibetans had received from the Government in Delhi.

'When were you last there?' Maggie said.

'Yesterday morning. I took a delivery to the kitchen block.'

'Is he conscious?'

Kapil shrugged. 'They were still preparing meals for him.'

That meant very little, Maggie knew. She'd filmed the Dalai Lama, shot documentary material in Lhasa. She knew a fair bit about Tibetan history. The Tibetans were good at keeping secrets. The death of the Fifth Dalai Lama, in the seventeenth century, had been concealed by the prime minister for an incredible fifteen years without anyone discovering the deception. Covering up a serious illness for a few weeks was child's play for such skilled dissemblers.

Maggie took out five hundred rupee notes, worth about ten pounds to her but a lot more to Kapil. He folded the bills in half and slipped them into his pocket.

'What else can I tell you?' he said.

Kapil was astute, observant. And he was good at ingratiating himself with people. Maggie had noticed that the first time she'd encountered him. Fleshing out the piece on the Dalai Lama's sixty-fifth birthday, they'd done a few interviews with the residence staff, getting a feel for how he lived. Kapil had been in the kitchens, talkative, a natural in front of the camera. Maggie had recognised a fixer when she saw him and, following a practice she'd found paid dividends on other jobs, left him her phone number and a small retainer.

'Remind me again of the layout,' Maggie said.

'Of the residence compound, or Gangchen Kyishong, the administrative area?'

'Both.'

27

'You are going to go over there?'

'Maybe,' Maggie replied ambiguously.

'If you are, I know a good way in.'

Kapil waited.

'How much?' Maggie said.

'Another five hundred.'

'Make it three.'

'Four.'

'Okay.'

She handed over the notes.

'It might be dangerous,' Kapil said.

'Now you tell me.'

Maggie crouched down behind the bushes and waited a moment, breathing heavily, listening for any sign of activity, any sign of an alert. Kapil had said there was no alarm wire on the wall where she'd just come over, but she wanted to be sure. The Indian and Tibetan security guards who jointly patrolled the perimeter of Thekchen Chöling – Island of the Mahayana Teaching – the Dalai Lama's residence compound, were armed and well trained. Maggie had no intention of confronting any of them if she could help it.

She squatted motionless in the undergrowth. There was an earthy smell of damp soil and vegetation, a slight breeze bringing with it the scent of pine and cedar from the forested slopes behind her. She snaked forward on her belly and gently parted the lower branches of a shrub, peering out across the garden. The compound was on a steep hillside, the kitchen block, office buildings and security blocks on different levels and at the top the small one-storey cottage where the Dalai Lama lived. It was gone midnight, but one or two lights still glowed in the windows of the kitchen complex and guard room. The Dalai Lama's cottage, though, was in darkness.

Maggie paused, her eyes roving the hillside, searching for figures, for any movement. Then she crept out from the bushes and ran across the terraced garden, her camcorder clutched to her side. She'd removed the camera from its protective case and attached a small battery-powered light to the front, above the lens. The whole thing was smaller, and lighter, than a woman's handbag. She took shelter behind the trunk of a pine tree and paused again. It was an overcast night, the peaks above McLeod Ganj obscured by a blanket of cloud, but there was enough light for her to see the layout of the garden. There were steps just above her, a rockery, then a terraced lawn outside the Dalai Lama's cottage. Kapil had told her there was normally a security guard on duty outside the front door of the cottage. Maggie could see no sign of him.

She studied the modest brick building. It looked like a suburban bungalow, not the residence of a political and spiritual leader of the Dalai Lama's stature. But it was in keeping with his simple, unostentatious lifestyle. Anything grander would have felt incongruous and false. She recalled what the interior was like, picturing it from her previous visit. The Dalai Lama's bedroom was small, almost as bare as a monk's cell, then there were offices for his personal staff, a bathroom, an audience room, reception area and a tiny workshop where the Dalai Lama indulged his hobby of dismantling and repairing watches. She remembered the certificates and citations, the souvenirs of his overseas visits adorning the walls of the public rooms, and the blackened wood-burning stove whose meagre warmth did little to ease the chilly atmosphere in the building.

Her gaze moved along the exterior of the cottage, along the deep verandah where pots of geraniums were blooming. The Dalai Lama's bedroom overlooked the garden. There was a bird table just below the window where he liked to watch the parrots and pigeons feeding. Maggie waited five, ten minutes, still searching for the security guard assigned to the bungalow. Even if he'd gone for a walk around the perimeter of the building he should have reappeared by now.

There was no point in delaying any longer. Edging out from behind the tree, she flitted up the steps and across the lawn to the cottage. She climbed stealthily up on to the verandah and looked in through the bedroom window. The shutters were open, the glass panes swung back a little to let air into the room. She saw at once why the security seemed so lax. The Dalai Lama wasn't there. His bed was neatly made, an embroidered Tibetan quilt pulled up over the pillows.

Maggie retreated across the lawn and took cover behind a rhododendron bush. Where was he? Had they moved him to another bedroom somewhere? Or had he been secretly moved to hospital? She looked across towards Namgyal Dratsang, the Dalai Lama's personal monastery. There was a faint emanation of flickering light around the gold-pinnacled Tsuglagkhang temple and she could hear a distant murmur which she thought at first was the sound of the wind in the trees then realised was monks chanting. Her detailed knowledge of Buddhist monastic ritual was hazy – perhaps they had ceremonies that took place at the dead of night – but it still struck her as odd.

Curious to know what was happening, she climbed back over the wall of the compound and skirted round to the flagstone *chora*, the debating courtyard, in front of the temple. The sound of chanting was louder now. She looked around. The temple precincts appeared to be deserted. Maggie ran across the courtyard and up the steps at the side of the Tsuglagkhang. She found a wooden door in the stonework and tried the handle. It was unlocked. Very carefully, she pushed the door open a few inches and peeped in. There was a darkened room inside, like a vestry. Maggie stepped through and closed the door behind her. She went across to a door on the far side of the room and eased it open. The scene beyond took her breath away.

In the main chamber of the temple, just in front of the altar and the huge gilt statue of the Buddha, was a raised dais covered in rich yellow silk. Around the base of the dais, hundreds of tiny butter lamps were burning, filling the vault of the temple with an ethereal light and a drifting mist of scented white smoke. Outside the rows of glimmering lamps was a circle of Gelukpa monks, maroon-robed, heads shaven so their pates shone like polished ivory in the dim light. They were sitting cross-legged on the floor, their eyes half closed, chanting mantras in unison. It was an astonishing sight that touched her with a profound sense of awe.

But it was the figure on top of the dais that stunned her most: a man sitting cross-legged, clad in plain maroon and yellow robes, just like the monks, except that his eyes were fully closed and he wasn't chanting. His face looked familiar. With a shock that hit her like a blow, Maggie realised who he was. He wasn't wearing his spectacles, but his features were unmistakable. It was the Dalai Lama himself.

For a fleeting instant, Maggie thought that Kapil had got it wrong. The Dalai Lama wasn't terminally ill, wasn't ill at all, for here he was participating in a religious ceremony. Then she noticed something about his posture, his absolute stillness. And his face. His face had a shiny, unreal patina as if it were a wax mask. She stifled a gasp of surprise, realising with wide-eyed horror what she was witnessing. The Dalai Lama was lying in state, his body arranged in the meditation position which Buddhist tradition prescribed for high reincarnate lamas.

Maggie stared at him, her skin going cold. So he was gone. Tenzin Gyatso, the reincarnation of Chenresig, the Buddha of Compassion, had passed from the world. Maggie remembered him from their brief meeting those few years ago. Remembered him as smiling and full of joy. His Tibetan nickname, Kundun, meant 'The Presence' and it was true that his personality, the aura of goodness that surrounded him, could light up a room. Even in death that presence still seemed to fill every lofty corner of the temple. Yet there had been something sad about him too. A lost soul in exile who had never returned to his homeland, and who had now died without seeing it again. However much Buddhists believed in the preeminence of the spirit, there was a desperate, heart-rending poignancy to his death here in an alien land.

Maggie pulled back into the vestry and closed the door

quietly, remembering why she was there. She could walk away now and leave the monks to their mourning. A part of her wanted to, believed that that was the proper thing to do. But her professional instincts were strong, more powerful even than her sense of right and wrong. She was witnessing something that few others were privileged to see. The chance to record it for posterity, and perhaps for her own personal glory, was too good to miss.

She checked the settings on the camcorder and pressed the 'record' button. A tiny red bulb lit up on the side of the camera. The motor was just a faint, almost inaudible whir. It would not be heard over the sound of the monks' chanting. Softly, Maggie opened the door again. She crept out into the temple and began to tape the scene.

Tsering paused at the edge of the courtyard, wondering if he'd imagined it. He looked around the temple precinct, his eyes probing the darkness. He'd seen something, he was sure. Coming up the path from the *Kashag* building, he'd seen a figure crossing the *chora*. Only a fleeting glimpse, a flash of clothing, of a shape in the night, but he knew it hadn't been a monk or a security guard, the only categories of people with any good reason for being in the area at this time.

He headed for the temple, his leather sandals slapping against the stone slabs beneath his feet. The wind was gusting up from the valley, plucking at his robes, chilling the exposed flesh of his arms. He did a full circuit of the Tsuglagkhang without seeing anything untoward and came back to the main entrance. He went into the temple porch and hesitated. Was he just using this as an excuse to go in, a pretext for his own gratification? Or was his intuition right?

Slipping off his sandals, he walked through into the chamber of the temple and stopped. He gazed in reverence at the figure on the raised dais, the butter lamps sending flickers of light over the Dalai Lama's immobile body like fingers reaching up to touch him. Tsering couldn't take his eyes off the face, moved to the depths of his soul, aware not of personal loss but of something much greater, of something more universal. A beacon had been extinguished not just in his life, but across the earth.

He stood motionless for a long time. Then he became aware of another light in the temple. Away to one side, in the shadows, was a tiny pinprick glowing red. Tsering squinted at it, trying to make out what it was. Behind the light the shadows were denser. He began to discern the outline of something, a recognisable shape. He padded softly towards it. The stone floor was cold on the soles of his bare feet. As he drew nearer, the outline changed shape. Tsering saw a gleam of pale skin, a face turning to look at him. Then the outline melted away. A door opened and suddenly the shadow was gone.

Tsering started to run. He reached the doorway in time to see a figure disappearing through the side door of the temple. Tsering ran across the vestry and out on to the path. The figure was heading away from the Tsuglagkhang. Tsering raced after it, ignoring the pain of the sharp gravel on his naked soles. The figure ahead changed direction, taking a path through the forest. Tsering gained on it, nearer and nearer, then threw himself forwards, grabbing the figure around the waist and knocking it to the ground. He heard a cry of pain – a woman's voice – felt a body underneath him. He rolled off and bent down, hauling the woman to her feet. He stared at her in surprise. Maggie gazed back at him, out of breath, hurting. She saw a tall, lean monk, a handsome face set hard with anger. Then he took her roughly by the arm and dragged her back along the path.

A man in the uniform of the Tibetan Security Police conducted the interview. Maggie was open with him, giving straight answers to all his questions.

'I'd heard he was unwell, perhaps terminally ill, so I came over to have a look for myself.'

Maggie fingered the graze on the side of her head. The skin was broken but it wasn't bleeding. Her ribs were hurting more, bruised from the weight of the monk who'd caught her. He was in the small security block office with them now, standing by the door. He was big, muscular, surprisingly aggressive for a Buddhist monk. Maggie wasted no time on self-pity. She had no one to blame but herself.

'You're lucky your injuries aren't worse,' the police officer said. 'You could have got yourself shot.'

He picked up the camcorder, ejected the cassette and placed it in an envelope. This is becoming a habit, Maggie thought.

'What are you, a tourist?' he asked.

Maggie considered saying yes, but rejected the deception. She was better off being honest.

'It's my job. I'm a professional camerawoman.'

'Whom do you work for?'

'A television news agency in London.'

'With a little camera like this?' The police officer was sceptical.

'Look at the tape,' Maggie said. 'You'd be surprised.'

'You filmed inside the temple.' It was the monk who spoke. 'Have you no respect for the dead?'

Maggie turned to look at him. He was older than she'd first thought. Late thirties, maybe early forties. He wore the robes of a simple monk, but there was authority in the way he spoke and carried himself. She shrugged. 'It's a body,' she said. 'You're Buddhists; you believe his spirit has already departed. How can I be disrespectful to an empty vessel?'

Tsering's lip curled. 'I think you know what I mean. You play with words, but all decent people know what respect for the dead is. Whether we are Buddhists or not makes no difference. He was a great man.'

'I know,' Maggie said.

'Then how can you intrude like this?'

'I didn't know he was dead when I came over.'

'You knew he was ill.'

'He was a public figure. He was used to cameras. He was expert at using the world's media for his own purposes. His life was lived in the glare of the press. Do you really think it won't be the same in death?'

34

'Don't try to justify what you did,' Tsering said. 'It was contemptible, dishonourable.'

'Look, maybe you're right,' Maggie said. 'Maybe I shouldn't have done what I did. You're right. It was insensitive, wrong. But do you really think you can keep all this secret? Why don't you announce it now? Let me tape the announcement, shoot some more footage of the Dalai Lama lying in state. It will be the cleanest, least intrusive way of doing it.'

Tsering looked at her. 'I have to admire your tenacity, but don't try to dress up your own self-interest as doing some kind of favour to us. We're not that naïve.'

'Aren't you?' Maggie said. 'I'm not sure you know how these things work. The moment you announce his death – or it leaks out, and it will very soon, believe me – every news organisation in the world will be banging on your door demanding access. It won't just be me with a small camcorder. It will be hundreds of people. Have you ever seen a media mob in action? They're not a bunch of meek, mild-mannered characters with notebooks and pencils. They're a travelling circus – reporters, producers, technicians with more hardware than you can imagine. This whole hillside will be covered with floodlights, satellite dishes, generators and communications vans. Why not do it now, keep the disruption to a minimum?'

Tsering gave a dismissive shake of the head and turned to the police officer. They had a brief discussion in Tibetan which Maggie, though she had a smattering of the language, couldn't follow. Then Tsering headed for the door.

'What are you going to do with me?' Maggie asked.

Tsering paused. 'That is not my decision,' he said.

He went out. The police officer locked the door behind him and put the key in his pocket. He sat down at the desk and stared inscrutably at Maggie.

'What now?' she said.

'We wait.'

*   *   *

Tsering walked quickly down the hill towards Gangchen Kyishong – the poetically named Abode of Snow-Happy Valley – which was the administrative compound of the Tibetan Government in exile. He could have used the road, but he preferred the shortcut through the trees. Although the path was unlit, impossible to see clearly in the darkness, he knew every inch of the twisting, rocky descent.

The lights were on in the National Assembly building where the *Kashag*, the Tibetan cabinet, held its regular meetings. Tsering entered the building and conferred with another monk who was sitting on a chair outside a committee room. The monk knocked once on the committee room door and entered. A few minutes elapsed before he re-emerged accompanied by an older monk who held the office of Minister of Security. Tsering repeated his story and the minister frowned, his whole face wrinkling like a piece of crumpled hide.

'Where is she now?' he said.

'In the security block,' Tsering replied. 'But we have no facilities for detaining her.'

'Did she come alone?'

'As far as we can tell, yes.'

'You have her camera?'

Tsering nodded. 'And her tape.'

'Keep them both,' the minister said. 'Contact the police in Dharamsala. Report her as an intruder, a trespasser. Have them send someone up for her. I will speak to the commissioner as soon as I am free.'

'She knows about His Holiness. She will talk,' Tsering said.

'Then we must ensure that no one listens to her,' the minister replied.

He pushed open the door and went back into the committee room. The seven men seated around the conference table inside broke off their discussion and looked up at the Minister of Security as he returned to his chair.

'We have a problem,' he said mildly. 'A Western journalist, a camerawoman. She was caught filming inside the Tsuglagkhang. I fear our time is running out.'

The First Minister, sitting at the head of the table, studied the faces of the others in turn. When he got to the last, the weatherbeaten, lined face of Pasang Rinpoche, he stopped.

'Well, Rinpoche?'

The old man's mouth moved as if he were chewing. He sucked in his cheeks, making his face even more cadaverous.

'We are going round in circles,' he said firmly. 'Achieving nothing. Let us summon the Medium of the State Oracle and ask him for guidance.'

The ceremony was ready to begin. The preparations had taken several hours and it was now almost dawn. The jagged peaks of the Dhauladar mountains were starting to emerge from the night, their contours growing sharper as the sky behind them slowly lightened, suffused with the first warming touch of the day. Inside the assembly hall it was dim. Butter lamps burned around the perimeter of the room and at one end the members of the *Kashag* were gathered, sitting cross-legged on thick red cushions.

Suddenly, two monks blew a sustained, deafening blast on *thungchen*, ten-foot-long horns whose curving bells – too heavy to hold up – rested on the floor of the hall. The silvery tinkle of tiny cymbals and the thud of drums intermingled as monks from the Nechung monastery – the home of the Oracle – began a recitation, calling on the oracular deity to descend. A maroon curtain parted and a figure stepped out, supported by three monk attendants. He was clad in red brocade trousers and a red silk shirt covered with a heavy robe striped in blue, white, red and gold. His boots were knee-high, made of white leather, the toes curled up, and around his ankles angry eyes of crimson silk stared out menacingly. Over his chest he wore a tunic of gold-leaf ringlets, like the chainmail of an ancient Tibetan warrior. In the centre of the tunic was a shimmering gold mirror, surrounded by clusters of turquoise and amethyst, and emblazoned with the Sanskrit mantra of Dorje Drakden, the Dalai Lama's divine protector. At his left side was a silver sword and sheath, at the right a golden quiver filled with arrows. Strapped to his back in a harness were four flags and three victory banners, their gold tips towering above the Medium's head. The whole outfit was so heavy the Medium could barely stand, let alone move unaided.

Slowly, the Medium shuffled forwards and stopped. His attendants drew back. As the files of monks continued their chanting, the Medium's body began to quiver. His face contorted into a grimace, the skin stretched tight over his cheekbones, his mouth twisted into a silent scream of horror. His eyes stared out wildly, fixed on some terrifying vision of another world. The possession was beginning.

The monks began a new cycle of prayers, the cymbals and drums beating out their sombre accompaniment. Another long blast of the *thungchen* shook the foundations of the hall and the Medium began to hyperventilate. His breath hissed out between his contorted lips, so violently it could be heard above the voices of the monks. It grew louder, like compressed gas escaping from a cylinder. The Medium started to gag, as if he were about to choke. Then suddenly, his legs began to twitch, lifting his body high into the air in a series of exaggerated leaps. Beneath the heavy robes his heart started to race, the polished mirror on his chest pulsing with every beat.

Recognising that the Protector had taken hold of the Medium's body, one of the attendants stepped forward and placed a three-foot-high iron helmet on the Medium's head. The helmet was coated with gold and adorned with a circle of ruby-eyed skulls and a bear-fur crest surrounded by peacock feathers. More flags and banners, these topped with silver bells, were attached to the back of the helmet, the whole ensemble crowned with the three jewels of the Buddha, Dharma and Sangha.

The helmet securely strapped under his chin, the Medium drew his sword and began the *cham*, the ritual dance of Dorje Drakden whose spirit was now in full control of his earthly *kuden*, the receiving body. The weight of the costume – more than a hundred pounds – counted for nothing now. The

Medium danced as if he were naked, leaping from side to side in enormous bounds, bowing low from the waist so he was almost bent double then straightening up and throwing himself into the air, his burnished sword sweeping above his head in great arcs.

The elaborate dance became more and more frenetic. The Medium seemed transformed into a superhuman being, endowed with an unearthly strength and stamina. Up and up he leaped, round and round he twirled, his gyrating form casting grotesque shadows across the walls and ceiling of the hall, until it seemed that no mortal body, however possessed, could withstand the agonising strain. Then abruptly he stopped. He threw down his sword, took a white silk *khata*, a greeting scarf, from an attendant and offered it to the First Minister.

The minister accepted the offering and the Medium stepped back a pace. A silver goblet of black tea was handed to him. He offered it to the First Minister who took a sip before returning the cup. The Medium drank and then lifted his eyes to the minister.

'Speak!' the Medium intoned.

The First Minister swallowed nervously. It was normally only the Dalai Lama himself who addressed the Medium in his trance. The minister composed himself to ask the three questions that were allowed.

'Great Protector,' he said, his voice trembling, 'we seek your help and your wisdom and your divine insight. Gyalwa Rinpoche has departed this world. Will he be reborn?'

The Medium gazed at the minister. His eyes were glassy, the pupils dilated, a mere conduit for the Protector's vision. When his voice came it was high-pitched, quavering, the shrill timbre of a spirit.

'He will be reborn,' he said.

'Where will he be reborn? Will it be outside Tibet?'

'It will be inside the motherland,' the Medium replied.

The First Minister flinched visibly. This was a blow none of them had expected.

'Inside the motherland?' he repeated, seeking clarification.

'The true Dalai Lama will emerge through hardship and struggle. His rebirth must strengthen him for the fight against oppression. His truth will come only with the freedom of his people.'

The First Minister glanced at his colleagues and clasped his hands together in his lap, preparing to ask the third and final question.

'When will he be reborn?'

The Medium's breath hissed like a serpent. His eyes blazed and his voice seemed to come from an immense distance.

'He has already been reborn,' he said to audible gasps from the watching ministers. 'I see a child. A baby. I see his face. Wait ... it is fading. I see water now. A lake. I see a lake surrounded by high mountains. There are images in the surface of the water but they are cloudy. They are fading. They are gone ...'

The Medium went suddenly rigid. His body began to sway under the weight of the helmet. He gave one final violent shudder as Dorje Drakden released the *kuden*'s body and returned to the spirit world. Then he started to topple over backwards. His attendants rushed in and caught him before he crashed to the floor. They quickly removed the helmet to prevent the straps suffocating him. Then they lifted the Medium's stiff body on to their shoulders and carried him unconscious from the hall.

The eight members of the *Kashag* – the inner core of the Tibetan Government in exile – sat down again at the conference table. For a long time no one spoke, they were all in a state of shock.

Eventually, the First Minister cleared his throat. 'What can I say?' he said, still dazed by what had happened in the assembly hall. 'We did not expect this.'

'Why?' the Minister of Security asked. 'Every indication he gave us in life was that he would choose to be reborn outside Tibet, away from the influence of the Chinese. Why has he chosen the motherland?'

'He has chosen,' said Pasang Rinpoche quietly.

'But it makes it all the more difficult for us to find his re-incarnation.'

'Perhaps that is why he did it.'

The ministers were subdued, demoralised by the Medium's revelations. None of them doubted for an instant the truth of his words. The Oracle was sacred, infallible.

'He is trying to test us?' the First Minister asked.

Pasang Rinpoche nodded. 'He must be found inside Tibet to be a credible choice. It is the only way to unite our people in exile and those in the homeland. He must be legitimate and be seen to be legitimate.'

Pasang Rinpoche looked around the table, making sure he had everyone's undivided attention.

'We do not want another—' he searched for the right word '—"fiasco" like the case of the Panchen Lama. If the new Dalai Lama is found outside Tibet, the Chinese will question his legitimacy. They will find another child inside Tibet and declare him the real Dalai Lama. There would be two competing reincarnations. That would bring our whole faith into disrepute. To have undeniable authority, the Dalai Lama must be found by us, and inside Tibet.'

For a moment there was complete silence. Then the Minister of Information spoke.

'Can we do it?'

'We must,' the First Minister declared emphatically. 'We need a new leader, both spiritual and temporal. Our people need a new leader. Already we are dispersed across the globe. The Chinese are destroying our homeland, killing our people, wiping out our culture. If the Tibetan nation is to survive, we must have a new Dalai Lama. Our future, and our children's future, depends on our finding him.'

'The Chinese will never let a search party enter Tibet,' the Minister of Security said. 'If we ask, they will either insist on being a party to the search – in which case it is worthless – or they will block us for years until we become irrelevant and forgotten.'

'So we will go there in secret. He is waiting for us.'

'Go where? We do not even know where to begin.'

'We do,' said Pasang Rinpoche. 'The Medium's vision. The lake surrounded by mountains. It is Lhamo Latso, the oracle lake. We must go there.' The lama paused, correcting himself. '*I* must go there.'

The others turned to stare at him.

'You, Rinpoche?' the First Minister said.

The old man sat up straight, the years falling away from his bowed shoulders, and looked defiantly around the table. 'Only a high lama can see the visions in the water. I am the senior lama. It is my duty to go. And it is my right.'

'That may be, Rinpoche,' the First Minister said gently. 'But you are seventy-five years old. You are no longer a young man.'

'Then send some younger men to accompany me,' the lama retorted tetchily. 'I came out of Tibet with His Holiness in '59. I was at his side when we climbed the high mountain passes, I was at his side during these long years of exile and I was at his side when he died. If anyone can see the signs of where he will be reborn, it is I.'

There was no denying his resolve. His eyes burned with a fierce determination. He was old and frail, but he would overcome those handicaps by sheer force of willpower. He would not be deterred from his chosen path and no one in the room would be rash enough to oppose him. As the senior religious figure in the exiled community he commanded the utmost respect, even from the lay ministers. And besides, they knew he was right. The oracle lake revealed its secrets to the highest incarnate lamas and to no one else.

'Time is of the essence,' Pasang Rinpoche continued. 'We must soon reveal the death of His Holiness to his people. The moment we do, there will be great mourning, both here and in Tibet. The Chinese will close the borders to shut out the gaze of the outside world and try to suppress any show of devotion to the faith. It is their way. When the announcement is made, we must already be inside Tibet.'

He paused. 'The Dalai Lama is gone. We must begin the search for his reincarnation immediately.'

THREE

Tsering took a last look around his cell. He had a premonition, a feeling in his gut, that it would be a long time before he saw it again. The room was no more than two metres square. The walls were whitewashed brick, the floor plain stone flags. A woven Tibetan rug provided a splash of colour, a patch of warmth in the otherwise stark, functional surroundings. Against one wall was a creaking iron-framed bed covered with a couple of coarse blankets and a quilt. In front of the window, which overlooked the courtyard of the monastery, were a tiny wooden desk and a chair. That was the only furniture apart from a small low table draped in yellow cloth on which were arranged a picture of the Buddha, a photograph of the Dalai Lama and seven small metal bowls filled with water, symbolic offering to the deities. Very few personal possessions were visible: a transistor radio beside the bed, some religious texts on the desk. It wasn't much to show for thirty-nine years of life, but Tsering had never for one moment felt deprived. The acquisition of objects meant nothing to him.

He picked up his bag and held it in his arms, studying the intricate pattern on the material, the rainbow-hued embroidery which his mother had painstakingly applied to the bag. She'd made it for him when he first left home to go into the local monastery thirty years earlier. He remembered watching her as she sat by a butter lamp in the evenings sewing, hunched over to see her needle dipping in and out of the cloth like a dancing silverfish. She'd intended it to be special.

Something colourful to counter the austerity of the *gompa*. And to remind him of her. It always did that. It was worn and faded now, but it was the only possession he really treasured. More than anything, it seemed to encapsulate his memories of Tibet, his memories of childhood. He couldn't look at it without being engulfed by painful visions of his mother. It was thirteen years since he'd last seen her, five since he'd last received word of her from the remote village in Kham where she lived. He wrote to her regularly but had heard nothing in return. He didn't even know whether she was still alive. He'd tried to obtain news of her, sought out refugees from the homeland, newly arrived in McLeod Ganj, to see if they hailed from anywhere near her locality, but to no avail. She was lost to him.

He ran his fingertips over the outside of the bag. This was the first time he'd taken it out since he'd escaped from Tibet. It reminded him not just of his mother, but of other faces from the past. His father, whose image he could still see clearly though it was nearly thirty-five years since he'd died. His teachers at the monastery, his fellow novices, the friends who'd shared those years with him. He'd lost touch with them all. He'd made his choice, but he wondered daily if it had been the right one. He had got out. They had not been so fortunate. Reconciling that with his conscience was something Tsering had never managed to do with any degree of equanimity. He was physically free, but what true liberty was there in exile, and when others were still prisoners?

Slinging the strap of the bag over his shoulder, Tsering went out of the cell and closed the door firmly behind him. Outside in the courtyard, two other monks, Lobsang and Jigme, were waiting for him. They too were carrying bags. The three of them walked down to the road where a dark green four-wheel-drive Jeep was parked, its driver – another monk in maroon robes – seated behind the wheel. Tsering, Lobsang and Jigme loaded their bags into the rear of the vehicle and waited in silence by the doors. It was 7 am. On a normal day the monastery would have been awake for hours, morning prayers completed, breakfast eaten, the monks going about their duties. But this wasn't a normal morning. The whole area was deserted. The main body of monks was still holding its vigil in the Tsuglagkhang.

A group of figures came down the path. At the front, walking slowly with the aid of a stick, was Pasang Rinpoche. Next to him was the abbot of the monastery and behind them came the members of the *Kashag*. As they reached the Jeep, Pasang Rinpoche stopped and turned to face the rest of the group. Tsering, Lobsang and Jigme fell in behind him. The lama bid a polite, restrained farewell to the abbot and the ministers, then the abbot took a handful of yellow barley grains from the pocket of his robe and cast them over the feet of Pasang Rinpoche and the three monks, intoning a prayer of protection for them.

The formalities over, the abbot stepped forward and added a more personal touch to the parting by throwing his arms around Pasang Rinpoche and embracing him. Tsering saw that there were tears in the abbot's eyes.

'May the Buddha be with you,' the abbot said. 'May he give you strength and guidance.'

The old lama bowed his head. 'Pray for us in the days to come, for we will need your support.'

'We will, Rinpoche.'

Tsering pulled open the front passenger door of the Jeep and helped Pasang Rinpoche inside, leaning over to fasten his seatbelt. Then he climbed into the back seat next to Lobsang and Jigme. As the vehicle pulled away, Tsering glanced back through the rear window. The abbot and the ministers were rooted to the spot, watching the departing Jeep with grave, anxious faces. Tsering turned away, breathing deeply, trying to loosen the talons of apprehension that were clawing at his belly.

The first part of their journey took them down the hill to Dharamsala, then forty miles due west to the railway station at Pathankot from where they caught the train to Delhi. They stayed overnight in the Indian capital and in the morning took a specially chartered plane to Guwahati in the Brahmaputra Valley in eastern India. Another Jeep, also driven by a monk, was waiting for them there. They drove north-east for two hours and reached the provincial frontier of Arunachal Pradesh in the late afternoon. There was an Indian army checkpoint on the frontier, soldiers stopping all vehicles attempting to cross. Disputed territory still claimed by China, Arunachal Pradesh was a restricted area closed to visitors without a special permit. Tsering climbed out of the Jeep and went into the roadside hut to show the entry documents the Tibetan Government in exile representative in Delhi had obtained for them. The soldier on duty took in Tsering's maroon robes and barely glanced at the papers. A Buddhist monk was nothing to worry about. He stamped the permits, handed them back and gave a bored, dismissive wave of the hand. Tsering returned to the Jeep and they drove on into the foothills, ascending a steep, winding road which, as they left the plains behind, became ever more precipitous. On one side was a sheer drop into a deep gorge, on the other the rocky slopes of the mountains rising in craggy steps towards the clear blue sky.

Nearly three hours later, as dusk was falling, they left the main road and began a precarious climb up a rough dirt track to the monastery at Tawang. The abbot welcomed them and discreetly refrained from asking any questions about the purpose of their journey. He'd been told only that they were on a pilgrimage and needed assistance to cross the border into Tibet. He provided them with food and beds for the night and in the morning, before dawn, they were driven down the hill again and north to the village of Chutangmo, the last settlement before the frontier. This was Indian territory, but it had long been the home of Tibetan tribes who farmed the valley slopes and, in the past, moved freely between the two countries to trade. Since the Chinese occupation of Tibet, and the long-running border dispute between Beijing and Delhi, this freedom of movement had been severely curtailed. But this hadn't stopped the Tibetans. Trading was in their blood and if they couldn't do it legitimately, they would do it clandestinely. The Chinese border guards, whose penchant for corruption was legendary, were willing partners in a symbiotic smuggling racket which, so long as the kickbacks kept coming, they allowed to flourish virtually unchecked.

At Chutangmo, the monks left the Jeep and were introduced to a Tibetan trader named Topgyal. They had already changed out of their religious robes at the monastery and were now wearing traditional *chubas* and caps to hide their shaven heads. Topgyal, on the instructions of the Tawang abbot, had provided four sturdy ponies and a guide to take them over one of the high passes into Tibet.

Under cover of darkness, they rode out of the village and began the long climb towards the border. The guide led the way, Tsering and the others following. It was years since Tsering had been on a pony, even longer since he'd worn a layman's *chuba*. It felt strange, bobbing around in the saddle, the cool air gusting against his legs. He was nervous; about the crossing, but also about Pasang Rinpoche. The elderly lama rode just behind him and Tsering kept turning round to make sure he was all right. Pasang Rinpoche was too old, too feeble for such an arduous journey. The responsibility of looking after him weighed heavily on Tsering's shoulders.

Dawn was breaking when they came up the final few metres of the ascent and paused on the highest point of the pass. The guide, a thick-set Monpa who spoke a Tibetan dialect that was almost unintelligible to the monks, gestured into the distance.

'Tibet,' he grunted.

In front of them, the Himalayas stretched as far as the eye could see, a vast ocean of rolling peaks, their summits daubed with snow like the crests of breaking waves, their lower slopes smothered in dense cloud so they appeared to be floating in mid-air. A cold sunlight bathed the horizon, spreading out to enfold the mountains in a shadowy embrace, making their icy tops gleam like shards of shattered crystal.

Pasang Rinpoche gazed at the view from his pony, then turned to Tsering. 'Help me down,' he said. 'Let me feel the ground beneath my feet.'

Tsering slid down from his own pony and lifted the lama from his saddle. The old man was light, little more than skin and bone. Tsering kept hold of his arm to support him, but Pasang Rinpoche shook it off.

'Down there,' he pointed, 'is the way His Holiness came in '59. We rode south from Lhasa, crossing the Tsangpo in yak-skin coracles. Khampa warriors came with us, draped with pistols and swords and gilt charm boxes. It was cold, bitterly cold. On the Karpo-La the Khampas let down their long braids to shield their faces from the glare of the snow.'

The lama's eyes were moist, his voice unsteady as he remembered. It was more than forty years ago but every detail of that desperate flight was indelibly etched on his memory.

'The Chinese were shelling Lhasa. The Potala, the Norbulingka, the Jokhang Temple. The dead were lining the streets, the city was burning. We'd made camp in Mangmang. His Holiness was ill – dysentery. I sat with him that night, fearing he would not survive. In the morning we received word that the PLA were closing in on us. We had to move. We put His Holiness on a *dzo* and he rode over the border like a peasant, sick and weary and full of sorrow. He never saw the homeland again.'

Pasang Rinpoche stared bleakly out into space, seeing only the dark vestiges of that tragic time. Then he lifted his cupped hands to his chest and began to pray. Tsering stood beside him, reciting the mantra in unison.

When the lama was ready, Tsering lifted him back on to his pony. Then Tsering stepped over the unmarked frontier, bent down and picked up a handful of earth. Tibetan earth. He rubbed it between his fingers and touched it to his forehead in symbolic obeisance. After thirteen years of exile, he was going home.

* * *

48

The hatch in the door snapped open and a hand reached in holding a bowl of food. Maggie pushed herself up off the bed and walked across the cell. She could see the face of the police officer outside through the narrow opening.

'You can't keep me here, I have rights,' she said. She tried to sound angry, but she'd been through this so many times already that she found it hard to summon the necessary energy. Two days and nights in this stinking cell had drained her will. 'Do you hear me? I want to see the senior officer. Who's in charge here? Take me to him.'

The police officer looked at her patiently. 'Do you want this or not?'

'I'm a British citizen. You can't detain me here,' Maggie snapped, realising how pathetic she sounded. In post-imperial India her nationality was anything but an advantage. 'You haven't questioned me. You haven't charged me with any offence,' she went on. 'What grounds do you have for keeping me in this dump?'

The police officer didn't say anything. He merely looked at her with mild, slightly bored eyes. His imperturbability infuriated Maggie; the calm, good-tempered way in which he refused to engage in any kind of dialogue with her. She would almost rather he came into the cell and roughed her up. Anything was better than being shut away and ignored.

'There are laws here, aren't there?' Maggie demanded. 'You've got to give me a reason for holding me. Take me before a judge, a magistrate or something. This is supposed to be a democracy.'

'Your dinner is getting cold,' the police officer said equably.

'Dinner?' Maggie almost laughed. 'You call that shit dinner?'

'Okay, your shit is getting cold.'

Maggie snatched the bowl from his grasp. 'When are you going to let me go?'

'Enjoy your meal.'

The hand withdrew and the hatch clicked shut.

Maggie hammered on the door with a fist. 'Let me out of

here, you bastards,' she yelled, a gesture of defiance, a way of releasing her pent-up frustration rather than because she believed it would have the slightest impact on the man outside.

Still livid, she carried the bowl of food back to her bed – a wooden board, like a door, which folded down from the wall on chains – and sat down. The cell was insufferably hot and airless, the only ventilation a barred window high up on one wall. The bare earth floor was crawling with flies, great big Indian flies the size of swollen raisins, and the stench from the slop bucket in one corner made her gag. But she'd been held in worse cells; had been more frightened in a cell before. The Dharamsala police didn't scare her. They were just keeping her out of the way. That was what she found particularly enraging.

She looked down at the food in the bowl. More bloody rice and watery lentils. Could they cook nothing else here? Maggie dipped the spoon into the unappetising slush and chewed a mouthful slowly.

In the evening of the fourth day, they reached the oracle lake of Lhamo Latso. They'd left their ponies and guide a day's ride beyond the frontier and continued north in the back of a lorry heading for Lhasa. It was cold and uncomfortable, but quicker and less taxing than trying to complete the journey on horseback. Near Choekhorgyal, the closest settlement to the lake, they left the lorry and hired another pony for Pasang Rinpoche. There was a Buddhist monastery at Choekhorgyal where they could have asked for help, but they kept well away from it. Destroyed by the Chinese, and later partially rebuilt by Tibetan monks, the monastery – like most others in Tibet – was too full of Chinese placemen and informers to be safe.

For several hours they went north-east up a narrow valley fringed with high, scree-covered slopes, Tsering leading the skinny mountain pony over the rocky terrain. Lobsang and Jigme brought up the rear, their backs laden with their luggage – tents, a stove, food, spare clothes. Even on a pony, Pasang Rinpoche struggled with the physical demands of the trek. They were close to 13,000 feet high now and the old lama – his lungs afflicted with asthma and accustomed to the lower altitudes of McLeod Ganj – was finding it difficult to breathe. He clung to the reins, swinging from side to side with the motion of the pony, his face contorted with pain as he gasped for air. The three younger monks, fit though they were, were also finding the going tough. Each breath they took was starved of oxygen, each pace an effort. Tsering was surprised at how hard it was. He'd lived most of his life in Tibet, had thought his body would be permanently acclimatised to the thin air, but the years in India had softened him more than he'd expected.

Dusk was falling as they climbed over a low rock lip and saw the lake before them. It was set in a deep basin almost completely surrounded by mountains, the highest capped with snow that never melted even in summer. They paused, taking in the awesome panorama. Tsering had never seen Lhamo Latso before – nor had Lobsang and Jigme – but the oracle lake held a mythical and mysterious place in their faith. It was here that visions were seen, that destiny could be glimpsed by those with the power to decipher it. The signs that had guided previous search parties to both the Thirteenth and Fourteenth Dalai Lamas had been found in the crystal waters of this lake. Now they were here to seek out a portent of the Fifteenth.

Tsering helped Pasang Rinpoche down off the pony and seated him on a rock while he took out a small butane stove from one of the packs. Lobsang and Jigme busied themselves with pitching their two tents on a patch of flat ground in the shelter of an enormous boulder, clearing away the surface layer of rocks to make a smooth bed for the groundsheets.

Tsering took a kettle down to the edge of the lake. It was the clearest water he'd ever seen. Every pebble, every grain of sand and gravel was visible in the shallows along the shoreline. Further out the surface was opaque, turning silver like a mirror as the sun dropped below the encircling mountains. He dipped his hands into the water. It was as cold as melted ice. He took a sip and felt the freezing liquid numb his throat, taking his breath away. He shuddered and swallowed a few times to ease the raw pain. Then, after filling the kettle, he returned to the camp, ignited the stove and set the kettle on the top.

'How are you, Rinpoche?' he asked.

The lama gave a feeble nod, too exhausted to speak. Tsering saw that he was shivering and fetched a blanket to wrap around the old man's shoulders. A wind was picking up as the daylight faded. A cold, gusting breeze that started to break up the surface of the lake, sending tiny waves out to lap the shore.

Tsering made black tea, strong and hot, and they curled their hands around their tin mugs, feeling the warmth seeping through their tired bones. Over to one side, the hobbled pony nuzzled the stony earth, searching for scraps of vegetation to eat. No one spoke. Conversation was too draining. Then Tsering fetched more water from the lake and made a pan of vegetable soup from a packet, adding dried noodles to fill it out. Pasang Rinpoche shook his head when he was offered a bowl.

'You must, Rinpoche,' Tsering insisted. 'You've eaten almost nothing all day.'

'I'm not hungry.'

'Here, let me.'

Tsering took a spoon and forced some soup between the lama's lips, feeding him like a baby. Pasang Rinpoche managed only a few mouthfuls before turning his head away, too weary to swallow any more. Between them, the other monks carried him to his tent and wrapped him in blankets. Then they returned to the stove and huddled around the butane flame, finishing their soup. It was an extravagant use of scarce fuel, but they were cold and there was no wood or anything else with which to make a fire. They were above the tree line, in a rocky, barren desert. Only moss and a few alpine flowers and grasses could survive here.

In time, they extinguished the stove and prepared themselves for bed. Tsering walked to the lake and sat down crosslegged on the shore. It was dark now. He could see the water in front of him, black and shadowy, stippled with pinpricks of starlight which ebbed and flowed with the ripples on the surface of the lake. It was so quiet he could hear every tiny movement of the water. He stared into the distance. The mountains were all around him, their summits silhouetted against the paler hues of the night sky like huge jagged fingers cradling Lhamo Latso in the palm of a vast hand. He closed his eyes and began to meditate, murmuring a mantra as he emptied his mind, letting the stresses of the day drain away. His breathing eased, his heartbeat slowed, and for a time he lingered in the peaceful limbo between sleeping and waking. When he returned to full consciousness, he felt rested, ready to face the rigours he knew the next day would bring.

Lobsang and Jigme were already inside their tent. Tsering quietly unzipped the flap of the second tent and crawled inside. Pasang Rinpoche was sleeping fitfully, his breathing laboured and rasping. Tsering lay down beside him, not bothering to undress, and wrapped his blankets around himself. The ground was hard and uneven. He turned on his side, trying to find a hollow for his hip bone. The tent was small, claustrophobic. Outside, the wind moaned, catching at the sides of the tent so that they flapped and billowed.

Tsering closed his eyes and tried to sleep. He saw the lake in his mind. No longer limpid, it was growing cloudier, murkier. Darker and darker it became, the waves swelling and washing over him, until he was submerged in absolute blackness.

They rose at first light. Tsering went down to the lake and stripped off his *chuba* to wash himself. The water was even colder than the night before. Gasping with shock, he splashed his shoulders and arms and chest, then rubbed himself vigorously dry with a towel. Replacing his *chuba*, he knelt down again and washed his face, massaging the icy water into his skin like an ointment until he tingled all over. Then he stood up and looked out over the lake. The wind had died. The air was still, the sky cloudless. It was going to be a fine day. It was a good omen.

When he returned to the camp, Lobsang and Jigme were emerging from their tent, bleary-eyed and yawning. None of them had slept well and they were not in the mood for talking. They nodded at each other and while Lobsang and Jigme went to the lake to wash, Tsering lit the stove and made tea. He took the first cup in to Pasang Rinpoche who was lying on his back in the tent, awake but too weak to get up. Tsering helped him into a sitting position and supported him while the lama took a few sips of the sweet tea.

'The day is warm and clear,' Tsering said. 'The Buddha is smiling on us.'

'Help me up,' Pasang Rinpoche said. 'It is time to begin.'

Tsering assisted the lama from the tent and held him around the waist as they walked slowly down to the water's edge. The old man barely had the strength to stay upright. Tsering lowered him to a rock and washed his face and hands.

'Thank you,' Pasang Rinpoche said, struggling to find enough breath for even a few words. 'I am sorry to be a trouble to you.'

'You are not a trouble, Rinpoche,' Tsering replied. 'It is an honour to help you.'

'Is everything ready?'

'It will be shortly. But you must eat something first. You must prepare yourself for the day.'

The old man smiled feebly. 'You bully me, Tsering.'

'I know, Rinpoche. Someone has to.'

They walked back to the camp and Tsering coaxed the lama into drinking more tea and nibbling a couple of biscuits. By the time they'd finished, Lobsang and Jigme had laid out the lama's ceremonial robes on a rock and were taking off their laymen's clothes to change back into their monk's robes. Tsering helped Pasang Rinpoche remove his *chuba* and put on the long maroon and yellow robe, the thick maroon cloak

54

and the high yellow hat with a crest like a horse's mane which was the distinctive headwear of the Gelukpa sect, the dominant force in Tibetan Buddhism.

'Where are the items?' the lama asked.

'They are here, Rinpoche.'

Carefully, Tsering unpacked a silk parcel to reveal a rosary, a pair of metal-framed spectacles, a silver pencil, a wooden eating bowl and a small ivory finger drum used in religious rituals – all of them possessions of the late Dalai Lama. The pencil and drum, in fact, had been passed down from the Thirteenth Dalai Lama. Pasang Rinpoche picked each item up in turn and held it in his hands, feeling it between his fingers as if drawing some hidden message from its contours. Then he nodded and the items were placed back on the silk and wrapped up again.

Tsering and Lobsang stood on either side of the lama, taking an arm each, and helped him up the steep path that led to a large flat boulder overlooking Lhamo Latso. Normally the watch for visions took place on the Throne, a ridge a thousand metres above the lake, but Pasang Rinpoche was too frail to make such a demanding climb. When they reached the rock, Tsering and Lobsang continued to support the lama while he purified the area by chanting mantras and sprinkling the surface of the rock with water from the lake. Then all three of them recited the refuge prayer – *Pay ngo wor jur pa, Cho chi pung po tong trak jay chu tsa shi jung nay* . . . kneeling down and performing three full body prostrations symbolising devotion to the three jewels of the Buddha, the Dharma and the Sangha. Each time, Tsering and Lobsang lowered Pasang Rinpoche to the rock, and helped him up again. The prayer completed, they recited in unison the Bodhisattva vows, pledging themselves to the search for enlightenment for all sentient beings. Then Pasang Rinpoche was lowered again, this time into the meditation position. His cloak was arranged around him to shelter him from the elements and a long leather belt was strapped around his back and crossed legs to stop him keeling over with fatigue during the long vigil. In one of the lama's hands was placed a tiny brass bell, in the other a *dorje*, the ritual brass thunderbolt that symbolised the indestructibility of the Buddha's teachings.

Jigme brought more water from the lake and poured it into seven small silver bowls which were lined up in front of Pasang Rinpoche. A stick of incense was wedged into a crack in the rock behind the bowls and lit. The smoke curled slowly into the air, the fine tendrils drifting out over the lake and disappearing into a haze of sunlight.

The watching began. Tsering and the other two monks took it in turn to sit beside the lama as he gazed at the surface of the lake. Pasang Rinpoche was in a semi-trance. His eyes were open but he was sealed inside a world of his own, watching for something that only he could see and understand. Tsering studied the water too, knowing he would not share in the vision if it came, but wondering for a moment whether he might see some small sign. Immediately he berated himself for his vanity and presumption. He was there to serve, not to participate.

The morning passed. At intervals, the monks would make tea for themselves, and at midday they prepared a simple lunch of rice and spiced vegetables. Tsering took a bowl up to the rock and made Pasang Rinpoche eat some. The lama swallowed a little without speaking, then returned to his trance, his eyes fixed unwaveringly on the water below.

As the afternoon progressed, the wind picked up. The surface of the lake became choppier. It was no longer possible to see the bottom, even in the shallows. The sky clouded over. A mass of swollen cumulus rolled in from the east, obscuring the sun. The temperature dropped. The whole lake was in shadow now, its surface torn by the wind. Waves moved across it, dipping and surging, the eerie light picking out strange shapes in the water. Tsering watched intently, but he couldn't discern anything recognisable in the churning swell.

Pasang Rinpoche could.

There was something different about the lama. He hadn't

moved for hours. His body remained in exactly the same position, his gaze still riveted on the lake. But something had changed. His posture was a little more upright, his neck tilted forwards as if he were craning to see something. His eyes were wide open, unblinking, concentrating with such a fierce intensity they seemed to be burning with light. It was happening.

Tsering watched, his eyes flicking back and forth between the lama and the lake. He kept very still, hardly daring to breathe for fear of disturbing Pasang Rinpoche. The lake was changing. A swathe of cloud broke apart and for an instant the sun blazed down on the water, searing a line across the surface that seemed to cut the lake in two. On either side of the line the waves rose in a bank, spreading outwards so that it appeared as if the waters were parting and a giant crack opening up down the centre of the lake. The waves rolled out, racing towards the shore, but along the sunlit line the water was absolutely still, so clear that it seemed as if it were not there.

Pasang Rinpoche was staring directly up the line which began just below the outcrop on which he was sitting. Tsering followed his gaze but could see nothing in the water. The lama stiffened, his torso going rigid as though some unseen force were pulling him upwards. His mouth opened, the lips drawn back from the teeth. His eyes bulged, gaping into a chasm; draining, emptying, so that there was nothing at all between his consciousness and his vision. The two were the same.

Then a cloud obliterated the sun. The line in the lake disappeared in an instant, like a torch beam snapping suddenly off. Pasang Rinpoche gave a shudder. A moan escaped from his lips and his head slumped down on to his chest as he lost consciousness.

Tsering shouted down to Lobsang and Jigme and they scrambled up the path on to the outcrop. Between them, the monks carried Pasang Rinpoche down to the lake. They removed his hat, loosened his robes and bathed his face with water. The lama's heart was racing, Tsering could feel it when he laid his hand on the old man's chest. His breathing was shallow, rapid. Tsering was alarmed. It was too much for someone as old and feeble as Pasang Rinpoche. Tsering wondered whether he should have forced the lama to break his vigil and rest, whether he should have intervened before the old man passed out.

'Rinpoche, Rinpoche, wake up,' Tsering murmured, splashing more cold water on the lama's forehead. 'Rinpoche.' Tsering patted the lama's hollow cheeks. 'A cup of water, quickly!'

Jigme dipped a cup in the lake and passed it to Tsering who lifted the old man's head and forced some water between his lips. Pasang Rinpoche stirred. He coughed a little as the water slipped down his throat. Then his eyes opened. Tsering raised him into a sitting position and supported his back with an arm around his shoulders.

'We are here, Rinpoche.'

The lama blinked and peered around as if trying to work out where he was. Then he saw the monks looking down at him and sighed with relief.

'It is over,' he said.

His eyes closed and he lapsed into a deep sleep. Tsering and Lobsang lifted him up and carried him to his tent. They laid him down on the groundsheet, wrapped him in blankets and left him in peace.

Jigme was waiting anxiously outside the tent. 'Will he be all right?'

Tsering nodded. 'He just needs rest.'

'Did he see anything?'

'I think so. We must be patient. He will tell us when he is ready.'

It was twilight before Pasang Rinpoche awoke. He emerged unsteadily from his tent and walked across to where the monks were gathered around the stove, eating soup and bread. Lobsang and Jigme helped the lama sit down while Tsering poured him a mug of black tea.

'How are you, Rinpoche?'

'I am recovered.'

The old man sipped his tea. He seemed somehow less frail, and there was a serenity about him that had not been there earlier. They sat in silence, eating their meal. A few metres away, Lhamo Latso was still once again, barely a ripple disturbing its surface.

Finally, Pasang Rinpoche put down his mug and looked around at the three monks. They waited expectantly for him to speak.

'The Buddha has blessed us,' he said. 'His compassion knows no bounds, his wisdom exceeds all understanding. When we needed him most, he came to our aid.'

The lama paused. The monks watched his face which radiated a mixture of devotion and wonder.

'He has given me a sign,' Pasang Rinpoche continued. 'Four signs. I saw them in the water. The first was a mountain. A high mountain with snow on the top and a distinctive shape. Like this.'

He leaned forward and swept away a clutch of stones on the ground, revealing the gritty sand underneath. With his finger he drew the outline of the mountain in the sand. It had a high peak in the middle and two lower peaks on either side, the three summits separated by V-shaped valleys, so in profile the mountain looked a bit like a king's crown.

'The second sign was a bear, a white bear standing on its hind legs with its paws outstretched. I do not know what it means. It was shadowy, difficult to see clearly.

'The third sign was a blue mountainside. I could not see whether it was the same mountain I saw in the first sign or whether it was a different one. It was a hillside, a steep slope covered in blue, as if the rock had been painted or a piece of the sky had fallen on it. And the fourth sign was a lotus flower.' He paused again. 'We should pray now, offer our thanks to the Buddha.'

They cupped their hands to their chests and chanted in unison for several minutes. Then Pasang Rinpoche turned his eyes to the lake which was fading away in the dusky light.

'Walk with me, Tsering,' he said.

They went down to the shore and stood together by the water.

'The Buddha has given us what we came here for,' Pasang Rinpoche said quietly. 'He has shown us the way. I have fulfilled my role. Now it is your turn.'

Tsering turned his head to look at the lama. 'My turn, Rinpoche?'

'I will not be coming with you on the next stage of the search.'

For a moment Tsering was too stunned to speak. Then he stammered, 'Rinpoche . . . I do not understand. What do you mean?'

'I would only be a burden to you,' Pasang Rinpoche went on. 'I am old, my health is not good. I have seen the signs. Now the responsibility for finding the child is yours.'

'Finding the child?' Tsering whispered. 'But I thought we were here only to seek guidance from the oracle lake, not to begin the search.'

'We cannot afford to delay. Now we have the signs, we must press on at once. *You* must press on.'

'It is too much, Rinpoche,' Tsering protested. 'I am not worthy of such an onerous task.'

'You are ready, Tsering.'

'But, Rinpoche . . .'

The lama held up a hand to silence him. 'Listen to me. You are ready. That is why I chose you to accompany me. I have taught you these past ten years. I have seen you grow. This is a task for the strong. It will need great physical and mental resilience to complete it. You are the strongest monk, Tsering. You must do it.'

'No, Rinpoche, I am not worthy,' Tsering repeated. 'Only a high lama can undertake the search. That is how it has always been.'

'Things are different now. The Chinese control Tibet. It is

hostile territory. We cannot send out high lamas to find the chosen child as we did in the past. We must do it by stealth. We must use cunning and guile. Religious distinction is no longer enough. The search must be carried out by men of resource and courage. You have those qualities in abundance.'

'But I am not learned enough. I am too young, too lacking in wisdom for such a task.'

'You have wisdom enough. One day you too will be a high lama. Perhaps you may come here again and see the visions for yourself. The responsibility is great, but you can carry it out.'

Tsering shook his head. 'You honour me, Rinpoche. But I don't even know where to begin.'

'Begin with the signs. Follow them.'

'How?'

'The Buddha will guide you. Have faith, Tsering. We are but the vessel of his wisdom and compassion.'

Tsering turned away. His initial shock had given way to anxiety. He felt sick with worry and fear.

'Look at me, Tsering,' Pasang Rinpoche said gently. 'Look at me.'

Tsering swung back. The lama was regarding him with warm, affectionate eyes. There was a bond between them. Of teacher and pupil, mentor and disciple. But it was more than that too. There was real love there.

'I do not do this lightly,' Pasang Rinpoche said. 'The task is difficult, but I believe in you. You must believe in your-self.'

The lama lifted his hand and touched his fingers to Tsering's forehead, conferring a benediction on him, blessing him.

'You have been chosen, Tsering. I know you will not fail.'

That night, Tsering had a dream. He was standing by a lake, crystal clear like Lhamo Latso, only it was surrounded not by mountains but by lush green pasture. In the middle of the lake grew a majestic tree, its boughs laden with glistening wish-granting gems. The refuge tree. On the central branch was a bejewelled throne supported by eight magic lions and on the throne sat Pasang Rinpoche in the form of a perfect Buddha. On the other branches were yidams and Bodhisattvas and other enlightened beings surrounded by a radiant rainbow of the Dharma teachings whose light dazzled Tsering as he gazed up at the tree. He felt the warmth of the light, felt his fears and worries melt away. A serene calm settled over him, purifying him, filling his body with a quiet euphoria. Then the gems started to fall from the tree like raindrops. Tsering held out his hand and caught some and saw that they were not jewels but tiny Buddhas. They sat on his palm, gleaming like tears, but when he tried to touch them they dissolved and slipped away through his fingers.

When he awoke, that sense of peace was with him still. He looked up at the roof of the tent and felt strong and invigorated. He glanced to the side and saw that Pasang Rinpoche wasn't there. His blankets were folded neatly in the place where he'd been sleeping.

Tsering unzipped the door and looked out. The lama was down by the lake, sitting cross-legged, meditating. Tsering crawled out and stretched his limbs. He took the kettle down to fill with water, moving further along the shore to avoid disturbing Pasang Rinpoche, then brought it back and boiled it on the stove to make tea. The lama hadn't moved. Tsering wondered how long he'd been down there. He thought about taking him some tea, but decided against it. Breaking another person's contemplation, especially someone as venerable as Pasang Rinpoche, was an inconsiderate act that no monk would undertake lightly.

It was only when Lobsang and Jigme had come out of their tent and they were eating their breakfast that Tsering's thoughts turned back to Pasang Rinpoche. The lama was still deep in meditation, immobile as a statue. Tsering watched him and a tremor of unease passed through his mind. There was something about the lama that struck him as odd. Tsering wasn't sure what it was, but it disturbed him.

Putting aside his bowl, Tsering walked down across the rocky foreshore and stopped beside Pasang Rinpoche. The lama's hands were cupped in his lap, his ivory rosary clutched between his fingers. His eyes were open, fixed on a point at the far side of the lake, but they seemed empty and lifeless.

'Rinpoche?'

The old man didn't stir. Tsering leaned down and touched his bare arm. The skin was cold, the limb stiff and curiously detached, as if it were no longer part of his body.

'Rinpoche?'

Tsering touched the lama's face and an icy chill of realisation lanced through him. He fell to his knees and stared at Pasang Rinpoche. Stared in disbelief and horror and pain.

FOUR

Maggie's stomach muscles were aching, but she forced herself to continue. Five more. Just five. She gripped her fingers behind her head and curled her body upwards in an arc until her forehead was almost touching her knees. How many sit-ups was that? Fifty-one? Fifty-two? She'd lost count. She uncurled backwards and lay flat on the floor, panting for breath. Her abdomen felt red hot, a burning strip underneath her grimy T-shirt. Just four more. She could do it. Gritting her teeth, she jerked her head up again and stretched forwards, closing her eyes and concentrating on the exercise, a mental as well as physical challenge. A fly landed on her nose but she ignored it. Three more. Now two. One. She collapsed backwards and flung out her arms and legs. Oh, the blessed relief! Her chest was heaving, her face streaming with sweat, but it felt good. It always felt good when it was over.

She lay there on the dusty floor until her breathing was back to normal. Then she stood up and wiped her face with the bottom of her T-shirt. It was early morning, but already the cell was like an oven. She spread her legs and lifted her arms, ready to start one of her yoga exercises, staving off the tedium of incarceration with a gruelling regime of callisthenics . . . and became suddenly aware of the eyes watching her through the hatch in the door. She lowered her arms and glared at the police officer.

'Enjoying yourself?' she asked scathingly. 'Have you nothing better to do than spy on me?'

The hatch banged shut and a key turned in the lock. The cell door swung open.

'You can go,' the police officer said.

Maggie looked at him without moving. 'What?'

'You're free to go. We're releasing you.'

'Just like that. No charges.'

'No charges.'

'Where's my camcorder?'

'You can collect it at the desk.'

Maggie picked up her sweat top and took a last look around the cell – a reflex action for there was nothing about it she wanted to remember. She followed the officer down the corridor to the front of the police station and waited while he gave her back her belongings – just her camcorder, her jacket and the money she'd had on her when she was caught. She counted the money and wasn't surprised to find that half of it was missing.

'Where's the rest of it?' she asked.

'The rest?' the police officer replied innocently.

'Keep it,' Maggie said. 'For services rendered. I've had such a great time here it was cheap at the price. Make sure the chef gets his cut. He could buy a few more sacks of bloody lentils with it.'

The police officer pushed the camcorder across the desk. Maggie checked it over.

'What happened to the tape?'

'What tape?'

Maggie didn't pursue it. She hadn't seriously expected the Tibetans to give her back the material she'd taped.

'Enjoy your journey, Miss Walsh,' the police officer said politely.

'Pardon?'

'You'll be leaving Dharamsala this morning. You have outstayed your welcome.'

'My things are still at my hotel in McLeod Ganj.'

'You may collect them. But if you go anywhere near the Tibetan compounds, you will be arrested again. Next time we may not be so lenient with you.'

Maggie picked up her camcorder. 'Thanks for having me,' she said sourly.

The police officer smiled. 'The pleasure was all ours.'

She walked out into the street and paused to let her eyes adjust to the glare. She inhaled deeply, trying to clear her lungs of the fetid stench of the cell. Her five days inside had been uncomfortable and boring rather than truly unpleasant, but she was nonetheless relieved to be out.

Then she noticed a newspaper seller across the street, read the crude handwritten billboard next to his stand, and froze for an instant. So it had happened. Shit! Burning with anger, she strode across, dodging the traffic, and bought a copy of the English-language *Times of India*. The front page was emblazoned with the headline, 'Dalai Lama Dies', a strapline above it reading, 'Tibetan leader suffers massive stroke'.

Maggie glanced at the text and bit her lip, swearing under her breath. She'd missed it. Missed the whole bloody story. She rolled up the newspaper and walked down the street to a café where she bought some cigarettes and a bottle of beer. She sat at a table, chain-smoking her way through the packet and reading the newspaper.

The official announcement by the Tibetan Government in exile had been made the previous day. It said very little except that the Dalai Lama had had a stroke and fallen into a coma from which he never recovered. It gave no specific time for either the stroke or his actual death. Most of the newspaper article was taken up with photographs of His Holiness and reactions to his death from around the world. There were further pieces on the inside pages recounting the Dalai Lama's life history and speculating about what might happen next to both Tibet and the Tibetans in exile.

Maggie threw down the newspaper and finished her beer. If anything, she was angrier now she'd read the reports: with herself for getting caught inside the Tsuglagkhang Temple; with the Tibetans – particularly the monk who'd apprehended her – for confiscating her tape; and with the Indian police who'd so helpfully kept her out of the way until it was all over. 'Bastards!' she muttered resentfully, repeating the word a few times like a mantra. She'd blown it, that was the worst of it. She'd had a head start on the world's media, a prestigious exclusive all lined up, and she'd thrown it away. Flushed it down the toilet. The only question that remained was what she was going to do about it – and nothing was more certain than that she was going to do something. Inertia had never been one of Maggie Walsh's faults.

Picking up the paper, she walked out of the café and took a taxi up the hill to McLeod Ganj. As she'd predicted in her conversation with the tall monk, the road outside Gangchen Kyishong was already jammed with cars and communications vans. And this was only the vanguard. When the legions arrived in force, congregating ghoulishly for the Dalai Lama's funeral, there would be standing room only on the mountain.

The owner of the hotel in which she'd been staying before the Dharamsala police made her their guest had removed all her luggage from her room and relet it to a producer from an Indian television network. Maggie reclaimed her possessions and went to the post office to make a phone call. After trying for an hour, she finally got through to David Ackland in London.

'Maggie, where the hell have you been?' Ackland demanded bluntly. 'Everybody in the bloody world has got the story except us. What the fuck are you playing at?'

'I'm sorry, David.'

'Have you got any pictures?'

'No.'

'What do you mean, no? What did you go out there for? What was that three grand I gave you for? What've you been doing? I've been trying to locate you since yesterday morning. Where've you been?'

'I've been in jail.'

'You've *what*?'

Maggie told him what had happened. Ackland was silent for a moment. Then he said, 'You screwed up, Maggie. We were supposed to be first to the kill. That was the deal.'

'I've been in a police cell for five days, David.'

'You missed it. You've got nothing, Maggie. Sweet fuck-all.'

'I'll make it up to you.'

'How? Everybody's there now. The pictures are all over CNN, the BBC, Sky. What can you give us that's not already being covered?'

'I can give you Lhasa.'

'What?'

'Lhasa,' Maggie repeated.

She heard nothing except a crackle on the line for so long she thought they'd been disconnected.

'David?'

'Lhasa?' Ackland said eventually. 'Maggie, the Chinese have closed the frontiers with Tibet. Every foreign journalist in the country has been expelled.'

'That's the point,' Maggie replied. 'There's no one there to record what happens. There's going to be trouble, I can guarantee it. The Tibetans will take to the streets. There'll be a huge outpouring of grief. The Chinese will send in the riot police, the army. There's going to be violence and the Chinese don't want any Western news organisation witnessing it.'

'You'll never get in.'

'I'll find a way.'

Ackland didn't reply. Maggie waited, sensing he was still there on the line. When his voice came, it was faint, emerging indistinctly through the interference.

'I hope you know what you're doing.'

'So do I,' Maggie replied. 'I'll be in touch.'

'Stay out of trouble.'

Maggie smiled. 'Don't I always?'

Pasang Rinpoche's body was laid out on the shore covered with a blanket. Tsering, Lobsang and Jigme sat in a huddle a few metres away, trying not to look at the shapeless bundle. They were tough, resilient monks, but the lama's death had shaken them.

'We cannot take him back to India,' Tsering said. 'It's at least a four-day journey, more if we attempt to do it all on foot or horseback. It's too dangerous. One Chinese checkpoint and that would be the end. How would we explain a body?'

'Yet we cannot leave him here,' Lobsang countered. His face was screwed up into a deep scowl of anxiety.

'We must find a *ragyapa* village,' Tsering continued. 'Make sure he has a proper burial.' He paused, glancing uncomfortably at the shrouded body. 'It is what Pasang Rinpoche would have wanted. He was always a stranger in India. Like all of us. He would have wanted to be buried here in the motherland.'

Jigme shook his head in bewilderment. The youngest of the three monks, he was finding it hard to think in terms of what came next. His mind was still dwelling on the past.

'Why?' he asked. 'He seemed fit and well last night. In better health than he had been for a long time.'

'He had completed his task,' Tsering said with a fatalistic shrug. 'There was nothing more left for him to do. He died happy. And he will come again.'

'And what about us?' Lobsang demanded. 'What do we do?'

'We start the search,' Tsering replied.

Lobsang and Jigme turned to look at him, their faces puzzled, then incredulous.

'The search?' Lobsang repeated. 'What do you mean?'

'What I say,' Tsering answered. 'Pasang Rinpoche spoke to me yesterday evening. I think he knew even then that he would not see out another day. He charged me with beginning, and completing, the search.'

'That is madness,' Lobsang said vehemently. 'Three lowly monks like us? It is not for us to take on such an important task.'

'That is what I told the Rinpoche,' Tsering replied. 'He would not have it. It was his wish that we should do it. He *entrusted* us with the task. We cannot betray that trust.'

Lobsang stared at him. 'You realise how vital this is to the future of our people?'

'I realise. I have thought of nothing else since he spoke to me. But Pasang Rinpoche was right. If we leave Tibet now, who knows when another search party might get back in? It could be years. In the meantime, the Chinese will begin their own search, as they did with the Panchen Lama. At the moment, we have the advantage. No one knows we are here. The Chinese will not expect us to be beginning our search so soon. We will never again have such advantages on our side.'

Lobsang and Jigme were silent. Tsering knew he had to overcome their scepticism, convince them the way Pasang Rinpoche had convinced him.

'We have the signs from the oracle lake to guide us. We have His Holiness's possessions for the tests. We have been chosen by Pasang Rinpoche, the most senior incarnate lama of our sect. If he thought we could do it, then we can. We *must.*'

Still the other two were silent. Tsering turned to Lobsang first, knowing that he was the key. If Lobsang could be persuaded, then Jigme would follow without question.

'We are monks. We have taken vows of obedience. We have pledged to devote our lives to the Buddha. We are here to serve. It is not for us to doubt the wisdom of Pasang Rinpoche, our teacher and our mentor. He has honoured us with this task. We must honour him in the fulfilling of it.' Tsering paused. 'The responsibility is onerous, but we are blessed to have been given it. The call has come. We must answer it.'

Lobsang frowned pensively and looked away across the lake. The tops of the mountains were hidden in cloud, a grey mist hanging low over the surface of the water.

'I give you a choice,' Tsering continued more gently. 'It is for you to decide. I do not ask you to accompany me. You may return to India. But if you stay, you must be fully committed. You must have no doubts.'

Tsering waited. To doubt was human. Only fools lived their

lives in absolute certainty. Humility, the abnegation of individual will, were integral parts of the monastic path. They had been trained to doubt themselves, to overcome their base instincts, their unworthy impulses, and trust in the Buddha. That trust, the basis of their faith, was the rod and staff that would help them through the task ahead.

Eventually, Lobsang spoke. 'If it is the Buddha's will, then it must be done. And done with all our strength and determination. But I would ask one thing: that we contact Dharamsala and make sure that we have their approval. They must be told.'

Tsering nodded. 'We will go to Lhasa, make contact with the Underground, and send a message to the *Kashag*. We will not proceed without their full backing. Jigme?'

'I am with you,' Jigme said simply.

'Then let us strike camp and move out.'

They saw the vultures gathering on the escarpment long before they reached the *ragyapa* village. The dark shapes circled and glided gracefully down on to the cliff top, perching on the edge like finials carved from the rock. Perhaps fifteen or twenty birds, waiting patiently for the next offering to arrive.

The monks pressed on up the narrow gorge. Pasang Rinpoche's body, still wrapped in the blanket, was strapped to the saddle of the pony. It was approaching evening. They'd been on the move all day, coming down from Lhamo Latso to the outskirts of Choekhorgyal where Tsering had left the others and gone into the village to find the location of the nearest sky burial site. And then a four-hour walk up an uninhabited valley to the fleshcutters' settlement, a remote outpost where the *ragyapa*, the shunned but indispensable pariahs of Tibetan society, lived.

The village was at the top end of the gorge where it opened out into a deep basin surrounded by high cliffs. A small stream cascaded down one of the rock faces, collecting in a pool before flowing out down the side of the stone houses.

Even in the middle of the day, parts of the village would have been in shadow but now, as dusk neared, the whole area was dark, pervaded with a damp chill that cut to the bone.

As the monks entered the village, a tall, skinny man came out of one of the houses and watched them silently. He had a face ingrained with dirt and, over his *chuba*, he wore an apron that was soiled with blood and human remains. He noticed the bundle draped across the pony's saddle and gestured towards the far end of the village, walking ahead of them to lead the way.

A couple of filthy, snot-nosed children appeared in the doorway of another house and stared at the group with blank, indifferent eyes. Tsering nodded at them, but they didn't respond. Smoke drifted out of the chimney of the house and Tsering caught a whiff of something he hadn't smelt for years: burning yak dung. It was still in his nostrils when they entered a building set apart from the others and another, more pungent, aroma displaced it: the raw, fetid stench of the mortuary. In the centre of the building – a small one-roomed stone structure with bare walls and an earth floor – was a long wooden table whose surface was deeply incised with knife cuts like a butcher's block. Hanging around the walls were various tools: mallets, hammers, saws and huge, gleaming cleavers.

Another man had joined them by now, a stocky, squat little fellow with a pronounced limp. The two *ragyapa* untied the bundle from the pony and laid it out on the table, unwrapping the blanket to reveal Pasang Rinpoche's body.

'When did he die?' the skinny fleshcutter asked. His Tibetan was so thick and guttural that Tsering struggled to understand him.

'When . . .'

'When did he die?' the man repeated.

'This morning.'

'We will need to get a monk. For the rituals. I will send to the monastery at Choekhorgyal.'

'No,' Tsering said.

He'd given this a great deal of thought on the walk from Lhamo Latso. The rites of death, the rituals to help a deceased person through the *bardo*, the interim existence before rebirth, required a monk to perform them. Tsering knew the *ragyapa* would have someone they used regularly, but he didn't want an outsider becoming involved. The fewer people who knew about Pasang Rinpoche's death, who knew about Tsering, Lobsang and Jigme, the better. On the other hand, Tsering didn't particularly want the *ragyapa* to know he was a monk himself. He was in layman's clothes and suspicions would undoubtedly be aroused. But what choice did he have? The rituals had to be performed and Tsering, weighing up the alternatives, thought it wiser to do them himself. He wanted to do it, in any case, as a last service to his mentor: speeding Pasang Rinpoche on his way to rebirth.

'No,' Tsering said again. 'I am a monk. I will carry out the ceremonies.'

The *ragyapa* shrugged. 'As you wish.'

The two fleshcutters withdrew from the building and Tsering changed out of his *chuba* into his maroon robes. With Lobsang and Jigme at his side, he stood over Pasang Rinpoche's body and began the ritual chanting, the ceremonial recitations, to take the lama's spirit through the *bardo*. It was a lengthy process and by the time he'd finished, the room was in complete darkness.

The *ragyapa* returned with a paraffin lamp and buckets of warm water. The monks stripped off Pasang Rinpoche's clothes and washed his body with the water which was scented with saffron and camphor. They dried him with towels and wrapped his body in a cotton robe, leaving his face uncovered. Then they left him there on the table and pitched their tents on a patch of grass outside the village.

At dawn the next day, the corpse was taken to the sky burial site, a large flat rock at the base of the cliffs. Tsering, Lobsang and Jigme carried Pasang Rinpoche between them, with the *ragyapa* following behind. They placed the body on

73

the rock and removed the robe, exposing the dead lama's naked, emaciated body. Above them, the vultures gazed down eagerly from the crags, awaiting their moment. One of them, braver, greedier than the others, took off and dived down. The *ragyapa* with the limp drove it away with a swinging rope, then stood at one side of the rock and continued whirling the line above his head to keep the birds at bay.

Tsering made the mark of the mandala on Pasang Rinpoche's chest and stomach and stepped back. The *ragyapa*, the skinny man from the previous evening now supplemented by three more, crouched down and began to slice the body into pieces, cutting off the flesh with knives and then crushing the bones with hammers and mixing the powder with *tsampa*, roasted barley flour, to make it more palatable to the vultures.

The three monks watched from a distance. Tsering and Lobsang had witnessed sky burials before but for Jigme, most of his adult life spent in exile, this was the first time. He knew the rationale behind what was, to Western eyes, a rather gruesome funeral practice: that in a country where the ground was too rocky or frozen for ordinary burial, and where there was little wood for cremation, a sky burial was the only practical solution, as well as being a final act of charity – providing food for other living creatures. But he still found it difficult to stomach. He looked away, watching the vultures on the clifftop instead. They were stretching their wings, adjusting their talons on their precipitous perches, their hard, beady eyes fixed on the feast being prepared for them below.

When the *ragyapa* had finished their bloody work, they drew back from the rock, their knives glinting in the sunlight. The man with the limp stopped swinging his rope and the vultures, taking this as a signal, descended *en masse*, swooping down and settling over the flat rock like a voluminous black cloak.

The *ragyapa* with the limp watched through the window of

his house as the three men departed. They walked away with their pony, taking the path back down the gorge. There was something strange about them. One was a monk who dressed like a layman, that was peculiar. And the other two? Perhaps they were not what they seemed either.

The *ragyapa* went out into the muddy clearing in the centre of the settlement where the village leader was dividing up and distributing the money they'd been paid. The dead man's clothes, as was the tradition, had also been left as a gift, along with his *mala*, the rosary he'd used for counting off his prayers. The *ragyapa* caught sight of it. It was old and each of its one hundred and eight beads was beautifully carved out of ivory. Not a poor man's *mala*. Maybe not even an ordinary layman's.

The *ragyapa* returned to his house and waited, giving the three strangers enough time to get through the gorge. He didn't want to catch up with them by accident. Then, when no one was looking, he slipped out of the village and limped away down the path, moving as swiftly as his crippled leg would allow.

Four hours later, he reached Choekhorgyal, avoiding the monastery and continuing on to the nearby village. On the outskirts, looking incongruous amidst the rough stone Tibetan houses, was a modern concrete building, an ugly one-storey structure of unmistakable Chinese origin. Over the entrance was a sign in Chinese characters which read *Gong An Ju*, Public Security Bureau. The *ragyapa* paused on the threshold, then went inside.

FIVE

The room was bare, characterless, just a sagging wooden-framed bed under the window and a couple of hooks behind the door for hanging clothes. How many of these squalid hotels had she stayed in over the years? Maggie wondered as she walked in and threw down her bag. Dozens, maybe hundreds. In different places, different continents, yet somehow they all contrived to be the same. At the other end of the scale from the Hiltons and the Sheratons and the Holiday Inns, they seemed as much part of a worldwide chain as those ubiquitous hostelries. Instead of specialising in homogeneous Western comfort though, they had a niche market in fleas, bedbugs and other assorted vermin.

She sat down on the bed, feeling the springs of the frame through the thin mattress, and pulled back the dirty blanket to examine the sheets. They were creased, spotted with various unidentifiable stains and, when she lowered her nose to sniff them, impregnated with the distinctive odour of human sweat. The room was cold and had a dank, depressing atmosphere that reminded Maggie of a rundown English seaside boarding house in the middle of winter. Except that this was Kodari in north-east Nepal, a frontier town in the Himalayas on the Kathmandu to Lhasa highway. It should have been exotic, exciting, a vibrant trading post where different cultures and peoples intermingled in a colourful throng. Instead, it was an ugly collection of shabby wooden huts inhabited by unwashed, surly shopkeepers, grasping hoteliers and so many unscrupulous rogues it seemed to

Maggie as though a lawyers' convention was in town. The glamour of travel. Maggie had believed in it once, but somehow the illusion never survived your first rat in the toilet.

She unpacked her bag and sorted through the contents, spreading them out on the bed, calculating what was essential and what she could leave behind. Her camcorder, spare batteries and tapes were top of the list of items to keep. Next came toothbrush and toothpaste and packets of American cigarettes she'd bought in Delhi – not just to smoke but to use as bribes. Marlboros were as good as hard currency, sometimes better, when you needed to grease a few open palms. Then came a few basic toiletries, spare underwear and her first aid kit. Just about everything else was dispensable: a couple of books she'd bought in Dharamsala to read on the train journey to Delhi and then on the flight to Kathmandu; most of her clothes. She was going over the border on foot and wanted as little weight on her back as possible.

Stowing the camcorder in her battered canvas shoulder bag, she went out to find something to eat. It was growing dark, the twilight exacerbating the town's gloomy feel. The actual border with Tibet was two kilometres down the road at the ironically named Friendship Bridge, but there were no houses or hotels there. Kodari was where everyone stayed. The hotels were full of lorry drivers and merchants, suspicious, unfriendly individuals waiting patiently for the Chinese to reopen the frontier.

In a teahouse off the main road, Maggie had a plate of *dhal bhat*, the rice and lentil dish that was the staple meal in rural Nepal, followed by sweet black tea served in a thick glass tumbler. No one gave her a second glance. They were used to Western travellers here, even unaccompanied women. Maggie didn't linger. She went back to her hotel and washed perfunctorily in cold water. Then, shivering, she went to bed fully dressed and tried to sleep.

She was awake long before dawn. She stayed under the blanket watching the sky growing lighter through the gaps in the wooden shutters and running over in her mind the route she was going to take. She had it clearly mapped out, the information provided by a garrulous local on the bus from Kathmandu who'd spent most of the five-hour journey practising his English on her.

When she could bear the discomfort of the bed no longer, she crawled out and slipped on her shoes. Her watch read 5.40 am. She picked up her bag and left the room, making her way quietly downstairs. She'd paid for her bed on arrival, saying she had to leave early, though not saying why, and the hotel owner had left the front door unlocked for her. She stepped out into the street. The town seemed deserted. A pall of woodsmoke hung over the houses. Somewhere in the distance a dog was barking.

Maggie crossed the street and cut down a narrow alley between two buildings, skirting round the edge of the town to avoid the Nepalese customs post on the main road. Lanterns burned in some of the houses, but she encountered no one outdoors. Climbing over a low stone wall, she walked quickly across a patch of rough open grazing and began to drop down towards the river. She'd expected the border with Tibet to be high in the mountains, on the top of some snow-covered pass perhaps, and she'd been surprised to find it was actually deep in a gorge. The area, far from being barren and rocky, the way she'd imagined, was lush and fertile, the hillsides – where they weren't cultivated – blanketed in green, almost tropical vegetation. As she walked, the mist started to lift and she saw the valley below her. The Friendship Bridge was hidden from sight, but she could see the road on the Chinese side climbing in a series of hairpin bends to a notch in the ridge of mountains where it disappeared behind a rock spur. Zhangmu, the first town in Tibet, where the Chinese border station was located, was nine kilometres up that road. Between here and there was a largely unpopulated no-man's-land policed by neither the Chinese nor the Nepalese.

Maggie made good time. She was going downhill and the path was clear and well trodden. After half an hour she reached a bluff overlooking the river. Below her the water flowed swiftly down a steep gorge, swirling and foaming around submerged rocks. It was too wide and dangerous to attempt to swim: the powerful current would have swept her away instantly. But she knew there was another bridge upstream, an old Nepalese footbridge. The man on the bus, a trader who'd boasted of profitable smuggling excursions over the border, had told her about it. Turning on to another worn path that followed the steep bank above the river, Maggie began to climb the gorge.

The incline was gentle to start with, then it became steeper. The path kept to the easiest, least hazardous line but it was still tricky to negotiate. In places steps had been worn into the bedrock by generations of feet, in other parts the path had been washed away completely by rain and landslides. Maggie had to edge cautiously across the treacherous open slopes, all too aware of the river racing past a hundred metres below her. The valley was forested, like an alpine gorge, the pine and fir trees forming a canopy over the path. Maggie was glad of the shade. As the sun had risen higher, the day had become stiflingly hot. She had two bottles of boiled water in her bag but she was drinking so much she feared they might run out.

For two hours she climbed. She saw no one, heard nothing except the occasional rustle of a bird in the undergrowth and the roar of the river. Then she saw the bridge. It was strung across the narrowest point of the gorge, a crude, rickety-looking affair constructed of four thick ropes – two for the handrails, two with wooden planks tied across them for the feet. Maggie climbed up to it and looked across to the other side. She tested the ropes. They seemed secure enough. The planks were a little wobbly and in the middle there were a couple of gaps, but it appeared solid and safe. Grasping hold of the handrails, she inched cautiously out across the bridge. She felt it vibrate under her feet and tightened her grip. Three metres out it started to sway and Maggie paused, suddenly conscious of the white water and rocks beneath her. She glanced down. She could see the river through the cracks in the planks. She took a few more steps, the handrails sagging, the whole construction rocking like a cradle as she moved across it. She reached the gaps where the planks had either rotted or fallen away into the torrent below. This time she didn't look down. She stretched across with her hands and one foot. The gap was only eighteen inches wide but it seemed more. She took a deep breath and swung her other leg over, pausing again to regain her balance. Then she pressed on, taking each step slowly, carefully, trying to stop the bridge from swinging too much. Finally, she reached the other side and stepped on to solid ground again with an exhalation of relief. Her legs were shaking, her muscles trembling with tension. She sat down and ate a chunk of the stale loaf of bread and one of the small Nepalese bananas she'd brought with her. It was hot, the sun beating down from a cloudless sky. The air was fresh, laced with the scent of pine. Maggie was tired and could easily have lain back and gone to sleep, but she had a long way to go across hard, rugged terrain. She didn't want to be out here when darkness fell.

For another hour she climbed up the path away from the gorge, getting deeper into Chinese territory. Then suddenly she heard a noise and froze. She listened. It was a voice. Two voices now. They were above her, higher up the path. Getting nearer. Maggie dropped off the path and clambered down to conceal herself behind a rock outcrop. The voices were coming down the hill. Several voices. A Chinese border patrol? Maggie peered out tentatively and caught a glimpse of a figure on the path. He wasn't a soldier. He was barefoot, wearing a checked shirt and baggy trousers and on his back was a huge canvas sack supported by a band looped around his forehead. Behind him came five other men carrying similar packs. Porters. Porters no doubt working for one of the organised smuggling operations in the area. From their clothes Maggie guessed they were Nepalese, not Tibetan, though in this border country their high-cheekboned Mongoloid faces were the same.

She ducked back behind the outcrop and waited, listening to the voices getting fainter as the porters descended the hill towards the bridge. Only when they were well out of earshot did she scramble back up on to the path and continue her climb.

In the late afternoon, her limbs heavy with fatigue having struggled up several thousand feet of mountain, she had her first sight of Zhangmu. It was across the other side of a deep ravine, a collection of ramshackle stone and wooden buildings perched hazardously on the hillside above the twisting main road. The slope was so steep it seemed from a distance as if the buildings were constructed one on top of another. Any sudden disturbance, an earth tremor or a violent downpour, and it was easy to imagine the whole lot being washed away into the ravine. On the southern edge of the village, just below a structure which looked like a hotel, was the Chinese border station and customs post. Maggie could see uniformed soldiers with rifles loitering around on the forecourt outside the post. Higher up the road was a long line of parked lorries. Maggie studied them closely, trying to identify the cargoes loaded into their open backs. But she was too far away to make them out.

Leaving the path, she slithered down into the ravine, grabbing on to tree trunks and branches to slow her descent. When she reached the bottom, she found a dry, sheltered hollow well hidden from inquisitive eyes, and lay down on the ground. She ate a little more bread and a couple of biscuits, closed her eyes and dozed off for a while.

The sun had dipped below the horizon when she woke up again. The temperature was cooling rapidly so she put on her fleece jacket and zipped it up to the neck. She waited until it was almost dark before she started to climb up the side of the ravine. Forty minutes later she reached the top. She lay flat in the undergrowth just below the edge of the main road and looked out. She was next to the line of parked lorries. No one was about and there was no traffic. With the border closed there was nowhere for it to go. Maggie hauled herself up on to the road and looked inside the back of the nearest lorry. It was empty. So was the next. The third contained gravel and the fourth sacks of cement. She continued on down the line, keeping low so that the lorries shielded her from the buildings on the other side of the road. The fifth lorry's load she smelt before she got to it and saw the mound rising up behind the driver's cab: turnips, the one vegetable she loathed. The sixth and seventh lorries were again empty and the one after, the final one in the line, had a flat back bearing a single large wooden crate. Maggie paused to consider. None of them was really suitable. Maybe she'd try the ones higher up the road. She retraced her steps and was thirty metres on when there was a sudden burst of noise from across the road, as if a door to a crowded room had opened. She crouched down instinctively behind the turnip lorry and peeked out. A man had come out of a teahouse and was walking across in her direction. Maggie dropped to the ground and rolled underneath the lorry as the man went to the edge of the road and urinated into the ravine. When he'd finished he headed round to the cab, pulled open the door and climbed in. The engine turned over and started. Maggie had to make a quick decision. The other lorries might be here for days. At least this one was on the move. She rolled out between the rear wheels and threw her bag into the back of the lorry. It was already starting to pull out in to the road. Maggie grabbed hold of the tailgate and scrambled over the side. She crawled forward over the mound of vegetables and burrowed down into it so that only her face was exposed. She lay back and pulled the collar of her jacket up over her nose, trying to shut out the stench of ripe turnips.

When the time came for him to leave Tibet, it was the skies he would remember most, Shen Tzu reflected as he looked out of the window of his office. The thin, high-altitude air gave the atmosphere a clear, translucent quality, a brilliant azure hue that he'd seen nowhere else in China. When you looked up, it seemed as if you were staring into a vast, pure emptiness that had no beginning and no end. The sky was there, filling the horizons with its silky blue sheen, yet it wasn't there. It had colour, but no substance, like a mirage stretching to infinity.

There was little else he wanted to remember about his five years in Tibet. He regarded it as a hardship posting, a necessary rung on the ladder of his career that he wanted only to put behind him. The people here were primitive barbarians, the climate and landscape harsh and inhospitable. He missed the warmth, the familiarity of the east and longed to return to the civilisation of his native Shanghai. He did not understand the Tibetans. They had a truculent mentality, an attachment to a culture he regarded as feudal and reactionary. Their hostility to the Chinese continued both to puzzle and anger him. Had the Han not brought progress and modernisation to a backward territory? Had they not freed its people from servitude, from enslavement by monks and the landed aristocracy? The benefits were as clear as the skies above Lhasa, yet the Tibetans remained stubbornly ungrateful.

Shen could see the Tibetan Quarter of the city from his window. A squalid neighbourhood of twisting alleys and muddy courtyards, it seemed to Shen to epitomise the uncivilised nature of the indigenous population. If it had been up to him, he would have razed the whole area and replaced it with Chinese-style housing blocks. But decisions like that were made in Beijing. He was just a colonel in the Public Security Bureau; a faceless, unnoticed policeman. They've forgotten about me, he thought bitterly. Five years I've been here. I should have moved on by now, been promoted, transferred to a more important post. They've dumped me here in this shitty little backwater and left me here to rot.

He moved back to his desk as the intercom buzzed.

'Yes?'

'Major Chang is here, Comrade Colonel,' his secretary's voice replied.

'Send him in.'

The door opened and Chang entered. He was a lithe, slightly built officer who moved with such a feline grace that

83

it came as something of a shock to see how coarse his face was. His head was lumpy and misshapen, his ears sticking out, and his complexion was so pockmarked by acne it looked as if his skin had been peppered with gravel.

'You asked to see me, Comrade Colonel,' Chang said.

'Yes, take a seat.'

Shen searched around on his desk and pulled out a sheet of paper covered with typewritten Chinese characters.

'This report. From Choekhorgyal.' Shen slipped a pair of wire-framed spectacles on to his nose and glanced at the paper. 'It intrigues me.'

'I thought it would,' Chang said. 'That's why I forwarded it to you.'

'You have made further enquiries?'

'Yes, Comrade Colonel. I telephoned Choekhorgyal first, to check the facts.'

'They are accurate?'

Chang nodded. 'Three strangers, at least one of them a monk. Perhaps all of them monks. An old man dead. The flesh monkey informer said he looked like a monk too. He had a rosary that looked special. Something only a monk – maybe a senior monk – would have possessed.'

'You have contacted the Religious Affairs Bureau?'

'I received their report this morning. They have had no notification of any monk dying in that area. All licensed monks are accounted for, and none of them had been granted travel permits for that district.'

'So . . .' Shen mused for a moment. 'What do we have? Monks travelling through the area without authorisation?'

'Or simply four unlicensed monks,' Chang added.

'Is that likely?'

Chang shrugged. 'You never know with these people. They do not all come forward to be registered. Certainly, they cannot be attached to any monastery.'

Shen took a map of the Tibet Autonomous Region out of his desk drawer. He unfolded the map and spread it out.

'There is another possibility,' he said. He ran a finger over the map, searching for something. 'Choekhorgyal. A small, insignificant place,' he said, his finger coming to a halt. 'But here, close by, we have a lake. Lhamo Latso, the Tibetans call it. Do you know of it?'

'The oracle lake,' Chang replied.

Shen looked at him over his spectacles. So Chang had already worked all this out for himself. The major was always one step ahead of his superiors. That was what made him so good at his job. And he was confident enough not to feel obliged to conceal it. That was what made him dangerous.

'Yes, the oracle lake,' Shen said impassively. 'You know what the Tibetans believe happens there?'

'Yes, Comrade Colonel.'

'And your conclusion?' Shen decided to give his subordinate the opportunity to show off.

'The same as yours, Comrade Colonel. They have come from outside Tibet.'

'What about the dates? Do they make sense?'

'The announcement from Dharamsala was made four days ago. The monks were probably already at Lhamo Latso when it happened. They must have crossed the border at least two or three days before that.'

'Before the Dalai Lama died?'

Chang shook his head. 'They delayed the announcement to give them time to get to the lake.'

'They have moved more quickly than we expected,' Shen said pensively.

'What do you wish me to do?' Chang asked.

'Speak to the Religious Affairs Bureau again. Get them to send us an expert on Buddhist practices. The better informed we are, the easier it will be to decide on our course of action.'

The professor was a tiny, delicate-looking man with huge black-framed glasses containing lenses so thick they appeared almost opaque. He had a perfectly round face, a beaky little nose and a strange way of turning his neck that made him look a bit like a short-sighted owl. He was perched on the edge of a chair, his feet only just reaching the floor, blinking inquisitively at Colonel Shen.

'Professor Mah,' Shen said. 'You are a teacher at the university, I believe.'

'That is correct.'

'In Tibetan studies?'

Mah looked horrified. 'Oh, no. There are no Tibetan studies at the university. The Tibetan culture is a thing of the past. We do not teach such reactionary matters. I thought you would have known that, Comrade Colonel.'

Shen scowled, not taking kindly to being patronised by this diminutive academic.

'So what *do* you teach?' he growled.

'I teach the History of the Socialist Revolution, the People's Struggle and Political Theory,' Professor Mah replied precisely.

'I asked for an expert on Buddhism,' Shen said irritably. 'Why have they sent me you?'

'Ah, because to understand the history of the People's Republic it is necessary to have some knowledge of the inferior systems that came before it.' Mah had a slow, pedantic way of speaking, as if he were addressing an audience of particularly dim schoolchildren. 'You see, here in Tibet, for example, it is impossible to fully understand the achievements of the People's Revolution without knowing something of the primitive, misguided political system that was in place when we liberated the region. As that system was based on the imperialistic domination of the Buddhist monasteries, you will understand why it has been necessary for me to educate myself in that particular religion. In other parts of China – in Xinjiang or Qinghai, for instance – I would similarly have to acquaint myself with the traditions of Islam.'

'So you know something about reincarnation?'

'Indeed I do. The belief in reincarnation is fundamental to Tibetan Buddhism. They believe in a cycle of existence, which they call *samsara*, in which they are constantly born, die and are reborn. The cycle is broken only when an individual achieves enlightenment, or *nirvana*, and is no longer reborn. Unless they choose to be reborn, that is. There are those, Buddhas and Bodhisattvas, who have achieved enlightenment but nevertheless return to this world to help others break their cycle of suffering.' Professor Mah gave an apologetic shrug. 'It is an ignorant, feudal superstition, of course, but the Tibetans believe it. You have to understand that their whole religion was devised to keep a privileged élite of landowners and monks in comfort while the peasants slaved to provide for them. The proletariat did all the work so that the monks could spend all day doing nothing except meditating.' Mah snorted contemptuously. 'As if sitting cross-legged with your eyes closed is likely to bring you enlightenment. The whole thing is ridiculous. Now in socialist theory . . .'

'Yes, yes,' Shen interrupted tetchily. He got quite enough socialist theory from the monthly political education classes he was still expected to attend. The last thing he needed was a lecture from this pompous little man. 'What we need to know is how it applies to the Dalai Lama?'

'Well . . .' Professor Mah sucked in his cheeks as if considering where to begin, how he could make it easy for these obtuse policemen, '. . . the Tibetans believe that the Dalai Lama is the incarnation of the Buddha of Compassion. Chenresig, they call him in Tibetan. Or Avalokitesvara, if you prefer the Sanskrit name. Many of the concepts in Tibetan Buddhism also have Sanskrit equivalents because, of course, the religion has its origins in India. Indeed . . .'

'Will he be reborn?' Shen broke in abruptly.

Professor Mah started, taken aback to be cut off in mid-flow. 'Not necessarily,' he said. 'He always has been in the past, but it is possible that he may choose not to be reborn.'

'But if he is reborn, when will it happen?'

'That's a difficult question.'

Shen sighed inwardly. That was what he'd feared.

'You see,' Mah continued, 'in Buddhism there is the concept of the *bardo – antarabhava*, in Sanskrit – which is the interval between death and rebirth. When you die, you are reborn into the *bardo* which is a spirit state that can last from a moment to seven days. If, however, during that time you are unable to find a suitable rebirth situation on earth, you go through a small death and take a second rebirth in the *bardo*. This cycle can happen up to seven times, making a total of forty-nine days.'

'So he has to be reborn within forty-nine days of his death?' Shen said.

'Not necessarily,' Mah said again.

'What do you mean, not necessarily?' Shen snapped. He glanced at Chang who was leaning on the wall behind the professor, keeping well out of the discussion. Was that a faint trace of a smirk he saw on the major's face?

'With someone like the Dalai Lama,' Mah explained, 'it is always possible for him to be reborn before he dies.'

'*What*?' Shen barked. 'What are you talking about? How can he be reborn before he dies?'

Professor Mah adjusted his spectacles on his nose and rocked back on the edge of his chair. 'How can I explain this?' he said slowly. 'These things are not easy to understand. There is a precedent, you see. The Seventh Dalai Lama, for example, was born before the Sixth Dalai Lama had died. A realised being, like the Dalai Lama, can manifest himself in many forms at the same time. He need not rely on the passage of his previous body's consciousness. In Buddhism, both the premature and belated birth of a reincarnation is possible.'

'So what you're saying,' Shen snarled, finally losing patience with the professor, 'is that the Dalai Lama could have already been reborn, or could be reborn years from now?'

'Yes, you could put it like that,' Mah conceded.

'Then why didn't you say so at the beginning?'

Mah looked hurt. 'I am sorry, Comrade Colonel. I was merely trying to answer your question. What you say is quite possible, although the forty-nine-day period is the most likely. Please accept my apologies if I have inadvertently . . .'

'Yes, thank you, Professor, that is all. Major Chang will show you out.'

Mah stood up and bowed. 'I hope I have been of some assistance to the *Gong An Ju*.'

Shen gave a dismissive wave and turned away as the little man padded across the office and out of the door. He waited for Chang to come back in.

'An annoying fellow,' Shen said acidly. 'What did you make of it all?'

Chang shrugged. 'These Buddhists, they seem to make the rules up as they go along. Anything is possible if they want it to be.'

'That is the nature of all religion. It depends on extreme gullibility in its followers. An irrational belief in something that cannot possibly exist.'

The colonel fell silent, pondering what to do next. The Chinese State was a slow-moving behemoth. Since the announcement of the Fourteenth Dalai Lama's death there had been little reaction from Beijing except to expel all foreign journalists from Tibet and to close the frontiers. The People's Liberation Army and the PSB had been put on full alert throughout the Tibet Autonomous Region and in Lhasa in particular. But these were knee-jerk reactions; protective measures that the Communist leadership took automatically at times of potential crisis. What they hadn't done was address the question of what came next. They hadn't looked beyond the immediate short term. Shen had expected word from his superiors, some kind of official direction, but there had been none. They had given him no instructions, yet he knew they would not expect him to remain idle. When the behemoth finally roused itself, it would lumber forth and crush those who had been too slow to anticipate its arrival. Shen had no intention of being trampled under its cumbersome feet.

'I want a list drawn up of every male Tibetan child born since the death of the Dalai Lama,' Shen said. 'And every male child born from now until the forty-ninth day of *bardo*.'

'That could be many thousands,' Chang said.

'I know. The information will be there anyway, given that all births have to be registered. I just want it collated and sent to us.'

The proposal made little practical sense, Shen was aware of that. So was Chang. There was no way even the PSB, with its thousands of officers, could keep an eye on all the newborn baby boys across such a vast territory. But it gave the impression that action was being taken. Whether it was of any use or not was irrelevant.

'And the monks near Lhamo Latso?' Chang prompted.

'Ah yes, the monks.'

'They may have nothing to do with the Dalai Lama's death.'

'That is true,' Shen admitted. 'But I don't think so. The location, the timings, it's too much of a coincidence. They've started the search already.'

'You want them found?'

'Yes, Major. I want them found.'

SIX

It was thirteen years since Tsering had last seen Lhasa, and the changes that had come over the Tibetan capital in the interim shocked and depressed him. Some things were still the same. The skyline of the city was still dominated by the radio mast on the Chakpo Ri and the gleaming gold roofs of the Potala Palace. But the outskirts had been transformed. Where once there had been open land between the city and the mountains, now there were dozens of sprawling housing estates; vast ugly developments built for the thousands of Chinese immigrants Beijing had relocated to Lhasa. It was a Chinese city now, not a Tibetan one. The relentless colonisation that had been going on for fifty years was swamping the native residents, destroying their buildings, their history, their culture. The Fourteenth Dalai Lama had once remarked: 'China has eaten Tibet, but it cannot digest it.' That was no longer true, Tsering reflected sadly. Slowly, everything Tibetan was being dissolved and absorbed into the greedy Han gut.

Surveying the city from the cab of the truck that was bringing the three monks in through the suburbs, Tsering could see little sign of a Tibetan presence. The architecture was indisputably Chinese – row after row of barrack-like concrete buildings that had been knocked up on the cheap, their walls unfinished, rusty iron girders protruding from their roofs. The shops, the businesses were all Chinese; the signs were in Chinese; the people wandering the streets and cycling along the broad, charmless thoroughfares were all Chinese. It wasn't until they neared the centre of the city that Tsering saw any Tibetans. The truck driver – a Tibetan who'd picked them up on the highway west of Choekhorgyal – dropped them off near the Potala and they made their way on foot towards the Tibetan Quarter. Tsering found himself staring around like a tourist, noting familiar landmarks, gaping at the locals, absorbing the atmosphere, the smell of the city.

As they walked, Tsering noticed the soldiers standing in groups at road junctions, the PLA canvas-backed trucks parked by the kerbs, more armed soldiers sitting stiffly inside. The Chinese army was always to be found on the streets of Lhasa, but Tsering had never seen such a large and obvious contingent. At the Jokhang Temple, the holiest shrine in Tibet, there were yet more soldiers. They were gathered in the corners of the square – fidgety, nervous troops waiting for something to happen. The temple forecourt was crowded with people, mostly Tibetan but one or two Chinese who were almost certainly plain-clothes PSB officers from the *Gong An Ju* sub-station across the square.

Tsering could feel the tension, an undercurrent of hostility in the crowd. He pushed his way through the throng with Lobsang and Jigme just behind him. The Jokhang was a modest, unostentatious, white-painted building. On the flat roof above the main entrance was a golden *ritak-choekor*, the eight-pointed wheel of the Dharma flanked by two golden fawns; a reminder that the Buddha's first teachings had been given in a deer park. In front of the entrance, pilgrims were prostrating themselves, lying full length on the stone slabs which had been worn into smooth hollows by centuries of devout visitors. Many of the pilgrims had protective leather pads on their hands and knees – one even had pieces of cut-up truck tyre tied to his palms. Some would have come hundreds of miles, prostrating them-selves and praying the whole way. Tsering felt his heart soar. Despite decades of brutal Chinese repression, the Buddhist faith remained strong and resilient.

The three monks bought white silk *khata*, offertory scarves, from one of the stalls in the square and went into the temple. At the entrance they passed a monk standing like a sentry by the doors. Tsering caught a glimpse of a T-shirt beneath his maroon robes. He was a 'day monk', a layman paid a salary by the Chinese to give tourists and foreign visitors the impression of religious freedom in the country. At the end of his shift he would go home and change back into his layman's clothes.

Inside, the temple was still and cool. If anything, there were even more people here than outside; a great swelling body of visitors moving slowly clockwise around the chapels. As they shuffled along, the pilgrims murmured mantras, counting off the prayers on their rosaries, their humming voices reverberating as one around the darkened chambers. Butter lamps burned in every part of the temple, their flickering light illuminating the gold on the statues and the vault of the richly decorated ceiling. The three monks followed the crowd to the chapel of the Jowo Sakyamuni. They rang the bell at the entrance to alert the gods to their presence and climbed the steps, touching their heads to the feet of the sacred statue of the Buddha before offering their *khatas* and withdrawing.

Back outside the crowd was growing. So too was the number of soldiers. Several more PLA trucks had pulled into the square and were disgorging their troops. Tsering watched them with concern.

Lobsang came up to his shoulder. 'We should go,' he said quietly.

'I know.'

They moved away from the temple on to the Barkhor, the pilgrims' circuit that ringed the Jokhang. More pilgrims were circumambulating clockwise around the circuit, many of them prostrating themselves. There were market stalls along the edges selling colourful rugs, huge slabs of yak butter, jerry cans of yoghurt, spices, tea, barley flour, dried apricots. A tall trader wearing sunglasses and a wide-brimmed hat held out arms dripping with coral and turquoise jewellery. On other stalls great chunks of raw yak meat crawling with flies were displayed in the sun, their vendors standing guard with sticks to keep away the hungry neighbourhood dogs.

Tsering approached a stall selling wooden carvings – of bears and yaks and dragons and other animals as well as several beautifully crafted sculptures of the Buddha. The elderly man seated on a canvas stool behind the stall was hunched forward over the table putting the finishing touches to an intricate carving of a demon. Tsering watched the old man work for a while, admiring the skilful way he handled his knife, moulding the wood with easy, practised strokes as if it were as simple to shape as a piece of butter. The demon had four arms with huge claw-like hands on the ends, its feet were like the talons of a vulture and its face was twisted and ugly, the mouth gaping open in a fearsome snarl. If you studied it closely, you could see that the features, though distorted and exaggerated like a caricature, were unmistakably Chinese.

The old man sensed Tsering watching and looked up. Tsering nodded at him. 'Are you Wangchuk?'

The old man put down his knife and glanced around guardedly, his gaze coming to rest on Lobsang and Jigme.

'We are together,' Tsering reassured him.

'And you are?'

'My name is Tsering.'

'From?'

Tsering gave a shake of the head. 'Are you Wangchuk?' he asked again.

'Yes, I am Wangchuk.'

'We are looking for Thondup.'

The old man stiffened. His eyes flickered around once more, to the adjoining stalls, to the pilgrims passing by. Very casually he picked up his knife again. He ran a calloused thumb over the blade, testing the sharpness of the edge. Tsering noticed that he was no longer holding the knife as a tool, but as a weapon.

'We are friends,' Tsering said calmly.

'Friends from where?'

'From a long way off.'

Tsering removed his cap briefly to give the wood carver a glimpse of his shaven head. The old man gave no obvious sign that he'd seen, but his shoulders seemed to relax a little and the hand holding the knife dropped to his side. He pulled himself to his feet and asked the neighbouring stallholder to keep an eye on his things, then murmured, 'Follow me', to Tsering.

They walked a short distance around the Barkhor before plunging off down one of the narrow alleys that criss-crossed the Tibetan Quarter. Emerging into a tiny square hemmed in by two-storey stone buildings, they ducked through a low doorway and found themselves in a smoky teahouse. The old wood carver gestured at an empty table and disappeared through a curtained door at the rear of the shop. He returned a few minutes later.

'You wait,' he said curtly and went back out into the square.

The three monks settled themselves at the table and looked around the dim, dilapidated interior. There were Tibetan teahouses in McLeod Ganj, but they were sanitised imitations catering for Western tourists who liked their ethnic watering holes to be picturesque and quaint but not too insalubrious. This was the real thing. The floor was bare earth, littered with discarded cigarette stubs and glistening globules of saliva and mucus where the clientele had cleared their throats and noses. The walls were rough, unpainted plaster, discoloured by tobacco smoke and the fumes from the open yak-dung fire which burned in the hearth on one wall. The wooden tables, their surfaces polished smooth by thousands of elbows, exuded the aroma of garlic and onion and the sweet pungent flavour of marinated yak meat. The customers, gossiping in groups over bowls of greasy butter tea and *momos*, dumplings stuffed with spiced meat, were all men, all Tibetan. The few foreign tourists who visited Lhasa in carefully escorted groups would have ventured nowhere near this part of the city, and certainly no Chinese would have come here unless he wanted to leave with a knife between his ribs.

One or two of the men glanced inquisitively at the three monks, but it was no more than a passing curiosity. Even the teahouse owner, a short, leathery individual in a dirty apron, paid them no attention, standing aloof in the doorway of the kitchen with a mangy *apso*, a Tibetan terrier, curled at his feet.

Twenty minutes had elapsed when two men entered the teahouse, one through the front entrance, the other through the door at the rear. They were big men wearing *chubas* and sheepskin boots. Both carried daggers in elaborate, bejewelled sheaths on their belts. One of them stood over the table and inspected the three monks with dark eyes plugged deep into his fleshy cheeks.

'This way,' he growled.

Tsering, Lobsang and Jigme picked up their bags and followed the man through the back door, the second man sandwiching them from behind. They crossed a courtyard and went out through a gate into an alley which turned and twisted its way between the closely packed houses. They took another alley to the right, then another, cutting across a triangular intersection and into a third alley which seemed to double back on itself and return them towards the point from which they'd started. After ten minutes of changing direction, dipping in and out of innumerable courtyards and passageways, the main purpose of the exercise was completed – there was no danger that any of the three monks would ever be able to retrace their steps and pinpoint exactly where they'd been taken. They were led through yet another courtyard into a building which seemed to be a storeroom of some kind. Boxes and cardboard cartons were stacked on the floor next to bales of straw and sacks of barley. At one side of the room a wooden staircase led up to the first floor. The man in the lead stopped and turned to the monks.

'Hands on the wall,' he said tersely.

The three monks were thoroughly searched and their bags taken away from them. Then they were escorted up the stairs into a second room, the same size as the store but furnished like a home. There were colourful rugs on the wooden floor; and around the walls, about waist height, were painted bands of blue, red and green, representing the elements. In the centre of the room was a low wooden table with a carpeted couch on either side. Sitting on the furthermost couch, his arm resting casually on one of the curved wooden arms, was a striking figure of a man. He had the tall, rangy build of a Khampa, the inhabitants of the mountainous region of eastern Tibet who were renowned for their height and their courage in battle. He wore embroidered felt boots, a plain grey *chuba* over a bright red shirt, and his long black hair was tied in plaits with red silk tassels at the ends – another distinctive sign of the Khampa. Like the other two men, he wore a dagger in a jewelled sheath on his belt.

Tsering pressed his palms together in front of his chest and bowed his head. *'Tashi delek.'*

The Khampa didn't return the greeting. He studied the three men with a languid ease. He seemed relaxed but his eyes were alert and wary.

'Sit down. Take off your caps,' he said.

The three men lowered themselves on to the other couch and removed their caps to expose their cropped hair.

'You are monks?' the Khampa asked.

'Yes. You are Thondup?' Tsering replied.

'Your names?'

'I am Tsering Gyaltso. This is Lobsang Namgyal and this is Jigme Lhasang. Are you Thondup?'

'Where are you from?'

'I can speak only to Thondup.'

'I am Thondup.'

'We are from Dharamsala.'

Thondup looked at them impassively. Then he glanced at the two men who had stationed themselves by the stairs and nodded almost imperceptibly. The men picked up the monks' bags. They opened the bags and took out the contents: the maroon robes, the tents, the stove, the food supplies. Then they came to the yellow silk parcel.

'Not that!' Tsering cried.

The two men paused and turned to Thondup for guidance. He inclined his head towards the low table and they put the parcel on its surface.

'Let me see the other things,' Thondup said. He examined the robes, the camping equipment. 'How long have you been in Tibet?'

'A week.'

'You are fools,' Thondup said caustically. 'Either that or you are incredibly naïve and ignorant, which amounts to the same thing.' He picked up the robes. 'You travel in laymen's clothes and yet you have monks' robes in your bags. That makes you instantly suspicious. All monks have to be licensed, registered with the Religious Affairs Bureau, and they have to be attached to one of the state monasteries. You knew that, surely. Do you have licences with you? No? Then why carry your robes?'

'There were reasons,' Tsering said defensively.

'Were there indeed? And this stove, it is not Tibetan nor Chinese. It clearly comes from the West. So does your food. This bag of rice is marked "Produce of India".' Thondup tossed the items down in disgust. 'You're very lucky you haven't been picked up by the *Gong An Ju*. They're swarming all over Lhasa. There's a curfew in force, they're setting up checkpoints all round the city. I wouldn't care if it was just you, you mean nothing to me. But you've put others at risk.' He leaned forward, an expression of raw anger on his face. 'You have my name, you know how to contact me. The *Gong An Ju* would have had it out of you in a matter of hours.'

'We are not as weak as you seem to think,' Tsering said.

'Aren't you? Who gave you my name?'

'Thupten Norbu.'

Thondup's eyes opened wide in surprise. He leant back on the couch again and looked at the three monks with a new interest.

'You know the First Minister?' he asked.

Tsering nodded. 'He gave me the information for use only in an emergency.'

'And this is an emergency?'

'We need your help. To send a message to Dharamsala.'

'I think you'd better tell me everything.'

Tsering hesitated. There were risks involved, but he had no real option but to trust this Khampa. Sensing Tsering's unease, the Underground leader said: 'Nothing you say will go beyond this room.'

Tsering nodded and explained where they'd been and what had happened. Thondup listened in silence. When Tsering had finished, the Khampa leaned forward over the table and untied the yellow silk parcel. He spread out the folds of material and looked at the objects inside, but he didn't touch them.

'These were His?' he said.

'Yes.'

Thondup studied the items: the spectacles, the pen, the rosary, the bowl, the drum. The two other men moved closer, peering down at the table too, all of them infected with the curiosity and reverence the Dalai Lama had aroused throughout his life and could still command in death. Then Thondup refastened the parcel and gave a signal to one of the men who disappeared through a door in the back wall. A few minutes later he returned accompanied by a woman in a long *chuba* and the multi-coloured striped apron that signified she was married. Her hair was braided and tied in a circle around her head, held in place by a coral clasp that matched the rings dangling from her ears. She was carrying a tray of butter tea and *tsampa* which she placed on the table. She gave a slight bow and withdrew to the kitchen. Thondup gestured to the bowls.

'You must be hungry after your journey.'

The monks took a bowl each, adding a handful of *tsampa* to the butter tea before drinking the thick, salty brew. For a time, no one spoke. Then Tsering put down his empty bowl.

'We will need somewhere to stay.'

'I will make the necessary arrangements,' Thondup said. 'You have come at a dangerous time. Feelings are running high.'

'We sensed it near the Jokhang. We saw a lot of soldiers in the square.'

'They are everywhere, but particularly there. They are

waiting for an opportunity to show their strength. The slightest excuse and they will move in with a vengeance.'

'Will they get that excuse?'

Thondup shrugged his shoulders. 'The Dalai Lama's death has brought all our suppressed resentment to the surface. And it has removed the greatest restraint on our freedom to act.'

Something in his voice, his manner, alarmed Tsering. 'You surely do not intend to fight?'

'Whatever we do, they crush us. They kill us when we demonstrate peacefully. How much worse can it be if we fight back?'

'A lot worse,' Tsering said quickly. 'It will be a bloodbath.'

'Sometimes bloodshed is necessary.'

'That was not the Dalai Lama's view.'

'The Dalai Lama is dead. For fifty years he preached the doctrine of non-violence, but where did it get us? It's exactly what the Chinese want, a docile, compliant Tibet. Look around the world at all the other peoples seeking justice. The men who choose peace get nowhere. Did the Palestine Liberation Organization get anything by lying down and doing nothing? You think the Israelis, the Americans, would have done anything for the Palestinians if they hadn't waged a war against their oppressors?'

'It's not the same situation. The PLO had arms, wealthy backers in the Arab nations. Who will help us? The Americans? The British? India? We tried it once from Mustang and look what happened.'

Thondup's eyes blazed, his anger flashing across the room. 'Don't tell me about Mustang. I know all about Mustang,' he said bitterly. 'Don't lecture me. You are a monk, and I respect you for that, but we are tired of listening to monks. We are tired of doing nothing, getting nowhere. It is not the Khampa way.'

'I too am a Khampa,' Tsering said.

Thondup shook his head. 'No, you are a monk. And you are an outsider now. You've got out. We are still here. Remember that.'

Tsering looked him directly in the eye. 'I will never forget it.'

For a moment they held each other's gaze, one defiant, combative, the other seized by a melancholy regret. Then Thondup looked away.

'It is no longer your fight,' he said.

It was Lobsang who responded, unable to contain his fury. 'Don't tell us it's not our fight,' he spat across the table. 'It will always be our fight. Our methods may be different, but our objectives are the same.'

'Lobsang,' Tsering cautioned.

'No,' Lobsang replied heatedly. 'They bring us here, they search us as if we were common criminals, they check our bags. And now they insult us. We do not have to take this. If they will not help us, we will do without them.'

A fleeting half smile touched Thondup's lips. 'So prayers and meditation haven't entirely eliminated your spirit, I'm glad to see.'

'They have made my spirit stronger,' Lobsang retorted forcefully.

'And your stomach? This is not for the squeamish.'

'You think you are the only ones who have suffered? You think that because we have chosen exile in India we do not know what pain is?' Lobsang demanded.

Thondup scrutinised him quizzically, taking in his heated expression, his aggressive posture. Then he noticed Lobsang's left hand. Parts of the fore and middle fingers were missing.

'What happened to your hand?'

'Never mind what happened to my hand. Do you intend to help us?'

'Yes, I will help you,' Thondup said. 'But there are other, more pressing, matters to deal with first.'

'You cannot hope to win, you know,' Tsering said.

'No? The *Chushi Gangdruk* has returned. And the Chinese will know it.'

'You called us fools,' Tsering said, shaking his head in disbelief. 'Yet you propose a course which is the greatest folly of all. A course which goes against everything our faith stands for. Everything His Holiness believed in.'

'His death has released us from our duty of loyalty.'

'Your loyalty is to the faith, not to the man.'

'I am not a monk,' Thondup said simply. 'We have spent too many years on our knees. Now it is time to stand up and fight.'

Maggie had thought that nothing could quite compare with the smell of rotting turnips, but she'd reckoned without the putrid delights of mature yak dung. That the latter was by far and away the more noxious substance she could confirm unreservedly, having spent nine hours in the back of a lorry with several tonnes of the stuff.

It had been her free and conscious choice to travel with it, but that was little consolation when she was lying next to a steaming mound, the rank odours stinging her nostrils and turning her stomach. The reality was that she'd had no other option. The turnip lorry from Zhangmu had taken her only as far as an agricultural depot in Shigatse, Tibet's second largest city, where she'd clambered out and secreted herself behind a pile of wooden crates. Inspecting the various other trucks in the depot under cover of darkness, she had selected the dung lorry because in the Tibetan script on the cab door she'd recognised the word Lhasa and because she thought it was least likely to be searched by the Chinese.

She'd been proved correct on that last point though she'd paid for the advantage many times over during the journey to the capital. Using sacks and a sheet of polythene she'd found in a corner of the agricultural depot, she'd constructed a hidden cavity immediately behind the driver's cab, digging out the mixture of dung and straw and lining the cavity with the polythene before climbing in, wrapping the sheet around her and scooping the dung back into place. She'd left an opening for her head, concealed by a hemp sack, and settled down to wait for morning. It was snug and warm and she managed to cut out the worst of the odours by stuffing plugs of toilet paper up her nostrils.

At daybreak, when the lorry departed, she was completely hidden, safe from all but a very thorough search. As she'd calculated, even the diligent Chinese drew the line at sifting through a cargo of yak shit. They'd been stopped twice at checkpoints, once near the turn-off for Gonggar Airport and once on the outskirts of Lhasa, but on both occasions the PLA soldiers had taken one look in the back of the lorry and waved it through. Now, rattling along the streets of the capital, Maggie felt a surge of exhilaration. She had reached her destination.

When the jolting finally stopped and the lorry's engine was turned off, she lay still for several minutes, listening intently. She heard other truck engines, doors slamming, voices talking – in Tibetan, not Chinese, that was comforting. She waited, trying to work out from the sounds where she was. Somewhere in the centre of Lhasa, she guessed. Maybe close to the Tibetan Quarter. The Chinese residents of the city had no need for yak dung, they had electricity supplied to their homes. It was the Tibetans, excluded from the power system, who still relied on dung for cooking and heating their houses.

Very carefully, Maggie lifted a corner of the sack concealing her head and peeped out. It was dusk. She could see a few stars beginning to twinkle in the darkening sky. She was in an open yard, a haulage depot, with a number of other lorries. A light was burning in a low wooden building at one side of the yard, presumably an office of some sort. Maggie could see figures moving behind the window, but the yard itself appeared to be deserted. She pushed back more of the sack to uncover her whole face and took a deep breath of the clear, fresh air blowing across the rear of the lorry. She looked around, ensuring she wasn't observed, and slowly lifted the polythene sheet, pushing up with her knees and hands to force back the layer of dung that was covering her. She clambered over the side of the lorry and paused to get her bearings.

Lhasa was an easy city in which to navigate. There were no high-rise buildings obscuring the horizon and wherever you were you could nearly always see the Potala Palace, its thirteen storeys towering over the surrounding area. Maggie could see it now, silhouetted against the setting sun. That put her in the eastern part of Lhasa. She looked to the south. The steep slopes of Chyakyag Karpo Ri and Bumpa Ri, two of the mountains ringing the city, seemed very close. She knew she must be somewhere near the Kyichu River, probably on the southern fringe of the Tibetan Quarter. It wasn't a perfect position, but it was better than she'd expected.

She glanced around and flitted across the yard, keeping down behind the rows of parked lorries. She'd sneaked out of the main entrance gates and was leaning against the fence on the other side when a siren went off. Maggie went rigid, thinking it was some kind of an alarm she'd accidentally triggered inside the depot. But then she realised the noise was coming from a distance, echoing over the whole city. She noticed the street was virtually empty. The few pedestrians she could see were hurrying away, disappearing through doors, down alleys. Shit! She should have thought of this. There was a curfew. And she was out in the open, a long way from where she wanted to be.

She headed down the street, walking briskly but trying not to draw attention to herself. She was aware of an aroma hanging over her and sniffed her clothes. The Chinese army wouldn't need to see her, they could probably smell her without leaving their barracks.

Reaching a junction with a wider street, she stopped, recognising where she was from her previous visit to Lhasa. This was part of the Lingkhor, the outer pilgrims' circuit around the ancient city. The Chinese had demolished a lot of it to build new roads and housing but this section was still intact, a characteristically Tibetan street fringed with whitewashed stone houses, their windows broader at the base than the top. An image of the Buddha was painted on a wall opposite her, a butter lamp burning in an alcove just below it. Maggie checked in both directions and hurried across the street. It was getting dark quickly. That was her only hope, that the night would cover her movements.

She cut down a side street and felt suddenly faint. She stopped and took a few deep breaths. She'd forgotten about the altitude. A day lying down in the back of a lorry was no effective way of acclimatising herself to Lhasa's thin air. She'd have to slow down, avoid running if she could. The dizziness passed, but she was still breathless. She could feel the beginnings of a headache throbbing behind her eyes. Moving at a more measured pace, she continued on down the street to where it met a much larger thoroughfare, the broad boulevard the Tibetans called the Chingdrol Shar Lam. Maggie pressed herself into a doorway and considered her next move. The river was ahead of her, little more than a quarter of a mile away, but the University of Tibet, where she was headed, was probably three times that distance and to get there she had to cross the Chingdrol Shar Lam.

Headlights were coming towards her down the avenue. She heard the roar of truck engines. She retreated deeper into the doorway and watched as a convoy of three PLA lorries rumbled past. Another two trucks followed a short distance behind. Their canvas backs were rolled up, soldiers with steel helmets and rifles sitting on benches inside.

Maggie looked out. The road appeared clear. Civilian traffic would have stopped when the curfew began, so any vehicles moving around would be PLA or PSB. The street was utterly deserted, something she'd never seen in Lhasa before: no cars, no bicycles, no people. She braced herself and ran out into the avenue.

Halfway across, she saw more headlights approaching. They were too far away to pick her out, but they gave her a jolt nevertheless. She accelerated and ducked behind the wall of the first building she reached. The exertion made her gasp. Her lungs felt so starved of oxygen she wondered if she was going to black out. The headlights drew nearer. They belonged to another PLA convoy. Two of the trucks drove past but the third stopped almost level with her on the far side of the boulevard. For one heartstopping moment Maggie thought she'd been spotted. She pulled back into the shadows and stared across the street. A squad of soldiers was jumping down from the truck, but the men were heading into the Tibetan Quarter she'd just left. She almost sobbed with relief. If she'd delayed any longer, she'd have been trapped.

She waited a while to recover her breath, then moved off down the street. This was an area of offices and commercial premises, its centre dominated by the People's Stadium which was ringed by walls and chainlink fencing. Maggie walked cautiously, keeping to the shadows next to the buildings as much as she could. This wasn't one of the Tibetan residential areas which she knew would be the main focus of the curfew restrictions, but she kept a watchful eye out for PLA foot patrols all the same. The Chinese had thousands of troops stationed in Lhasa. Many of them would be out on the streets.

She reached the Lingkhor Shar Lam without seeing any people or vehicles. It was a curious feeling, walking the empty streets, only the sound of her shoes on the pavement breaking the eerie silence. She stopped at the side of the avenue and pondered which way to go next. She could head south past the Himalaya Hotel, then follow the road along the river to the university; or she could keep going in a straight line. She chose the second option. The river was too exposed. She preferred the cover of buildings, a network of streets into which she could melt if necessary. Her headache was getting worse, her breathing constricted by a tight band of tension around her chest. Every few metres she had to pause to rest. Ahead of her she saw another broad avenue crossing at right angles. She slowed, more alert now, listening hard. Hugging the side of a building, she edged cautiously towards the junction. She pressed her face to the wall and slid an eye out to inspect the avenue.

She pulled back quickly.

Coming towards her, only a few metres away, were two Chinese soldiers. Maggie looked around in a panic. There was nowhere to hide: no doorways, no side-streets, no yards to dive into. She could hear the soldiers' boots scraping on the ground, the staccato exchanges of their muted conversation.

They would reach the junction in a matter of seconds and couldn't fail to see her. She contemplated running, but that would have been suicidal. They'd hear her, see her on the exposed street. She was cornered.

Then she glanced up. The building next to her had only one storey and a flat roof. Maggie tossed her bag up on to the roof and pulled herself on to a windowsill. Reaching up, she grasped the top edge of the wall and hauled herself on to the roof, rolling over out of sight as the two soldiers stopped at the junction. They were right below her. Maggie lay on her side, her cheek resting on the gritty surface of the roof, one hand over her mouth to try to muffle the sound of her laboured breathing.

The soldiers waited on the corner for several minutes. Maggie heard the scratch of a match striking. The smell of cigarette smoke wafted up. They chatted for a while in the intermittent, casual way of bored soldiers. Killing time, eking out their small talk to fill the interminable hours of their shift. Maggie forced herself to relax, to control her respiration, inhaling deeply then exhaling slowly, counting to herself to keep the rhythm even.

Finally, the soldiers moved off. Maggie waited until the sound of their boots had receded down the avenue before she dared to move. She crawled to the front of the roof and peered over the low concrete parapet. Across the avenue was the campus of the University of Tibet. She studied it, reminding herself of the layout, the location of the teaching buildings, the administration and accommodation blocks. Then she lowered herself back down on to the side-street and scanned the avenue once more. The soldiers had disappeared from sight. The avenue was deserted.

Taking a last look around, she clutched her bag to her side and sprinted across the road. The western entrance to the campus was a hundred metres up the avenue, but Maggie knew it would be manned by a night-watchman. The only safe way in was over the wall. She tossed her bag over first, then scrambled up on to the top, straddling the wall with her legs.

The noise of an engine made her twist round suddenly. Headlights were racing towards her down the avenue. Not a lorry this time but an army Jeep. Maggie whipped her leg over the wall and dropped swiftly to the ground on the other side of it. She crouched in the darkness, listening as the Jeep went past. Then she ventured out on to the campus.

The foreign accommodation block – where all the non-Chinese teaching staff lived – was a two-storey building near the central administration department. There was always a porter on duty at the desk inside the front entrance to the block, a PSB employee whose job it was to monitor the comings and goings of the foreign teachers. But there was another way in round the back which Maggie had been shown on her previous visit: a fire exit which the foreigners, and their visitors, utilised at appropriate moments to protect their privacy.

Maggie tried the door. It slid open easily and she stepped inside. She went up the back stairs to the first floor, hoping, praying, that he was still on the staff, that he still had the same room. She checked the name-plates on each of the identical doors as she walked along the corridor. Halfway down she found it: 'Patrick Monroe', handwritten in English, Tibetan and Chinese. Maggie closed her eyes momentarily. Thank God! She put her ear to the door. She could hear no sound inside. She knocked softly. Then again. There was a scuff of feet on the other side and the door swung open.

Monroe stared at her, stifling an exclamation of surprise. Then a look of alarm passed across his face. He put his finger to his lips and pointed down the corridor. Maggie nodded and followed him. The foreign teachers' rooms were all bugged by the PSB. The communal bathrooms were the only safe place to talk. Monroe pushed open the bathroom door and locked it behind them. He turned on the shower. He was pretty sure the bathroom was clean of listening devices, but you could never be absolutely certain. Covered by the noise of splashing water, he said softly: 'What the hell are you doing here?'

'Working,' Maggie replied.

'You know all foreign journalists have been expelled?'

'Yes.'

'Christ, how did you get here?'

'I'll tell you later. I need somewhere to stay.'

Monroe looked at her. He was in his forties, balding, with a reddish complexion, his skin and lips chapped from the dry Lhasa air. He'd been in Tibet for five years, one of those itinerant Englishmen who wandered the world teaching their native language. On her previous visit, filming secretly for a documentary, Maggie had used him as an interpreter for interviews with the local Tibetans.

'You're expecting me to shelter you?' he said incredulously.

'I don't know anyone else in Lhasa.'

'You know what will happen to us if we're caught?'

'We won't be caught.'

'You shouldn't have come here.'

'I'm sorry, Patrick, I know it's put you at risk, but I had no choice.'

'You could have stayed at home. How on earth did you get here? There's a curfew from dusk until dawn. The PLA are all over the city.'

'What's happening? Any confrontations?'

'That's what you want, isn't it? Violence. A good riot, or a massacre you can film. It makes better television that way, doesn't it?'

'I report what happens,' Maggie said. 'I don't make it happen. Can I sleep on your floor for a couple of nights? Please.'

Monroe sighed. 'I can hardly say no, can I?' His nose wrinkled. 'What's that smell?'

'It might be either turnips or yak dung. Probably yak dung.'

'The shower's running,' Monroe said. 'I'll get you some soap.'

SEVEN

Maggie slept badly and awoke feeling tired and sluggish. She'd taken a couple of paracetamol tablets the previous evening but her headache was still there, a nagging throb behind her forehead that was uncomfortable rather than painful. She was used to sleeping well, even on hard floors like Monroe's, and waking raring to go. Slowing down, taking things gently, she found difficult, even though she knew it was essential to do so. What was worse was having to go without smoking. Her body craved her regular morning fix of nicotine but she knew a cigarette would only exacerbate her mild symptoms of altitude sickness.

Monroe's accommodation consisted of just one room, about four metres by three. It contained a single bed, a cheap chest of drawers, a sink and a two-ring electric stove. He wasn't a man who went in for home comforts much, but he'd put a Tibetan rug on the wooden floor and a couple of *thangkas* – religious cloth hangings – on the wall to alleviate the bare white plaster. Over the bed he'd hung a framed aerial photograph of the Himalayas.

On waking, the first thing Monroe did was switch on his transistor radio to mask the sounds of two people in the room. They dressed with their backs to each other, Monroe innately reserved, Maggie not wanting to embarrass him. Then Monroe made black tea and watery barley porridge on the stove for breakfast. Maggie consumed them gratefully, relieved that, despite his years in Tibet, Monroe hadn't taken to the local staple diet of butter tea and *tsampa*. Of all the cuisine she'd sampled across the world, Tibetan had to be one of the worst.

Maggie found a pad of paper and a pencil and scribbled a message on it. Monroe read the note and pulled a face. Maggie gave him an imploring look. He clicked his tongue in irritation but nodded. Shortly afterwards, he went out.

Maggie locked the door after him and sat down on the bed, checking through her camera gear whilst the radio continued to broadcast an insufferable stream of tinny Chinese pop music.

Forty minutes later, Monroe returned. He was carrying a plastic carrier bag with Chinese characters printed on the outside. He pointed to the door and silently mouthed the word 'bathroom'. They went down the corridor, locked the bathroom door behind them and turned on the shower again. Maggie opened the carrier bag and pulled out the forage cap and plain blue worker's jacket and trousers that many of the Chinese in Lhasa wore.

'Thanks, I really appreciate this,' she said.

'I had to guess your size.'

Maggie held up the outfit. 'It looks okay. How much do I owe you?'

'Forget it.'

'No, take this.' She thrust a ten-dollar bill into his hand. 'What's it like out there? Many soldiers?'

'A lot.'

'Something happening?'

Monroe shrugged. 'The Tibetans have been gathering outside the Jokhang every day since they announced the Dalai Lama had died.'

'And the Chinese have tolerated it?'

'So far. It's all been very peaceful.'

'That hasn't stopped the Chinese intervening before.'

'What are you planning to do?'

'Tape whatever I can.'

'Not openly?'

'Of course not.'

Monroe gave her a puzzled look. 'The risks don't bother you, do they? Why do you do this?'

'It's my job.'

'And the people you film, what about them?'

'What do you mean?'

'The last time you were here, the people you interviewed. How many of them do you think are still walking the streets?'

Maggie went very still. She licked her lips. 'What happened?'

'The Chinese Embassy in London taped the programme when it was shown in England. They sent it to the *Gong An Ju* who came looking for everyone who'd appeared on camera.'

'We deliberately didn't identify them for that very reason.'

'The *Gong An Ju* are thorough. They have informers, a photo archive of potential agitators. They have ways of finding out these things.'

'How many?'

'I don't know. But some are in jail. One or two have simply disappeared. Doesn't that trouble you? Journalists, people like you, you fly in somewhere, stay a few days, talk to a few locals and suddenly you're experts on the country. You pick up a few facts, a few half truths and you think you're qualified to pronounce on everything: the people, the politics, the culture. Then you fly out again without a thought for what you leave behind. You can walk away, Maggie; the people out there can't.'

'You're wrong if you believe I don't give a thought to what I leave behind. I do,' Maggie said. 'I didn't know that's what had happened.'

'You could've expected it.'

'Would you rather we did nothing? Took no photos, shot no film, reported nothing? That's what the Chinese want: to conceal from the outside world what they've done, and are continuing to do, to Tibet.'

'I suppose so,' Monroe conceded.

Maggie put her hand gently on his arm. 'I'm grateful for

your help, Patrick. Like I was last time I was here. I know you're taking a risk. But I'm probably the only Western reporter left in Lhasa. If something happens, it's important that the rest of the world knows about it.'

'You think it makes a difference?'

'I have to believe it does,' Maggie said. 'It's the one thing that keeps me going.'

Camp-fires had been lit on the Lingkhor. Maggie could smell the scent of burning juniper, see the smoke rising into the hazy morning sunlight. Pilgrims were prostrating themselves around the circuit, lying full length in the gutters while cars and trucks sped past in the middle of the road. A woman with two dirty-faced ragged children crouched by a smouldering fire making butter tea in a small wooden churn. Maggie walked past them. She was wearing the blue worker's suit and cap and had used the soot from a burnt match to make subtle alterations to the shape of her eyes. With her straight black hair and tanned complexion she could pass as Chinese provided no one examined her too closely. At any rate, the disguise had been convincing enough to get her safely off the university campus, mingling with a group of Chinese students who were leaving through the western entrance. But now she was in the Tibetan Quarter it was more of a liability. She removed the cap and jacket and stowed them in her shoulder bag, using the jacket to conceal the camcorder whose lens was protruding covertly through a slit in the front of the bag.

Ahead of her she saw a PLA truck parked at the side of the road, a dozen or more armed soldiers seated in the back. She cut down a narrow alley to avoid it and made her way towards the centre of the Quarter. It was quiet. The streets seemed very empty. Through an open gate she caught a glimpse of an elderly woman in a muddy courtyard, sitting on a stool moulding yak dun and straw into patties for cooking fuel. An *apso* scampered forward and snapped aggressively at Maggie's heels.

In one of the tiny squares a crowd of Tibetans was gathered, watching something. Maggie pushed through to the front and saw a squad of Chinese soldiers going into the surrounding houses. They were coming out with prayer flags and *thangkas*, images of the Buddha and other religious artefacts which they threw down in a pile. Maggie reached into her shoulder bag and turned on her camcorder, taping what was happening. A few prohibited Tibetan national flags were brought out of one house, their owner bundled away and tossed roughly into the back of an army truck which was blocking one of the side streets. A low murmur of protest emerged from the group of watching Tibetans. The Chinese officer in charge swung round, a sub-machine-gun cradled in his arms, and shouted at them angrily in Chinese.

The pile of objects on the ground was growing larger. Maggie saw several photographs of the late Dalai Lama among them. The Chinese officer barked a command and a soldier doused the pile in petrol and set light to it. The crowd pulled back as the flames licked into the air. The photographs of the Dalai Lama started to burn first, curling up and shrivelling until only a sprinkling of charred ash was left. Then the flags and the religious pictures and texts were burnt away to nothing. The crowd watched in horror, one or two of them weeping. The soldiers rounded on them, prodding at them with their rifle barrels to disperse them. Maggie backed away, swinging her bag round to get a shot of another Tibetan man being dragged from his house and forced at gunpoint into the back of the army truck.

The resentment, the tension were almost tangible. The Tibetans were moving away, muttering under their breath, scowling at the Chinese soldiers. A man in a *chuba* spat on the ground and yelled contemptuously at the soldiers, then dived down an alley before they could catch him.

Maggie didn't linger. She didn't want either the Chinese or the Tibetans to take an interest in her. She continued taping, her bag clutched under her arm, as she headed towards the Jokhang. She noticed other groups of Tibetans going the same way. As she neared the temple, the streets became so crowded they were like rivers of people, flowing steadily between the houses and flooding out into the square in front of the Jokhang. Maggie stayed close to the edge of the square, taping the milling throng. Above them, the roof of the PSB building overlooking the square was lined with armed police. An officer in the middle was holding a large video camera with which he was filming the crowds below. Maggie clambered up on to a low wall to get a better view. Across the far side of the square was a long row of green, canvas-backed PLA trucks. In front of the trucks were armed soldiers and a company of riot police dressed like medieval warriors in metal helmets with leather neck protectors, leather cuirasses and gauntleted hands in which they were holding long wooden batons.

The crowd grew larger, filling the space outside the Jokhang and spreading across the square so that only a narrow strip of open ground separated the Tibetans from the Chinese security forces. Then suddenly, as if some unseen signal had been given, the multitude stopped moving. A strange, unnatural silence descended over the square. For a few minutes no one spoke or stirred. Even the police on the surrounding rooftops seemed petrified, like stone gargoyles gaping down on the motionless crowd. Maggie's body was still but her eyes were flickering ceaselessly over the faces nearby, darting to the rooftops, to the phalanx of soldiers and riot police across the square. Her neck was prickling. The moment seemed to go on for ever.

Then it broke. All over the crowd banners were lifted into the air. Maggie couldn't read the Tibetan script, but she'd seen similar signs before and knew they were calling for independence for Tibet. Huge photographs of the late Dalai Lama were raised above people's heads. Tibetan flags appeared everywhere, fluttering in the breeze. Maggie lifted her shoulder bag, the camcorder still taping, to get the images into shot.

As one, the crowd began to chant, every single person

intoning the same words: *'Bo Rangtsen, Bo Rangtsen'*. Freedom for Tibet. Repeating their demands for independence like a mantra. All of them praying together, united in their defiance. Maggie watched the spectacle in astonishment and awe, moved by the peaceful dignity of the protest.

The Chinese, for a moment, seemed paralysed and impotent. Then the reaction came so quickly, and with such force, that it had to have been prearranged. The riot police on the other side of the square charged forward without warning, wading into the crowd with their batons swinging. At the same time, the doors of the PSB station were thrown open and more riot police poured out. Maggie had a clear view of them laying into the demonstrators, smashing people to the ground and beating them senseless with their batons. The Tibetans were felled like cornstalks, whole rows of them going down as the police advanced, trampling over the bodies of those they had flattened.

Maggie watched with a grim, appalled fascination, her concealed camcorder recording everything. Attacked on two fronts, the cornered Tibetans panicked, turned to flee, but the only way out of the square was into the streets around the Jokhang which were too narrow to take the swollen volume of people. Many sought sanctuary inside the temple, but Chinese soldiers were now surging along the sides of the square, outflanking the riot police to attack the demonstrators as they tried to escape.

A few metres in front of Maggie, a man was hit on the head with a baton. Blood gushed from his face as a second blow knocked him unconscious. Another man was shielding his young son with his arms, backing away, screaming for mercy. Two riot police floored him with vicious blows to the head and neck, then, as the father collapsed, administered the same brutal punishment on the terrified boy. Maggie closed her eyes as the child was knocked out and his limp body kicked and battered where it lay on the ground.

There was blood everywhere. People were screaming, shouting, struggling desperately to retreat, but there was nowhere to run. Trapped in the bottleneck, unable to hide or get out of the square, the Tibetans were picked off in droves by the police and soldiers.

Then, in the midst of the pandemonium, Maggie saw something extraordinary: a group of Tibetan men fighting back. There were perhaps thirty or forty of them, young men standing firm together, holding the riot police at bay. In their centre, leading the resistance, was a tall Khampa in a wide-brimmed Tibetan Stetson, his red-tasselled plaited hair swinging around his shoulders. The Tibetans were pushing forward now, attacking the riot police with nothing more than their bare hands. The tall Khampa snatched one of the police batons and knocked its owner to the ground. More police officers went down.

Throwing caution to the wind, Maggie moved away from her sheltered position to get a better shot of the fighting, holding her shoulder bag high to raise her camcorder lens above the heads of the crowd. She saw another riot policeman go down. Then another. The young Tibetan men had grabbed more batons and were driving the police line back. Other Tibetans joined in, mostly young men but a few girls as well. The police retreated, trying to regroup. The Tibetans came at them from all sides, retaliating furiously.

Then suddenly, there was a burst of gunfire. Maggie spun round and saw the police on the roof of the PSB station aiming their rifles into the seething crowd. They fired a second volley. The Tibetans went down like skittles. Six, seven, eight . . . Maggie tried to count how many but it was impossible to see. The Khampa leader waved an arm above his head and his men pulled back, splintering off into smaller groups and retreating across the square. A couple of tear-gas grenades landed on the ground, their smoke billowing up and adding to the overwhelming confusion. Maggie squeezed her eyes shut and ran through the choking clouds of gas. The square was emptying now, the demonstrators fighting frantically to escape into the surrounding streets. Some were knocked over in the stampede and crushed underfoot. Maggie looked around for the Khampa, coughing violently as a gust of tear-gas hit her in the face. The tall man seemed to have melted away into the crowd. The ground was littered with fallen banners, flags and photographs of the Dalai Lama. And bodies. Lots of bodies. They were scattered across the square, some dead, others just unconscious. The wounded, their faces smeared with red, were dragging themselves to their feet and staggering away before the police could arrest them. The more seriously injured were being picked up by friends and carried to safety.

Maggie paused to get one last shot of the carnage, then ran into the tail-end of the dispersing crowd. The Chinese police were re-forming for a final attack. A line of them charged, shouting a fearsome war cry, relishing the opportunity for another go at the defenceless demonstrators. Maggie forced her way through the fringes of the crowd. The police were right behind her, picking off the wounded and the stragglers, beating them savagely with their batons. Maggie found her escape blocked by a wall of terrified people. She dodged to the side and in through the open doors of the Jokhang Temple.

The dimly lit chamber inside was crowded with demonstrators, the noise of sobbing women and children echoing around the chapels and vaults. Some were injured, nursing broken limbs and bleeding gashes. All were traumatised by what they'd just experienced. A group of PLA soldiers rushed in and started dragging people out, hitting them with their rifle butts. Maggie hid behind a pillar, then ran to the back of the chamber and out into the courtyard in the centre of the temple where more Tibetans were taking shelter. Maggie squeezed through the throng, looking for a way out. She spotted a door to one side and pushed it open, going back into a different part of the temple. She ran across a shadowy chamber and stopped abruptly as she heard a loud hiss. She turned. An elderly monk was standing by a curtain, beckoning her urgently. He pulled back the curtains slightly to reveal another door. As Maggie hurried across to him, she heard the thud of boots outside the chamber, caught sight of more Chinese soldiers bursting in. The monk whipped aside the curtain. Maggie threw herself through the door and closed it behind her, leaning on it for a moment to recover her breath.

She was in another, smaller courtyard. Looking up, she could see the flat roof of the temple and clouds drifting across the vivid blue sky. Beyond the far wall of the courtyard there were people's voices ebbing and flowing as if they were moving past. Maggie went to the gate in the wall and wrenched it open. On the other side was the street, filled with jostling people. Maggie slipped in amongst them and let them carry her along. She was out of breath, numb with shock, but underneath there was a sense of elation, of professional pride because she'd captured everything on tape. She had the evidence in her shoulder bag.

She craned her neck to look behind and in front. The stream of people extended as far as she could see. Ahead of her she noticed a Tibetan Stetson floating along above the surrounding heads, a fringe of plaited hair with red silk tassels hanging down below the hat. She kept her eyes on it. As the crowd moved deeper into the heart of the Tibetan Quarter, it grew less dense. Groups broke off, disappearing down side-streets, into houses. Maggie could see the tall Khampa more clearly now. He was only a few metres in front of her, in a group of five or six men who were carrying two injured colleagues between them. When they veered off down an alley, Maggie followed, keeping well back. The men turned right into another twisting alley. Maggie lost sight of them for a moment, then saw the Khampa's distinctive hat ducking through an arched gateway. She crept cautiously up to the entrance and peered into a secluded courtyard filled with bales of straw and planks of wood. A door on the far side was just closing. Maggie waited a couple of minutes, then darted across and squinted through the grimy window next to the door. She saw more bales of straw inside, a flight of wooden stairs. She straightened up.

And felt an arm snake around her chest – a hard, muscular

arm with a silver bracelet on the wrist. The tip of a knife pricked her windpipe and a man's voice growled something incomprehensible at her in Tibetan. Maggie swallowed. She could feel the man's body behind her, smell the onions and dried yak meat on his breath.

'I'm a British journalist,' she said in halting Tibetan, a phrase she knew in at least fifteen other languages.

She felt the man back away. With his hand he spun her around and studied her face, her Western features. Then he pulled open the door and pushed her roughly inside. He gestured at the staircase. Maggie went up and emerged into an open living room at the top. Two men in *chubas* and sheepskin boots wheeled round, drawing their knives as they heard her footsteps. The man with the silver bracelet came up behind her and said something to the two men who fixed Maggie with mean, belligerent stares. She was pushed into a corner and her shoulder bag was confiscated.

The room was like a field hospital ward. There were bodies lying on the two couches and on the floor. Some were bleeding badly, their injuries being dressed by Tibetan women. One was slumped against the wall, the shoulder of his *chuba* soaked with blood from what looked like a gunshot wound.

A door in the back wall opened and the Khampa came out, snapping off orders to the two lieutenants who accompanied him. In the room he was leaving, Maggie saw more bodies on the floor. The Khampa glanced around, noticed Maggie in the corner and walked across to her. He moved with an easy grace, his felt boots making almost no sound on the floor. He had dark skin, a broad mouth and fierce penetrating eyes that contrasted markedly with his calm, relaxed demeanour. He examined Maggie curiously while the man with the silver bracelet explained to him what had happened.

'You say you're British?' Thondup said in excellent English, revealing a couple of gleaming gold teeth.

'Yes.'

'A journalist?'

Maggie nodded. 'Camerawoman.'

'Where's your camera?'

'In my bag.'

Thondup reached out an arm for the bag and pulled out the camcorder.

'You followed us,' he said. 'Why?'

'I saw you in the square, fighting. I wanted to know more about you.'

'You were in the square? Filming?'

'Yes.'

He turned the camcorder around. 'With this little thing?'

'I'll show you.'

Maggie took the camcorder from him and rewound the tape. Then she flipped out the tiny viewing monitor on the side and held up the camcorder in front of his face.

'Watch.'

She pressed the 'play' button. Thondup gazed intently at the pictures on the monitor. The other men gathered round, not having followed the conversation in English, but curious to see what was going on.

Maggie let the tape run. It was shorter than she'd thought, no more than ten minutes in total. But she'd captured everything of consequence: the people chanting for independence, protesting peacefully; the riot police attacking; the panic, the demonstrators fleeing; the gunfire and the bodies strewn across the square. Thondup and his men watched the images with rapt, open-mouthed concentration. Then the monitor went blank and Thondup turned to Maggie.

'You can show this?' he said. 'In the West?'

'If I can get the tape out of Tibet.'

'Film here too.' He gestured at the wounded. 'This needs to be shown.'

Maggie checked the settings on the camcorder and switched it to 'record'. The Tibetans seemed unsophisticated people but they knew the value of propaganda – that was one thing living under Chinese occupation taught you. Slowly, she moved around the room, taping the bodies, the bloodied survivors. Most of them needed proper hospital attention but she knew they would never get it. The PSB would be waiting, ready to arrest any Tibetan who showed up in Casualty.

'There are more in the back,' Thondup said, opening the door.

Maggie stepped into the room, letting the camcorder pan around the wounded figures on the floor. Three men were kneeling down, attending to the injuries. One of them looked up and Maggie started. She stared at him, too stunned to move. It was the monk who'd caught her outside the Tsuglagkhang in McLeod Ganj. He was as surprised as she was, but he recovered first. He leapt to his feet and snatched the camcorder away from her.

'What are you doing?' he demanded angrily in English.

Thondup said something sharply. Tsering snapped a reply and the two men had a heated exchange in Tibetan. Then Tsering shook his head, disagreeing vehemently with the Khampa, and turned back to Maggie. He handed her the camcorder.

'You can film the injured, but not me and my two colleagues. You understand?'

Maggie nodded. The other two men stood up and moved out of shot while she finished recording the scene. Then Thondup took her by the arm and led her out into the front room.

'I will talk to the camera,' he said.

Maggie hesitated, Patrick Monroe's accusation still fresh in her mind. 'You know the Chinese will record this when it's broadcast in the West and be able to identify you?'

'They can identify me already from the film they took in the square. I'm not afraid. Start the camera.'

He waited for Maggie to give him a signal, then addressed the camcorder in fluent English.

'My name is Thondup Tempa. I am just an ordinary Tibetan. This morning, I went to the square outside the Jokhang Temple, our most sacred shrine, with thousands of my fellow countrymen. Our intention was to demonstrate our loyalty to the late Dalai Lama and to demand independence for Tibet which has been illegally occupied by the Chinese for the past fifty years. You have seen what happened. We were unarmed. We were peaceful. The Chinese attacked us without any provocation. We fought back only to protect ourselves. I believe at least twenty Tibetans were killed when the Chinese police opened fire on the crowd. Many more were injured. You see some of them here around me.

'This will happen again. There is no true political or religious freedom in Tibet; the Chinese will not allow it. And they will not tolerate any kind of opposition. But we will not be crushed. We will continue to demand the independence for our country which is rightfully ours. You have seen what the Chinese do to peaceful, unarmed demonstrators. How much more do we Tibetans have to suffer before the rest of the world takes notice of our plight? I urge you in the West to come to our aid. Please help us.'

Thondup gave a nod to indicate that he had finished. Maggie switched off the camcorder.

'How soon can you get the tape out of Tibet?' he asked.

'I don't know,' Maggie replied. 'It might be difficult. I'm here illegally. The borders are closed.'

'Will you entrust it to us?'

'Can you get it out?'

'Over the Black Route to India. If you tell us where you want it to go, we will do our best to make sure it reaches them.'

Maggie pressed the 'rewind' button on the camcorder. 'I'll write a covering note to go with it.'

Thondup turned to one of his lieutenants and had a brief conversation in Tibetan. Then he looked back at Maggie who ejected the tape from the camcorder and handed it to him.

'Where are you staying in Lhasa?' the Khampa asked.

Maggie took a decision not to involve Monroe any further. 'I don't have a place,' she said.

'We will find you somewhere. There are other things you can film. Now, excuse me, I must see to my men.'

An elderly Tibetan man – obviously a doctor – had arrived and was making his rounds of the wounded, assessing what kind of treatment was required. Thondup knelt down beside him and they conversed in low, urgent tones.

Maggie looked across the room. The monk from McLeod Ganj was standing in the doorway of the back room, watching her with hostile eyes. She stared back at him without flinching. He turned away and retreated through the door.

Shen Tzu watched with mounting alarm the videotape he'd been sent by the PSB Lhasa City head office. The telephone reports he'd received from the field had been disquieting enough, but it was only now, seeing the pictures, that he realised fully the dangerous implications of what had happened outside the Jokhang. Quite simply, this was potentially another Tiananmen Square.

The orders to suppress ruthlessly any show of Tibetan nationalism had come from Beijing, and the PSB had carried out the orders with its customary zeal and efficiency. The actions had been officially sanctioned at the highest level of the Chinese Government, but Shen knew all too well that when things went wrong the blame had a tendency to fall on those lower down the pecking order.

The videotape made disturbing viewing. The demonstrators had broken the law by displaying the banned Tibetan flag and photographs of the late Dalai Lama, but they'd presented no physical threat to the Chinese security forces. At least, not initially. In Shen's view, the riot police had moved in precipitately. An order to the demonstrators to disperse should have been given first. Loss of life and injury were unfortunate consequences of opposing the authorities, but he was acutely aware that it placed the PSB in a bad light. Appearances mattered, even more so now that Beijing was so sensitive to world opinion. Fortunately, they'd had the foresight and good sense to expel all foreign journalists from the region, so there would be no outside witnesses to the slaughter. But word would inevitably leak out. The Tibetan nationalists would see to that.

The intercom on Shen's desk buzzed and his secretary informed him that Major Chang had arrived.

'Send him in,' Shen said.

The major's pockmarked face was grave, worried, his mouth set so tight his lips were barely visible.

'Watch this,' Shen said grimly, rewinding the videotape and playing it through again for his deputy.

Chang stared impassively at the television screen, careful not to let any emotion show. When the screen went blank, he remained silent, waiting to see the line the colonel took.

'It's a disaster,' Shen said emphatically. 'A complete disaster.'

'Yes, Comrade Colonel,' Chang agreed.

'The officers on the rooftop panicked. There was absolutely no need to open fire.'

'Do we have a casualty figure?'

'The Tibetans carried away many of their wounded and dead so it's hard to tell. At least fifteen fatalities is the current official total.'

'Has Beijing been informed?'

'That is for Comrade Huang to undertake,' Shen replied, the relief apparent in his voice.

'Of course.'

The manoeuvring had begun. Shen had no direct responsibility for policing in Lhasa City itself. He was head of intelligence for the Tibet Autonomous Region. Colonel Huang Shu Hua was in charge of operational matters in the capital and Shen was already beginning to distance himself from his colleague.

'But there will be repercussions that affect us,' Shen said. 'This demonstration was not spontaneous. It was carefully organised and orchestrated by the nationalists. We must find the ringleaders and deal with them.'

He picked up the video recorder remote control and

searched through the tape. The cameraman on the roof of the PSB station opposite the Jokhang had had a perfect aerial view of the events in the square. He had zoomed in close as much as possible, getting clear images of dozens of Tibetan demonstrators. One particular figure stood out in the midst of the chaos. Shen found the section he was looking for and froze the frame on the tall figure of a man in a wide-brimmed hat.

'That one,' the colonel said, jabbing a finger at the screen. 'Do you recognise him?'

Chang studied the grainy picture. 'There have been rumours of a new leader. Our informants have mentioned a tall man with tassels in his hair. A Khampa.'

'You have a name?'

'No. He has kept a low profile until now. We have been unable to penetrate his inner circle.'

'Find him. And find him quickly. Someone must pay for what happened this morning. Use whatever means are necessary.'

Shen gave a curt nod of dismissal, but Chang didn't move.

'There is something else,' the major said. He held out a sheet of paper he'd been holding in his hand. 'The Lhasa monitoring station picked up this message yesterday evening. A radio transmission to Dharamsala.'

Shen took the piece of paper and read the transcript. 'It was encrypted?'

'Yes. But they are amateurs. It took us only twelve hours to break.'

'The source?'

'Impossible to pinpoint. They move the transmitter around all the time.'

Shen put the paper down on his desk. 'So we guessed right. And the monks are in Lhasa? The Tibetan Quarter?'

'Without doubt.'

'Our Khampa friend in the hat too?'

'I would stake my career on it.'

A morbid smile touched Shen's lips and was gone. 'Strong

words, major. But let there be no mistake, both our careers are on the line here. If we don't find this man, and the monks too, we'll spend the next twenty years freezing our balls off at some miserable outpost on the Mongolian border. If we're lucky.'

Shen didn't dwell on the prospect. The penalities for failure were harsh, but he had no intention of failing.

'Mobilise every officer we have,' he continued. 'Wait till after dark, then seal off the Tibetan Quarter and search it from top to bottom. If they're there, we will have them.'

EIGHT

Throughout the rest of the day, a steady stream of men arrived at the house, coming upstairs to talk to Thondup with the wounded and dying all around them on the floor of the living room. Most of the men were young, but a number were well into middle age and one or two even older. They came carrying weapons: daggers, swords, clubs, revolvers, British Lee Enfield rifles that must have been fifty years old, handed down from fathers to sons and locked away in dusty chests until the time came when they were needed again.

Maggie couldn't follow the conversations in Tibetan, but it was easy enough to work out what was happening.

'These are new recruits, aren't they?' she said to Thondup during a lull in all the activity.

'Yes,' he replied. 'Many of them were in the square this morning. They saw what the Chinese did. Others weren't present, but they've heard what happened. They are all angry. They want to do something.'

'You mean fight?'

Thondup shrugged. 'Whatever is necessary.'

'You know the Chinese will answer violence with more violence.'

Thondup looked at her with his dark, fiery eyes; eyes that burned with a fervent sense of injustice.

'It will show they are frightened,' he replied. 'That is progress – for the Chinese to fear the Tibetans.'

'You cannot hope to win,' Maggie said.

'Winning is not the only reason for fighting.'

In the mid-afternoon, two more of the injured demonstrators died. Their bodies were wrapped in shrouds and carried
out of the house. Maggie knew that before nightfall several
more would die. She'd seen too many casualties of war, too
many gunshot wounds, to believe that the bleeding, semi-
conscious victims around her had much hope of survival. They
needed surgery, transfusions, drugs, not the bandages and
unsophisticated Tibetan medicine that they were being given.
Herbs and poultices and faith were not much use when your
flesh was shattered and your life blood was draining away on
to the floor. There weren't even any painkillers to ease the
victims' suffering. In a red haze of agony, they moaned and
twitched, crying out and screaming before lapsing back into a
disturbed unconsciousness. It was harrowing to witness.

Maggie tried to distance herself from it all by concentrating
on writing a report to accompany her camcorder tape. But it
was difficult to stand back when people were dying next to
her. She'd known cameramen and journalists who'd managed
to insulate themselves from the distressing events they were
covering, but it was an ability she'd never acquired. Objective
reporting was a myth to Maggie. It was impossible not to
take sides. Sometimes, indeed, she regarded it as essential.
There was a moral dimension to news journalism that no
practitioner could ignore. Reporters had a duty to probe
beyond the mere facts and provide an ethical perspective on
a conflict that necessarily meant making judgements about
the participants. Were there two sides to the Holocaust? Were
there two sides to the killing fields of Cambodia, to the genocide in Rwanda or to the rape and slaughter of civilians in
Bosnia? To even attempt to be objective and impartial in such
circumstances seemed to Maggie to be an obscene abroga-
tion of her responsibility as an independent witness.

And in Tibet? Maggie had absolutely no doubt that the
Chinese had conducted a campaign of genocide in the
country since their invasion. The figures, verified by independent sources, supported that conclusion. More than a
million Tibetans, a fifth of the population, had been killed,

either directly in conflict or through execution, maltreatment and starvation in the vast network of prisons and labour camps the Chinese had set up. Were there two sides to the killing of monks for wanting to continue to practise their faith? Were there two sides to the gunning down of civilians who had the temerity to wave their national flag? Maggie couldn't see it. Truth was a notoriously elusive concept whose appearance depended less on its intrinsic constituents than on the agenda of the person seeking it, but what she'd witnessed outside the Jokhang Temple could not be interpreted in any way that was remotely favourable to the Chinese. It had been a bloody, unprovoked massacre of unarmed civilians. No amount of professional objectivity or journalistic independence could deny that.

Towards evening, before the curfew began, the injured were evacuated from the house.

'We have been here long enough,' Thondup told Maggie when she asked what was going on. 'No place is safe indefinitely. There are too many Chinese informers around. For all I know, some of the new recruits to our cause might be traitors.'

'And me?' Maggie enquired.

'You will be taken to another safe house for the night.'

'What about my tape?'

'A courier will take it across to India. He is ready to leave any minute. You have your covering note?'

Maggie handed him the four-page report she'd compiled, and the instructions for delivery of the tape.

'With luck, it will be there in two days,' Thondup said.

'Your English is very good. Where did you learn it?' Maggie asked.

'From my father.'

'He's English?'

'No, but he spent some time with the Americans. "An optimist learns English, a pessimist Chinese," he used to say to me when I was a boy.'

'You're an optimist?'

'I'm a realist. We can make our pleas, but no one in the

outside world is going to help us. I know that. But that won't stop us helping ourselves.'

There was something magnificent about Thondup, Maggie thought, this tall Khampa with his Stetson and silk tassels in his hair; his charisma and defiance and courage. Something magnificent, but also something hopeless.

One of the big men in sheepskin boots escorted her across the Quarter to the new safe house, moving quickly through the maze of streets to get there before the curfew began. She found that the monk from McLeod Ganj and his two companions – who from their appearance and demeanour she was sure were also monks – had been taken there before her. They were sitting on a couch in front of the hearth, being served butter tea and *tsampa* by a woman in a *chuba* and striped apron. They looked round as Maggie was brought in, then pointedly turned their backs on her and got on with their meal. The woman glanced tentatively at Maggie and said something to her in Tibetan.

'Please could you help me?' Maggie asked the monks. 'What did she say?'

For a moment there was no response. Then without looking at her, Tsering said grudgingly, 'She asked if you wanted tea.'

'Butter tea?'

'Yes.'

'Could you ask her if she has black tea instead?'

'This isn't a hotel, Miss Walsh.'

'I'll have hot water then, please.'

Tsering said something to the woman who nodded and lifted a kettle off the fire. Maggie walked across to the hearth and crouched down with her back against the wall. The Tibetan woman exclaimed and shook her head, coming forward with a stool and insisting that Maggie sit down on it. Then she presented her with a bowl of black tea.

'*Tujaychay*,' Maggie said, thanking her politely.

The woman's lips moved in a melancholy smile that matched the sadness in her eyes. Then she rattled off another phrase in Tibetan.

'She wants to know if you're hungry,' Tsering said without being asked.

Maggie shook her head. *'Maray.'*

But the woman wasn't prepared to take no for an answer. She lifted off the lid of a bamboo steamer which was keeping warm by the fire and removed a plump *momo*. She placed the dumpling on a plate and held it out to Maggie, urging her to take it.

'Tujaychay,' Maggie said. She took a bite of the *momo*, tasting the heavy dough and the strong salty yak meat inside. *'Yago,* good,' she said and the woman acknowledged the compliment with a bow of her head.

'Thank you for asking for black tea,' Maggie said to Tsering who shrugged indifferently and rolled another ball of *tsampa* between his fingers and popped it into his mouth. His hands and lips were greasy with yak butter.

'You know my name,' Maggie continued. 'What are yours?'

She looked at the three men. Only the youngest one met her gaze. He had a boyish, open face. His manner was friendlier, more receptive than the other two.

'I am Jigme,' he replied.

'Are you all from Dharamsala?'

'Yes, we . . .'

Tsering interrupted sharply in Tibetan. A warning. Jigme fell silent. He looked down at his bowl, mopping up the last of his butter tea with *tsampa*.

'What are you doing here?' Maggie asked, undeterred by the overt hostility. They ignored her. 'We're here together. We can be civil to each other, can't we?'

'We are being civil,' Tsering said.

Maggie took another bite of her dumpling, realising only now how hungry she was. It was gloomy in the room, the only light the glow from the fire, but at one end Maggie could see a makeshift altar with the traditional seven bowls of water placed before an image of the Buddha. On the wall next to the altar were photographs of a Tibetan man and two smiling children, presumably the woman's husband and sons.

Maggie wiped her mouth with the back of her hand and tried to break the ice again.

'You're not still angry about what happened in McLeod Ganj, surely? I spent five days in a police cell. Isn't that enough?'

They didn't respond. The monk in the middle, with the battered, ugly face, scowled at her, then growled something which didn't sound very complimentary in Tibetan to his companions.

Maggie turned back to her food. She finished her *momo* and black tea and handed the plate and bowl to the woman in the *chuba*. The woman stood up and gestured to Maggie to follow her. They went outside into the muddy yard which had a standpipe in the centre, shared by all the families in the surrounding houses. The Tibetan woman filled a plastic bowl with water and gave Maggie a thin piece of soap and a rough towel. Maggie washed her hands and face while the woman looked on, chatting to her amiably in Tibetan, unconcerned that Maggie could understand almost nothing of what she said.

Maggie had an aptitude for languages, though she was fluent only in her own. She'd acquired passable Spanish, French and Russian and smatterings of maybe a dozen others, mostly tourist phrases and a few more esoteric expressions particular to her work. Like young Victorian women on the Grand Tour, taught by their governesses to say, 'But sir, this is so sudden' in every major European language, Maggie had memorised certain phrases which she was able to use when necessary. Among them were: 'I want to speak to someone from the British Embassy'; 'Where is the toilet?' and 'Piss off, you arsehole.' She utilised the second of those stock phrases in Tibetan now and the woman pointed to a hut on the other side of the yard. Maggie braced herself, trying not to breathe through her nose, and pulled open the door.

When she returned to the house, the three monks were sitting cross-legged on the living room floor. Eyes closed, rosaries clutched in their hands, they were chanting mantras in subdued tones. The Tibetan woman showed Maggie up the stairs. There was just one room on the first floor, a small room with a raised wooden platform at either end. There were woven mats and neatly rolled blankets on each platform. A window at the front overlooked the courtyard and at the back, leaning against the wall, was a wooden ladder leading up to a trapdoor in the flat roof.

Maggie walked across to the furthermost platform and sat down on the edge. She slipped off her shoes and lay down fully clothed, pulling the blanket up over her legs. It was still early, but she was tired. The thin air and lack of oxygen in Lhasa sapped the body's energy yet at the same time made it difficult to sleep. Maggie could feel her heart beating, the throb of the blood in her head. She closed her eyes and tried to relax.

She was dozing lightly when the monks came up to bed. She awoke with a jerk and rolled on to her side, watching them sleepily across the room as they worked out how the three of them were going to fit on to the narrow platform intended only for two.

'There's room for one over here,' Maggie said.

The monks stopped talking and looked round briefly, then they continued their discussion in Tibetan as if she hadn't spoken.

'You have my word I won't molest you,' Maggie promised.

She expected them to refuse the offer and squeeze up together like sardines, but to her surprise the tall monk came across and sat down on the other side of her platform. He removed his boots and lay down, using his bag as a pillow.

'Where's the woman who lives here going to sleep?' Maggie asked.

'On the couch downstairs,' Tsering replied.

'And her husband and children? They're staying elsewhere tonight?'

From the silence, Maggie knew she'd said the wrong thing.

'Her husband is in prison,' Tsering said. 'A labour camp.'

'For what?'

'He was caught putting up a poster in support of a jailed monk. He was given eight years.'

'And her children?'

'The Chinese took them away. For re-education.'

It was a common occurrence, Maggie knew, the Chinese taking Tibetan children away from their families to be brought up in state orphanages in China. It was all part of Beijing's programme of cultural indoctrination. The children would be taught to reject their Tibetan heritage, to speak Chinese and adopt Chinese culture. If they ever saw their parents again, they would be strangers to each other.

'I'm sorry,' Maggie said. 'I didn't know.'

'How could you? Goodnight, Miss Walsh.'

He rolled on to his side, his back to her. Maggie stared up at the ceiling, listening to the monks breathing, thinking about the woman downstairs all alone.

The shout was sudden, terrified. Maggie jolted upright immediately, thinking it was part of a nightmare. Then it came again.

'*Gyami!*'

Chinese! The woman's voice coming up the stairs, her feet thudding on the wooden planks.

Maggie threw back her blanket and swung her legs off the platform, bending down to pull on her shoes. The door banged open and the woman burst in.

'Gyami!' she cried again.

The monks were out of bed now, fumbling for their boots in the darkness, barking questions at the woman, their voices urgent, anxious. The woman crossed to the ladder and gesticulated towards the roof, jabbering frantically in Tibetan. Maggie grabbed her bag and stood up, skirting round the end of the platform. Through the window she saw torches entering the courtyard, shadowy figures moving behind them. Someone banged loudly on the door downstairs, shouting in Chinese.

Maggie hurried to the foot of the ladder, her bag swinging from her shoulder, and shinned up it rapidly, sensing from the vibrations that the monks were following. She rammed open the trapdoor at the top and scrambled out on to the roof, dropping to her belly to avoid being seen from the courtyard. One after another the three monks clambered out behind her. They lowered the trapdoor back into place and lay down flat next to her. There was a thud down below, as if the front door were being smashed open, then more shouting in Chinese. Maggie looked around. There were no streetlamps in the Tibetan Quarter, but in the reflected light from the sky she could see the closely packed rooftops stretching away on all sides. The tall monk was only a couple of feet away. She could see his face, tense and worried.

'Do you know where to go?' Maggie whispered.

'No.'

'You have other friends nearby?'

'None.'

'They'll check the roof. We have to move.'

The monk looked at her and nodded. He seemed shocked, still half asleep. Maggie knew she'd have to take the lead. She snaked across the roof on her stomach and peered over the parapet. The roof of the adjoining house was on the other side, a few feet lower but with no intervening gap. Maggie slithered over and crouched down, watching the three monks coming over after her. Through a gap in the parapet next to the chimney, Maggie peered back across the roof they'd just left. The trapdoor banged open and a man's head emerged. She saw his peaked cap silhouetted against the skyline, his face turning to scan the roof. Maggie held her breath. The policeman had only to climb out and take a few paces and he was certain to find them.

A minute passed, or maybe it was only a few seconds. The officer was taking his time, making a slow 360-degree turn. Maggie glanced at the monks. They were doubled up against the parapet, lying completely still. The policeman snapped something in Chinese to someone below him in the house. Then he ducked back down the ladder, pulling the trapdoor shut above him.

Maggie started to breathe again. The monks uncurled their bodies and sat up straight.

'How did they know we were there?' Tsering murmured to Maggie.

'They didn't. It was a random search. Look, they're all over the Quarter.'

Dotted across the entire neighbourhood were dancing pinpricks of light; torchbeams bobbing through the narrow streets, probing courtyards and hidden corners of the Tibetan enclave.

'They didn't single out that house,' Maggie said. 'They're searching them all. A show of strength after this morning's demonstration.' She picked up her bag. 'We'd better go. There are other trapdoors on other roofs. Sooner or later they'll come up somewhere else and spot us.'

'Where are we going to go?' Tsering asked.

'I know a place. But first we have to get out of the Quarter.'

Maggie surveyed the surrounding area, looking at the torchbeams, searching for a pattern, for an area of houses that the PSB had not yet penetrated. They seemed to be moving in from all directions, but there looked to be more activity to the west around the Jokhang Temple. A swathe of territory to the east of their rooftop was in virtual darkness, the PSB only just getting to the fringes. Maggie knew they had to move quickly.

Dropping on to all fours, she crawled across to the other side of the roof and peeped over the edge. There was an alley fifteen feet below her – a dark, empty corridor joining two courtyards. It was maybe a metre across, no more. Narrow enough to jump. Maggie got cautiously to her feet and looked around. There was never going to be a perfect time, she just had to take a chance. Her bag clutched under one arm, she took a couple of paces back then launched herself forwards, leaping out over the alley and landing easily on the roof on the other side.

The three monks followed, dropping lightly down beside her with their own bags slung over their shoulders. We have to get off the roof, Maggie thought. We're too exposed, too vulnerable to being seen. She crawled to the edge and looked down into a small enclosed yard. The drop was too great to contemplate jumping – they would certainly break a leg or sprain an ankle if they attempted it. But further round, in a corner of the yard, was a one-storey outbuilding attached to the main house. Maggie scuttled across the roof in a low, simian crouch and checked over the edge again. The outbuilding was only a couple of metres below. She swung her legs off the roof and hung full length from her hands, dropping the last few feet to the flat roof of the outbuilding. From there she repeated the manoeuvre to reach the yard. She retreated into the hidden depths of the corner and waited for the monks to join her. Tsering came first. He was a big man, burdened by his pack, but surprisingly agile.

'Where are you taking us?' he whispered.

'The university.'

'It's too risky.'

'They've sealed off the Quarter,' Maggie said. 'If we stay here, they'll have us like rats in a trap.'

She didn't wait for a reply. She took off across the yard and eased open the wooden exit gate, peering out into the alley beyond it. There was no one about. Very cautiously, she slipped out into the alley and hurried along it, moving quickly but not recklessly fast. She heard the monks behind her, the soft squelch of their boots on the muddy, unpaved ground. After fifty metres they reached a junction. Maggie paused, getting her bearings. The Tibetan Quarter was a complex labyrinth of passageways and squares which, in the dark, all looked confusingly similar. It was easy to get lost. She turned right down a wider lane, sticking close to the houses. Behind the wooden shutters paraffin lamps were burning. Faint strips of light seeped between the slats, playing over the whitewashed stonework and the rough, potholed surface of the street.

At the next junction, she paused again. Which way next? There were three routes to choose from, no time to make a considered decision. She went for the right fork, another narrow alley hemmed in by solid stone buildings. They were twenty metres in when Maggie saw a torch flash at the far end of the alley. She stopped abruptly, pressing herself into a doorway. The torch flashed again. She caught a distant glimpse of a face, a uniform. Then more figures milling around in the darkness. She signalled to the monks and they retreated back to the junction. This time they took the middle path, a narrower passageway little wider than a man's shoulders that twisted and turned so much it was impossible to see more than a few metres ahead. There was no light here, just a claustrophobic blackness that seemed to fill the alley with its thick, oppressive weight.

Maggie heard them before she saw them: the thud of boots, the harsh rasp of an order given in Chinese. She stopped dead, then edged carefully forward and peered round the next bend. A PSB squad was thirty metres away, maybe ten or twelve uniformed officers splitting up into pairs and searching every house along the alley. Maggie returned to the monks and pointed urgently back the way they'd come. They started to retreat.

Then stopped suddenly.

There were more voices in this direction too. Somewhere back near the junction. Maggie crept to the curve in the alley that blocked their view and risked a quick look out. Another PSB squad was beginning its search at the other end of the alley, working its way in to link up with the first squad. Maggie pulled back and met the anxious gazes of the monks. She shook her head. She could feel a tight knot of fear in her stomach. Her legs were trembling. They were trapped.

Maggie estimated how much time they had. A few minutes, no more. The Chinese were closing in from both ends, moving swiftly through the houses. Their voices were getting nearer. Maggie looked around. There was nowhere to run, but maybe there was somewhere to hide. On one side of the alley the buildings had two storeys. Their walls were sheer, smooth, unclimbable. On the other side they were the same, except for a small gap where the stonework was interrupted by a short length of wooden fencing about eight feet high. There was a gate in the fence – Maggie tried it. It was locked. She looked at Tsering and he gave a nod of understanding. He leant back on the fence and cupped his hands in front of him – just below waist level – like a stirrup. Maggie put her right foot into his hands and he hoisted her up into the air. She grabbed hold of the top of the fence and swung herself over, dropping to the ground on the other side and rolling over like a parachutist to break her fall. Jigme came next, then Lobsang. Finally, Tsering threw his bag over to leave his hands free for climbing. Jigme attempted to catch the bag, but it slipped from his grasp, hitting the ground so that the contents spilled out. A silk parcel came undone and a few items fell out. Jigme scrambled to retrieve them, but not before Maggie had seen the rosary and a pair of metal-framed spectacles.

Tsering appeared at the top of the fence, straddling it for a moment, then jumping nimbly down. He saw Jigme retying the parcel and threw a brief anxious glance in Maggie's direction before taking the parcel and stowing it safely back in his bag.

Maggie turned to inspect their surroundings. They were in another courtyard, ringed not with homes but with what looked like workshops. The yard was cluttered with lengths of timber and assorted junk, the bare earth round about sprinkled with sawdust and wood shavings. Maggie tried the door of the nearest workshop. It wouldn't budge. Tsering and Jigme were trying other doors. All were locked.

'Break it open,' Maggie whispered to Tsering. 'Quickly.'

Tsering lifted his foot and smashed the sole of his boot hard against the lock. The wood splintered with a sharp crack and the door burst open. They hesitated, ears cocked towards the fence, wondering how far the noise had travelled. Then they ran inside the workshop and shut the door behind them. It was a small room. In the centre was a workbench with a vice bolted to the side. Next to it was an old-fashioned pedal lathe and on the walls were racks of tools. But there was nowhere to hide. Maggie cursed under her breath.

'Let's try one of the other workshops.'

She went back to the door and pulled it open. She stopped. There were voices in the alley on the other side of the fence. The gate handle rattled as someone tried it. Maggie pulled back and quietly closed the workshop door.

'They're here,' she said softly.

Her eyes were already roving around the room again, probing the corners, the hidden recesses, in case she'd missed a possible hiding place. There was nothing.

A sudden bang from the yard made her spin round. The Chinese were breaking down the gate.

Then Tsering said: 'The window.'

Maggie followed his gaze. High up on the back wall of the workshop was a small window.

'Hurry!' Tsering said, taking hold of the workbench.

The three monks heaved the heavy bench back until it was below the window. Tsering leapt up on to the top of the bench and reached up. He undid the catch on the window and pushed it open.

'You first,' he said to Maggie. 'Quick!'

Maggie scrambled up on to the bench. Outside there was another sharp bang and the gate from the alley flew open. She didn't see what happened next for Tsering took hold of her legs and lifted her up, propelling her out through the window in one continuous movement. Maggie rolled over on the flat roof outside and twisted round to hold open the window for the others, Jigme first, then Lobsang, squirming through the gap and slithering to the side out of sight. Maggie peered back down into the workshop. The beam of a torch flitted across the interior from outside. Tsering had ducked down, taking cover next to the bench. She heard the PSB officers out in the yard trying the doors of the other workshops. They seemed to be over the other side. There was a heavy thud – a boot or a rifle butt, she guessed – the sound of breaking glass as a door banged open.

Tsering was back on top of the bench. He reached up, grabbing the window frame with his hands and hauling himself up. Maggie and Jigme grasped one of his arms, Lobsang the other, and together they dragged him out on to the roof. Maggie pushed the window closed and pulled back, hardly daring to breathe. Someone had entered the workshop. Light from a torch filtered out through the dirty panes of the window, then the full beam hit the glass, lancing up and out over the roof. Maggie waited. The monks were flat on their stomachs, their faces hidden. The noises from below continued. Maggie kept a hold on her nerves by trying to work out what was happening. One man, perhaps two, inspecting the interior of the workshop. She could hear their footsteps, the occasional clatter as they caught something with a stray hand or boot. Then a more distant voice, a voice out in the yard, barking an order. The footsteps receded, the window went dark again as the torches withdrew. The squad went back out into the alley, moving on to the next block of buildings.

Maggie exhaled for the first time in almost a minute. The monks lifted their heads, then sat up, looking at each other with expressions of subdued relief. Maggie scanned the rooftops. They were very close to the eastern edge of the Tibetan Quarter. She could see the break in the tight-knit sprawl of houses that marked the Lingkhor Shar Lam and the ugly modern Chinese buildings on the other side of the avenue. They waited a while longer, letting the PSB search parties get further away, then moved off across the roofs, skirting chimneys, negotiating courtyards and alleys, until they reached the last section of the Quarter. On the final roof before the Lingkhor Shar Lam, they dropped to their bellies and wriggled across to the parapet and looked over. Below them the avenue was quiet and deserted. A few metres away, two PSB trucks were parked at the kerb. Both were empty, but further up the avenue a couple of officers were standing guard by one of the entrances to the Tibetan Quarter. They were almost out of sight in the mouth of the alley, but their shoulders and the barrels of their rifles were just visible.

Maggie pointed at the trucks, motioning with her hands, explaining soundlessly what she had in mind. Tsering nodded. Maggie checked the pavement below, then the avenue, searching for patrols, for vehicles. Then she slid her legs over the parapet so they dangled in space. Tsering took hold of her hands and leant out, lowering as far as he could. He let go and Maggie dropped to the ground. She scuttled across the pavement and rolled underneath the nearest PSB truck.

One after the other the monks followed her until all four of them were lying on the road under the truck. The two PSB guards were thirty metres away. All Maggie could see of them now were their legs and boots. She felt both physically and emotionally drained, a mixture of fear and adrenaline keeping her going. The monks too were showing the strain, particularly Jigme. His face was taut, pale.

Maggie took a bearing on the guards, drawing an imaginary diagonal line from them to the other side of the avenue, running directly through the parked trucks. She pinpointed the exact place the line ended and fixed her eyes on it. Then she crawled out on the off side of the lorries, checked that the avenue was clear, and sprinted across it, the bulk of the two trucks covering her movements. She ducked into a side-street and bent over, her hands on her knees, gasping for breath.

She was still panting when Jigme came dashing round the corner and lurched to a halt, leaning back on the wall with his eyes closed. Lobsang took a little longer, lumbering awkwardly across the avenue with Tsering only a few metres behind him. They paused for a moment, to see if there was any reaction from the guards. When none came, they headed off down the side-street and circled round to approach the university from the north.

The campus was deserted, the curfew keeping everyone indoors. Maggie took the monks in through the fire exit of the foreign accommodation block and put them in the bathroom, warning them to keep quiet, while she went down the corridor to Monroe's room. She looked at her watch. It was twenty past midnight. She knocked softly on the door.

'Monroe, open up,' she whispered through the keyhole.

She heard him getting out of bed, shuffling across the floor. A key turned in the lock and the door swung open. Monroe was in his pyjamas, a paisley-patterned jacket and trousers that Maggie, marvelling at how her mind could stray absurdly on to trivia, recognised as Marks and Spencer at its finest. He looked at her blearily, too sleepy to get angry. She beckoned him out and, still in a daze, Monroe followed her to the bathroom. He gaped at the three monks, one sitting on the toilet seat, the other two on the edge of the bath. The sight seemed to jolt him fully awake for he reached out and automatically switched on the shower before he turned to Maggie and hissed: 'What the hell's going on? Who are these people?'

'Monks. From Dharamsala,' Maggie replied.

'*What?*'

'We had to get out of the Tibetan Quarter. The PSB are everywhere.'

'Monks? What're you doing, Maggie? Do you know what time it is?'

'Can we sleep on your floor?'

'My floor? All of you? Christ, what am I supposed to say?' Monroe ran a hand over his balding head in exasperation.

'Just the one night,' Maggie said. 'Please, Patrick.'

'Do I have a choice?'

'Thanks.'

'They know they have to remain silent in my room?'

'They're monks. They're good at silence.'

Monroe opened the bathroom door and gestured at the monks to follow him. Tsering lingered behind with Maggie.

'We are grateful for this, Miss Walsh,' he said.

'It's Maggie. What's your name?'

He hesitated, then gave a wry shrug. 'Tsering.'

Maggie smiled at him. 'Pleased to meet you, Tsering.'

She leaned over and turned off the shower.

NINE

'You know what happened yesterday?' Monroe said to Maggie. They were in the bathroom again, talking quietly under the noise of the running shower.

'Outside the Jokhang, you mean? I was there.'

'Not that. Afterwards. The PSB came over here and told all the foreign teaching staff that they had to leave. Classes have been suspended, the students have been told to stay at home.'

'You have to leave? When?'

'This afternoon. They're bussing us to Gonggar and putting us on a flight to Chengdu. God knows when we'll be allowed back.'

'It's the start of the reprisals,' Maggie said grimly. 'For the demonstration. First get rid of the journalists, then all Westerners. Remove the outside witnesses and it clears the ground for a massive clampdown on the Tibetans.'

'What I'm saying,' Monroe continued, 'is that after this afternoon there won't be a single Westerner left in Lhasa. You'll be pretty obvious if you stay.'

'I'll take that chance. But thanks for the warning.'

They returned to Monroe's room to find Jigme and Lobsang washing themselves at the sink. Stripped to the waist, the two monks were rinsing soap off their arms and chests. They covered themselves up hurriedly with towels as Maggie came in. The transistor radio was on again, spewing out its relentless diet of strident Chinese pop music. It grated on Maggie's nerves, but they had to endure it.

Tsering was standing by Monroe's bed, studying closely the aerial photograph of the Himalayas that was pinned to the wall. He turned to Monroe, his voice only just above a whisper.

'Where did you get this?'

Monroe turned up the volume on the radio to smother their conversation. Maggie moved a little nearer, eavesdropping discreetly.

'From someone I know at the university. I've been giving him English lessons,' Monroe answered.

'Chinese?'

'No, Tibetan. He works in the Geology Department.'

'How was this taken? From an aeroplane?'

'Satellite. Pretty spectacular, isn't it?'

'And your friend, how did he get it?'

'The Geology Department has a database of aerial photographs, for the Ministry of Geology and the Western mining corporations who are helping them exploit Tibet's mineral resources.'

Tsering glanced furtively at Maggie and lowered his voice even more. But the room was too small for her not to catch his words.

'Your friend, is he trustworthy? He's not a Chinese informer?'

'No.'

'How can you be sure?'

'Because once he was a distinguished professor here. A learned teacher respected in his field. The Chinese took away his post and gave it to a cadre with Party connections. My friend was kept on as a lab technician, cleaning benches and equipment, sweeping up after the Chinese. Would you act as an informer for them if they'd done that to you?'

'Can you take us to him?'

'Why?'

'Can you?'

'What's this about?' Monroe asked impatiently. 'Is it important?'

'Maybe.'

'I'm sorry, but I have to pack.'

'Please. It will be a great help to us.'

'Why would monks from Dharamsala be interested in aerial maps?'

'Just take us to him. I beg you,' Tsering said imploringly.

Monroe sighed and looked at his watch. 'It will have to be now.'

'We are ready.'

Tsering walked across to Lobsang and Jigme and they had a muted conversation in Tibetan. Monroe went to the door and waited for them, his fingers resting lightly on the handle. Maggie sauntered over and stood next to him. When Monroe opened the door she was right behind him, but Tsering stepped in to block her exit.

'You wait here, Miss Walsh.'

Maggie shook her head. 'Sorry.'

'This is our business. This is nothing to do with you.'

'What isn't?'

'Don't make things difficult. We don't want you with us. Do you understand?'

Maggie held his gaze, not in the least bit intimidated. 'How are you going to stop me? Call the police?'

The university Geology Department was across the other side of the campus in a shabby old building that was badly in need of a facelift. Inside, the laboratories were stark and uncluttered; plain white tiles on the walls, bare concrete floors and long wooden benches set out in rows. They reminded Maggie of her old school chemistry labs, right down to the smell of gas and unidentifiable chemicals that pricked the nostrils as you walked in.

The whole department seemed deserted – no students, no teachers – but at the end of one of the labs they found Monroe's friend, Chozom. He was in his sixties, slightly built with a wispy grey goatee beard. He was in the process of setting up some complicated piece of apparatus for an experiment, but he broke off and smiled broadly when he saw Monroe.

'Good morning, Patrick,' he said in slow, accented English. 'How are you today?'

'Very well, thank you,' Monroe replied, going through an exchange that was obviously part of some well-practised teaching exercise. Then Monroe changed to fluent Tibetan, introducing the three monks.

Chozom turned to the monks. '*Tashi delek*,' he said politely, but his eyes were wary, his manner guarded. In Tibet, it paid to be suspicious of all strangers.

The monks returned the greeting, pressing their palms together and bowing their heads formally. Then Tsering had a short conversation with Chozom. The lab technician glanced at Monroe and asked a question, apparently seeking corroboration or maybe reassurance. Monroe nodded and Chozom gestured at them to remain in the laboratory. He went out through a door and returned a few minutes later carrying a bunch of keys. Signalling them to follow, he led them across the lab and out into a corridor. He stopped outside a door and unlocked it, standing aside to let them all enter, before closing the door and locking it behind them.

The room they were in was a complete contrast to the tatty, old-fashioned laboratory. This was the new China, the dynamic, high-tech entrepreneurial China. There was carpet on the floor, tinted glass windows covered by designer blinds, strips of bright lights on the false ceiling. And mounted on large shiny desks, expensive adjustable swivel chairs drawn up before them, were several gleaming computer terminals. They could have been in the computer room of any giant Western corporation, Maggie reflected as she looked around. But then that wasn't so surprising given the purpose of all the equipment and the fact that most of it had probably been paid for by some multinational conglomerate. There was big money to be made in Tibet. The Chinese name for the region was Xizang, the western treasure house, and since their invasion they'd made a concerted effort to remove as much of the treasure as possible. Vast areas in the eastern province of Kham had been stripped of their forests, the timber shipped out to Beijing and other burgeoning Chinese cities. But it was the mineral reserves – the uranium, iron, copper, oil, platinum and diamonds – that would ensure that the Chinese never left Tibet.

Chozom had closed the blinds and was sitting at one of the terminals now, logging on to the system. Various icons with Chinese labels appeared on the screen and Chozom clicked on one.

Watching from a distance, Maggie said to Monroe: 'The Chinese let him use this?'

'No way. He's Tibetan.'

'If he's caught?'

'Yes, he's taking a big risk. But he's done it before. He designed most of the software so he knows how to hack into the system. He's a very clever man.'

Tsering was standing behind Chozom, looking at the screen over the lab technician's shoulder. Chozom asked him something and Tsering moved round to the side, taking a piece of scrap paper and a pencil off the desk and carefully drawing an outline on it. Maggie craned her head to see what it was. It seemed to be just a simple but meaningless pattern of zigzag lines.

'What are they doing?' she asked Monroe.

'Looking for a mountain.'

'A mountain. Why?'

'They didn't say.'

'This guy can help them find a mountain?'

'The Chinese have surveyed most of Tibet in detail. They know where everything is. These terminals access the Geology Department's database. He's seeing if he can get a match.'

Monroe glanced at the locked door. Maggie could tell he was nervous. This wasn't just some harmless academic enquiry he was assisting. The Chinese would undoubtedly view what they were doing as espionage. And espionage was a capital offence.

He said something in Tibetan – telling them to hurry up, Maggie guessed – and Chozom looked round and nodded. The lab technician had the mouse in his hand, tracing the exact outline of the pattern on the piece of paper and transferring it to the screen. He clicked on an icon and sat back in his chair, saying something to Tsering.

'What was that?' Maggie asked.

'He said it's searching,' Monroe replied. 'Going through the database.'

'What else did the monks say to your friend?'

'Just that it was important they identified this mountain. Who are they, anyway? How come they're with you?'

'It's probably better you don't know,' Maggie said.

'Yes, maybe.' He glanced at the door again. 'This is taking a long time. If someone finds us here . . .'

'Relax. The place is deserted. Like you said, the staff and students have all taken the day off.'

'The security men never take a day off.'

A photographic image appeared on the screen, an aerial view of a range of snow-capped mountains. Then the camera moved in closer, selecting a small section of the range and blowing it up to fill the screen. The search field became even narrower. The top of a single mountain came into view. Chozom manipulated the image, turning it backwards through ninety degrees so that they could see the mountain from the front. The zigzag outline made sense now. That was exactly what the mountain looked like, a high central summit with a lower peak on either side, separated by V-shaped valleys. Chozom indicated some Chinese characters at the top of the screen and said something to Tsering.

'What's he saying?' Maggie asked.

'That this is the only mountain in Tibet that matches the search parameters.'

Maggie studied the image. It was a striking peak, each of its summits rising to a needle-sharp point, the tips gleaming with ice.

'Does it have a name?'

'Mount Gebur,' Monroe replied, repeating what Chozom had said. 'Crown Mountain.'

Tsering looked round, hearing their words, and glared at them.

Maggie ignored him. 'Where is it?'

'In northern Kham,' Monroe said. 'Six and a half thousand metres high. He's giving them the coordinates now. Why do you think they want to know? A bunch of monks from India.'

'I don't know,' Maggie said.

But she had an idea. She was beginning to work out why the monks were in Tibet.

'What do you mean, you didn't find them?' Shen demanded, his narrow features tight with anger.

Chang stood to attention in front of the colonel's desk, staring at the photograph of Mao which hung on the wall of the office. There had been a time when the Great Helmsman had fallen out of favour and his image had been carefully removed from public view. Now his reputation had been restored, his photograph had once again resumed pride of place in offices across the country. But Chang knew no such rehabilitation awaited him if he lost the faith of his superiors. He would be cast out into the darkness, his career erased like chalk wiped from a slate.

'I am sorry, Comrade Colonel,' he said contritely. 'We sealed off the Quarter as you ordered and searched every building, every street. There was no sign of either the Khampa or the monks.'

'Nothing?'

'No. However, we did find a number of wounded Tibetans who had obviously taken part in the riot outside the Jokhang.'

Chang's voice had regained some of its normal assurance, but Shen wasn't going to let him off the hook. He enjoyed seeing his deputy squirm a little.

'I wanted the ringleader,' he snapped. 'Not the sheep who follow him. The Khampa, where is he?'

'I believe the rioters may be able to tell us that.'

'They are being interrogated?'

'Yes, Comrade Colonel.'

'Any results?'

'They are stubborn. But we will break them.'

Shen lit a cigarette, drawing on it and savouring the harsh flavour of the tobacco in his mouth. He said nothing for a long time. Let Chang stew a bit in the silence. The major was confident, a little too bumptious for Shen's liking. It would be good for him to dwell on his failure.

Eventually, Shen said: 'Someone must know who the Khampa is.'

'We have also arrested more than two hundred men. A random selection. One of them will crack,' Chang replied.

'Let us hope so.'

Shen didn't share the major's optimism. The Tibetans were a backward, primitive people, but their very simplicity made them difficult to handle. The only thing in the world they wanted was their independence, something which they knew they would never be granted. Yet they continued to struggle for it. Shen, an unquestioning obedience to authority deeply imbued in his character, didn't understand that. But he recognised that the Tibetans' single-minded pursuit of that unattainable goal was what made them so dangerous. There were no carrots he could use to tempt them, because the one carrot they wanted was not his to offer, so all he had left were sticks. Except for their freedom, the Tibetans wanted nothing. And people who wanted nothing were impossible to control. If they had no desires, what did you have to refuse them?

'Is he still in Lhasa?' Shen asked.

'I don't know, but I would guess he is.'

'Guess, Major? Guesswork is no sensible basis for apprehending criminals.'

'With respect, Comrade Colonel,' Chang said stiffly, 'a guess, when combined with sound psychological reasoning, can be most effective.'

'What "sound psychological reasoning" are you referring to?' Shen said. He distrusted such pretentious terminology, particularly as he suspected Chang used it to make him feel inferior. In the colonel's view, the criminal mind was so warped and unpredictable that it was impossible to apply any kind of reason to it.

'This man is a leader. He has a strong presence. He shows physical courage. We can see that from the tape of the riot. He does not strike me as a man who would run away. He is not a coward.'

'So?'

'What would his followers think of him if he fled while they stayed behind? No, he is too vain, perhaps too sure of himself, to leave Lhasa when remaining can only add to his status and prestige. He is still here.'

Shen tapped the ash off the end of his cigarette and raised his eyes to the major's. 'Then I suggest you try harder to find him.'

'Yes, Comrade Colonel.'

'And the monks. I want them too.' Shen looked away, adding casually, 'Reinforce our checkpoints around the city. Every vehicle and person leaving to be stopped.' He gave a thin smile. 'Just in case your "sound psychological reasoning" turns out to be wrong.'

Maggie stood by the window of Monroe's room and pulled back the curtain a little, looking down into the square in front of the foreign accommodation block. A blue and white coach – one of the tour buses that were used for transporting visitors to and from the airport – was just drawing up outside the building. Two Chinese men in grey suits and sunglasses – the secret policeman's favourite fashion accessory across the world – jumped down from the coach and walked purposefully in through the main entrance.

Maggie pulled back. 'They're here.'

Monroe threw the last of his belongings into the top of his suitcase and closed the lid, leaning on it with all his weight to snap the catches shut. He looked around the room. He'd left the *thangkas* on the wall, the transistor radio on the bedside table, still pumping out its discordant background noise, as small marks of his residence, superstitious tokens that would ensure he returned. He lifted the suitcase off the bed and put it on the floor next to his bulging holdall.

He turned to Maggie. 'You're out of your mind, but good luck.'

Maggie nodded. 'Thanks for your help.'

'Don't hang around. The PSB porter on the front desk downstairs will probably check all the rooms after we've gone.'

Monroe picked up his luggage. As he reached the door, there was a sharp rap on it from outside and a voice shouted something in Chinese.

'I'm ready,' Monroe called back in the same language.

He waited for the footsteps to recede, listening to the bangs and shouts further along the corridor. Then he walked over to the bed and turned off the radio. The sudden silence seemed to magnify the remaining sounds in the room: the rustle of clothes, the pad of Monroe's shoes as he went back to the door. Maggie was acutely aware of the noise of her own breathing, of the three monks squatting down on their haunches against the wall. Monroe opened the door and looked out into the corridor. The other foreign staff were leaving their rooms, making their way downstairs. He picked up his suitcase and holdall, gave a brief nod of farewell and was gone.

Maggie stepped across to the window and pulled back the curtain again, watching the teachers staggering out with their luggage, clambering up the steps on to the coach. Monroe was one of the last. He took a seat at the front of the coach, staring straight ahead as the men in the sunglasses stood in the aisle doing a head count. The coach door hissed shut and the vehicle pulled away. At the last moment, Monroe turned his head, glancing up expressionlessly at the window. Then the coach swung round in a loop and headed back across the square towards the campus exit.

For a long while no one moved. The three monks stayed

squatting against the wall, apparently unsure what to do next. Maggie caught Tsering's eye and pointed at the door. He nodded and stood up, his two companions following him. Maggie opened the door. The corridor outside was deserted. Picking up their bags, they flitted soundlessly into the bathroom and turned on the shower.

'We can't stay here, it's not safe,' Maggie said. 'We have to get back to the Tibetan Quarter.'

'"We"?' Tsering said and shook his head. 'This is where we part company, Miss Walsh.'

'Uh-uh,' Maggie said. 'You're not going to leave me here on my own with nowhere to go.'

'That's not our problem.'

'I think it is.'

Tsering didn't like that. 'We didn't choose to be with you,' he said caustically. 'Circumstance thrust us together. You're here for your own reasons which have nothing to do with us. You're not our responsibility.'

'You owe me,' Maggie said. 'Without me, where would you have gone last night? The PSB or PLA would have picked you up out on the streets. Don't you think you have a moral obligation to help me in return?'

'Help you how?'

'You know how to find Thondup. I don't. If I'm to get out of Tibet, I'm going to need his assistance.'

'You should have thought of that before you entered the country.'

'You're not going to dump me. Wherever you go, I'm going to be right behind you. Try to stop me, and I'll make a scene. You don't want to draw too much attention to yourselves, do you?'

'Nor do you,' Tsering retorted.

'True. But look at what will happen if we're caught. Me, I'm British, a woman. They'll probably just deport me. But you guys – three monks from Dharamsala – they'll say you're spies, or *agents provocateurs* sent here to stir up trouble. They might make things very hard for you.'

Tsering looked at her, saying nothing. He didn't know how to handle this.

'Miss Walsh . . .' he began, but Maggie put a hand on his arm suddenly.

'Ssssh.' She reached out and turned off the shower, one finger pressed to her lips.

Tsering heard it now. Footsteps in the corridor.

Maggie opened the door a fraction. The porter from downstairs was at the far end, pausing outside a room to open the door with his master key. Maggie waited for him to go inside. How long would he be? A couple of minutes? A few seconds? She counted. Fifteen seconds later he came out again, locked the door behind him and moved on to the next room.

'One at a time,' Maggie said quietly to Tsering. 'Wait downstairs at the back.' She pulled the door wider. The porter was inside the second room. Maggie signalled to Jigme. 'Go!' she whispered.

Jigme took off towards the back stairs, only just making it round the corner before the porter reappeared and continued his rounds. A key turned in another lock and the porter stepped into a third room. Lobsang shot out into the corridor and vanished. Monroe's room was next. The porter tried the handle and the door swung open. He went inside. Maggie gave Tsering a nod and he ran to the stairs and was lost from sight. The porter was getting dangerously close. Two more doors and he'd be level with the bathroom. Maggie picked up her bag. She took a look through the crack in the door. The porter was back in the corridor, locking Monroe's door, moving on. Maggie eased the bathroom door shut and listened, judging her moment as the porter went into the next room. She gave him a couple of seconds, then whipped open the door and sprinted for the stairs, flinging herself round the corner and descending two, three steps at a time.

The three monks were waiting for her outside the fire escape. They moved off immediately, crossing a strip of open ground behind the accommodation block and taking cover in the complex of faculty buildings. They sheltered behind a wall, getting their breath back. Maggie gave Tsering a look.

'Back there,' she said, 'you could have left me upstairs, run off without me, but you didn't.'

'That would not have been right,' Tsering replied, bridling a little at the suggestion. 'We are honourable men.'

'Thank you.'

They found a teahouse on the edge of the Tibetan Quarter and while Lobsang, Jigme and Maggie sat at a table in a dark corner, Tsering went off to the Barkhor to find Wangchuk, the wood carver, who they hoped might know how to contact Thondup again. The teahouse was crowded with elderly Tibetan men. Lobsang eyed them warily, watching to see if anyone seemed unduly curious about these three strangers: the two Tibetans and the Chinese woman. Maggie was wearing her blue worker's suit and cap and in the gloomy interior was confident that no one would recognise her as a Westerner. She kept well back in the shadows, the cap pulled low over her forehead, and concentrated on eating the bowl of noodles the monks had ordered for her. Lobsang and Jigme had butter tea and *tsampa*. They exchanged occasional remarks in Tibetan but were silent most of the time. They were all on edge, their gazes flickering continually towards the door, waiting anxiously for Tsering to return.

Close on an hour later, he reappeared and sat down at the table.

'You found him?' Lobsang asked.

Tsering nodded. 'He is sending someone for us.'

'When?'

'Shortly.'

'We've been here too long,' Lobsang said. 'If the *Gong An Ju* come, we have no papers.'

'Thondup is fixing papers for us.'

'And the woman?'

'She comes with us. Just for tonight.'

'One night only. Good. We are too conspicuous with her.'

'There is something else,' Tsering said, lowering his voice to a murmur. 'Dharamsala have replied to our message.'

Lobsang and Jigme leaned closer, staring at Tsering with such fixed concentration that Maggie, though she couldn't follow their Tibetan, knew something important was being discussed.

'Just one word,' Tsering went on. He paused, knowing the terrible significance of what he was about to say. '"Proceed".'

No one spoke. The news took a moment to sink in, the full implications a while longer. Jigme glanced at Lobsang, wondering if the other monk's stomach had knotted suddenly the way his own had. Lobsang let out a deep breath, the air hissing between his clenched teeth.

'So that's it,' he said fatalistically. 'We're on our own.'

'There are three of us,' Tsering said. 'We will support each other.' He started to think of the task ahead, but it was so daunting he made himself stop. Some things in life were so momentous, so frightening, it was better not to contemplate them but to simply let them happen.

'Three?' Lobsang said. 'Three against all these Chinese. What hope do we have?'

Tsering's face clouded. 'We have our faith,' he said resolutely.

Lobsang's lip curled. 'Oh yes, our faith, I'd forgotten.'

Tsering put his hand on Lobsang's arm, gripping the flesh tightly. 'Our faith is what makes us the men we are. Never forget that, Lobsang. It is our strength, our comfort, our courage. We have a task to complete and we will never, not for one moment, contemplate failing. Do you understand?'

Lobsang didn't reply. Tsering tightened his grip on the other's arm. 'Do you understand?'

'Yes, I understand.'

Lobsang pulled his arm away and rubbed it. Maggie watched, wondering what the argument had been about. She was beginning to work out the dynamics between the three monks. They were a curious mixture of personalities. Tsering, undoubtedly the leader of the group, had a presence that reminded her of Thondup though his charisma was less showy than the Khampa's. He wasn't flamboyant in any way, but you couldn't help noticing him. He had an aura of authority about him, a quiet tenacity that was also evident in Lobsang, the most overtly aggressive of the three men. Maggie knew he didn't like her. His antipathy was obvious from the way he looked at her, the scowl of distrust that contorted his features. He seemed a man wary of people and the world, a darkly brooding character whose misgivings about his fellow creatures bordered on misanthropy. Then there was Jigme, the youngest of them, who exuded a far greater warmth than the other two. He had an air of naivety about him, a childlike innocence that Maggie knew was deceptive. He was a Tibetan, and Tibetan innocence had long ago been shattered by the Chinese.

They waited a further half hour, justifying their occupancy of the table by ordering black tea and bowls of yak's-milk yoghurt that was so thick you could almost eat it with your fingers. Then a man in a *chuba* and sheepskin boots, one of the two who'd taken the monks to Thondup before, came in and signalled them to leave. They followed him to the edge of the Quarter where a white van with Tibetan and Chinese markings on the side was waiting for them. They climbed into the back. It was just big enough for the four of them and their bags and smelt strongly of disinfectant.

For ten minutes they drove around Lhasa, stopping occasionally before moving off again. There were no windows in the back so it was impossible to see where they were going, but Maggie was sure it was somewhere on the northern fringes of the city. She'd followed every turn of the vehicle, relating it to the rough plan of Lhasa she carried in her head.

Eventually, they slowed and came to a halt. The engine was cut and they could hear doors banging shut outside. The doors of the van were opened and they climbed out, stretching their limbs. They were in what looked at first sight like a garage, but from the double doors at either end seemed more like a loading bay.

The man in sheepskin boots led them through a smaller access door, down a short corridor and into a large, cool, high-ceilinged hall that smelt of the same disinfectant as the van. Along the edges of the hall, laid out on wooden trestle tables, were shapes wrapped in white sheets that could only be one thing. Maggie realised they were in the city morgue. The Tibetan morgue – there was a separate one for the Chinese who, even in death, feared contamination by the unclean natives.

They were taken into a windowless office off the hall and the man in sheepskin boots handed Tsering a key and said something in Tibetan before leaving. Tsering locked the door after the man had gone and stowed the key in one of the folds of his *chuba*.

'What's happening?' Maggie asked.

'We stay here for the night,' Tsering replied.

'And then?'

'Then?' Tsering shrugged. 'Thondup will try to get you out of Tibet.'

'And if I want to stay?'

'Why would you want to stay?'

'To see what happens next. It's not going to end here, is it? I've got plenty more tapes in my bag.'

'You will have to talk to Thondup about that.'

'And what about you guys? What are you going to do next?'

'What we do need not concern you.'

Tsering turned away to indicate the conversation was at an end. He moved to the other side of the room and sat down cross-legged on the floor. Lobsang and Jigme joined him. Their eyes closed, their rosaries held loosely between their fingers, they began to meditate, murmuring the mantra *Om mani padme hum* over and over again, each recitation being counted off on their rosaries as if they were totting up figures on an abacus.

Maggie sat down on a chair and lit a cigarette, watching them, envying them their ability to shut themselves off from the outside world. She'd tried meditation a few times, as a stress reliever rather than a religious practice, but she couldn't sit still long enough to manage it successfully. It always seemed such a waste of time to her, but maybe that was the point: life itself was a waste of time so sitting doing nothing somehow encapsulated the futility of it all. Not that the monks believed that. To them, meditation was the path to enlightenment, a way of calming the mind, of focusing on the tenets of their faith.

Maggie inhaled on her cigarette, listening to the soothing hum of the monks' voices, the gentle click of their rosary beads. She always thought of Buddhism as a numerical religion. Its followers believed in repetition. Repeating mantras, performing endless prostrations, circumambulating sacred shrines time and time again, each cycle accruing merit that would help them to a better rebirth and ultimately *nirvana*. It had a comforting simplicity to it. No great intellectual ability was required, no great education. You just performed the specified acts a sufficient number of times and a better new life was almost guaranteed.

Three cigarettes later, Maggie was bored. The incessant chanting was getting on her nerves. She stood up and paced around the room, feeling cramped, claustrophobic. She would have liked to get out, find more space somewhere, but the door was locked and Tsering had the key. Besides, where would she go? Strolling around the shrouded bodies outside held no appeal whatsoever. She wished she had a book to read, but she'd left them all behind in Nepal. There was nothing to do except endure the tedium.

An hour later – every minute of it noted by Maggie on the dial of her watch – the monks ended their meditation. To give herself something to do, Maggie asked Tsering for the key to go and find a toilet. He resisted the idea, but when she insisted, went out himself to explore the morgue first, returning with directions to a washroom he'd found on the ground floor. He came with her, to deal with any Tibetan staff she happened to encounter, but the building seemed deserted. When they returned to the office, Maggie positioned herself close to Jigme and went to work on him.

'How long have you lived in McLeod Ganj?' she asked.

'Six years.'

'And before that? You were a monk in Tibet?'

'Yes.'

'Whereabouts?'

'Jigme!' Tsering barked a warning, shaking his head.

'What's the problem?' Maggie said irritably. 'This is just harmless conversation.'

'You ask too many questions.'

'Is there anything you'll allow us to talk about? Or do we have to sit in silence?'

'What's wrong with silence?'

'I know,' Maggie said, as if the thought had just occurred to her. 'Let's talk about Mount Gebur.'

Tsering stiffened. 'That is not your business.'

'Anything's my business if I want it to be. What's so special about Mount Gebur?'

Tsering looked away, not deigning to reply.

Maggie probed a little further. 'Okay, let's try another topic. How about eyesight?' That had him for a moment. Maggie saw his eyes glance back at her, wondering what she meant. 'You all seem to have good vision. You don't appear to be long-sighted, or short-sighted. I can't see any signs of astigmatisms.' She was enjoying herself, watching the puzzled looks on their faces. 'I know I'm not an expert so I might be mistaken about this, but if there's nothing wrong with your vision . . .' she paused, wanting their full attention '. . . what is that pair of spectacles doing in your luggage?'

They did their best not to react, but Maggie caught the sudden starts, the jolts of surprise in their faces and knew she was right.

'Spectacles?' Tsering said calmly.

'Wrapped up in cloth in your bag. Along with a rosary which I don't think belongs to any of you either.'

'Then whom do they belong to?'

'Let's not play the innocent,' Maggie said. 'When they fell out of your bag last night, they just looked like an ordinary pair of metal-framed spectacles to me. It was only later I began to think about them, especially this morning when you were so anxious to identify a particular mountain. Then I realised they weren't ordinary spectacles. And I knew I'd seen them somewhere before . . .' They were staring quizzically at her, waiting for her to go on. 'I'd seen him in the flesh, you see. Spoken to him face to face. I know what his spectacles look like. Metal-framed with a tortoiseshell trim along the top edge.'

'Him?'

'You know who I mean. Of course, there are probably millions of similar pairs of glasses in the world. But these are in your bag. And you are a monk – probably a senior monk – from McLeod Ganj. You're here in Tibet, illegally, just a matter of days after his death. And you're looking for a special mountain. What are you, the advance search party?'

In the silence that followed, Maggie looked at each of the monks in turn. 'You're on the young side, I suppose, but maybe that's how it has to be with the Chinese controlling the country. You wouldn't want some elderly, infirm lama to have to scour the country with the Chinese breathing down his neck. Circumstances make this one different, don't they. The last time was before the invasion. I'm right, aren't I?'

When no one replied, she went on: 'I know how it works; the signs you follow, maybe seen in a vision or prophesied by the Oracle, the objects you ask the chosen child to identify as his. That's how it's always been done, and you're a very traditional people. You're looking for his reincarnation, aren't you?'

Tsering found his voice. 'As I've said, what we are doing here is none of your business.'

'Why deny it? You're monks, you've taken a vow not to lie. I'll ask you straight. Is that why you're here? Yes, or no?'

'We do not have to answer any of your questions, Miss Walsh.'

'No, but I think you just answered it.' She paused. 'I'll offer you a deal.'

'A deal?'

'You let me accompany you on the search, and I'll tape it for you.'

Tsering squinted at her, his forehead creased into fine wrinkles. 'That seems a very one-sided deal. We do not wish to be taped.'

'You need it. You need a record,' Maggie explained. 'A few years ago, when they were searching for the new Panchen Lama, the monks from Tashilhunpo Monastery videotaped how they went about it. I've seen some of the footage. Why did they do it? Not because they wanted to be film stars, but for authenticity.'

'We do not need that kind of authenticity.'

'Don't you? I said back in McLeod Ganj that you were naïve. This is the twenty-first century, the television age. No one believes anything has happened unless they've seen pictures of it on a screen. You know the Chinese will question whoever you choose. They may even produce a rival claimant, as they did with the Panchen Lama. You need to be able to prove categorically that your choice is valid. I'll give you that proof.'

She saw the uncertainty in Tsering's face. Her argument was having some impact on him.

'There's another reason why you should let me come with you,' Maggie continued. 'Because I'm coming whatever you say.'

Tsering stared at her incredulously. 'I don't think so.'

'I know where you're going. I know about Mount Gebur. I'm going to follow you there and you can't stop me.'

'This is blackmail.'

'It's negotiation. Why don't you discuss it with your friends?' Maggie turned away and lit another cigarette.

Tsering looked at Lobsang and Jigme.

Lobsang scowled and shook his head. 'It's out of the question,' he said unequivocally in Tibetan. 'She is not coming with us.'

'How do we stop her? I'm getting to know her. She is stubborn, tenacious. She will certainly follow us.'

'We could ask Thondup to smuggle her out of the country.'

'What, against her will? That would not be easy. And she would only come straight back, perhaps be picked up by the Chinese. That's what worries me. If she's interrogated, she may be forced to betray us. She knows who we are, she knows our destination. Can we afford to take that risk?'

'She is a liability,' Lobsang snarled.

'Jigme?'

Jigme hesitated, unsure whether his opinion counted for anything. 'She has nerve and courage,' he said haltingly. 'And she has helped us. Without her we might not have escaped from the Quarter last night. Her pictures of the killings outside the Jokhang will help our cause too. She is on our side. She may be right that some filmed evidence of our search – if it succeeds – will strengthen the position of the new Dalai Lama and our people in exile.'

'She is on no one's side but her own,' Lobsang snapped. 'She will use us for her own ends.'

Tsering turned his gaze back to Maggie. She was watching them coolly, a trickle of cigarette smoke seeping between her lips.

'Well?' she said.

'You are an unscrupulous, manipulative woman, Miss Walsh,' Tsering replied.

'Yeah, I know. So what do you say? Do we have a deal?'

TEN

Maggie had seen dead bodies before, seen men and women and sometimes children who'd been shot, or killed by shrapnel or exploding shells. She'd filmed them lying in the street, in the wreckage of burnt-out buildings or in holes in the ground where they'd been dumped by their killers. But she'd never been this close to them before.

They were all around her in the truck. Eight bodies in total, wrapped from head to toe in white shrouds. Maggie could feel one of them pressing against her, feel the cold rigid shape through the thin cotton material. The scent of them was in her nostrils too. And it really was a scent, not the putrid stench she'd expected. The bodies had been washed in perfumed water and she could smell the camphor and saffron. No preservatives or disinfectant had been used, for the vultures were fastidious scavengers who disliked the taint of chemicals, refusing to touch a body that had been contaminated by them – a singularly bad omen for the rebirth of the deceased person's spirit.

Maggie too was wrapped in a shroud, as were the three monks next to her. It was a strange sensation, lying swaddled like a baby, her arms pressed tight to her sides, the sheet folded across her face. She could breathe, could see light through the shroud, but her movements were constricted. She could turn her head and wiggle her toes, but her torso, her arms and legs were immobilised.

They'd been woken before dawn by Thondup and two of his men who'd been let into the office at the morgue by one of the Tibetan porters. Maggie and the monks had thrown aside the blankets with which they'd been provided and got to their feet quickly, reaching for their bags. All had been sleeping fully dressed, ready for the hurried departure they knew might be forced on them.

Thondup held up a calming hand. 'We are not leaving yet,' he said in English. Then to Tsering, in Tibetan, he added: 'The arrangements are all in place.'

He explained what he had planned and saw the looks of doubt on the monks' faces. 'It is the only way. The city is ringed by checkpoints, PLA and *Gong An Ju*. The Chinese have imposed martial law. They're tightening the screws on us.'

'And once we're out of Lhasa?' Tsering asked.

'A van will be waiting for you. You will be given false identity papers and travel permits and a contact point in Nyingchi.'

'And after that?'

'You are on your own.'

Thondup turned to Maggie and switched back to English. 'You have your camera? There are people who wish to tell their stories to you. To tell the West what the Chinese have done to them and their families.'

'I'm staying with them,' Maggie replied, nodding at the monks.

Thondup raised an eyebrow. 'Is this true?' he asked Tsering.

'Yes, it's true,' was the reluctant reply.

'I have no false papers for you,' Thondup said to Maggie.

'They'd be no use, anyway,' she replied. 'If I'm stopped, they'll see immediately I'm a Westerner.'

'You have thought carefully about this?'

'Yes.'

Thondup shrugged. 'Then there is nothing further to discuss. We must get you ready before the truck arrives.'

Their baggage had been taken away by Thondup's lieutenants and then the morgue porter had ushered them out into the hall and made them lie down on sheets draped over four trestle tables. Jigme had been wrapped up first, much to Maggie's alarm.

'What's going on?' she'd whispered to Tsering who was stretched out on the adjoining table.

'We're being smuggled out of Lhasa in the sky burial truck,' he'd answered. 'The Chinese won't search a truck full of dead bodies.'

Lying next to the corpses now, the truck rumbling towards the outskirts of the city, Maggie prayed he was right. She heard the engine note change, felt the lorry begin to slow and then stop. Through the canvas sides of the truck she heard a high-pitched voice yapping something in Chinese, a question, an order, she couldn't tell which. Boots pounded on the road and the rear flap of the truck was flung aside, letting in a sudden flood of light. Maggie held her breath, staying absolutely still. Her heartbeat seemed loud enough to alert the Chinese to her presence. Surely they would hear it throbbing and come to investigate. But the flood of light was abruptly extinguished as the rear flap was dropped back into place. The truck moved off and Maggie sucked in a deep lungful of air, then exhaled hard to ease the tension in her muscles.

They drove for another ten minutes before stopping again. The flap was pulled back once more and the lorry rocked a little as someone clambered inside. A voice said something – in Tibetan this time – and Tsering answered, his voice muffled by the sheet over his mouth. Maggie sensed someone climbing over her, then the shroud was pulled away from her head and she blinked up at a dark, weatherbeaten man's face. The man unfastened the bindings around her ankles and chest and Maggie wriggled out of the shroud. Stumbling over the rows of dead bodies, she reached the rear of the truck and jumped down.

The truck had pulled in on the dirt track which led to the sky burial site. They were well out of the city now, on the flat fertile plain that surrounded Lhasa. Parked behind them was a battered white Toyota camper van with a second Tibetan man standing beside it. He beckoned urgently to Maggie, pulling open the door of the van. She hurried across and scrambled in, squeezing between the front seats into the back. There were curtains drawn over the windows, but she lay down instinctively on the floor, noticing with relief that their baggage had been transferred to the van.

The three monks climbed into the front, Tsering sliding behind the wheel. They had a brief conversation with the Tibetan man by the door who handed them each a thin wad of documents, then walked away and clambered into the cab of the truck. The truck drove off down the track, leaving a billowing cloud of dust in its wake. By the time the dust cleared, the truck was nowhere in sight.

Tsering examined the dashboard and controls of the van, familiarising himself with the layout. Then he found the ignition key and turned it. After several attempts the engine gave a throaty cough and turned over. Tsering tried to find first gear, but the stick wouldn't shift. Then he remembered the clutch. The gear engaged with a grinding rasp. Tsering brought up the clutch pedal and stalled the engine. He had another go, this one a little more successful. But as he turned across the track he stalled again.

Maggie knelt up and looked over the back of the front seats. Through the windscreen she could see the wide, empty plain, the barley fields just stubble now. A few patches of sparse grass and isolated clumps of willow trees added a touch of green to the stark vista. Tsering was attempting to restart the engine.

'Where did a monk like you learn to drive?' Maggie asked.

'I didn't,' Tsering replied.

For the next four hours they drove steadily north, then east, looping around the mountains to join the main Tibet–Sichuan highway well away from Lhasa. Most of the time there was no proper road, just a dusty track littered with rocks and treacherous potholes deep enough to snap the axles of the Toyota van. Tsering kept his speed low, to avoid the obstacles in their path, but also because the van wouldn't go much more than fifty kilometres an hour. Even below that speed, it juddered and rattled, its engine sounding ominously as if it were about to fall to pieces.

The interior too was in a bad state of repair. The upholstery on the bench seats in the back was shabby and torn, the covers ripped apart to expose slabs of mouldy grey foam rubber. The curtains covering the windows were frayed and full of holes and the wooden lockers along the sides – their varnish chipped and faded – had doors which either wouldn't open or hung forlornly from broken hinges. Maggie had inspected everything in the first half hour of their journey, finding two spare cans of petrol, a large plastic jerrycan of water, a kerosene stove and pans and a cupboard containing rice, *tsampa*, noodles, a brick of tea and a slab of sweaty yak butter which was borderline rancid. At least they would eat – not very well, but they were lucky to have anything at all.

Maggie sat on one of the tatty seats, hanging on to the locker next to her as the van bounced along the unmade track. The cushions were thin, the van's suspension shot, and every bump sent a jarring shudder through her body. She smoked a couple of cigarettes and looked at the monotonous view through a gap in the curtains. There was no conversation, even between the monks. The van was much too noisy for talking. Occasionally, Tsering would shout something, presumably a request for directions, and Lobsang would consult the map spread open on his knees and jab a finger at the horizon. It wasn't difficult navigation; it was simply a question of following the track wherever it took them. There were almost no junctions or turn-offs. In places the track seemed to disappear altogether and they drove across open ground, their route dictated by the angle of the sun and the position of the mountains which rose all around them as they got further away from Lhasa.

Towards noon, they stopped for a break. Tsering turned off the engine and leaned back in his seat, stretching his neck and shoulders. His arms were aching from gripping the steering wheel. The sudden silence was unnerving. It was so quiet it seemed to Maggie as if she'd gone deaf, but then she realised there was nothing to hear: no traffic, no people, no birds, not even any wind, which was unusual for Tibet. She slid open the side door of the van and stepped out. It was a clear, warm day, not a trace of cloud in the sky. She looked around, feeling the vast emptiness of the country, under-standing why its people had such a tradition of meditation. There was something in the air, in the sheer space, that was conducive to a contemplative life.

Jigme got the kerosene stove burning and boiled up hot water, making first a bowl of black tea for Maggie, then mixing the tea with a chunk of the yak butter for himself and the other two. Maggie sat in the open doorway of the van, watching him.

'You really like that stuff?' she asked.

'Butter tea? Of course. It's our national dish. You want to try some?'

'I've tried some before. It's definitely an acquired taste.'

'In parts of Tibet it's all there is to eat.'

'You eat it in McLeod Ganj?'

'Not so much. There are other things there. Rice, vegeta-bles.'

'Black Forest gateau.'

'Pardon?'

'You've obviously never been in one of the teahouses.'

'They are for tourists.'

'The Dalai Lama didn't drink butter tea. It upset his stomach.'

'How do you know that?'

'He told me.'

Jigme turned to stare at her. 'He told you? Ah, yes, you said you'd met him.'

'A few years ago. He did an interview on camera.'

'What did you think of him?'

'I thought he was a great man. But sad.'

'Sad?' Jigme reflected for a moment. 'Yes, I suppose so. We are all sad.'

'Do you think you'll ever come back here permanently?'

He shook his head firmly. 'Sometimes I dream of it, but that's all it is. A dream.'

They drank their tea in the back of the van, then Maggie got out her camcorder and recorded a few minutes of tape, walking away from the van to get some shots of the landscape before returning to focus on the three men.

'No close-ups,' Tsering said tersely. 'We do not wish to be identified.'

'Okay. But I really need the human side of this, not just pictures of mountains and some clapped-out old van. I need people.'

'We are simply servants of the Lord Buddha. Your film should be about the search, not us. We are nothing in this.'

Maggie switched off the camcorder. She was prepared to be patient. This was only the beginning. In time she would either wear down their resistance, or tape them when they weren't aware of it.

'So how come you three got picked?' she asked.

Tsering shrugged. 'We just were.'

'You must be very special monks?'

'No, we are very ordinary monks.'

'Come on, to be entrusted with something as important as this?'

'As I said, we are servants. It is not we who will find the chosen one but the Lord Buddha. We are simply being guided by his invisible hand.'

'Mount Gebur, is that where he's told you to look?'

'He has given us signs, yes.'

'And the other signs?'

'You will see in time.' Tsering climbed back into the driver's seat. 'Finish your tea, we must be on our way.'

Two hundred kilometres east of Lhasa – after they'd joined the Tibet–Sichuan highway – they encountered a PSB roadblock near the town of Gongbogyamda. Rounding a tight curve in the highway, they came upon it suddenly, a group of uniformed officers straddling the carriageway, stopping vehicles in both directions. There was no hope of avoiding it. To turn round and head back the way they'd come would have been too obvious, an action inviting pursuit by one of the police cars parked on the verge by the checkpoint.

'*Gong An Ju*,' Tsering said over his shoulder as he applied the brakes and joined the line of vehicles crawling towards the roadblock.

Maggie lowered herself off the bench seat and pulled open the two locker doors underneath it to reveal a long storage compartment running virtually the whole length of the van. It was just wide enough to accommodate her body. She rolled inside the compartment and pulled her bag in after her, stowing it by her feet. If the PSB decided to inspect the luggage, it wasn't a good idea to let them find tampons and women's underwear. As for the storage compartment, it would protect her from a perfunctory search by the police, but anything more thorough and she would certainly be discovered.

Tsering wound down his window as they reached the checkpoint. A buck-toothed PSB officer with a clipboard under his arm held out his hand.

'Papers.'

Tsering watched the officer examining the documents, writing down the details on a form attached to the clipboard. Tsering's pulse was racing. He concentrated on controlling his breathing, as he did during meditation, trying to appear calm. He knew this was a routine police check, a normal everyday part of the PSB's work. He'd seen the drivers in front being given identical treatment, but that didn't stop him being nervous.

The officer was taking his time, copying down the names on the identity papers, the serial numbers and issue dates. He was a policeman, but at heart, like all Chinese public officials, he was just another bureaucrat.

'Where are you going?' the officer said, looking up from his clipboard.

'Chamdo,' Tsering replied.

'Purpose of travel?'

'We are being transferred from our work unit in Lhasa to one in Chamdo.'

'Which one?'

'In Chamdo? The Fifty-Third.'

'Your jobs?'

'We are building labourers.'

Tsering lowered his hands out of sight in case the officer noticed they didn't look like those of a labourer.

'Your transfer documents.'

Tsering handed over the forged papers and the officer took more laborious notes, writing very slowly as if even copying Chinese characters was a huge mental effort for him. Behind the van, the line of waiting traffic was growing steadily longer.

Finally, the officer finished writing and gave back the documents. He glanced into the back of the van through a gap in the curtains, then slid open the side door and gave the interior a superficial inspection. He closed the door and waved his clipboard.

'You can go.'

Shen studied the message on the sheet of paper his deputy had handed him and glanced up inquiringly.

'This is it? Just one word, "Proceed"?'

Chang nodded. 'It was repeated twice. The same word.'

'When was it intercepted?'

Chang shuffled his feet uncomfortably. 'I have only just seen it.'

'When was it intercepted, Major?'

'Late yesterday afternoon.'

Shen tossed the piece of paper down on to his desk in disgust. 'Late yesterday afternoon,' he repeated, rolling the words around his mouth as if they were laced with vinegar. 'That was – what? – eighteen, twenty hours ago? And how long did it take our cryptographers to decode it? This one word. Not twenty hours, surely?'

'I don't know, Comrade Colonel. It was sent to the Lhasa City office in the evening, then here. The night duty officer

174

had it transferred to my office, but it was not drawn to my attention until a few minutes ago. I have been out all morning, touring our checkpoints around Lhasa.'

'And in the meantime, the monks may have slipped through our fingers.'

'Every road is manned. We are stopping every person, every vehicle leaving the city as you ordered. There is little more we can do.'

'We have a description of them, from the informer at Choekhorgyal, the flesh monkey?'

'We have, but it is next to useless. Too vague and general. It could apply to almost any Tibetan in the region.'

'Nevertheless, have it circulated to all our district offices. Tell them to be on the lookout for three men travelling together.'

'You think they have evaded our checkpoints and got out of Lhasa?'

'I don't know, Major. But I think we should cover the possibility, don't you?'

It was growing dark now. The dusk wouldn't linger. Once the sun dipped behind the mountains the day would pass quickly into night. If they were to find somewhere to stop, they would have to do it soon.

They drove straight through Gongbogyamda and kept going until off the highway a few kilometres further on, Tsering spotted a rough track. He slowed and turned down the track, fording a shallow stream and dropping into a gulley which ran almost parallel to the main road but was separated from it by a large rocky outcrop. A hundred metres into the gulley, Tsering stopped and turned off the engine. He killed the headlights. In the distance they could hear the faint, intermittent rumble of traffic on the highway.

'We'll stay here for the night,' he said.

They lit the stove and made more butter tea and a bowl of plain noodles for Maggie. She ate them standing up outside the van, looking up at the clear, star-spangled night sky. There were sheer cliffs on either side of the gulley, maybe ten metres high, and up above the cliffs the dark bulk of the mountains seemed to enfold them in a heavy, louring embrace.

The harsh, barren terrain reminded Maggie of Afghanistan, her first time in the Panjsher Valley, making camp with the *mujahideen*. Eating tough goat meat stew and nan bread, Alex sitting next to her telling her she'd get used to the food, joking that when they got back to England they'd write a book on Afghani cuisine – *A Hundred and One Ways to Cook Goat*. A vivid image came to her then, sharp as a photograph: his eyes shining in the firelight, the grime on his cheeks, his beard and hair getting long and untidy. Turning to her and smiling, his hand on her leg. She dwelt on it for a moment, thought of other things, then put him out of her mind. She ate the last of her noodles. They were soggy and tasteless. Compared to Tibet, Afghanistan was a gourmet's paradise.

The monks were in the back of the van, making greasy dough balls with their butter tea and *tsampa*. Maggie watched them, admiring their dexterity, the way they rolled the balls between their fingertips, finding just the right consistency of mixture before they shovelled the dough into their mouths. It was inelegant and messy, but it worked.

She opened her bag and took out her wash things, then made her way back up the gulley to the stream. She climbed down into a hollow where the water cascaded into a pool. She was below the level of the highway here, safe from the headlights of passing vehicles. Removing her shirt and bra, she knelt down by the pool and washed herself, shivering as the icy water touched her skin. She dried herself, put her shirt back on and brushed her teeth. Then she dipped her bra in the water and scrubbed it with the bar of soap before rinsing it and wringing it out.

The monks were outside the van when she went back down the gulley. From a distance, in the dark, it was difficult to make out what they were doing. Only as she drew nearer did she see that they were prostrating themselves on the rock-strewn ground. First, standing next to one another, they cupped their palms together, the thumbs between them forming the symbol of the wish-fulfilling gem. Then they lifted their hands to touch their foreheads, throats and hearts before kneeling down and stretching out full length to press their foreheads to the stony earth. With each prostration, they chanted a mantra which Maggie recognised as the refuge prayer.

She walked quietly behind them and climbed into the van, spreading out her damp bra on the rear locker to dry. It was getting cold. She slipped on her sweater and jacket and clicked on the overhead light to work out how she turned the seats into a bed. There was very little space, but she reckoned the van was big enough for at least two of them to sleep, perhaps three if one lay down in the front. But not Tsering. He was too tall to fit in anywhere.

'The van is yours, Miss Walsh. We will sleep outside.'

Maggie looked up. Tsering was watching her through the open door.

'Don't be silly. There's room in here.'

'No, we have tents, blankets. We will be fine on the ground.'

He moved away to help Lobsang and Jigme pitch the two tents. He felt troubled. Normally, the ritual of prostration relaxed him, cleared his mind of its worries. But not tonight. He thought about the checkpoint they'd passed back up the road. The papers Thondup had supplied them with were good forgeries – good enough to fool the PSB officer who'd examined them – but they were forgeries nonetheless. If someone chose to examine the information they contained more closely, the deception would be readily apparent. But *would* anyone examine it? The PSB was a notorious collector of useless bits of paper, most of which were filed away somewhere and forgotten. It was quite conceivable that the form the officer had filled in would never be looked at again. Even if it were, it might take days for anyone to get round to it and the checks might only be so cursory as to be useless. But could the monks rely on that?

Tsering knelt down, automatically hammering in a tent peg with a chunk of rock, but his thoughts were elsewhere, one question agitating him: *how long did they have?*

ELEVEN

Maggie awoke at first light. She pulled aside one of the curtains and peered out of the van. The ground outside was still in darkness, but the sky above the mountains was turning grey, a pale wash of distant sunlight seeping gradually between the peaks and trickling down into the shadowy valleys.

She slid open the door and climbed out, slipping on her jacket against the early-morning cold. It was mid-October. The days were still bright and warm but at night the temperature plummeted, a chilling presage of the long winter that was only weeks away. Picking up her washbag and towel, she walked up the gulley to the stream.

Tsering had got there before her. He was crouching naked in the pool, splashing water over himself, his *chuba* discarded on the bank. Maggie watched him. He had a good body: powerful shoulders, narrow waist, long, muscular legs. He straightened up, turning, and saw her. She expected him to be embarrassed, to reach for the towel lying next to his *chuba*, but he just stood there looking at her. Then, without haste, he stepped out on to the bank.

'I'm sorry,' Maggie said, feeling like a voyeur. 'I didn't know you were here.'

Tsering picked up his towel and rubbed himself dry. 'I am finished. The pool is yours. But be warned, the water is very cold.'

He pulled on his *chuba*, knotting the cord around his waist, and clambered up the steep bank. Maggie waited for him to disappear back down the gulley before she slithered down the slope to the pool. He was right, the water was freezing; just dipping her fingers in it took her breath away. How Tsering had stood in it naked was beyond her. A handful scooped up on to her face was about all she could bear.

She washed quickly, and perfunctorily, and returned to the van, shivering beneath her fleece jacket. Tsering was sitting on the ground in front of his tent, murmuring mantras with his eyes half closed, his fingers counting off the beads on his rosary. Maggie lit the kerosene stove and boiled a pan of water to make tea. She felt refreshed, wide awake. She'd slept well for the first night since entering Tibet. The nagging headache she'd had all that time had gone and she was no longer so short of breath. Full acclimatisation would take several more days, but she was getting there.

By the time she had the tea ready, Jigme and Lobsang were emerging from their tent. She offered them a bowl each. Jigme took his gratefully, mumbling his thanks, but Lobsang hesitated, glowering at her with his hooded, hostile eyes. Maggie shrugged and put the bowl down on the locker next to the open door of the van.

'It's there if you want it,' she said.

She sipped some of her own tea. Although the water had boiled, the altitude meant it was nothing like a hundred degrees centigrade. But it warmed her through, melting away the damp chill of the night that had leached into her bones. Jigme sat near her, his bowl cupped between his hands, watching Tsering praying.

'You're not going to join him?' Maggie asked.

Jigme gave a boyish grin. 'It's too early. And too cold.'

'You get up this early in McLeod Ganj, don't you?'

'Because they make me. I'd be punished if I stayed in bed.'

'You don't want to pray?'

'I want to drink my tea. I'll pray later.'

'I thought monks were supposed to be disciplined.'

'Away from the monastery it's harder.'

'Tsering manages it.'

'Tsering? Yes, Tsering manages it. He's different.'

'In what way?'

'Tsering is a *tulku*.'

'Ah.'

Maggie wasn't surprised. Tsering's manner, his self-assurance and authority were all consistent with his being a reincarnate lama.

'He is very devout, very strong,' Jigme continued.

'Is that why he was chosen for this task?'

'I suppose so.'

'And you? Why were *you* chosen?'

'I don't know. I think the Rinpoche asked for me.'

'Rinpoche?'

'Pasang Rinpoche. We accompanied him to Lhamo Latso, the oracle lake.'

Suddenly, Maggie understood. 'He had a vision?'

Jigme nodded. 'Then he died.'

'Leaving you three to continue the quest?'

'Yes. To complete it if we can.'

'You have doubts?'

Jigme turned his head to look at her, his face troubled. 'Wouldn't you?'

They'd struck camp and were loading the tents into the back of the van before the sun had risen high enough to penetrate into the gulley. Tsering saw the strip of white, lacy material spread out on the rear locker and leaned over in the gloom to take a closer look.

'It's a bra,' Maggie said.

'I know what it is,' Tsering replied. 'What's it doing there?'

'Drying.'

'You're not leaving it there?'

'What do you take me for?'

Maggie lifted the damp bra off the locker and hung it out of sight on one of the cupboard door knobs.

'You're a monk,' she said. 'How come you know what a bra looks like?'

Tsering gave her a weary glance, not amused, and climbed into the driver's seat. He turned the key in the ignition. Nothing happened. He tried again. The engine didn't even turn over; it was completely dead. He frowned and tried a third time.

'Why won't it start?' he asked, throwing the question out in a bemused state of helplessness. 'What's the matter with it?'

Maggie sat quietly in the back, watching Lobsang and Jigme shaking their heads and shrugging, then Tsering trying the key again. Still nothing happened. Tsering sat back, studying the dashboard carefully as if hoping to find some magical solution to the problem.

'What do we do?'

'One of us will have to walk back to Gongbogyamda and find someone who can fix it,' Lobsang said.

'That will take hours.'

'What choice do we have?'

Maggie listened to them talking, not following the Tibetan, but getting the gist from their body language.

'You don't know much about engines, do you?' she said.

Tsering swivelled round in his seat. 'What?'

'Let me take a look.'

She climbed out and clicked open the bonnet of the van. Inside was one of the dirtiest engines she'd ever seen. It looked as if someone had thrown a bucket of oil over it, then sprinkled it with grit for good measure. Maggie checked the electrical connections.

'What's wrong with it?' Tsering asked. He'd come out and was standing behind her, looking over her shoulder.

'You turn the key and nothing happens,' Maggie said. 'That might be because the battery's flat.'

'Is that serious?'

'In a city, no. You'd either recharge it from the mains or fit a new one. Out here, yes, it's a problem. But it might be some-thing else.'

She located the wire from the battery to the ignition switch and pulled it. It seemed to be firmly attached at both ends. Then she searched for the wire from the switch to the ignition coil and found the problem.

'Here you are,' she said. 'Loose wire. Have you got a knife?'

Tsering reached into the pouch of his *chuba* and pulled out a bone-handled pocket knife. Maggie used the tip as a screwdriver, undoing the terminal on the ignition coil and re-securing the wire.

'What does that do?' Tsering asked, watching her closely.

'The ignition coil? It's like a transformer. It turns the twelve volts from the battery into the twenty thousand or so volts you need to ignite the petrol-air mixture in the engine.'

He stared inside the bonnet, trying to make sense of all the cables and machinery. 'Will it work now?'

Maggie slammed the bonnet shut and climbed in behind the wheel. She turned the key. The engine coughed into life. Maggie gunned the accelerator a few times.

'Get in the back,' she said to Tsering.

'You are driving? If someone sees you . . .'

'Just get in. We don't want it stalling.'

She rammed the gearstick into reverse and backed up the gulley and out on to the main road. She applied the handbrake and left the engine idling.

'It's all yours,' she said, scrambling over the seat into the back of the van.

Tsering nodded at her respectfully. 'Your knowledge of engines is most impressive.'

'I have my uses,' Maggie said.

Zhao Yu had known for many years that he was neither an exceptionally gifted nor a particularly bright police officer. But he was thorough and methodical and followed orders to the letter. In the Public Security Bureau, those were great virtues which many – including Zhao himself – regarded as more important than intelligence. A great intellect was of little use in the tedious, day-to-day work of the Bureau. If anything, it was a handicap. Shooting stars shone brightly for a short period and then burned themselves out and fell to earth. Those who survived, and prospered, were the less dazzling lights who glowed dully but endured. Zhao was a stolid, plodding officer who would never go any higher than his present rank of district captain, but his paperwork was fault-less. If there was one thing he excelled at, it was the careful sifting of documentation, the bureaucracy that formed a large part of the PSB's daily work.

On the desk in front of him, stacked in neat piles, was a collection of official forms. The pink ones were hotel and guest-house registration records, the white ones residence permits, the peach ones vehicle and driver questionnaires and the yellow ones crime and anti-social behaviour reports. Next to the piles was a single sheet of white paper which bore the letterhead of the Public Security Department for the Tibet Autonomous Region and below that the words, 'For the urgent attention of all district commanders'. It had been faxed through from Lhasa late the previous day and instructed all PSB personnel to be on the lookout for three Tibetan men travel-ling together. A description of the men followed, with the order to arrest them if they were identified. The fax did not give any reasons for detaining the men, just the instruction to notify Lhasa immediately they were apprehended.

Zhao had read through the fax several times, making sure he absorbed every detail. Orders from Lhasa were not unusual – directives came through to Gongbogyamda every day of the week – but Zhao sensed there was something more important about this particular missive. Today, he would be especially conscientious in carrying out his duties.

He started with the pink forms, the hotel and guesthouse registrations, which were filled in by the hotel managers and collected every evening by the PSB. He read each form in turn, working slowly through the information they contained: the names of the guests, their home addresses, their identity numbers, their destinations and the registration details of their vehicles if they had one. As each form was finished, he placed it in another orderly pile at the far side of his desk.

After two hours' concentrated work, he took a short break. His secretary brought in his customary bowl of black tea and he moved away from his desk to sip it – he was a fastidious drinker, but one never knew when a spillage might occur, soiling the papers which he regarded as sacrosanct.

The pink forms completed, he moved on to the white ones, the residence permits. These were unlikely to be of any relevance to the search for the three men travelling together, but Zhao was a creature of habit. This was the order in which he always scrutinised the documents and he saw no reason to change it today.

At noon, he walked across to the mess for his lunch – potato soup with noodles, a bowl of tea and two dried apricots – before returning to his office to start on the peach forms which were filled in by the road traffic division whenever they stopped a vehicle.

An hour and a half later, he found it.

He read the form twice just to make sure. It matched the parameters of the directive from Lhasa exactly: three men, Tibetans, travelling together in a van.

Zhao took a clean sheet of paper from his desk drawer and a fountain pen from his breast pocket and wrote out a message by hand, the characters scrupulously laid out on the page. Then he called in his secretary.

'Type this out and fax it to Major Chang, in Lhasa.'

'Is it priority, Captain? I am in the middle of preparing your weekly report.'

Zhao hesitated. The weekly report was the most crucial document his district produced, the benchmark by which his performance was judged. But the directive from Lhasa was also important. He weighed the two options up mentally, his fundamental conservatism winning out.

'Finish the report first,' he said. 'Then send the fax to Lhasa.'

They made good time, heading almost due east along the Tibet–Sichuan highway at a steady fifty kilometres an hour.

It was a wide, well-made road, one of the first the Chinese had constructed after their invasion – to bring in matériel and supplies for the PLA divisions stationed in the region, and to ship out the timber and minerals they began extracting as soon as they had quelled the local population.

Army lorries and freight trucks still made up the bulk of the traffic on the road. Hidden in the back of the van, peeping out occasionally through one of the many holes in the curtains, it seemed to Maggie that they passed a PLA convoy every ten or fifteen minutes – long lines of dark green trucks going towards Lhasa, their rear flaps rolled up to reveal the soldiers sitting inside. And as they came down off the high plateau to below the tree line, they overtook dozens of huge lorries heavily laden with logs. Some of them joined the highway from dirt tracks cut into the hillsides, descending from logging camps hidden away higher up the valleys. The slopes next to the road had already been stripped bare, every single tree removed, exposing the thin topsoil which the wind and the rain were gradually eroding.

Once, at a point where the side of the highway had crumbled away, they slowed to a crawl and Maggie saw a gang of Tibetan prisoners repairing the carriageway. They were dirty and bowed, their clothes hanging in tatters from their emaciated bodies. She thought about getting out her camcorder and taping the scene, but decided it was too risky.

They stopped only twice – for toilet breaks – Tsering keeping the engine going, terrified of being unable to start it again, while they took it in turns to duck behind one of the large boulders beside the road, and they reached the outskirts of Nyingchi in the late afternoon. They pulled off the highway and parked the van in a dead end adjoining some kind of small housing estate. Maggie could tell it was a Chinese estate because it had electricity lines strung from poles and the houses – long rows of identical concrete blocks – were enclosed by high metal fences to protect the inhabitants from the surrounding Tibetans.

Tsering left them and went off to find the contact they'd

been given by Thondup. When he returned, he was accompanied by a youth who climbed into the back of the van and gave directions to the safe house, deep in the Tibetan section of the town.

They left the van in a yard and walked the last few hundred metres. Maggie tied a handkerchief over her face – a common practice in Tibet where the wind and dust could be choking – to hide her Western features and followed the youth down a muddy alley. At the end was a two-storey stone house with a flat roof on which white prayer flags fluttered in the breeze, dispersing the message of the Buddha far and wide.

Inside, the house was dark and draughty. A yak-dung fire smouldered in the hearth, the smoke stinging the eyes. The youth gestured to them to sit down on a low wooden couch and crossed to the hearth to make them tea. Maggie pulled the handkerchief from her face and looked around. Signs of poverty were everywhere – in the bare earth floor, in the faded shutters over the windows, the wads of yellowing newspaper plugging holes in the walls. A butter lamp glowed in front of a makeshift altar, illuminating an image of Chenresig, the Buddha of Compassion, and a photograph of his earthly incarnation, the late Dalai Lama. It was a brave display of devotion to the faith. The photograph of the Dalai Lama alone was enough to earn the occupants of the house a substantial term in jail.

At one end of the room, a curtain had been hung from a sagging length of rope, partitioning off a small area as a bedroom. There was a movement behind the curtain, the noise of a cough – a harsh, painful cough. The youth by the fire called out something. The curtain parted and a man came out into the room. He was old and hunched, shuffling slowly forwards with the aid of two sticks. The youth went over and grasped the old man's arm, lowering him gently into a chair by the fire. The old man leaned his sticks against the wall and took a moment to recover. Even that short walk from his bed had left him out of breath. He looked at Tsering, then Lobsang and Jigme. Finally, his gaze – firm and steady despite his fragility – came to rest on Maggie. She was stunned to hear him address her in English.

'You're not Tibetan, you're not Chinese, so what the hell are you?' he said. His accent was poor, but it had a distinct American intonation.

'I'm British,' Maggie replied.

'British? Ah.'

He started to say something else, but broke off as another fit of coughing racked his body. He held a dirty rag over his mouth and Maggie noticed there was blood on it. Finally, the coughing stopped. The old man took a few breaths, the sound of wheezing hissing around the room.

'It's been a long time since I spoke English,' he said, struggling a little to find the words.

'You speak it very well.'

He seemed pleased by the compliment. 'I had no choice. The Americans could not say a word in Tibetan.'

'The Americans?'

He nodded. 'Very bad at languages. You speak Tibetan?'

'Only a little.'

The youth interrupted them, firing off something in Tibetan which Maggie guessed was a plea to the old man to rest. But the old man dismissed his concerns with an impatient shake of the head.

'So you've seen my son,' he continued. 'How is he?'

'Your son?' Maggie was puzzled.

'In Lhasa. He sent you, didn't he?'

She realised who he meant. 'Thondup is your son?'

'Yes, my son.' The old man's eyes gleamed with pride. 'A fine boy. He's revived the *Chushi Gangdruk*. You know what that was?'

'Yes.'

He was surprised. 'You do? How?'

'I've read books. I've been here before.'

'He's going to continue what we started back in the Fifties.'

He coughed again, pressing the soiled rag to his lips. The youth brought him a bowl of tea and urged him to drink some. The old man took a few sips, then settled back in his chair. He closed his eyes, fatigued by the effort of talking, and lapsed into a shallow sleep.

'He's ill,' Maggie said to Tsering. 'He should be in hospital.'

Tsering nodded. 'I know. But the hospitals are for the Chinese, not Tibetans.'

'But he has tuberculosis.'

'That makes no difference.'

'What about a doctor? There are treatments for TB.'

'Expensive treatments. The Chinese will make him pay – and pay a lot. He doesn't have the money for medicine. Few Tibetans do.'

Maggie looked curiously at Tsering. 'You're so calm about everything, so dispassionate. Doesn't the injustice, the cruelty, make you angry?'

'Yes, it makes me angry. But what is my anger to a dying man? What is my anger to one and a half billion Chinese? If anger counted for anything, Tibet would have been free years ago.'

They drank their tea and for supper were given noodles and dried yak meat and chunks of yak's-milk cheese so hard they were impossible to chew but had to be sucked like sweets. By now it was dark outside. A paraffin lamp was lit and hung from a hook on the wall. More yak-dung patties were thrown on to the fire and Maggie and the monks huddled closer to the hearth, trying to keep warm.

The old man – whose name was Samdrup – woke up and suffered another agonising fit of coughing. The youth offered him a bowl of hot water to drink, but Samdrup waved it away irritably.

'Not water, boy. Give me some *chang*.'

'But uncle, are you sure . . .'

'*Chang*, boy. Some for our guests too.'

The youth produced a flagon of barley beer and half filled a glass for Samdrup.

'To the top, boy. What are you saving it for? We don't have visitors very often.'

The monks declined the offer of a glass, but Maggie accepted some. The beer was cloudy and bitter to the taste. Samdrup took a gulp, then wiped his mouth with a trembling hand and looked across at Maggie. His tired face was pallid and waxen in the harsh light from the paraffin lamp.

'I was there at the beginning,' he said in English, resuming their conversation as if it had never been interrupted. 'At Jomdha Dzong. You know about that too?'

Maggie gave a nod, but the old man told her anyway, reminiscing nostalgically about his youth. Maggie let him talk. The past was all he had left.

He'd been there in the summer of 1956, one of the *pons*, the tribal chieftains of Kham, who'd been held hostage by the PLA in the fortress of Jomdha Dzong, near Chamdo, until they agreed to Chinese reforms. But the chieftains, all 210 of them, had escaped one night and taken to the mountains, forming the guerrilla resistance force they called *Chushi Gangdruk* – 'Four Rivers, Six Ranges', the traditional name for Kham and Amdo.

From their isolated strongholds, the Khampas, poorly armed but courageous, had launched a series of attacks on PLA garrisons and convoys, sweeping down from the hills on horseback to confront the Chinese before retreating back to their hidden bases. In response, the Chinese had begun a campaign of reprisals so savage that much of the region had been turned into a wasteland. Villages and towns were bombed indiscriminately, killing thousands of innocent civilians. Entire communities were rounded up and executed, their houses razed. Buddhist monks and nuns were forced to copulate together in public, others were crucified, dismembered or dragged to their deaths behind galloping horses. Those lucky enough to be shot had their tongues ripped out with meathooks to prevent them shouting 'Long Live the Dalai Lama' as they awaited the executioner's bullet.

'Those were terrible days,' Samdrup said, shaking his head. 'People like me, we are the leftovers of death. Most of my family, my friends, were wiped out by the Chinese.'

'And Thondup?' Maggie said.

'He came later. After Mustang.'

'You were in Mustang?'

Samdrup nodded. 'The CIA smuggled groups of us out to Guam and Okinawa. I went on to Camp Hale in Colorado. They trained us how to fight, to use a radio, to kill Chinese, then parachuted us back into Tibet. We still believed then that the Americans were on our side.' He gave a contemptuous snort. 'What fools we were. We should have known they would betray us. The Americans have never helped anyone but themselves.'

Mustang was a disaster for the Tibetan resistance movement. For most of the Sixties they had continued their guerrilla war from that tiny, semi-independent kingdom on Nepal's northern frontier. Then Nixon had made his peace with Mao, drunk tea with him in Beijing, and suddenly the Tibetan fighters were an embarrassment. The CIA had cut off its support for the guerrillas and the Chinese had pressured the Nepalese into curbing the Tibetans' activities. The Nepalese army, reneging on a promise to let the guerrillas go if they disarmed and surrendered, moved into Mustang, forcing the Tibetans over the border into Tibet where the grateful PLA were waiting to finish them off.

'Everyone betrayed us,' Samdrup said. 'The Americans, the Nepalese, the Indians. The whole stinking lot of them.' He gathered the phelgm in his throat and turned and spat into the fire, the sputum sizzling on the glowing yak dung.

'But you escaped,' Maggie said.

'I never believed the promises. I got out before the end. Went over the mountains and walked back to Kham. It took me six months. Now my son is taking up where we left off. He is strong, determined, the way I used to be.'

He broke off, another sudden spasm of coughing convulsing his frail body. Maggie could see something of Thondup in the old man. They had the same fiery eyes, the same courage, the same refusal to lie down and give up. She could admire those qualities. There was something awe-inspiring in this broken, dying man who still had hope.

'You've talked enough,' Maggie said gently. 'Save your breath now.'

Samdrup looked at her, defiance tinged by sadness. 'Save my breath for what?' he said.

Teng Wei-Kuo rubbed the bridge of his nose with his finger-tips, smoothing the skin upwards between his eyebrows, massaging his forehead to try to ease the throbbing pain of his headache. It was the air in Lhasa, the damned altitude that only *mantze* – barbarians – like the Tibetans could live with. A Han like him needed a richer atmosphere, a warmer, more humid climate that didn't desiccate the skin and brain and cause such terrible migraines.

He was in a foul mood, and not just because of his headache. He'd been hoping for a quiet evening; a few routine bits of paperwork, maybe the opportunity for a crafty nap later on when things slackened off. But that bastard Chang had left him a mountain of chores to do, and strict instructions to complete them all before the end of the night shift. No reasons given. The major never deigned to explain his orders to his subordinates. He just yelled at them to get on with it.

Teng could make no sense of the task he'd been assigned: going through a daunting pile of faxes which had come in throughout the day from PSB district offices all over the TAR. Each one was a report of sightings or detentions of Tibetan males travelling in groups of three. There were probably fifty of them, from places as far afield as Nyalam in the south, Golmud in the north and Kailas in the west. Teng was surprised there weren't more. After all, the Tibetans always travelled in threes: one to piss, one to shit, and the third to make butter tea from the ingredients, as they joked in the PSB barracks. Not that Chang would have heard the joke – the major would only acquire a sense of humour when the Party started running classes in it.

Teng's job was to scrutinise all the reports and send out more faxes to the appropriate government departments, asking for verification of identity numbers, travel permits, vehicle registration details and anything else that might help establish the credentials of the Tibetans in question. He'd completed six of the reports and was now moving reluctantly on to the seventh: a long-winded dispatch from Gongbogyamda, in Kham, a poxy little dump on the highway to Sichuan that Teng had passed through several times without feeling the slightest urge to linger there.

He read the report, then typed out the same series of inquiries he'd produced for the previous reports. He could have put them all together in one longer fax for each of the ministries involved, but that wasn't the way things were done. There had to be a separate inquiry for each report. His headache getting worse, Teng pulled the sheets of paper out of the typewriter, placing the carbon copies into one tray on his desk and the top copies into his out-tray for his clerk to take over to the fax room. At least he wouldn't have to deal with the replies. That would be the responsibility of the poor sods on the day shift. With that cheery thought to comfort him, Teng moved on to the next report in the pile.

TWELVE

The sound of the old man coughing kept Tsering awake for half the night. The monks and Maggie had been put upstairs, squeezed together on a couple of straw palliasses laid out on the floor. Tsering found it hard to settle. The mattresses were lumpy and uncomfortable, stalks of straw poking out through the threadbare covers and spiking the skin of his arms and legs. Each time he started to doze off, he was jolted back by a sharp burst of coughing from downstairs. The noise was jarring, too loud to ignore, and Tsering found himself stiffening, lying tense and anxious as he waited for the next bout to reverberate up the stairs.

It was with relief that he saw the first glimmers of daylight through the cracks in the shutters. Careful not to disturb the others, he slid out from beneath his blankets and crept downstairs. He could hear the hoarse wheeze of Samdrup's breathing on the other side of the curtain as he crossed the living room to the hearth. The fire was cold, a few crumbs of yak dung remaining in the grate. Tsering took some sheets of newspaper from a pile next to the hearth and crumpled them into balls. The old man's nephew was asleep on a mat in front of the crude altar. He stirred and rolled over, but didn't wake.

Tsering lifted out a couple of thin yak-dung patties from a bucket and placed them over the balls of paper. Then he lit the paper with a match and watched it burn, the flames licking up over the patties, igniting the dung. It was years since he'd lit a yak-dung fire. He inhaled the pungent aroma, remembering his mother's house, remembering the times he'd helped her cook, the smell of the food, the touch of her hand on his head; a casual, affectionate caress as she busied herself with the pans. Lighting the fire had been one of his chores – before he left home for the monastery. Even then he'd taken his duties very seriously, rising before his mother to make sure the living room was warm for her, that the fire was hot enough to boil the water he'd drawn fresh from the well in the centre of the village.

They'd been very close, the two of them. They'd needed each other, looked after each other. Then the monks had come to take him away. He'd been only nine years old, still just a child. He hadn't wanted to go. Nor had his mother wanted to lose him. But the monks had insisted, and their authority was absolute. They'd done tests, questioned him and declared him a *tulku*, the reincarnation of a devout lama who had died several years earlier. He had been chosen. It was a privilege, a great honour, to enter the monastery, to learn to read and write and serve the Buddha. But Tsering didn't see it then as a privilege, he saw it as a cruel punishment – being wrenched away from his widowed mother and shut up in the *gompa*. And now? He wondered still how his life would have turned out if he had never become a monk.

He leaned forward and blew gently on the fire, nursing it until it began to blaze. Then he put a kettle of water on to boil. He sat back on his haunches and stared into the flames, thinking about what lay ahead. He'd slept badly in part because of the old man's coughing, but also because he wasn't at peace with himself. His inner equanimity, which normally was the source of his strength, had been disturbed by anxieties. And by fear of the unknown. They were in Tibet illegally, and there was no telling how long they would have to remain. They could get to Mount Gebur, but what then? How long would the search take thereafter? How would they identify and interpret the other signs Pasang Rinpoche had seen at Lhamo Latso? How would they find the child? And once found, how would they get him out of the country? There were too many questions that couldn't be answered, yet they continued to swill around in Tsering's brain, tormenting him with uncertainty.

A sudden noise on the stairs broke his reverie. He turned his head and saw Maggie coming into the room. She crossed to the fire and knelt down beside him, shivering. She held her hands out to warm them.

'You couldn't sleep either?' she said.

'No.'

'The old man's coughing?'

'And other things,' Tsering admitted.

'Worries?'

Tsering didn't answer. He felt no need to share his thoughts with her: this aggressive, scheming Western woman who had foisted herself on them through guile and threats. He didn't understand her. She was an alien species to him; a woman and a foreigner, two groups of which he had had very little experience.

'I'd be worried too,' Maggie continued. 'How far is Mount Gebur?'

'Some distance,' Tsering replied vaguely.

'You'd better show me on the map.'

'That won't be necessary.'

He felt her steely gaze on his face and turned to look at the fire.

'I know I'm unwelcome here,' Maggie said. 'You don't want me to come along. You resent the way I've intruded on your search. I can understand that. But we're in this together. If you're caught, I'm caught too. So why don't we forget our differences and start to cooperate?'

'Cooperate?'

'Put all the antagonism behind us. We don't have to be friends, but we can help each other. We can work together to make sure you complete your task. That's in all our interests.'

Tsering put another yak-dung patty on the fire, wrestling with his emotions. What she said made sense. She was with them, he couldn't ignore that fact. And she was tough and resourceful. The way she'd fixed the van, the way she'd got them out of the Tibetan Quarter, showed that clearly. Somewhat reluctantly, and slightly to his annoyance, he was forced to admit that she might be an asset rather than a liability.

'Mount Gebur is five or six days' journey,' he said.

'By road?'

'Some of it. The final stages we will have to do on foot.'

'The checkpoint we passed – the *Gong An Ju* will check the authenticity of your papers.'

'Maybe.'

'No maybe about it,' Maggie said firmly. 'They will. That's how the Chinese operate.'

'I *know* how they operate,' Tsering replied irritably. 'I lived here until thirteen years ago.'

'Then why delude yourself with wishful thinking? They'll check your identity papers, the vehicle registration, everything. I think we should think about dumping the van.'

'We need the van. How else will we reach Mount Gebur? Without a vehicle it will take us weeks to get there.'

'We'll have to find another.'

'That won't be easy. This isn't the West, you know. You can't just hire vans, especially out here in the provinces.'

'What about the old man, Thondup's father? Can he arrange anything?'

'He's hardly in a fit state to give us much help. This was just a safe house, a place for us to stay the night. After here, we're on our own.'

'You've no other contacts?'

'None.'

Maggie swore softly under her breath, wondering what the hell she was doing. She'd taken risks before, done stupid things, but she had a feeling that this was probably going to be the most hazardous gamble of her career.

'We'll have to be careful from now on,' she said. 'Very careful.'

* * *

They left soon after breakfast – a bowl of tea and some barley porridge prepared for them by Samdrup's nephew. The old man stayed in bed, hidden away behind the curtain, but they could hear the rasp of his breathing, the sudden explosions of coughing. Tsering took a wad of currency out of the pouch of his *chuba* and peeled off some notes to give to the nephew.

'Get him some medicine,' he said. 'Some Chinese medicine.'

The youth stared at the money. He'd never seen such a sum before. He nodded. 'I will do what I can for him.'

A stick poked out through the curtain and Samdrup muttered something inaudibly. The nephew pulled back the curtain and went to fetch a bowl of tea for his uncle. Samdrup struggled to sit up in his bed, panting with the exertion. The partitioned-off area had the smell of the sick bay about it, a stale, slightly sweet odour of illness. Samdrup said a few words to Tsering, then turned to Maggie.

'So you're going?' he said in English.

'Yes. Thank you for your hospitality. *Kâlishu.*'

'*Kâlishu*? Yes, it's goodbye. You think I'm a dreamer. I saw it in your eyes last night.' He paused to gather enough air to continue. 'It may take generations – and I shall not live to see it – but there will come a time when Tibetans *shall* be free again.'

'I believe you,' Maggie said, and she meant it.

They gathered up their bags and walked back to the van. The air was damp, a fine mist obscuring the tops of the mountains. But as they drove out of Nyingchi and on north-east, the mist lifted and the peaks shone clear and white in the dazzling sunshine. One mountain in particular stood out from all the others, a towering mass of ice-capped rock whose summit was so high it was lost in the clouds.

'That's incredible,' Maggie said, leaning over the front seats of the van. 'Look at it, it must be twenty-four, twenty-five thousand feet high.'

'Namjaqbarwa Feng,' Tsering said, glancing sideways. 'The highest mountain in this part of Kham.'

'It's beautiful. You've been this way before?'

'A few times.'

'You're from Kham? From near here?'

'No, not near here.'

Tsering looked away, concentrating on the road. Over to the east, the mountain filled the horizon, its gleaming sides soaring higher and higher into the cobalt sky until its pinnacle seemed to puncture the heavens.

At another time, the drive might have been pure pleasure. The road snaked between mountains, dipping into verdant gorges in which rivers cascaded over huge cataracts, the roar of the water echoing off the high rock edges; then it rose again, twisting and climbing over spectacular passes where the snow lay deep on the slopes and solitary eagles floated on the unseen currents. But none of them was in the mood for sightseeing today, for dwelling on the beauty of the scenery. They were all nervous, aware of their vulnerability and the distance they had to travel. Above all, they were on the lookout for checkpoints on the road. Lobsang had the map open on his knee, reading off the names of the towns and villages along their route. If the police were going to set up roadblocks, they would almost certainly do it on the outskirts of the settlements, not in the open countryside. The PSB liked to stay close to its bases, to be able to call for back-up if it was needed.

Fortunately, the towns were few and far between. This was mountainous, inhospitable terrain, most of it unpopulated except for wandering groups of nomads. For kilometre after kilometre they drove along the almost empty highway. There were freight trucks and buses and the ubiquitous PLA convoys on the road, but virtually no private vehicles. It made the driving easy, but it also made them conspicuous. How many other white Toyota vans were there heading towards Chamdo? Maggie wondered.

As they approached each town, they slowed and pulled off to the side. Tsering climbed to the nearest vantage point, looking ahead to see if there was a checkpoint. Then they drove on, moving cautiously through the town, relaxing only when they were back on the open road on the other side. Exactly what they would have done had they encountered a roadblock, Tsering didn't know. In their precarious circumstances it was impossible to predict the best course of action.

By evening, they had just passed the town of Rawu, some three hundred kilometres south of Chamdo, when Tsering saw a track forking off to the right. He pulled off the highway and followed the track down into a ravine. There were deep tyre ridges in the mud and he guessed the track probably led to a logging camp. After two hundred metres he left the track and parked the van in the lee of a small copse, a pocket of immature trees which the loggers had left untouched. Tsering climbed out and checked the surrounding area, confident that they could not be seen from the track.

They pitched the tents and sat in the back of the van drinking tea and eating bowls of plain boiled rice. Afterwards, Maggie and Jigme took the dirty pan and crockery down to the stream below the copse to wash them. It was still warm. They found a sheltered pool and knelt down, dipping their hands in the water. The insects were out in force. Maggie swatted them away but she noticed Jigme ignored them, letting the flies and mosquitoes settle on his arms and head. Even when the mosquitoes started to bite and suck his blood, he left them alone, unwilling to harm a living creature. It was the Buddhist way. Before the Chinese invaded, every building project in Tibet – even the tiniest excavation – had taken months and months to complete because each worm and beetle uncovered had to be carefully removed from the soil and carried out of harm's way.

'Where in England are you from?' Jigme asked.

Maggie dipped a bowl into the stream and rubbed it with her fingers. 'London.'

'I had a sponsor from London. Tim Jepson. Do you know him?'

Maggie smiled at his naivety. 'It's a very big place.'

'I suppose so.'

'He sends you money?'

'He did. He stopped a few years ago. I think he lost interest in Tibet. People do.'

A lot of the younger Tibetans in McLeod Ganj had foreign sponsors; people from the West who'd visited and wanted to help an individual with education or living costs. On her stays in the village Maggie had been approached several times with requests for help. She'd made donations, but never established a formal link with any one person. There seemed to her something colonial, condescending, about sponsorship.

'Did you need the money?' she asked.

'Not really. But I don't think that's why he sent it. It made him feel good. He came to McLeod Ganj to see the Dalai Lama. He took some classes in Buddhism, bought a rosary, tried some meditation. He thought it would bring him enlightenment. You know the kind of person I mean?'

Maggie nodded. 'Package tour Buddhists, I call them.'

India, and Dharamsala in particular, was full of them: backpackers, travellers, most young but many much older, who thought the East offered spiritual peace, some kind of meaning to their lives that they'd been unable to find back home in Basingstoke or Baltimore; dreamers who thought a fortnight of incense and chapatis would bring *nirvana*.

'He stayed a short time, then went back to London,' Jigme went on. 'He worked in . . . I think it was called public relations. What is that?'

'No one knows,' Maggie said. 'Including the people who do it.'

'He meant well, but it felt like charity. I'd done nothing to deserve it except be a Tibetan exile. It made me uncomfortable.'

'How did you get out of Tibet?'

'I walked.'

'As simple as that?'

'For me, yes.'

'That can't have been easy, crossing the mountains. What about the border guards?'

'I bribed them. Gave them some gold jewellery, my grand-mother's jewellery I'd kept with me in the monastery. The Chinese are very corrupt. These were young conscripts. Bored, underpaid soldiers. I felt sorry for them. They didn't want to be in Tibet any more than we wanted them there.'

'You felt sorry for your oppressors?'

'Compassion for all is the fundamental tenet of our faith.'

Maggie submerged the dirty pan in the pool and used a clump of grass as a scourer, scraping off the remains of the rice.

'Are you happy being a monk?'

'Happy?' Jigme hesitated. 'No one has ever asked me that before.'

'You must have asked yourself.'

'Yes, I have.

'And . . .'

'I don't know. It's the only life I know. I was seven years old when I entered the monastery. To change now would be difficult.'

'You've thought of changing?'

Jigme rinsed a bowl in the pool and watched the current take away a few grains of leftover rice, carrying them through a tiny channel between the rocks and away downstream.

'Yes, I've thought about it. In Tibet, being a monk is part of our culture, our society. It has meaning. In India, well . . . sometimes it feels like an act. The tourists come and stare at us. We perform our rituals, maintain our traditions, but it's not the same. Sometimes I wonder why we're doing it.'

'That's understandable.'

'Perhaps I'm not meant for it. I don't have the discipline, the commitment of monks like Tsering and Lobsang.'

'You could do something else.'

'What?'

'What would you like to do?'

'If I could start all over again?' He took a moment to reflect. 'I'd like to be a musician. A jazz musician.'

'Jazz?' Maggie sat back on her heels, surprised. 'You play an instrument?'

'I've been teaching myself the clarinet. I'm quite good. Tim sent me tapes: King Oliver, Jelly Roll Morton, Louis Armstrong, The Hot Five and Hot Seven. I love that stuff. "Potato Head Blues", "Muskrat Ramble". I can play them, you know.'

'They let you?'

'I play it very quietly. The abbot disapproves but he doesn't stop me. The monastery in McLeod Ganj, it is not like the ones in Tibet.'

That was true. In McLeod Ganj Maggie had seen monks drinking Coca-Cola, wandering around with Walkman headphones clamped to their ears, even riding motor scooters. But it was a diverting image nevertheless: Jigme, shaven-headed, wearing maroon robes, sitting in his cell playing New Orleans jazz.

'You got any friends who play?' she asked, only half joking. 'You could be big. The world's first Buddhist jazz band. Blues with a hint of spirituality. The girls would love those haircuts.'

'You're mocking me now.'

'I mean it. You just need the right manager.'

Jigme splashed water on to another bowl and rubbed it clean. 'We should get back to the van.'

'Why? I'm enjoying this.'

'Tsering doesn't like me talking to you.'

'Why not?'

'He thinks you might corrupt me.'

'And will I?'

Jigme grinned and gave her a look; a childlike, utterly sexless look. 'Sometimes, I think my life could do with a little corruption.' He gathered up the bowls and got to his feet. 'I'll race you back up the hill.'

Shen Tzu did not consider himself a philosopher, but he knew that Marx had got it wrong; it was not religion that was the opium of the people, but work. It was work that dulled the senses, that soothed the troubled mind, that provided the comforting illusion that there was some purpose to life. Man was born in darkness and would die in it. Between the two was another void that had to be filled with something and Shen, like many before him, had chosen the anodyne drug of unremitting labour. That way lay, if not happiness, then certainly contentment of a kind.

He had a deep-rooted fear of leisure, of time wasted. He dreaded the boredom and purposelessness that inactivity brought, but most of all he dreaded having the opportunity to think and reflect. He immersed himself in his work because he didn't want even a single moment in the day when he might be forced to question the wisdom or the point of his labour. Freedom of thought led inevitably to doubts and uncertainties, and ultimately to rejection of and rebellion against the faith. The Party understood that. Like a religion, it understood the importance of doctrine and dogma and the blind, unquestioning obedience of its followers. But then what was communism but a religion without a God?

It was ten o'clock in the evening and he was still at his desk in the PSB building overlooking the Lingkhor Shar Lam. What else was there for him to do in Lhasa? His wife and child were two thousand kilometres away in Shanghai. He spoke to them infrequently on the telephone and had not seen them for two years. He didn't know when he might be permitted to visit them. His requests for leave had always been turned down in the past and he could see no likelihood of being allowed a break from his duties – even for just a few days – in the forseeable future. Tibet was too tense. All leave had been cancelled for both the PSB and the PLA. The martial law decree was being enforced with ruthless efficiency and the hunt for the ringleaders of the Jokhang Square riot was continuing. Numerous Tibetan splittists had been rounded up and detained but not, so far, the Khampa in the hat.

Shen badly needed a result – Beijing expected it, demanded it. Colonel Huang Shu Hua, the commander of the Lhasa City PSB, had already been removed from his post and severely criticised – not for the way his officers had handled the demonstration, but for letting it happen in the first place. Shen knew only too well that other scapegoats might be needed to pacify the old men in Beijing and that he was next in the firing line. He was responsible for intelligence matters. In Beijing's view, that meant he should have been aware in advance of what was about to happen and nipped it in the bud. He should have known who the troublemakers were likely to be and made sure they were safely out of the way.

Shen picked up his smouldering cigarette from the ashtray and sucked on it abstractedly. Through the open door of his office, he saw Chang walk in from the corridor. In his hand the major was clutching a sheaf of papers and what looked like a map of Tibet.

'We have something,' Chang said, careful not to sound too confident. He approached the desk and opened the map. 'With your permission, Comrade Colonel?'

Shen gave a nod and Chang spread the map out on top of the desk.

'The day before yesterday, at a routine traffic division checkpoint outside Gongbogyamda, a white Toyota van was stopped. It contained three Tibetan men who said they were being transferred from their work unit in Lhasa to one in Chamdo.'

Shen sat up a little. His cigarette was in the corner of his mouth, the smoke drifting up into his eyes, but he didn't notice.

'They were detained?' he said.

Chang shook his head. 'This was several hours before our directive went out to all the district offices. There was no reason to detain them, but the district commander sent in the information yesterday. The details were checked. I have the replies from the Ministry of the Interior and the Ministry of Labour here.'

'And?

'Their identity papers were false. As were their transit papers and work transfer documents. The Fifty-Third work unit in Chamdo is not expecting any new workers from Lhasa.'

'It's them?'

'It may be. We can't be a hundred per cent certain.'

'What are you proposing?'

Chang leaned over the map, his finger following the route of the Tibet–Sichuan highway. 'They were in Gongbogyamda two days ago. That's here. The road traffic division had checkpoints at Ranglu, here, and Bamda, here, both yesterday and today. The three men passed through neither.'

Shen slipped on his spectacles and studied the map. 'So they're somewhere between Gongbogyamda and Ranglu.'

'Unless they turned off here, taking the road south-east towards the border with Myanmar. I've already alerted the office in Zhowagain to be on the lookout for them. And I have ordered additional checkpoints to be set up along the Sichuan highway – at Rawu and Gyitang as well as the two at Ranglu and Bamda. They have to pass through one of them. They have no alternative if they're still on the road.'

'And if they're not?'

'We will tighten the net and start a search of all the towns and villages along the road.' Chang drew a circle over the map with his finger. 'They're somewhere in here.' The major straightened up and looked at Shen. 'I'd like permission to fly out there and take personal charge of the case.'

Shen removed his cigarette from his mouth and stubbed it out in the ashtray. He had said nothing to Beijing about the three monks, or about his theory as to where they came from and why they were in Tibet. Nor did he have any intention of doing so until he had something more definite to flesh out the theory. He wanted the three men in custody, a confession on the record before he committed himself. A success here would be a way of redeeming himself for the debacle outside the Jokhang.

'Permission granted, Major,' he said.

THIRTEEN

During the night it rained heavily. Sleeping alone in the van, Maggie was disturbed by the noise of the raindrops drumming on the metal roof, at times so loud it sounded as if pebbles were dropping from the sky. At daybreak it was still raining. A thick wet mist enveloped the mountains and even at ground level the visibility was down to a hundred metres or less.

Maggie pulled open the door of the van and poked her nose out. The air smelt of damp pine and soggy earth. It seemed to cling to her skin in a moist film, penetrating the pores and refrigerating her blood. She put on her fleece jacket and lit the kerosene stove, using it to heat the interior of the van.

Jigme was the first of the monks to arrive, dashing across from his tent and clambering in, smoothing a hand over his shaven head to wipe away the rain. Lobsang and Tsering weren't far behind. They brushed the moisture off their *chubas* and squeezed on to one of the bench seats, their breath steaming up the windows until it was impossible to see out. Maggie opened the door a couple of inches to provide some ventilation and made tea. They drank in silence, listening to the steady rhythm of the rain.

'This could go on all day,' Tsering said. 'We'd better make a move or we'll never get the van out.'

No one bothered to wash. Even Tsering dispensed with his usual morning ritual of bathing followed by meditation and prostration. They struck the tents and dumped the dripping canvases inside the van, then prepared to move out. The ground was sodden, a mass of puddles and sticky mud. The wheels of the van skidded a little before finding sufficient purchase to negotiate the short distance from the copse to the logging track. It was when they reached the track that the problems started. The deep ruts made by the logging trucks were full of water, their sides turned to mud. There was nothing for the van tyres to grip. The wheels spun round in vain, churning up the ground without moving the vehicle one iota. Each time Tsering gunned the throttle he succeeded only in burying the back of the van even deeper into the quagmire. Worse, it started to slide out of control down the hill.

'Put the handbrake on!' Maggie yelled.

Tsering jerked up the lever. The van slithered another metre and came to a stop. Maggie jumped out, her feet sinking ankle-deep into the slush. The rear wheels were partially submerged, the chassis only inches above the ground.

'We need some stones under the wheels,' Maggie said, scrambling up the side of the ravine to collect an armful of loose rocks. The three monks climbed out of the van and stood looking at it for a moment as if it were some strange alien beast they'd never seen before.

'Come on,' Maggie shouted. 'Stop gawping and give me a hand here.'

They packed stones behind and in front of the rear wheels, laying a firm base beneath the layer of mud and water. Then Maggie pulled open the driver's door.

'You three push,' she instructed, sliding in behind the wheel.

She put the van in gear and depressed the accelerator, easing up the clutch pedal to the biting point.

'Now!' she shouted.

The monks put their shoulders to the back of the van and pushed with all their strength. The wheels started to spin, sending up a shower of mud. The monks dug in their heels, trying to find a firm footing, and pushed harder. The wheels skidded, then suddenly found some purchase on the bed of stones. The van jolted forward and up the hill. Maggie kept going, using the momentum to get the van as far as possible before it hit the next patch of mud. Twice more they had to put rocks under the wheels and push the van out. By the time they reached the main road, the three monks were soaked through and bedraggled, daubed with mud from head to toe. They cleaned themselves up as best they could and Tsering took over the driving. It was still raining heavily and the mist, if anything, had got thicker.

Tsering drove cautiously, the headlights on though they made little impact on the wall of impenetrable fog before them. The surface of the road gleamed with so much rain-water it seemed in places as if the whole carriageway were moving like a river.

They'd gone less than twenty kilometres when they rounded a bend and saw the brake lights of the truck in front glowing red as it slowed. Tsering edged out into the middle of the road. Ahead of them were lines of traffic cones, a cluster of figures in dark blue waterproof capes and a flashlight being swung to and fro to signal motorists to stop.

'Checkpoint,' Tsering said in alarm. He braked and swung back in behind the bulk of the lorry in front.

'It might be routine,' Lobsang said. 'Like the last one.'

'I don't think so.'

Tsering slowed. He had a bad feeling about this. They'd had a couple of days' grace, but now their luck had run out.

'They're waiting for us,' he said. 'I'm sure of it.'

He checked his rear-view mirror. There was nothing behind them. There was nothing coming the other way either, though in the distance he could see the headlights of a lorry that had been stopped at the checkpoint. He hauled the steering wheel over hard and did a clean U-turn, heading back the way they'd come.

Chang peered out through the rain-spattered window of the Landcruiser and stifled a yawn. He'd been on the move for most of the night, taking a PLA helicopter – an American-made Blackhawk especially adapted for high-altitude flying – from Lhasa to Chamdo, then driving south to the PSB checkpoints at Gyitang, Bamda and now Ranglu. He was tired, irritable and hungry.

He looked ahead through the windscreen, trying to make out the figures through the opaque film of streaming water. Where the hell was his driver? It must have been five minutes ago that he'd gone to fetch the major some tea from the catering wagon. How long did it take to make a bowl of tea? Chang turned his head, looking up the road now. A lorry was just coming to a halt at the checkpoint. Behind it . . . what was that behind the lorry? Something was turning. A white shape. Turning round in the road. Chang rubbed the misted glass with the palm of his hand. There was still too much rain on the outside. He wound down the window and stared.

A van. A white Toyota van. Disappearing back into the mist up the road.

Chang threw open the door of the Landcruiser and started yelling.

Tsering floored the accelerator. The speedometer crept just above the fifty kilometres an hour mark and stayed there. The engine was whining, the whole van vibrating under the strain. Tsering looked in his rear-view mirror. The road behind was clear. So far. He wondered if they'd been seen turning round, if even now the PSB were setting off in pursuit. If it came to a straight chase, there was no way the van could outrun the police.

'Look on the map,' he said urgently. 'Find a turn-off, another road, anything to get us off the highway.'

Lobsang bent over the map, studying the details.

'Quickly!' Tsering snapped. 'They could be right behind us.'

His eyes went to the mirror again. There were no headlights to be seen, just the swirling blanket of mist.

'There's a side road,' Lobsang said.

'Where?'

'Two, three kilometres. On the right.'

Tsering gripped the steering wheel, hunched forward as if the posture might force more speed out of the recalcitrant van. But it remained stubbornly on the fifty mark. Maggie moved to the back window and pulled aside the curtain. There was still no sign of any vehicle behind, but then the visibility was so poor that she could only see a short distance. She watched, every muscle tense, expecting a police car to erupt out of the mist any moment.

'How much further?' Tsering demanded.

'A kilometre.' Lobsang's voice seemed unnaturally calm.

'On the right, you said?'

'Yes.'

'Where does it go?'

'North-west. It's very small. It may be just a track.'

'I don't care. We're not staying on the highway.'

Tsering kept his eyes fixed on the road. In the adverse conditions, even fifty kilometres an hour seemed a danger- ously high speed. The mist was like a wall in front of them, a white, billowing cloud that rushed towards them, concealing the hazards beyond. Once or twice the highway turned unexpectedly and Tsering nearly drove off the side. Had there been a slower vehicle ahead of them, they would certainly have run into the back of it.

'Here!' Lobsang cried.

Tsering braked hard. The tyres skidded on the slippery surface, the back end of the van slewing sideways. Maggie was thrown on to the floor, banging her shoulder on one of the wooden lockers.

'Jesus!' she exclaimed. 'You trying to kill us?'

But Tsering wasn't listening. He was turning off the road on to a rough, unmetalled track that rose steeply up the hill- side, climbing higher into the mist.

Chang was on the edge of his seat in the back of the Landcruiser, leaning forward and peering intently through the windscreen. In the front, his driver was concentrating on the road whilst the PSB lieutenant in the passenger seat was on the radio, telling the checkpoint further south beyond Rawu to close the highway. The Landcruiser, a big, powerful beast with four-wheeled drive to give it extra grip on the greasy road, was touching ninety kilometres an hour. It could go much faster, but even Chang was content with the speed. They were driving almost blind as it was. Any faster would have been suicidal. Behind them, struggling to keep up, was another PSB vehicle, a canvas-topped Beijing Jeep, and behind that, lost from sight, was a Jiefang truck carrying a further ten armed police officers.

'How far have we gone?' Chang snapped.

'About ten kilometres, Comrade Major,' the lieutenant replied.

'Pull over.'

The lieutenant swivelled round in his seat. 'Comrade Major . . .'

'*Pull over.*'

The driver eased on the brakes and pulled off on to the hard shoulder. The Jeep came to a halt just behind them.

'Give me the map,' Chang ordered. He examined it closely. 'We should have caught up with them by now. They've turned off somewhere.' He jabbed a finger at the map. 'Here. Five, six kilometres back. There's a track. That's where they've gone.'

The track rose steeply up the mountainside in a series of tight hairpin bends. If there'd been mud on it, it would have been completely impassable, but the topsoil had been washed away long ago to expose the greyish, uneven bedrock which gave the van something to grip on to. It was still a treacherous ascent. There was rainwater pouring down the slope, lubricating the already precarious surface, and on one side the ground fell away into nothing. Glancing out of the window as the van negotiated yet another hair-raising bend, Maggie saw a sheer cliff below her and was glad that the mist concealed the full extent of the drop.

Gradually the track began to level out, cutting horizontally across the side of the mountain before it started its descent into the valley on the other side. At the highest point, Tsering stopped the van abruptly and applied the handbrake, staring in dismay out of the windscreen.

In front of them a landslide had completely blocked their path.

A slice of the mountain had broken away and slipped down in a river of earth and boulders that had flooded over a twenty-metre-wide stretch of the track. The four of them climbed out of the van and gazed disconsolately at the blockage. There was no way around it. To the right was a steep mound of earth, to the left, only a few feet from the track, a precipitous drop off the edge of the mountain.

'How do we get across that?' Tsering asked.

'You got any shovels?' Maggie enquired.

'No. We'll have to go back.'

'To what?' Maggie said. 'There'll be checkpoints all along the main highway, in both directions. How far will we get without being stopped? Going back isn't an option.'

Tsering gave a nod of agreement. 'Any suggestions?'

'As we did before. We have to build a path over the mud.'

They threw themselves into the work, digging rocks out of the mudslide, bringing others from the surrounding slopes and bedding them down in two lines the same distance apart as the van's wheels. The rain continued relentlessly, turning the mud into a runny sludge like melted chocolate. Maggie was drenched to the skin, her fingers numb with cold. She dropped a boulder into place, plugging it into the saturated earth, and straightened up, glancing down over the edge. For one brief instant the mist parted and far below her, coming slowly up the track she saw headlights.

'Tsering!' she called.

He followed her gaze and went ashen. 'PSB?'

'I don't know. But I don't think we should wait around to ask.'

'We've done only a bit of the track.'

212

'We'll have to chance it.'

Maggie scrambled into the van and turned on the engine. She lined it up, then bumped slowly up on to the twin tracks of rock they'd constructed across the landslide. They'd completed only six or seven metres, less than half the distance they needed. The rocks gave a little under the weight of the vehicle, but they held firm, providing a solid base for the tyres. At the end of the tracks, however, the van squelched down into the mud and stuck fast. Maggie tried to extricate it, but the wheels just spun round uselessly.

'Try pushing,' she yelled.

Tsering, Lobsang and Jigme went to the back of the van and put their weight to it. Maggie opened the throttle. The engine screamed, the wheels flinging up mud in thick brown sheets. Then suddenly the tyres found something firmer underneath. The van lurched forward, slithering and sliding over the patina of liquid earth. It slewed sideways towards the precipice and Maggie looked down out of the window and saw nothing but thin air beneath her. She hauled on the wheel and the van skidded back away from the edge. It managed a few more feet then came to a standstill, stuck firm in the mud. They tried again, the monks pushing, but the van wouldn't budge.

Maggie opened the door and climbed out, manoeuvring her way carefully along the side of the van, the sheer drop less than a metre away. Her heart was racing, her legs and arms trembling as she realised how close she'd been to going over the edge. Through gaps in the mist, she saw the headlights below her again, caught a glimpse of three vehicles. They were getting nearer.

'Tsering . . .'

Maggie stopped and gaped in astonishment at the three monks. They were kneeling next to one another on the landslide, eyes closed, hands raised, touching first their heads, then their throats, then their hearts. They were praying.

'What the bloody hell are you doing?' Maggie screamed. 'The *Gong An Ju* are just down the hill.'

The monks didn't appear to hear her, they were so focused on their prayers.

'They'll be here in minutes,' Maggie shouted, her voice rising in exasperation. 'We can still get away. Take our bags and make a run for it. In this mist they'll never find us. Are you listening? Jesus Christ! Are you fucking crazy? The *Gong An Ju* are nearly on us. You hear me?'

Tsering opened his eyes and blinked. The rain had got heavier. His face was running with water. He stood up.

'We will try one more time,' he said calmly.

'*What*?' Maggie couldn't believe it. 'Look down there. *Look*.'

'One more time,' Tsering repeated. 'Get behind the wheel, please.'

'We have to run for it. Don't you understand, the van is stuck? We'll never get it out.'

'Trust in the Lord Buddha.'

'It's stuck, for Christ's sake.'

'Please, Miss Walsh.' Tsering gestured without urgency at the van. 'Have faith.'

The three monks walked over to the back of the van and pressed their shoulders to it.

'We're waiting,' Tsering said.

Maggie threw up her arms, her head ready to explode, but she inched her way back round to the door of the van. Just before she climbed in, she looked down once more. The PSB vehicles were a hundred metres below them now, clearly visible through the rolling curtain of mist. Two more bends in the track and they would be here.

Maggie slid into the driver's seat and switched on the engine and windscreen wipers. She rammed the gearstick into first and worked the clutch and throttle pedals as the monks pushed from behind. The wheels spun furiously, but the van didn't move. They tried again. The same thing happened.

'It's no use,' Maggie shouted. 'We have to get out now.'

'Once more,' Tsering shouted from the back.

Maggie closed her eyes, praying herself now. Please, God,

make it happen. *Make it happen.* The PSB vehicles would be rounding the final bend now, coming up the last stretch of track to the summit. Maggie didn't dare look. She squeezed the accelerator again, the clutch biting. The van started to vibrate, but it didn't move. Please, God, Maggie implored. *Please.*

The axles were spinning, the engine shrieking as if it were about to shatter. Then, with a shudder, the wheels broke free of the mud. The van lurched forward. Maggie was so startled she took her foot off the throttle, then rammed it back hurriedly to keep the vehicle moving. Sliding and swaying, the van bumped its way across the landslide, the wheels almost skating over the mud as though they were weightless. The front wheels jolted down on to the track at the far side, then the whole van was off.

Tsering and Lobsang ran to the passenger door, Jigme to the side door.

'Quickly!' Maggie urged.

In her mirror she saw a Landcruiser come over the crest. She hit the accelerator and the van skidded away down the track.

The driver started to slow as he saw the landslide blocking their way.

'Keep going!' Chang commanded from the back seat.

'But Comrade Major . . .'

'That's an order.'

The Landcruiser hit the edge of the landslide with a bang, moving easily over the rocks that had been laid in the mud. But when it reached the end of the makeshift track, it sank down heavily into the soft earth and stopped. The driver revved the engine but succeeded only in burying the vehicle even deeper.

'It's no good, Comrade Major.'

'Keep trying,' Chang barked. 'They got across. So can we.'

The rain was lashing across the mountainside, great waves of it battering the outside of the Landcruiser. Even with the wipers on double speed the windscreen was a foggy sheet of streaming water, almost impossible to see through.

'Get some help,' Chang rapped. 'Where's the truck? Get some men to push us.'

The lieutenant in the front forced open his door, fighting against the ferocious power of the wind. He dragged himself out and stopped, staring in horror across the landslide.

'Comrade Major . . .'

Chang saw it just in time. The slope above the landslide was breaking away from the mountain, a huge spur of earth and rock sliding inexorably down towards them like an avalanche. Chang felt the ground beneath the vehicle start to move. He threw open his door and hurled himself out, falling head first into the mud. He stumbled to his feet. Small rocks and boulders were bouncing towards him. A terrifying wall of earth was starting to collapse and pour across the track. Chang staggered sideways, almost falling again. The lieutenant grabbed his arm, pulling him upright. The moving earth caught at their ankles, dragging them towards the edge. Knee deep in mud, Chang scrambled unsteadily away from the Landcruiser and threw himself off the landslide.

Lying breathless on the rocky ground, Chang turned his head in time to see the driver struggling out of his door. But too late. The surging barrage of earth picked up the Landcruiser as if it were a pebble and in a roaring torrent like a vast muddy cataract swept both vehicle and driver out over the precipice.

FOURTEEN

'Slow down!' Tsering shouted, straining to make himself heard above the noise of the engine and the thunder of the rain outside. 'You can slow down now.'

'What?' Maggie's gaze was locked on the windscreen as she tried desperately to see through the semi-opaque smear of water and dirt.

'They're not following,' Tsering said.

'You sure?'

'Yes, slow down.'

Maggie touched the brake pedal. Her whole body was tense, the muscles knotted so tight they ached. Another bend loomed up and she slowed to a crawl, taking the corner gently. In the heat of the moment, in the blind panic that had overwhelmed her at the top of the hill, she'd simply careered down the track, too wound up to think about the consequences. Calmer now, she was horrified at her recklessness. Only chance, and her instinctive driving skill, had prevented the van from hurtling out into the void below. She kept her foot on the brake, the van going so slowly it was barely moving. Each new bend in the track filled her with terror and she wondered how they would ever get down from the mountain.

Tsering was watching her closely. 'Stop here,' he said.

'What?'

'Stop. I'll take over.'

'I'm okay.'

'You're not. Let me take over now.'

Maggie was tempted to protest – out of habit more than anything else – but she knew he was right. She was in no condition to continue. She stopped the van and climbed into the back with Jigme. Her legs were tired and shaking as if she'd just run a marathon. She collapsed back into one of the seats feeling utterly drained.

'Where does this track end up?' Tsering asked.

Lobsang showed him the map. 'It goes north-west, joining this road here about twenty kilometres on.'

'And Mount Gebur?'

'Is here. A hundred kilometres north of the road.'

Tsering studied the map, thinking out loud. 'Assuming the track behind us is impassable, the PSB will have to go all the way back down on to the Sichuan highway and drive north towards Chamdo, heading off west here near Baxoi. To cut us off would be a circuitous trip of maybe a hundred and fifty kilometres.'

'Unless there's a police unit further north that can get there quicker,' Lobsang said.

'That's a risk we have to take. I say we drive to the road and hide the van somewhere. It's outlived its usefulness.'

'And then?'

'We'll face that decision when we get to it.'

Chang stood on the edge looking down over the precipice, his driver's final scream still ringing in his ears, a scream of pure terror that would stay with the major for a long time to come. Far below him, appearing then disappearing in the eddying mist, the Landcruiser lay broken and crushed, half buried in the debris that had cascaded over the cliff. The driver's body was nowhere to be seen. It would be somewhere under the mound of earth and rock, a crumpled, pulverised mess of flesh and bone. They would have to dig him out – what was left of him – and give him a proper funeral, another policeman killed in the course of duty.

Chang stepped back. He was shaken by the incident. It

could so easily have been him down there. The hair's-breadth margin between life and death had never seemed so fragile.

He walked carefully across to the Jeep that had stopped only metres from the landslide, composing himself to face his men. His uniform was caked with mud, all insignia of rank obliterated. The lieutenant was waiting for him, one hand gripping the door of the Jeep, the knuckles so tight the bones seemed to be bursting through the skin. Chang glanced at the landslide. It was as if some malign giant had taken a bite out of the mountain; sunk its teeth into the rock and then spat it out over the track. There was no possibility of getting across to the other side.

'Give me a map,' Chang said, his emotions once more under control.

He bent over slightly, using his body to protect the map from the rain. Damn this infernal weather. There was no way he could get a helicopter airborne. They would have to do it all from the ground.

'Radio the district headquarters. Inform them what's happened,' he instructed the lieutenant. 'Get a unit out further north to cover this road here. Block both ends of it and start a search of the area in between.'

'Yes, Comrade Major.'

'Then deploy the men from the truck to recover the driver's body from the landslide.'

The lieutenant nodded and reached inside the Jeep for the radio. The other officers inside the vehicle were staring at Chang with blank, inscrutable faces, but he knew what they were thinking. He was the senior officer. He was responsible for the safety of his men and he had put them at risk. One of them had died. Chang knew his competence had been called into question by what had happened. That it had been caused by an unforseeable act of God was irrelevant. The men would blame him for the death.

Chang turned away, feeling the humiliation like a physical wound that would fester until he found a way to heal it. The rain beat against his face, stinging his skin. Water poured down his chest, washing the mud from his uniform. There was only one way to absolve himself, and that was to find the three monks who had brought this about. When he found them, he would have his revenge.

'How far to the road now?' Tsering asked.

Lobsang glanced at the map and shrugged. 'One, maybe two kilometres.'

'We should find somewhere to dump the van.'

Tsering braked, taking his eyes off the track to scour the surrounding terrain for a suitable hiding place. They were down off the exposed slopes of the mountain now, driving through a densely forested valley.

'Just here,' Jigme said, pointing at a slight hollow next to the track.

Tsering stopped the van and they climbed out. They removed their baggage, the kerosene stove that had come with the van and the remains of the food supplies – the tea, butter, *tsampa*, rice and noodles. Then they pushed the van down into the hollow, guiding it between the trees until it was a good fifty metres off the track. They found fallen logs, pine and cedar branches and pulled up shrubs and used them to camouflage the van with foliage, concealing all traces of its white bodywork. It was a crude job which, close to, would have fooled no one, but from the track it made the van almost invisible. They swung their bags on to their backs and started walking.

Twenty minutes later they reached the road. It was narrower than the Sichuan highway, its surface pitted with holes and deep cracks where the winter frosts had bitten into the asphalt. They stayed in the trees, watching for a time, but no traffic came past in either direction. Tsering spread the map out on the ground, pinpointing their exact location.

'We should split up,' he said, speaking in English for Maggie's benefit. 'The Chinese will be looking for three Tibetan men travelling together. Lobsang, you go with Jigme. Miss Walsh, you will come with me. In those clothes, with your cap on, you could pass for a Han. Not that I expect to encounter many Chinese from now on. Much of our route will be through the mountains, away from villages and roads.'

He traced a line on the map with his finger. 'We will make a loop to the west, heading up this valley here. Lobsang, you and Jigme will go to the east. We will join up again here at the village of Pangor in two days' time. We'll wait a further day for each other. If one party doesn't show up, the others go on alone to Mount Gebur.'

'And the PSB?' Lobsang said.

'Will be hunting us with all their resources,' Tsering replied grimly. He looked up. The rain had eased off a little, but the mist was still as thick as ever. 'The weather is on our side. If it clears, they'll use helicopters to try and find us. Be careful. Stay under cover, in the woods, as much as possible. If necessary, hole up for the day and walk only at night.' He passed the map to Lobsang. 'Take this.'

'What about you? How will you navigate?'

'We will manage. I have memorised our route.'

They divided up the supplies and equipment so each group had a tent, a stove and half the food stock. Then Tsering clasped hands in turn with Lobsang and Jigme, wishing them good fortune and the assistance of the Buddha in their journey.

'We'll see you in Pangor in two days.'

Lobsang and Jigme moved cautiously out across the road. On the far side, they turned briefly, their hands raised in farewell, before disappearing from sight into the trees.

'How are your legs, Miss Walsh?' Tsering asked.

'They're fine.'

'Good. It's a long walk.'

Tsering picked up his bag and strode across the road, Maggie close behind him. They walked west along the verge on the other side for a few hundred metres, then slithered down the earth embankment and plunged into the thick forest.

*   *   *

221

For the first two hours they walked uphill through dense pine woods, the canopy of branches over their heads cutting out most of the light so that the ground was cloaked in a shadowy gloom. Occasionally there was a break in the trees and they emerged into the open, the mist drifting low over the slopes, the damp smoky clouds ebbing and flowing across the treetops as if the forest were breathing. Then they struck a well-worn path which followed the course of a foaming mountain stream. For a further three hours they climbed the path, sometimes down by the stream, sometimes winding across the rocky escarpments above the torrent.

It was tiring work. Maggie guessed they were somewhere close to ten thousand feet high, a punishing altitude for someone from the lowlands of Britain. Tsering seemed unaffected by the thin air and he set a gruelling pace, striding ahead of her as if he were trying to break her. Maggie hung in behind him, too proud to ask him to slow down. He must have heard her panting, noticed the sheen of sweat on her face, but he gave her no relief.

Towards evening, even Tsering was becoming fatigued by their exertions. He threw his bag down on a patch of flat ground beside the stream and looked around, assessing the terrain.

'This will do,' he said. 'We'll camp here for the night.'

Maggie flopped down and lay on her back, staring up at the overcast sky. She was too exhausted to move.

'Tired?' Tsering asked.

Maggie rolled on to her side. He was looking at her with a slight curl of amusement at the corners of his mouth.

'I'm okay,' she said.

'You are feeling the altitude?'

'A bit.'

'Have you been this high before?'

'Yes.'

'In Tibet?'

'Afghanistan.'

'You've been to Afghanistan?'

'A few times. During the war against the Taliban, but also back in the Eighties. When the Soviets were there.'

'You must have been very young.'

'I was.'

'You were a camerawoman?'

'Not then. That came later.'

Maggie slipped off her shoes and socks and rubbed her sore feet, letting the cool, damp air soothe them.

'So what were you doing there?' Tsering asked.

'My boyfriend was a cameraman.'

'And where is he now? Is he still your boyfriend?'

'He's dead.'

'Oh, I'm sorry. How did he die? In Afghanistan?'

'In Bosnia.'

'You were with him?'

Maggie stood up. 'It was a long time ago.' She walked down to the stream and dipped her feet into the freezing water, watching her toes go white with the cold. Alex would have liked it here. He loved the mountains, the cool, clear air. It was heat and jungles he loathed: the insects, the snakes, the cloying humidity. He'd have felt at home here, the way he had in Afghanistan with the *mujahideen*. He'd had a mountain man's build: tough, wiry, rangy. He'd enjoyed the physical challenge of the Hindu Kush: the altitude, the arduous ascents. Even with his heavy camera gear on his back he'd raced up the mountains as if he'd been born there. And he'd expected her to keep up. He'd never pampered her, never patronised her, even at the beginning. He'd treated her as an equal, one of the boys. Except at night . . .

Maggie smiled at the memory. She'd been attracted to that masculine strength the moment she'd first seen him. She'd been nineteen, studying photography at the London School of Art. Alex – an old friend of one of her tutors – had come to talk to her class. He'd walked in, an impossibly glamorous figure in worn denim and desert boots, his face tanned, his beard neatly trimmed, and Maggie had fallen for him immediately. Afterwards, a few of them had gone to the pub with him, and Maggie – never one to vacillate – had gone back to his flat and spent the night with him. Three months later, preparing to go to Afghanistan, he'd asked her if she wanted to come with him. He'd wangled her a job as his 'field producer', the television euphemism for dogsbody. Her duties, apart from screwing the cameraman, were to look after the equipment, find accommodation and food for Alex and his sound man and arrange for the footage to be sent back to London. But the sound man was an alcoholic. One morning he'd been too drunk to work so Alex had given Maggie a crash course in sound recording and taken her with him into the Panjsher Valley. It was the beginning of a professional, and personal, relationship that would last a decade. Until Sarajevo in '92 . . .

'If you stand there much longer, your feet will drop off,' Tsering said.

Maggie looked round. 'What?'

'Your feet.'

Maggie glanced down. She'd lost all sensation below the ankles. She stepped hurriedly out of the stream and massaged her toes. Tsering was making a campfire, building a teepee of logs over a mound of dry bark and kindling. He lit it with a match and blew gently on the bark until the flames ignited the kindling. In a matter of minutes the fire was blazing. Maggie sat down beside it and warmed her feet. Since they'd stopped walking, the sweat had cooled on her body and she was feeling the dank chill of the evening.

They used the fire for heat, but did the cooking on the kerosene stove, boiling up water for tea and noodles. Then they pitched the tent under the trees and Maggie went back to the fire, a blanket wrapped around her shoulders. Tsering had moved a little way off and was sitting meditating, oblivious to everything around him. Maggie put more wood on the fire and watched it burn and crackle, the smoke wafting into her eyes. By the time Tsering had finished his contemplation, it was dark. He came back to the fire and leaned close to the glowing embers.

'Feeling better?' Maggie said.

'Better?'

'Isn't that why you meditate?'

'In part, yes. It calms the mind, relaxes it.'

'I prefer a glass of wine and a cigarette.'

'But it does more than that. It helps develop a clearer understanding of the true nature of reality.'

'Oh yes?'

'You sound sceptical.'

'Maybe I am. Sometimes it seems as if you're copping out of reality.'

Tsering frowned at her. '"Copping out"? What does that mean?'

'Escaping from reality. Refusing to take responsibility for it.'

'I think you misunderstand the purpose of meditation. Do you have no faith?'

'Religious faith?'

'Any faith.'

'No, I don't think I do,' Maggie said.

'Then you are impoverished. You Westerners have rejected spiritual riches in favour of materialistic poverty.'

'Is the East much better? Are you a better person than me? You monks shut yourselves away, live on charity and devote your lives to seeking enlightenment for yourselves. Not for anyone else. You live off others so you can find fulfilment at their expense. You think that's worthy, a life well spent?'

'You know nothing about my life,' Tsering said sharply.

'It's true though, isn't it? That's how it was in old Tibet. The farmers, the peasants, would work their fields and give food to the monasteries. They wouldn't have time to meditate, wouldn't know how as the technique was only taught to monks. They were too preoccupied with surviving, with supporting their families, to have the leisure for spiritual contemplation. The monks, on the other hand, didn't have to work. They were provided with food and shelter and the time to seek their own personal salvation. It was a cushy, selfish life. Why should other people support your search for enlightenment?'

Tsering stared into the fire. Maggie could tell he was angry. That was how she wanted him. She wanted to provoke a reaction, pierce a hole in his carapace of self-control.

'You show your ignorance of Tibet and our faith,' he said. 'It is not true that the monks did no work. They grew much of their own food, provided medicine and education and religious guidance to the local people. They worked hard. As for meditation, our prayers are worthless if they are only for ourselves. We pray for all sentient beings. True Buddhists understand that. You shouldn't judge everything by your own misinformed standards. That is the arrogance of the West. You confuse prejudice with fact.'

'You're defending the privileged pampering of the monasteries?'

Tsering gave an irritated click of the tongue. 'The people gave alms to monks because it gave them credit for their next life, like all acts of charity. The aim of all Buddhists is to keep being reborn and living a better, more compassionate life each time until finally, like the Buddha, they achieve enlightenment.'

'Isn't that selfish?'

'No, because it doesn't end there. You then come back out of choice, like the Dalai Lama does, to help others achieve enlightenment.' Tsering looked up at her over the flames. 'You should slow your life down, take some time to cultivate and nurture your spirit. Find a teacher and learn something deeper about the faiths and beliefs of others.'

'Find a guru? Me?' Maggie said, amused at the thought. 'I've seen a few gurus, the East is full of them, and they're all charlatans preying on weak, impressionable people. A straggly beard and some incomprehensible platitudes and suddenly they're fountains of wisdom. Isn't it funny how religious sects always seem to have one man at the top and a lot of gullible female followers, all of whom have to sleep with the leader? It's just a modern form of harem. The best way for a man to get laid is to start a religion.'

226

Tsering shook his head angrily. 'This discussion is not worth continuing. You are too cynical, too disrespectful. You seem to believe there can be nothing good in people, that no one does anything for others out of compassion or altruism.'

'That's my experience of the world,' Maggie said. 'You talk about meditating to understand the true nature of reality. But reality isn't in the mind. It's out there. Reality isn't a spiritual experience. Reality is a child dying unnoticed in a gutter, a jet plane bombing a village full of innocent civilians, babies dying of starvation and drought, a man lying in a ditch with his guts hanging out. Reality is what we do to each other.'

'You are speaking of conventional reality – how we perceive the world,' Tsering replied. 'Not ultimate reality, which is how things truly exist.'

'No, my perception of the world – the pain and suffering, the violence and self-interest – is how it really is. I've seen it.'

'And do your eyes never lie to you? Do you see so clearly that you have no doubts?'

'You think I'm wrong?'

'I don't know,' Tsering said, standing up from the fire. 'But are you so wise that what you alone see must be the truth?'

He walked across to the tent and ducked inside it. Maggie remained by the fire a while longer, poking at the dying embers with a stick. Then she went to the tent and pulled aside the flap. Tsering was stretched out on one side of the groundsheet, his head at the far end. Maggie crawled in and lay down with her head by his feet.

'I hope you don't snore,' she said.

Tsering didn't reply. Maggie sensed him lying there hidden in the darkness, stiff and resentful.

'You sulking?' she said.

'No, I am not sulking,' he muttered indistinctly.

Maggie smiled to herself and rolled over, pulling the blanket up over her shoulders and closing her eyes.

In the morning the mist still lay heavy on the mountains. Maggie couldn't see the tops of any of them, but she could feel their presence, sense the overpowering bulk of them through the mist.

They packed away the tent and stamped out the remains of the fire and continued walking up the path by the stream. Maggie asked Tsering what a path was doing there in the middle of an empty wilderness.

'It's not empty,' he replied. 'There are villages further up. And *drogpa*, nomads, on the high pastures. They use the track to bring their produce down to the road – yak meat and skins, butter, cheese. They take them to market to exchange for *tsampa* and knives and ammunition for their rifles. The Tibetans have always been great traders.'

'And your family? Are they traders?'

'No, my father was a farmer.'

'Was?'

'He died when I was four.'

'That must have been hard for you. And for your mother. Where is she? Is she still alive?'

'I don't know,' Tsering said.

He strode away up the path, abruptly terminating the conversation. Maggie let him go. It was obviously a sensitive subject.

The path continued to climb steadily through the woods. As they got higher the trees started to thin out, the dense slopes of fir and cedar giving way to more isolated patches of stunted conifers and dwarf rhododendrons. Maggie could tell from her lungs that they were gaining altitude. Walking was becoming harder. She was having to pause more often to rest.

Finally, they emerged above the tree line and stopped to have something to eat. Tsering filled a pan with water from the stream and boiled some rice on the stove. The mist was beginning to lift, the sun breaking through and heating up the ground. Maggie lay back, her jacket off, and basked in the warmth. She had her eyes closed and was dozing off when Tsering said suddenly: 'Someone's coming!'

Maggie sat up quickly, grabbing her Mao cap and pulling the peak down over her face.

'Pretend you're asleep,' Tsering whispered.

Above them, around a bend in the track, appeared a man on a pony. Tsering stood up and greeted him. They conversed for several awkward minutes in the polite, stilted tones of strangers. Curled up on the grassy bank, Maggie opened her eyes a fraction under her cap and watched them. The other man was Tibetan, a Khampa with plaited hair and a colourful blouse beneath his *chuba*. His pony, a short but sturdy animal, was laden down with bags and a couple of panniers slung behind the saddle.

Tsering offered him tea, as custom dictated, but the man declined, saying he had a long way to go before nightfall. Raising an arm in farewell, the Khampa headed off down the track, his pony moving sure-footedly over the rocky ground.

Maggie waited until the sound of hooves had faded before she sat up again and removed her cap.

'Who was he?' she asked.

'A merchant taking yak-hair rugs to market.'

'Did he ask about us?'

'I said we were visiting relatives further north.'

'How did you explain me?'

'I said you were my wife.'

'That must have been a novelty for you. Did he believe you?'

'He had no reason not to.' Tsering looked up. Patches of sky were starting to appear through the thinning mist. 'We should eat our rice and move on. The next stage of our walk is very exposed.'

They left the path by the stream and walked cross-country towards a col between two mountains. The ground was dry and arid, patches of yellowish grass poking out from the stony soil, clumps of pale purple flowers scattered here and there like amethysts. Maggie could really feel the altitude now. Her chest was heaving, her heart pounding heavily though they were moving at little more than a shuffle, each pace up the steep gradient a draining effort.

229

At the top of the pass they stopped to rest. Snow was lying deep in the hollows. A string of prayer flags, dangling between two stone cairns, was fluttering in the wind. Tsering drank some water from his canteen and offered it to Maggie. Then they started the long descent into the valley on the other side.

After the grind of the ascent, the walk down was almost a pleasure. The sun was warm, the mist had cleared, so all around the mountains stood out in bold relief against the cornflower blue sky. Only the knowledge that the PSB were looking for them marred their enjoyment of the journey. But even that depressing thought could be forgotten for odd moments, submerged by the sheer untouched beauty of the landscape.

Near evening, they came over a low ridge and Tsering stopped. Below them, spread across the slope, were the ruins of some man-made buildings, a sprawling complex of broken walls and rubble the size of a small village.

Maggie glanced at Tsering. He was staring at the ruins with an expression on his face she couldn't readily identify. It seemed a look of horror, of surprise, but there was more there too – a sense of something Maggie could only describe as loss.

'What's the matter?' she said.

Tsering didn't seem to hear.

'Tsering?'

He broke his gaze away from the fallen buildings. 'Did you say something?'

'What is that? An abandoned village?'

'It's a monastery,' he said.

Maggie gave a nod. Of course. There were thousands of them all over Tibet. Razed to the ground by the Chinese.

They walked down the hill. An archway at the back of the monastery was still standing, though the buildings on either side had been flattened. They passed beneath it and down a flight of steps which had been carved from the bedrock of the mountain itself. All around them were the stumps of walls and pillars and mounds of debris, the products of a wanton vandalism that was breathtaking in its scale. Further down was an open area which must once have been the courtyard of the monastery where the monks gathered to debate and listen to their lamas teach. Now it was piled high with rubble and the charred remains of the wooden beams that had supported the roofs of the surrounding buildings.

Tsering touched one of the shattered walls, feeling the stones with his fingertips. His eyes were screwed shut as if in pain.

'Why?' he said quietly, shaking his head.

He moved off past the courtyard, taking a passageway that cut horizontally across the hillside, his eyes roving over the ruins as if he were looking for something. He paused beside a long, narrow building that had once been divided up into rooms. The foundations were still there, but nothing else. Of the dozens, perhaps hundreds, of monks who had lived here there was no trace. It was just a desolate, empty carcass, filled with homeless spirits.

Tsering's lips were moving soundlessly. He was chanting a mantra to himself, praying silently so as not to disturb the uneasy hush that lay over the ruins. Maggie let him be. It was his faith that had been profaned here. He would make his peace with the desecration in his own way.

Grass and weeds had begun to colonise the fallen stones, sprouting from cracks, clinging to crevices where there seemed to be no soil. The tops of some of the walls were fringed with foliage. Somewhere, an alpine grasshopper was singing. Maggie let the sun bathe her face, burning off the damp vestiges of the mist and the rain that seemed to linger still on her skin. On the rocky slope beyond the monastery, a Himalayan marmot – snow pig, the Tibetans called it – popped out of its burrow and sniffed the air.

Tsering finished his prayers and walked quickly away down the hill as though he couldn't bear to dwell there any longer. Maggie chased after him, struggling to match his pace on the descent as much as she had on the way up. They lost height swiftly, dropping several thousand feet in the space of a couple of hours. Then ahead of them they saw a village perched on the slope just above the valley bottom.

'Pangor,' Tsering said.

'Are we going in?'

'We have to meet Lobsang and Jigme here.'

'Is it safe?'

Tsering nodded. 'There are no Chinese here. Believe me, we can trust the people.'

The village had been built on the incline to preserve as much of the available flat land as possible for agriculture. The valley floor was divided into small fields, the soil thin and impoverished. The barley crop had already been harvested, but the stubble remained, grazed by a few scrawny goats.

Nearing the first house, they saw an old woman sitting outside in a chair, making the most of the waning sun. Tsering stopped dead, staring at the old woman for a time as if he were in a trance. Then he shook himself free and walked on towards her. The old woman heard their footsteps and tilted her head to one side, listening rather than looking. Maggie realised she was blind.

'Who's there?' the old woman asked.

'We are friends,' Tsering replied. 'Have no fear.' He was regarding her gravely. 'Can you not see us?'

'I can see shadows, nothing else,' the old woman said. 'You are strangers? Where are you from?'

'We have come up from the Chamdo road,' Tsering said, evading the question. 'Is there somewhere in the village we can stay the night?'

'Nyima!' the old woman called out.

A young woman in her early twenties came out of the house. She had jet-black hair, braided into a plait with threads of fine coral beads and pinned in a coil around the top of her head. Her face was delicate and pretty, her high cheekbones flushed pink. Over her drab blue *chuba* she wore the plain apron of an unmarried woman, on her feet a pair of embroidered felt boots with upturned toes.

'Nyima?' the old woman said again, turning her head.

'I am here. What is it?'

'Make tea for these visitors. They have come a long way.'

Nyima smiled tentatively at Tsering and Maggie, her gaze resting a little longer on Maggie, taking in her Western features. Then she stood back from the doorway and gestured, waiting for them to go in before her. The old woman was pushing herself up from her chair, reaching for her walking stick.

'Wait a moment,' Nyima said.

'Let me help.' Tsering took hold of the old woman's arm and lifted her from the chair, then supported her as she hobbled unsteadily into the house.

The single room inside was sparsely furnished, very similar to Samdrup's house in Nyingchi. There was a curtained-off bedroom area at one end, a makeshift altar at the other and a hearth on the back wall, a wooden couch and a couple of chairs drawn up before it.

Tsering assisted the old woman to one of the chairs and eased her down gently, holding on to her hand for a time after she was seated.

'Thank you,' she said.

'Are you comfortable there?' Tsering asked solicitously.

'I am fine. You are very kind.'

Tsering moved away and stood by the hearth. He watched Nyima mixing tea with a chunk of yak butter, but every few seconds his gaze went back to the old woman. She was hunched in the chair, her sightless eyes fixed on the fire. Her face was lined, the skin dark and wrinkled like tree bark, and her hands, resting on the arms of the chair, trembled as if they were shrivelled leaves moving in a breeze.

'There are two of you?' she asked.

'Yes,' Tsering replied.

'And the other? Your companion?'

'She speaks no Tibetan.'

'No Tibetan?' the old woman repeated, frowning. 'She is Chinese?'

'No, she is from another country.'

'Your wife?'

Tsering hesitated. 'No, we are travelling together, that is all. When did you lose your sight?'

'It started to go a few years back. Then it became worse.'

'How do you manage?'

'My neighbours are good to me. One of them works my fields and shares the produce. And Nyima looks after me. She is very good to me.'

Tsering turned to the girl. 'You live here too?'

She shook her head. 'My family lives in the village. I just come in every day to cook and look after the house. She has no family of her own.'

Tsering gave a nod and looked away, his expression hidden. Nyima poured butter tea into bowls and offered them to Maggie and Tsering. Maggie didn't have the heart to refuse.

'*Tujaychay*,' she said.

Nyima smiled, exuding a serene, welcoming warmth. She continued to stare curiously at her as Maggie forced down the tea. It was thick and greasy and the taste of the butter almost made her gag. She'd sampled plenty of unappetising food around the world – sheep's brains, goat's testicles, pickled rats, iguanas, snakes and assorted reptiles – and knew how to close off her nose as she ate to prevent herself tasting what she was eating. She drank the tea quickly to bring the ordeal to an end. Nyima misunderstood her haste and held out the kettle to replenish her bowl. Maggie shook her head vigorously and thanked the girl again in her fractured Tibetan.

'You said she spoke no Tibetan,' the old woman said accusingly to Tsering.

'Only a little,' Tsering replied. He drank some of his tea, seemingly unable to take his gaze off the old woman. Once, he looked away briefly and the light from the fire gleamed on moisture in his eyes.

'Have any other strangers come to the village today?' he asked.

'I have seen none,' the old woman said. 'Nyima?'

'No, you are the first in many months,' the girl confirmed. She was studying Tsering carefully, a pensive crease on her brow. 'Where are you going?'

'To the north,' Tsering answered vaguely.

'You have family there?'

'We have business to see to.'

'Business?'

'Your tea is very good,' Tsering said, changing the subject before she could pursue her line of questioning. 'But we have imposed on you enough. Is there somewhere we can bed down for the night?'

'You will stay here,' the old woman said.

'No, we cannot do that.'

'There is room,' the old woman said firmly. 'Nyima, will you see to it?'

'Gladly.'

'It is too much,' Tsering said. 'You are an old lady. Is there not somewhere else we can go?'

'You are our guests. You will stay here,' the old woman insisted.

Reluctantly, Tsering acquiesced. 'You are most hospitable.'

Nyima stood up from her stool. 'I will fetch some water for you to wash.'

'No, let me,' Tsering said. He took the wooden pail from her grasp and went towards the door.

'The well is . . .' Nyima began, but Tsering had already gone.

Maggie glanced after him. She hadn't been able to follow the conversation in Tibetan, but she'd worked out some of the gist of it from the body language. So she wasn't surprised when the young girl beckoned to her from another doorway at the back of the room. They went out into a tiny stone-flagged yard and through a door into a stone outhouse which had been made into another bedroom. It was dark and claus-trophobic, only just big enough for a narrow raised wooden platform along one wall. It had a dry, musty smell as if it hadn't been used for years. Nyima gestured at the bed, miming a sleeping action. Maggie nodded and smiled to show she'd understood. Nyima went out, returning a few minutes later with some blankets which she placed on the platform. Then she left Maggie alone in the room.

Maggie pushed open the shutters over the small window and looked out. Behind the house the mountains rose steeply upwards. The lower slopes were in darkness, but higher up the rays of the setting sun still glowed on the bare rock outcrops and the shimmering iced peaks. Maggie gazed at them, absorbing the tranquillity of the scene, her eyes following the contours of the mountains, moving ever upwards towards the juncture of earth and sky, the point where the Tibetans believed you could pass from one cosmos to another. The peace, the emptiness seemed to filter into her mind and calm it.

As darkness fell, she became aware of the temperature dropping. Shivering a little, she sat down on the edge of the bed and wrapped a blanket around herself. Underneath the window she noticed a small wooden cupboard standing on the floor. She pulled open the door. Inside was a collection of what seemed to be children's toys: a rubber ball, a brass bell, a carved wooden bear with a chipped face and flanks polished smooth by years of handling. Beneath the toys was a black and white photograph, curling at the edges. Maggie took it out. It was old and faded, almost a sepia print. She carried it to the window where there was more light and looked at it.

It was a typical family snapshot of a young boy – slightly over-exposed, a touch out of focus. He was squinting awkwardly at the camera with a stone wall in the background. There was a sadness in his face, a dark melancholy in his eyes. Maggie studied the picture more closely and felt an icy chill creep down her back. She stared at the photograph, numb with shock.

Still in a daze, she put the photograph back in the cupboard and closed the door.

Tsering was outside at the front of the house, looking across the valley to the mountains on the other side. Maggie came out of the door and stood next to him in silence. She lit a cigarette and smoked it quietly. Nyima had put the old woman to bed and returned to her own home. It was just the two of them now. They seemed to have the whole valley to themselves.

'This must be very painful for you,' Maggie said.

Tsering turned his head. 'Why do you say that?'

'You know this place, don't you?'

She gave him time. When he didn't reply, she went on. 'The room I'm in, out at the back. I found some child's toys. There was a photograph of a young boy, taken years ago. The resemblance was unmistakable.'

Still he didn't respond. Maggie exhaled and watched the cigarette smoke drift into the indigo sky. 'Am I prying too much? You can tell me to shut up, you know.' She paused. 'The old lady . . .'

The question hung in the air over them for a long moment. Maggie didn't look at Tsering. She didn't want to see his face.

Finally, he spoke, his voice choking with emotion. 'She is my mother.'

This time Maggie didn't respond. Either the conversation ended here, or he had to go on unprompted. It had to be his choice.

'That was my bedroom,' he continued softly. 'Until I was nine, when the monks took me away.'

'To the monastery up the hill?'

'Yes. I knew the Chinese had destroyed it, but it was still a shock to see the ruins. To see where I'd lived for all those years turned into a pile of rubble.'

'When were you last here?'

'Thirteen years ago. I was living at Drepung Monastery, near Lhasa. I transferred there after I took my final vows. I came home for a short visit. When I returned to Lhasa, I got caught up in the disturbances at the Jokhang. You know about that?'

'In '89? Yes.'

'The Chinese were rounding up monks they suspected of

taking part. I fled to India. I didn't have time to say goodbye to my mother.'

'You've not heard from her since?'

'I have written regularly from India and for a time I got letters in return. But for the last five years I've heard nothing. I didn't even know she'd lost her sight.'

'The Chinese blocked her letters?'

Tsering nodded. 'And my letters never got through to her either. Can you imagine what that was like for her? Hearing nothing from her only son who'd abandoned her.'

'You didn't abandon her.'

'Didn't I?'

He looked away. Maggie glanced at him covertly. There were tears on his cheeks.

'She is all alone here,' Tsering said. 'Blind, frail, struggling to survive in poverty. And I am one of those pampered monks you spoke about, living in comfort in India.'

'She has no other children?'

'Just me. My two sisters died of smallpox in infancy.'

'And your father? How did he die?'

'He was just a farmer, as I said. Those are our fields down there on the valley floor. The soil is poor, stony. He broke his back trying to grow enough to feed us. But he could read and write a little. The monks from the monastery taught him. When the Red Guards came during the Cultural Revolution they singled him out as an intellectual and a landowner. They bound him and subjected him to a *thamzing* in the village square. We had to stand and watch while he was beaten. Then they made him kneel down and shot him in the head. They wouldn't let us take the body away for burial until we paid them the price of the bullet.'

Maggie felt her skin go cold. How did you live with something like that? How did a four-year-old child cope with such an experience?

'She doesn't recognise my voice,' Tsering said. 'She doesn't know it's me.'

'You haven't told her?'

'No.'

'Are you going to?'

'I can't. I am here with a task to complete, a task which is more important than either me or my mother. I can't tell her who I am and then leave her again. That would be the worst cruelty. To come back and then desert her again. To abandon her to her lonely old age. It would break her heart.'

He fell silent again. Maggie didn't look at him, but she knew he was weeping. She tossed her cigarette away and went back into the house. Leaving Tsering alone with his memories. And with his conscience.

FIFTEEN

Unlike most of his fellow PSB officers, Major Chang Wei did not regard Tibet as a hardship posting. He saw it as an opportunity to show his mettle. There were challenges in the region that gave an ambitious policeman scope to demonstrate his true talents. And Chang was ambitious. If he did well in Tibet, he knew he stood a good chance of a transfer back east to one of the big cities – Guangzhou, Shanghai, perhaps even Beijing itself.

He had Party connections in the capital. The wife of one of his uncles was related to the nephew of a Central Committee member: a fairly tenuous link but sufficient to gain him preferment over other less fortunate members of the *Gong An Ju* – provided he did nothing to blot his copybook. Political contacts would count for nothing if he made errors or disgraced himself in Tibet.

Not that he entertained the slightest notion of failing. His rise through the ranks had been swift, his promotions based largely on merit. He was a thorough, dedicated officer, blessed with a flair for intelligence gathering and a dispassionate ruthlessness which enabled him to act on that intelligence with a ferocious zeal. He had no time for diplomacy or negotiation. He believed in the iron fist inside the iron glove; a personal philosophy that had stood him in good stead for it was also the official state policy in Tibet. All opposition had to be crushed, all dissent suppressed, all enemies of the Party destroyed. And of all the enemies that were present in the region, the most pernicious, the most

240

dangerous were the monks. Which was why he was so implacably determined to catch the three who were at large in the mountains of Kham.

Their status alone made them foes, but it was their mission that presented the greatest threat to the supremacy of the Party. For more than forty years the Dalai Lama had led and orchestrated the opposition to Chinese rule in Tibet. If another leader, another 'chosen one' were found, the dissent would undoubtedly continue. But without a figurehead to rally around, a spiritual mentor to follow, the Tibetans' resistance, and the Buddhist faith that bolstered their resistance, would wither and die. Chang saw it as his sacred duty to prevent the monks from carrying out their appointed task.

But first, he had to find them.

It was almost forty-eight hours since the white Toyota van had slipped from his grasp on the landslide. The van had been found later, hidden in the woods, but of its occupants there had been no sign. Chang was getting impatient.

'They can't have disappeared into thin air,' he snapped at Chou Wo, the lieutenant who'd dragged him from the mud before the Landcruiser and its driver had gone over the edge.

'The area is heavily forested,' Chou replied in a conciliatory tone. 'To search it all on foot would take a whole division several months.'

'We have no sightings?'

'Just the trader we stopped yesterday. You've seen the report. He met a man and his wife heading north. No one else. We've had no other sightings since.'

Chang glanced out of the window of the office he'd commandeered in the PSB district headquarters in Chamdo. The sky was clear, the sun shining on the mountains.

'What's the weather forecast for the area?'

'Good. We should be able to get a helicopter up.'

'And the commandos?'

'On stand-by, as you ordered, Comrade Major.'

'Get me the map.'

241

Chang studied the layout of the area, noting the location where the abandoned van had been found.

'How far could a man walk in a day?' he asked.

'In this terrain, no more than twenty kilometres, I would say.'

Chang drew a pencil circle on the map. 'Concentrate the search in this area. From both the air and the ground.'

'If they are holed up somewhere in the forest, it may be difficult to find them,' Chou said. 'Perhaps impossible.'

'Impossible?' Chang snarled. 'Never mention that word again in my presence, Lieutenant. It is not part of the *Gong An Ju* vocabulary. Do you understand?'

'Yes, Comrade Major.' Chou hesitated. 'Comrade Major, these men, these monks . . . what is it they have done? What offence have they committed?'

'All you need to know at the moment, Lieutenant, is that they are very dangerous, and must be caught.' Chang looked back at the map. 'There are a few isolated villages in this area. Send the commandos in to search them, one by one.'

'As you wish, Comrade Major.'

'This one here.' Chang peered at the tiny characters on the map. 'What's it called?'

Chou leaned closer. 'Pangor.'

'Start there.'

Maggie watched the two specks in the distance drawing closer: two indistinct figures on the far side of the valley, walking along the pale ribbon of track that skirted the fields. As they came nearer, she could see they were men, could recognise their shapes, their gaits.

'Tsering, I think it's them.'

Tsering looked up from the hearth where he was talking quietly with his mother, then came across to the window. Neither of them had been outside since daybreak. The house was set apart from the others in the village, but it seemed wise to stay out of sight. The fewer people who knew they were there the better. Tsering studied the approaching figures and nodded. He turned to Nyima who'd come in earlier to help his mother out of bed and make her breakfast and asked her to go out and escort the two men to the house.

The girl walked down the slope to the valley floor and met Lobsang and Jigme at the bottom. Maggie watched her talking to them, pointing back at the house, and became suddenly aware of a noise. It was outside somewhere, getting louder. With a sickening jolt, she realised what it was: a helicopter.

'Tsering!'

He'd heard it too. He ran out of the door and yelled at Lobsang and Jigme. The two monks looked up in alarm and started to run. The clattering noise increased in volume, reverberating across the valley so that it was impossible to pinpoint the direction from which it was coming.

Lobsang and Jigme scrambled up the slope, their bags swinging from their shoulders. Jigme lost his footing and slipped backwards, one hand reaching out to stop himself falling. Lobsang grabbed his arm and dragged him back up. Tsering was in the doorway urging them on, his eyes scanning the sky for a glimpse of the helicopter.

'Hurry! Over here!'

The two monks reached the doorway. Tsering bundled them inside just as the helicopter came over the ridge behind the house. It passed over the village and started to descend, hovering down to land in one of the bare fields. A squad of men in dark green combat fatigues and steel helmets, submachine-guns slung across their chests, jumped out and headed for the houses. Tsering turned to Nyima.

'We have to hide! It's important. They must not find us. The barn?'

Nyima nodded and led them out through the back and across the yard to the small stone barn. Inside the barn were bales of straw and bundles of green oats used for fodder for feeding the animals in winter. Nyima dragged aside a couple of the bales to reveal a rectangle of wooden slats set into the packed earth floor. She pulled out a few of the slats.

Underneath was a shallow storage cavity, perhaps four metres by two, and about a metre deep. Lobsang, Jigme and Maggie dropped down into the hole. Tsering paused on the rim.

'You haven't seen us, remember? Any of us. Tell the old lady she mustn't say a word.'

'She won't. She hates the Chinese more than anyone.'

Tsering slid down into the cavity and Nyima replaced the slats, pushing the bales of straw back into place on top. There was just enough room for all four of them. They were squeezed together, half sitting, half lying, their legs and feet entwined, close enough to feel the warmth of one another's breath. It wasn't completely dark. Traces of dusty light seeped in through the gaps in the slats, playing across their faces, their tight, anxious features, as they waited.

Several minutes elapsed, then the intensity of the light increased abruptly. Someone had opened the door of the barn. There were footsteps, heavy boots thudding on the earth floor, the clink of a sub-machine-gun swinging against something metallic – a belt buckle or a brass button. No one moved. The footsteps got louder. Through a crack at the edge of the slats, Maggie saw the toe of a polished army boot coming to rest next to one of the bales of straw. It stayed there for a moment. Maggie imagined the soldier staring around the interior of the barn, scanning the corners, the rafters. Just don't look down, she prayed. Don't even think about shifting the bales.

The boot swung out of sight, moving away across the barn. Outside someone shouted a command in Chinese. The footsteps receded. The barn door banged shut and the dim light returned. In the cavity, there was an audible exhalation. Positions were adjusted, cramped legs and arms stretched to relieve the tension. Then they were still again, completely motionless, listening.

The minutes passed: ten, fifteen, thirty. Then in the distance, faint but unmistakable, they heard the helicopter engine start, the whirring crescendo of the rotor blades turning. The volume increased, swelling to a climax as the helicopter passed overhead, before dying away to nothing.

Someone else entered the barn. Different footsteps this time. Lighter, softer. The bales of straw were slid aside and the slats removed. Nyima looked down at them.

'They've gone.'

They hauled themselves out of the hole and brushed the dust and soil off their clothes.

'They searched the whole village,' Nyima went on.

'Did they say anything?' Tsering asked.

'They told us to be on the lookout for three men – three dangerous criminals on the run.'

'We are not criminals.'

'I know. To the Han, all Tibetans are dangerous criminals.'

'Did they mistreat you?'

'The officer shouted a lot. Warned us what would happen to us if we were caught sheltering the men. But they didn't mistreat us.'

'The old lady?'

'They ignored her. She is all right.'

'We are going north. We will leave now.'

'Wait till nightfall,' Nyima said. 'There is little cover in the valley. If the helicopter comes back, they will see you.'

'We will never find our way in the dark.'

'I will guide you. There is a hut up in the mountains. The herdsmen use it during the summer grazing season, but they have brought all their animals down now. You can hide there.'

Tsering looked the girl in the eye. 'You do not know us, you do not know what kind of men we are, yet you are willing to trust us like this?'

Nyima gave a careless shrug, as if the matter were not worth discussing. 'You are honest men, good men. I can see that. Why should I not trust you?'

For the rest of the day they stayed holed up in the house. The helicopter came back once more, making a pass up the valley and back, but it didn't land. Maggie spent the time sitting by the window, getting bored and smoking too many cigarettes. She thought about getting out the camcorder that had lain untouched in her bag for days now and taping something, she wasn't sure what, but she couldn't summon the necessary resolve. Somehow it didn't seem very important. Once or twice Jigme came over and chatted to her inconsequentially, but Lobsang and Tsering kept themselves to themselves, the former brooding by the fire or walking up and down in the yard, the latter talking quietly to his mother. Maggie watched Tsering every now and again, wondering what they were saying. She guessed he was catching up on the years they'd been apart, filling in the gaps, getting to know her again. But how did he do that without revealing who he was?

Nyima was always nearby, busying herself around the hearth, joining in occasionally with their conversation. In the middle of the day she returned to her parents' house for a few hours, but came back later in the afternoon to prepare the evening meal for them – more butter tea and *tsampa* with a side dish of spicy curried turnips. She seemed fascinated by Tsering. Perhaps more than just fascinated. He was a striking man. Tall, strong, handsome. There were moments when Maggie saw Nyima gazing at the monk with a look any woman could recognise – that age-old look of attraction: shy, uncertain, her expression a montage of deep, confused feelings.

At dusk, they slung their bags over their shoulders and prepared to leave. Tsering thanked his mother for her hospitality and clasped one of her hands in both his own, unable to find any words. He turned away, hiding the anguish in his face, and walked quickly to the door as if he feared that he would not have the strength to wrench himself away if he lingered any longer.

They went down the slope and across the fields, keeping clear of the village. For three hours they walked up the valley, then they began to climb. There was no path, but Nyima knew the way. Sure-footed as a mountain goat, she led them up the rocky slope, pausing every few minutes to let them catch up with her, giving instructions, pointing out the hazards to avoid.

They walked in silence, saving their breath for the ascent. Then, after four or five hours, they reached the herdsmen's hut. It was a small stone building nestling in the shelter of a slight hollow. Just below it was a spring where they quenched their thirst before going inside the hut. Nyima lit an oil lantern that hung from one of the roof beams. The interior was austere and Spartan. No furniture, no beds, just a few wooden planks laid out on the earth floor. Yak-dung patties were stacked in piles next to the hearth and the whole place stank of animals – of sheep and goats and yaks.

'No one will come here,' Nyima said. 'You will be safe.'

'We are grateful for your help,' Tsering said.

Nyima flashed a smile. 'I must go back down now.'

Tsering went outside with her and they walked a little way from the hut.

'You are very good to the old lady in the village,' Tsering said. 'You have a kind, generous heart.'

In the darkness, Nyima flushed. 'She is old, blind. She has no one else. The whole village looks after her.'

'Without you, we would have been caught by the Chinese. Please don't take offence, but we would like to show our gratitude.'

Tsering held out a wad of money he'd taken from the fold of his *chuba*.

'Please, take it.'

'I cannot,' Nyima said. 'You do not need to pay me for helping you against the Han. Any enemy of the Chinese is a friend of mine.'

'Then take it for the old lady. As payment for her hospitality.'

'It is not necessary.'

Tsering took hold of Nyima's hand and pressed the money into the palm.

'I insist. She is poor and frail. Money cannot compensate

her for having no family to take care of her, but it can alleviate some of the hardship of her situation. Use it as you think best.'

Nyima looked down at the notes in her hand. 'It is too much.'

'No,' Tsering said. 'It is not nearly enough.'

Nyima had her eyes on his face now. There was just enough light from the moon to see his taut, earnest expression.

'It's strange,' she said. 'We have only just met, and I have never been further than a week's walk from my home village, yet I feel I have met you before.'

'Perhaps it was in another life,' Tsering said.

'Perhaps,' Nyima replied, but she didn't sound convinced.

'Take care on the descent,' Tsering said.

Nyima laughed. 'I have been up here hundreds of times, bringing food to my father and my brothers while they tended the animals. I could walk it with my eyes shut.'

Tsering watched her climb up the side of the hollow. On the rim, she paused to wave briefly, then was gone.

Tsering remained where he was. He didn't feel up to facing the others again just yet. He needed the solitude of the open, the emptiness of the mountains around him. Never in his life had a parting from his mother been such agony. The ones before had been difficult, but none had compared to the pain of this one. At nine, he had been taken away to the monastery. He'd been a child, a scared child, but he'd had no choice. It was his destiny. And his mother had still been close at hand. She had visited him in the monastery, he'd come back to the village at intervals to see her. His transfer to Drepung when he was twenty-one had been even less of a trauma. He'd been wrapped up in his studies, the excitement of finally going to Lhasa. With the selfish preoccupation of young manhood he had barely given his mother a thought. He had a new life ahead of him and that was all that concerned him. Deciding to flee Tibet for India had been a more momentous decision, but again it had been forced on him by external circumstances. Had he stayed, he would have faced the risk of arrest and imprisonment, and for monks that meant the labour camps and almost certain death from cold and starvation and maltreatment. He'd felt he had no real option but to leave.

But now? He was a mature man now, responsible for his own decisions. He'd come back and seen how frail his mother was, how poor and lonely. And he'd walked away from her of his own volition. The guilt he felt was like a knife in his heart. He'd sat and talked to her for hours. She'd told him about the son she hadn't heard from for years and he had been unable to relieve her sorrow by revealing who he was. That was a cruel, inhuman thing to do, but the alternative – as he'd explained to Maggie – had seemed to him even more cruel. His mother believed he was dead. She had come to terms with it. It was probably better to leave things like that. Besides, in a way, perhaps he *was* dead.

They snatched a few hours' uncomfortable sleep during what remained of the night and at first light roused themselves and made breakfast, brewing tea and eating some of the coarse brown bread Nyima had given them. The three monks engaged in an animated discussion, the map unfolded before them, while Maggie watched, trying unsuccessfully to understand what they were saying. Finally, her frustration got the better of her.

'Please speak English,' she said. 'I'm included in this. What are you talking about?'

'It's none of your business,' Lobsang growled.

'You're discussing what to do next, aren't you? Well, that *is* my business. You can't cut me out of it.'

'You didn't have to come with us,' Lobsang retorted. '*We* didn't ask you.'

'You still on about that?' Maggie said. 'I thought we'd sorted that all out back in Lhasa. I'm part of the group now.'

'You'll never be part of the group as far as I'm concerned.'

'Let's calm down,' Tsering interjected. He turned to Lobsang: 'She needs to know what's going on.' Then to

Maggie: 'We're debating whether to stay here all day and walk on tonight when it gets dark, or walk on now.'

'If we head off now, what do we do if the helicopter comes back?' Maggie said.

'That is the main drawback. On the other hand, walking at night in terrain like this could be very dangerous. One wrong foot and we could go over a precipice. In addition, none of us knows the way and navigating in the dark will be difficult. We also have to consider what we do if we rest during the day. There's very little cover up here. The helicopter is quite likely to spot us.'

'Let me see the map.'

Maggie pulled the sheet on to her knee and pored over it. 'Where's the helicopter coming from? Where's its base?'

'Probably Chamdo,' Tsering said. 'There are no other major airfields in Kham.'

'That's more than a hundred kilometres away. It will take time getting here in the morning, and it will need time to get back to refuel in the evening. That gives us a few hours at each end of the day when it may be safe to walk. No guarantees, but it's probably our best bet.'

'You think so?'

'We rest in the middle part of the day. We don't use the tents except if the weather turns bad again and there's a mist to cover us. We find holes, gulleys, caves, anything we can, and sleep there.'

'What do you think?' Tsering asked the other two.

Lobsang gave a contemptuous snort, unwilling to consider anything Maggie suggested, but Jigme nodded his approval.

'It seems to make sense to me.'

'Lobsang? Your thoughts?'

Lobsang shrugged indifferently. 'Whatever. I don't mind. Sitting around here talking isn't going to do us much good.'

'Then let's walk on for a few hours.'

The terrain around the hut was high, undulating pasture, rolling folds of hills covered in coarse grass. In the summer it would have been scattered with herds of grazing sheep and goats, but now it was deserted. High above the pasture jagged, snow-daubed peaks and sheer rock edges rose twenty thousand feet and more into the hazy sky.

They filled their water canteens from the spring and set off in a northerly direction, taking their bearings from the sun and heading for a notch in the ring of mountains that encircled them. It was cool to start with, but as the sun got higher it warmed up, turning into a brilliant clear day. Maggie could feel the rays of the sun on her exposed face and arms, burning through the thin atmosphere and searing her skin.

A few hundred metres below the pass that led into the next valley they came across a rockfall at the top of a scree slope where part of an escarpment had collapsed. The boulders, some as big as cars, lay in a jumbled heap, propped one on top of the other at various angles so that underneath there were hidden cavities. Lobsang and Jigme crawled into one of the cavities and Tsering and Maggie clambered higher and found another just big enough for them both to sit up in. It was a relief to be out of the glaring sun. Maggie leant back on the cool rock. She was completely concealed from the air, but through a gap in the boulders she had a perfect view back over the fell they'd just crossed. She closed her eyes and tried to sleep, but her brain was too alert. She was impatient to move on. Tsering too was wide awake, staring bleakly into space.

'Can't sleep either?' Maggie said.

'Pardon?'

'You're thinking about your mother, aren't you?'

It was a moment before he answered. 'Yes. I'm wondering if I did the right thing. Perhaps I should have told her it was me after all. Given her a moment of happiness. She's had so few in her life.'

Maggie waited, sensing he wanted to talk, that for once he needed to talk.

'My sisters both died before they were five years old. Then my father was killed. Then I went into the monastery. For most of her life she has been alone. The monks should never have taken me.'

'You were a *tulku*,' Maggie said. Tsering glanced at her in surprise. 'Jigme told me,' she explained.

'Yes, I was a *tulku*. It was a great honour. My mother was proud of me, was glad that I would receive an education and have a good life. But it condemned her to a life of loneliness and unceasing labour. If I'd stayed at home, I could have helped her work the fields, look after the animals. I have repaid her love and devotion with neglect and selfishness.'

'You can't blame yourself.'

'Can't I?'

'You were just a child when you went into the monastery.'

'But later I could have done more for her.'

'Perhaps. But that's a universal regret, perhaps an unavoidable one. We all could do more for our parents, but how many of us do? We have to break loose, learn to be independent, and that inevitably creates a rift. Your mother would not have expected you to stay tied to her apron strings. Nor would she have wanted you to.'

'I'll probably never see her again,' Tsering said desolately.

'You believe she'll be reborn?'

'Yes. But that doesn't make it easier to leave her now.'

'I've always thought a belief in reincarnation would be a comfort in life.'

'No, it's a comfort in death. In life we are just as frail, just as prone to grief and sorrow as those who believe in a final extinction.'

Tsering knew that happiness was transient. The fundamental essence of his faith was that happiness could never be permanent for those trapped in the cyclical existence of life and death and rebirth. Only when true enlightenment released a soul from the sorrows of *samsara* was lasting happiness a possibility. Until then, what joy a person found could never be more than fleeting for it was always replaced in turn by pain and longing and suffering. Mortal ties were just that: thin threads that could be severed as easily as gossamer. A belief in reincarnation could not shield you from that reality. It could not spare you the anguish of loss. Tsering believed that death was not the end for the human soul, but in life it is not souls that we love.

In the afternoon, the helicopter returned. They heard it coming long before they saw it top the ridge at the southern end of the valley, a small buzzing insect silhouetted against the skyline.

'Pull your feet in,' Maggie said to Tsering whose boots were sticking out into the open.

'They won't see my feet from that height, surely?' he said.

'They don't need to see them. They'll have thermal imaging equipment in the helicopter.'

'What's that?'

'It detects body heat. Shows an image on a screen. Even from something as small as a human foot.'

'Then they will detect the rest of our bodies too.'

'It can't penetrate solid rock. Stay back under the boulder and we're invisible to it.'

'How do you know this?'

'Experience.'

Maggie knew better than to underestimate the Chinese. Their worldwide image was that of a Third World nation of backward peasants, but their military capability was awesome. The communist government might struggle to combat endemic poverty and malnutrition, but there was always plenty of money for the apparatus of state security, much of it targeted at Tibet.

The helicopter flew overhead and on into the next valley. Half an hour later it came back, a couple of kilometres away to the west. That was the last they saw of it.

Towards evening, they had a meal of boiled noodles and tea, then they emerged from their hiding places and walked on over the pass.

'Colonel Shen on the phone for you, Comrade Major.'

Chang composed himself, straightening the tunic of his uniform as if he were standing before his superior instead of sitting in an office a thousand kilometres away. He picked up the telephone.

'Major Chang here, Comrade Colonel.'

'Have you found them?' Shen demanded, getting straight to the point of his call.

'Not yet. But we are making progress,' Chang replied.

'Progress is not good enough. We want this brought to a conclusion. You understand?'

'Yes, Comrade Colonel.'

Chang could tell from his tone that Shen was getting jittery. And that could mean only one thing: Beijing.

'There has been a development,' Shen went on, confirming Chang's suspicions. 'The riot outside the Jokhang. Somehow a tape was made of it and smuggled out of the country. It's been on the television news all around the world – America, Europe, Japan, everywhere. The Party leadership is livid. The last thing they want is the human rights and Tibet issues back on the world agenda.'

'But our hard line is Party policy,' Chang said automatically, chastising himself silently the moment the words were out of his mouth.

'Don't be stupid, Major,' Shen snapped. 'I know it's Party policy. So does the leadership. But that's not the impression they want the outside world to have. The Central Committee is baying for blood. We're doing everything we can here. We have two hundred splittists in custody, we've shut down Lhasa tighter than a Mongolian's arse, but we need something more. Something to appease the leadership. We need the monks. Capturing them would be a great propaganda coup for us.'

'You will have them, Comrade Colonel,' Chang promised confidently. 'We have narrowed down our search to a very small area. I have men on the ground and a helicopter and spotter plane in the air. It will not be long now.'

'You have forty-eight hours, Major.'

The line went dead. Chang replaced the receiver slowly and gazed across the shabby office, its floor scuffed and dirty, the furniture fit only for firewood. He gave an involuntary shudder. This was what awaited him if he failed to deliver on his promise.

'Lieutenant!' he shouted.

Chou came in warily, still not used to the major's violent mood swings.

'What's the latest report from the field?' Chang asked.

'No sighting yet, Comrade Major. The officers on the ground are still combing the forested areas, but it's slow work.'

'And the air search? The helicopter and plane?'

'Nothing.'

'What about the villages?'

'We've checked every one. Examined papers, searched the houses. There were no outsiders present, no visitors passing through and none of the villagers questioned had seen any strangers in the vicinity.'

'Mmm.' Chang sat back in his chair, stroking his pock-marked jawline thoughtfully. 'Something puzzles me,' he said eventually. 'A few days ago we had a sighting of a man and his wife heading north up a forest track. Going to visit relatives, they claimed, if I remember correctly.'

'That's right, Comrade Major,' Chou said.

Chang looked at the lieutenant. 'So where did they go?'

SIXTEEN

They walked through the evening, crossing another deserted expanse of grass-covered fell, and kept going after night had fallen. The terrain was easy to negotiate – no cliffs, no treacherous drops, no hazardous climbs – and there was a bright moon to light the way.

Only when they were close to dropping with exhaustion did they stop to rest. Wrapping blankets around themselves to keep out the biting cold, they slept under the stars for an hour, then walked on.

When the first glimmers of the dawn crept over the horizon to the east, they were just coming up on to a high sinewy ridge. Tsering stopped, looking ahead, the wind buffeting his body. Far in the distance, one particular mountain stood out from the surrounding peaks. It wasn't the highest in the range, nor the most spectacular, but something about the way the sun was rising meant its summit was bathed in a pool of brilliant light as if some giant celestial torch were focused on it. The mountains all around it were still in shadow, but this one was like a beacon, its distinctive three peaks blazing in the dawn sky like an ice-diamond crown.

'Mount Gebur,' Tsering breathed.

They gazed at it for several minutes, entranced by its dazzling aura.

Then Maggie said: 'How far is it?'

'Two, three days' walk,' Tsering replied.

Maggie took her camcorder out of her bag and checked the light meter, the settings. Then she switched to 'record' and panned across the horizon, coming to rest on the sunlit mountain. She repeated the move as a backup and added some footage of the three monks standing on the ridge gazing intently at their destination.

The sighting seemed to invigorate them. They plunged down the slope with a renewed energy and pressed on across the high plateau. They continued as long as they dared and in the middle of the morning, when they reached a gulley cut deep into the ground, decided to stop and hole up for the day. The gulley was narrow, a knife-cleft in the mountain, with overhanging sides which offered protection against being spotted from the air. Once they were in the bottom, the rock walls closed in over their heads, leaving only a tiny strip of sky visible. They made butter tea and finished the last of their bread before lying down and going to sleep.

In the middle of the afternoon, Maggie was woken by the sound of an engine overhead. As the noise grew louder, she realised it wasn't a helicopter this time, but a plane. Looking up, she caught a glimpse of a wing high in the sky. Then the sound gradually receded and a silent stillness returned to the gulley.

'What was it?' Tsering asked. He was lying in the shadow of a boulder a few metres away.

'A plane,' Maggie said.

'A search plane?'

'Probably. Now would be a good time to move on.'

'What if it comes back?'

'If it's searching for us, it will work on a grid pattern, criss-crossing a square of territory, then moving on to the next square. It's already covered this area. There's no reason for it to come back.'

'You've encountered this before? Being hunted from the air?'

'I've been with people who were being hunted, yes. Rebels, guerrilla units. But never in such open country.'

'Will we be found?'

'Your guess is as good as mine.'

Tsering gazed at her quizzically. 'You are a strange woman, Miss Walsh. You puzzle me. You have no real need to be here with us. You have no real need to be anywhere in the world where people are fighting and dying, yet you choose to go there. Why? Why do you risk your life just to take a few television pictures?'

'I don't think about the risks,' Maggie said. 'If I did, I wouldn't do it.' She got to her feet and stretched. 'Let's get going.'

They climbed back out of the gulley and traversed the side of the mountain, descending into a corrie whose upper end was still filled with the previous winter's snow. The sides were too sheer to climb so they walked out of the open end and dropped down and around the lower edge of a rock spur. Below them, set in a deep basin, they saw an emerald lake with a village at its head.

Tsering set off down the hill at a rapid pace, the others following. Halfway down they had to make a detour around an escarpment and Tsering stopped. On the face of the escarpment was a fault line which widened at its base into a shallow cave. Tsering turned to Lobsang and Jigme and discussed something with them in Tibetan. Lobsang shook his head violently, obviously objecting to whatever was being proposed. Tsering gave a shrug, then he and Lobsang headed off towards the lake.

'We have to wait in the cave,' Jigme said to Maggie.

'You drew the short straw, eh?'

'What do you mean?'

'Having to stay with me.'

'I don't mind,' Jigme said. 'I've had enough of walking.'

They clambered up the loose scree and pulled themselves into the cave.

'You could have gone with them,' Maggie said. 'I don't need a babysitter.'

'That's not what happened. Tsering wanted to go alone, but Lobsang insisted on accompanying him.'

'That's what they were arguing about?'

'Not really arguing.' Jigme grinned. 'With Lobsang it just sounds that way.'

'I can't make him out. You and Tsering have a sort of calmness about you. Almost a serenity. But Lobsang seems so full of anger. Especially for a monk.'

'He's been through a lot. I can understand his anger. He was in prison for a long time.'

'How long?'

'Fourteen years.'

'For what?'

'The Chinese don't need a reason. Just being a monk is enough for them. He doesn't talk about it, but I've heard other monks describing what happened to him. He was sent to a labour camp in the Changtang. You know where I mean?'

Maggie nodded. The harsh, remote northern plateau of Tibet was notorious for its prisons. 'I'm surprised he survived. Not many do.'

'Lobsang is tough. The conditions up there are horrific. They give the prisoners no beds, no blankets. You lie together, keeping each other warm, and wake up in the morning and find your neighbours dead from the cold. Or you die of starvation, picking bits of undigested food out of your own faeces. If the cold or malnutrition don't kill you, then the brutality of the guards will. That's how he lost his fingers. The Chinese guards used to play games with an axe. They chopped them off.'

Maggie stared at him. 'Dear God. He had fourteen years of that?'

'Not all in the Changtang. He was transferred south later on. That's when he escaped. Broke out of the compound one night – I don't know how – and walked to India. Four hundred miles in the middle of winter. He lost four toes to frostbite. That's why he walks in that odd rolling way.'

'I think I can forgive him his anger,' Maggie said. She looked down the hill. The two figures were nearly at the lake. 'Where are they going?'

'To the village.'

'Why?'

'We have seen Mount Gebur. Now our search really begins.'

Maggie's head jerked round. 'You mean they're looking for the child? The reincarnation?' Jigme nodded. 'Jesus! Why didn't you tell me earlier?'

Maggie scrambled to her feet and grabbed her bag, cursing herself for her complacency.

'That's why I'm here,' she said angrily. 'That's the whole bloody point. I'm supposed to be taping it.'

She lowered herself over the rock lip at the entrance to the cave and slithered down the scree slope, leaning backwards into the hill and letting the loose rocks carry her down. She heard Jigme coming out of the cave behind her.

'Miss Walsh . . . wait . . .' Jigme called. 'Miss Walsh . . .'

Maggie slid off the bottom of the scree and glanced round. Jigme was stumbling unsteadily down the slope, his arms flapping sideways like wings as he tried to keep his balance. Maggie shouted a warning, but too late. Jigme leaned out too far and seemed to float for a moment in mid-air. Then he toppled forwards, twisting round and hitting the ground with his shoulder, glissading head first down the hill. Maggie moved aside as the rocks cascaded past her, skittering and bouncing into the valley. Jigme tumbled off the scree and lay there, gasping for breath, the straps of his bag wrapped awkwardly around his neck and shoulders.

'You hurt?' Maggie asked.

Jigme sat up, rubbing his bruised limbs. 'I don't think so.'

Maggie helped him to his feet. Then she took off down the hill, almost running towards the lake.

Tsering and Lobsang approached the first of the stone houses. A woman in a soiled *chuba* appeared in the doorway and regarded them suspiciously. Tsering smiled and bowed his head.

'*Tashi delek.*'

The woman returned the greeting, though with little warmth.

'What village is this?' Tsering asked.

'The village by the lake,' the woman replied. A small curious face peered out from around her legs. The woman shooed the child away.

'Are there many families here?' Tsering said.

The woman continued to gaze at them warily. She didn't reply. Tsering understood her reticence. Up here, visitors meant only one thing: trouble. He removed his cap, revealing his shaven head, trying to put her at ease. She relaxed visibly. Her expression became friendlier.

'You are monks?' she said.

'From Lhasa,' Tsering said.

'Lhasa?' The woman's eyes showed a spark of interest. 'You come from Lhasa?'

She understood now. These men weren't officials, weren't outsiders intent on prying into her life. They were simple monks from the holy city. Even here, deep in the mountains, it was the ambition of every single person to see the capital one day, to prostrate themselves before the image of the Jowo Sakyamuni in the Jokhang Temple. It was an ambition that most knew realistically would never be fulfilled, but could nevertheless be shared vicariously with those fortunate to have made the journey.

'What is the news?' the woman asked eagerly. 'We hear so little up here. What is happening in Lhasa?'

'We are tired. May we sit down for a moment?' Tsering said.

'Of course. Come inside.' She stepped back to let them enter.

'The bastards,' Maggie said with feeling. 'You should have told me what they were doing. How dare they try to stitch me up. I'm *part* of this. Whose idea was it? Tsering's? Lobsang's?'

Jigme didn't answer. He was struggling to keep pace with her as she hurried down the hill.

'What else aren't you telling me?' she demanded. 'What

other devious schemes are you plotting to keep me out of the way?'

'It wasn't deliberate,' Jigme said breathlessly.

'Of course it was deliberate. They didn't want me with them. What are the other signs? Have they seen one and not told me? Have they?'

'No. They have seen no other signs.'

'Don't lie to me, Jigme.'

'It's the truth. But we are close to Mount Gebur now. We have to check every village we come to. Seek out every new baby in case he is the one.'

Maggie surveyed the landscape in front of them, the tree-less, grass-covered fell, the lake with its deep viridian waters, the houses on the far shore squeezed tightly together like frightened animals clinging to the security of the herd. All around was a vast empty wilderness, a terrifying, hostile land that seemed to nibble at the fringes of the village, threatening to overwhelm it with its windswept desolation.

Maggie took out her camcorder and recorded the images, cutting them together in her head.

'Would you walk down the hill in front of me?' she said to Jigme.

'Pardon?'

'I need a person in the shot. Keep going until I say stop, please.'

Maggie taped him descending the slope, with the lake and village in the background. She could feel a fist of excitement, of anticipation in her stomach. At last, after all these days of travelling, they were getting close to their destination.

'Okay, that's far enough.'

Jigme stopped and turned, waiting for her to catch up with him. Maggie had gone very still, her gaze fixed on the horizon to the west. Out of the glare of the setting sun, a shape was emerging, a tiny black silhouette like a bird on the wing. Then the low, monotonous throb of its engine rolled across the fell in a wave.

'Shit!' Maggie said.

There was no point in running, the village was more than a mile away. And there was nowhere to hide, not even a boulder or a ditch that might shield them. Maggie stuffed the camcorder back into her bag and walked down the hill to Jigme.

'What do we do?' he asked anxiously.

'Pretend it isn't there.'

She walked on, pulling the peak of her cap down over her forehead, resisting the temptation to look up as the search plane passed by a thousand feet above her.

Tsering looked down at the baby in the woven osier basket. The child was asleep, lying on its back, swaddled in a yak-hair blanket. Its face still had the red, wrinkled features of a new-born infant, but it had a full head of fine black hair. With its squashed nose and flabby little mouth, it looked a bit like a pug-dog puppy, Tsering thought.

'When was he born?' he asked.

'A month ago,' the child's mother replied, gazing affectionately at the sleeping figure.

'Your first?'

'Yes.'

'A month, you say?'

That was too long. The Dalai Lama had been dead only three weeks. Tsering was reassured. He'd known instinctively, the moment he'd stepped into the house, that this was not the child. In part he'd had his doubts because they had not yet seen the remaining three signs from Pasang Rinpoche's vision at Lhamo Latso, but something inside him had also contributed to his uncertainty. He sensed very strongly – and whether this was vanity or self-delusion, he wasn't sure – that when they found the chosen one he would know it absolutely. There would be no doubts whatever.

'Is he . . .?' the mother asked.

Tsering delayed his reply, not wanting to hurt her gratuitously. In order to explain their undue interest in new-born boys in the village, they'd told the inhabitants they were searching for a *tulku*, for the reincarnation of a lama whose identity they left carefully unmentioned. Tsering studied the sleeping child again and shook his head gently.

'He is too old, born a week before our lama departed.'

The mother's expression flashed from disappointment to relief. It was an honour to have a *tulku* in the family – it conferred great status on his mother – but it was also a curse for it meant that in time the monks would claim him as their own. Tsering knew all about that dichotomy.

'Is this the only new baby in the village?' he asked.

The mother nodded. 'There are only twelve families. The others, they have all had their quota,' she said, referring to the Chinese population control measures.

'We are sorry to have disturbed you. We wish you joy of your . . .' Tsering broke off and spun round as the door to the house banged open and Maggie and Jigme burst in.

Maggie paused, taking in the scene. Then she marched across and looked down into the basket.

'Is this him? Is this the child? Have I missed it?'

'Miss Walsh . . .' Tsering began.

'We had a deal, remember? That's why I'm here.'

'This is not the child,' Tsering said defensively.

The baby, woken by the raised voices, started crying. The mother picked him up and rocked him gently in her arms.

'Let us go outside,' Tsering said.

'This was for you as much as for me,' Maggie said when they were out of the door. 'An independent record of the search to verify the authenticity of the child when you find him. *If* you find him. Yes, I want the story. But you also need my pictures. This is a symbiotic relationship and we're not going to get anywhere if we don't work together.'

Tsering looked away towards the lake. In the twilight the water was changing colour, turning from green to white so that it looked like a pool of spilt milk.

'You have to include me,' Maggie said, her anger waning. 'We need each other. Don't we?'

Tsering said nothing.

'Don't we?' she insisted.

Tsering sighed. 'Yes, we will include you, Miss Walsh. Anything is preferable to your yelling at me.'

'I don't yell,' Maggie said.

Tsering looked at her. She was almost smiling.

'And I don't stay angry for long,' she said.

'Good.'

Then Jigme said suddenly from the doorway: 'We were spotted from the air.'

Tsering turned. 'What?'

'We were coming down the hill when the plane came back.'

'You should have stayed in the cave,' Lobsang said reproachfully.

'It could have happened to you just as easily,' Jigme retorted. 'Ten minutes earlier and *you'd* have been caught in the open.'

'The damage is done,' Tsering interjected firmly before another argument could develop. 'They saw only a man and a woman. That is not unusual. We may have lost nothing. But we shouldn't linger here. By morning we must be as far from this village as possible.'

They picked up their bags and began to climb the hill away from the lake. In the distance, glistening on the horizon, the triple peaks of Mount Gebur seemed to beckon them onwards.

They walked for most of the night, snatching a few hours' sleep during the darkest hours after midnight, then continuing on without a break until dawn. Finding a sheltered hollow out of the wind that whistled across the fell, they lit the kerosene stove and made black tea and noodles, gulping down the unappetising food more because they felt they ought to than because they wanted to. They were all heavy-limbed and weary, their feet sore from the hard, unyielding ground, their lungs struggling to cope with the lack of oxygen. Maggie leaned against a rock and dozed fitfully, dreaming of a soft bed, a strong cup of coffee and a bacon sandwich, none of which she was likely to find in the forsee-able future.

'Miss Walsh? Wake up.'

Maggie opened her eyes to see Jigme leaning over her.

'We're going on now,' he said.

Maggie hauled herself to her feet and stretched her back and arms. The sky was growing lighter, a greyish hue spreading over the summits of the mountains. Maggie took out her camcorder and checked the meter reading. There was just enough light to record. She let the others set off without her and taped them as they walked away across the fell.

It took her half a mile to catch up with them, by which time they were descending a knife-edge ridge along the rim of another snow-filled corrie that was scooped out of the side of the mountain. It was a perilous descent. The wind was gusting over the ridge, flailing in their faces, battering their bodies hard enough to push them over the edge. For thirty terrifying minutes, they stumbled down the narrow hog's back, fighting to keep their footing in the howling gale. Then they dropped into the mouth of the corrie and the wind suddenly stopped. The air was completely still as if they'd entered a hermetically sealed micro-climate. They stood motionless, listening. But there was nothing to hear.

Below the corrie, the hillside sloped steeply down into a broad basin, bounded on the northern side by Mount Gebur which formed part of a chain of mountains encircling the basin. In the bottom of the depression was a group of tents, and the surrounding land was speckled with black dots which could only have been grazing yaks.

'*Drogpa.* Nomads,' Tsering said.

'Tsering . . .' Jigme was gazing intently across the basin.

'What is it?' Tsering said.

'Look . . . in the sky.'

High above them was a single white cloud, a billowing mass of cumulus with a distinct shape, like a great snow bear standing on its hind legs, its paws outstretched.

Maggie looked at the three monks, puzzled by their reaction to a simple cloud. 'What's so special about it?' she asked.

Jigme tore his eyes away for a moment. 'It is the second sign,' he said.

The film from the aerial camera in the spotter plane had been developed overnight, the prints greatly enlarged to show clearly the two figures walking down the hill.

'That's your missing man and wife, I think, Comrade Major,' Lieutenant Chou said.

Chang studied the photograph. One of the figures, from her build and shape, was obviously a woman. The other was bigger, wearing a *chuba* and a woollen cap. Chang examined him more closely under a magnifying glass.

'Take a look, Lieutenant. His cap covers only the crown of his head. Look at his scalp, around the ears and the back of the neck. Do you see much hair?'

Chou leaned over the print. 'Very little, Comrade Major. It seems to be cropped short.'

'Shaved, I believe. Where were they going?'

'Towards this village here.' Chou handed Chang another aerial photograph, this one not enlarged. 'By the lake.'

'We have been to this village already?' Chang said.

'Two days ago. It was searched like all the others.'

'I'd like to pay it another visit. Make the arrangements.'

'You will be handling it personally, Comrade Major?'

'Yes,' Chang replied. 'I've waited around in this office long enough.'

Chang stood in the centre of the village, the wind catching at the sleeves of his tunic, almost knocking him off his feet. How did anyone manage to live up here? he wondered. No, he corrected himself. How did they survive? This wasn't living by his standards, by any civilised standards. The houses were crude stone hovels, battered by the elements, the winter snows and the gnawing wind that blew ceaselessly over the high plateau. There were no fields for cultivation, the altitude was too great even for barley. In any case, the soil was too thin and barren to support anything richer than coarse grass. All the villagers had were a few sheep and goats and yaks to support them. They lived on tough meat and butter, yak's-milk cheese and barley flour they carried up from the farms in the lower valleys. No wonder they all looked so malnourished and miserable.

Chang looked around at them, shuffling out of their houses, the *Gong An Ju* commandos prodding them with their sub-machine-gun barrels. Their faces and hands were ingrained with dirt, their hair matted. Chang regarded them with open disgust. They were filthy, backward peasants. An *apso* came to the doorway of one of the houses and stood there barking at the commandos.

Herded into the clearing between the houses, the villagers stood in a silent group, their heads bowed, not daring to look the Chinese in the eye.

'Two people came to this village yesterday. A man and a woman. Where are they?' Chang said, nodding at the interpreter they'd brought with them from Chamdo. The interpreter, a Tibetan civilian, translated the question into the local dialect.

Chang waited. None of the villagers responded.

'Ask them again,' Chang said impatiently.

Still the villagers didn't reply. Chang gave the commando sergeant an order and the sergeant stepped over to one of the villagers – a middle-aged man in a fox-fur hat – and hit him hard in the stomach with the butt of his sub-machine-gun. The man doubled up in agony and toppled forward on to his knees, his hands clutched to his belly.

'Who is the headman here?' Chang demanded.

The interpreter translated and an elderly man with a silver beard shuffled reluctantly forward.

'Answer the question,' Chang said.

'They are not here,' the headman said through the interpreter.

'Where did they go?'

'Away.' The headman gestured vaguely with a hand.

'Who were they?'

The headman looked down without answering. Chang

snapped off another order. A small boy of about ten was dragged from the group. His mother tried to hold on to him, crying out in alarm, but was pushed roughly to the ground by one of the commandos. The sergeant gripped the boy under the arms and held a knife to the child's left ear.

'Answer the question, or we cut off the boy's ear,' Chang said.

The headman lifted his eyes to the major's. Chang was accustomed to seeing hatred in the faces of Tibetans, but rarely had he seen such an implacable loathing.

'They were monks,' the headman said.

Chang listened to the translation and frowned. '"They"?'

The interpreter had another exchange with the headman and turned to Chang. 'He says there were three men.'

'Three men and a woman?' Chang said, seeking to clarify the numbers.

'Three monks, and a Western woman.'

'Western?' Chang gave a start of surprise. 'Is he sure?'

'He is sure.'

'What were they doing here?'

'They were from Lhasa,' the headman explained through the interpreter. 'They were looking for a *tulku*, the reincarnation of a lama.'

'Did they find him?'

'No, they went away.'

'When?'

'Yesterday evening.'

'Which direction?'

The headman pointed north. Lieutenant Chou stepped close to Chang, alert and eager.

'They can't have gone far, Comrade Major,' Chou said. 'In the helicopter we should have no difficulty finding them.'

Chang gazed over the houses, focusing on the mountain tops beyond. But he saw nothing. His mind was fixed on something else, suddenly preoccupied with a thought that had only just occurred to him.

'Comrade Major,' Chou said. 'I can take the squad in the

helicopter. We can have these monks in custody in a couple of hours. Just give the order.'

'No,' Chang said. 'Let them go.'

'I don't understand.'

'You heard me, Lieutenant. I said let them go.'

'You did *what*?' Shen's voice on the phone was like a small explosion.

'If you would allow me to explain,' Chang said, flinching a little at his superior's furious reaction.

'I think you'd better, Major. We hunt these men across half of Tibet and when you finally locate them you let them go. I think that needs a damn good explanation.'

'I haven't let them go exactly,' Chang said.

'No? It looks that way to me.'

'We know where they are. Not the precise grid reference, but we know roughly the area in which they are located.'

'And what is the point of that?'

'If I might be permitted to finish, Comrade Colonel? These monks, they are not wandering the country aimlessly. They have a purpose in being here. I don't mean in Tibet, I mean in this particular part of Tibet. We know how they search for a reincarnation. They don't scour the entire country, they narrow down their quest to a small area. They seek guidance from oracles, from visions and other superstitious sources.' Chang paused. He could hear Shen breathing on the other end of the line, but the colonel did not interrupt. 'If they are here, then they must have a good reason. Why? There are very few people in this region. Most of it is uninhabited wilderness. It does not seem an auspicious place to search unless . . . unless they have had some strong indication that the child will be found here. I think they are very close to finding him.'

Chang paused again, knowing he had Shen's complete attention.

'We give them time and space,' Chang continued. 'Observe them from a distance without letting them know we are watching. Then, when they have identified the chosen child, we move in and seize them all. Not only will we have the monks from Dharamsala, but we will have the new Dalai Lama – the new Tibetan leader, chosen and authenticated by the official search party, but in our custody.'

Chang waited. It was a while before Shen responded.

'The idea has its merits,' the colonel conceded, unwilling to give too much credit to a subordinate. 'It has its risks too, but the benefits – if we can pull it off – far outweigh them.'

'You give your approval?'

'Yes, Major. We will bide our time. When they have found the child, then we will make our move.'

SEVENTEEN

The *drogpa* camp was much larger than the village by the lake they'd left the previous evening. There were perhaps twenty or thirty *ba* – the yak-hair tents in which the nomads lived – grouped together in the bottom of the wide basin. Beside the tents was a small stream which cascaded down the northern slopes of the surrounding mountains and exited through a narrow cleft on the south-eastern rim.

Maggie paused as they entered the camp, looking up at the encircling wall of jagged peaks, the bear-shaped cloud holding steady above them. There was something tranquil, something strange about the setting. It reminded her of the ancient Tibetan myth of Shambhala, the mystical kingdom surrounded by mountains which the Tibetans believed would be the fount of a universal Buddhist enlightenment. At the centre of Shambhala was the jewelled city of Kalapa from which, according to the story, King Rudachakrin would one day ride forth on his stone horse to vanquish the forces of evil and bring about the dawning of an age of *nirvana*.

There was no fabulous city in evidence, just a rude nomad encampment, but perhaps Kalapa was simply a metaphor for a place that was rich and blessed in other ways, as the stable in Bethlehem, in Christian belief, was more precious than the most opulent palace.

One by one, the nomads emerged from their tents to stare at the four visitors, their gazes lingering longer on Maggie whose Caucasian features were almost certainly a novelty for all of them. Even the Chinese rarely ventured into this wild, remote part of the country. A Westerner, and a woman at that, was as strange and rare a sighting as a yeti.

A *drogpa* in a thick sheepskin *chuba* took charge of the new arrivals, gesturing at them to follow him. They were led to a tent a little larger than the others and ushered inside. Another man, clad also in a heavy sheepskin *chuba* like all the nomad males, was sitting cross-legged on a rug by the open hearth. He had long dark hair and skin so weathered by the sun and wind that it was almost ebony. Around his neck was an ancient gilt charm box to ward off evil spirits; by his side, a Kalashnikov rifle of more recent provenance.

Tsering, Lobsang and Jigme raised their cupped hands to their chests and bowed their heads. '*Tashi delek*.'

The nomad leader grinned, revealing teeth so worn and black they looked like chips of charred wood.

'*Tashi delek*,' he replied, waving them to another rug beside the fire. It was dark and stuffy inside the tent. A slit in the roof provided a makeshift chimney, but clouds of smoke still drifted around the interior, perfuming it with the distinctive aroma of yak dung.

The nomad leader said a few words of welcome, then barked an instruction at his wife who was sitting on a low wooden stool next to the hearth. She took a *dhongmo* – a small wooden barrel hooped with metal – off a shelf and placed it between her feet. Into the barrel she put a large block of yak butter, a chunk of tea broken off a long brick and a sprinkling of salt. Then she lifted a blackened kettle off the fire and poured boiling water into the *dhongmo*. After putting the lid on the barrel and clamping it shut, she began pumping a handle like a piston in and out vigorously, mixing the ingredients together. The liquid she poured out into bowls was thick and greasy, more like porridge than tea. Maggie took hers with a sinking heart. A larger bowl of *tsampa* was passed around. Maggie watched the monks add a few handfuls of the roast barley flour to their tea and stir it around to make a thick dough. She did the same. That was the easy bit. It was as she attempted to roll the dough into balls with her fingertips that she realised the others were all watching her. Tsering said something to the *drogpa* chief, and the nomad and his wife, not to mention the other curious onlookers who'd crowded into the tent behind them, convulsed themselves with laughter.

'I'm glad they're amused,' Maggie said sourly, licking the sticky mess off her fingers.

The chief's wife leaned forward and gave Maggie a spoon, provoking another round of amiable giggling. Maggie thanked her graciously in Tibetan and earned herself a sudden, surprised look from the nomad chief. The *drogpa* had a lengthy exchange with Tsering then chuckled coarsely and gave Maggie a look, as if he were sizing up a mare at market.

'What are you talking about?' Maggie demanded.

'He wanted to know where you come from,' Tsering said.

'And what did you say?'

'From a country far away over the mountains. He has never heard of England. He wondered if you were married to all three of us.'

'I hope you put him straight on that.'

'I said we were monks, but that you were unmarried.'

'What did he say to that?'

'That you might make a good wife for one of his sons . . .' Tsering paused, eying her slyly. 'If you had more meat on you.'

Maggie snorted. Bloody men. Even up here in the back of beyond they were all the same.

'Tell him I don't think much to his figure either,' Maggie said.

Tsering was aghast. 'That would be most insulting.'

'Exactly.'

Only when the butter tea had been consumed and the customary small talk exhausted did Tsering broach the reason for their visit, telling the *drogpa* chief the same story about looking for a *tulku*.

'Have any children – any boys – been born to your tribe in the last month?' he asked.

274

'Month?' The nomad glanced at his wife. 'What about Dolma Tashi?' His wife gave a nod of confirmation. 'Yes, there is a child.'

'May we see him?'

The *drogpa* chief barked an instruction at one of the watching men. A few minutes later, a young woman, probably still in her teens, was brought in. She looked nervous, apprehensive. Clutched to her breast was a sleeping infant wrapped in a woollen shawl.

The *drogpa* chief told her why she'd been summoned. He called her over to the fire. The girl walked across reluctantly, her eyes flickering anxiously over the faces of the monks.

Tsering tried to put her at ease. 'Have no fear,' he said gently. 'There is nothing to worry about.'

The girl frowned, holding her baby tighter, unwilling to let go of him.

Tsering turned to the nomad chief. 'We need peace and seclusion for the tests.'

The chief ordered the onlookers to leave the tent. There were grumblings of dissent – nothing this exciting had happened to them in years – but the nomads shuffled out immediately.

'May we see the child?' Tsering asked.

Dolma Tashi hesitated.

'Do as you're told, girl,' the *drogpa* chief said impatiently. 'These are monks, holy men, from Lhasa. You must obey them.'

'Your son will not be harmed,' Tsering said. 'We just want to look at him.'

'Give him here.' The chief's wife took the baby from the girl and laid him down on the rug before the fire. The child opened his eyes and gazed around at the blur of faces above him. He started to wail. His mother knelt down beside him, murmuring reassuringly. She slipped her little finger into his mouth and the infant sucked on it. Maggie had her camcorder out now, recording everything.

'When was he born?' Tsering asked.

'A few weeks ago,' the girl replied vaguely.

Tsering felt a frisson of anticipation. They had not yet seen the remaining two signs from Pasang Rinpoche's vision, but perhaps this was the child nonetheless. Very carefully, he unwrapped the shawl and examined the baby's body, looking for the traditional signs of a reincarnate Dalai Lama – the distinctive physical characteristics such as large ears, long eyes with the eyebrows curving upwards, streaks on the legs like a tiger's stripes and a conch-shaped imprint on one hand.

Tsering's excitement turned to disappointment. The child had large ears, but none of the other signs was present. He glanced at Lobsang and Jigme. They knew what he was thinking, could sense his doubts.

'Bring me the parcel from my bag,' Tsering said.

He unfastened the yellow silk cloth and took out a beautiful carved ivory rosary. Jigme and Lobsang handed him their own rosaries and Tsering dangled all three over the baby's face. The child's eyes followed the strings of beads as they swung to and fro above him. He reached up with a chubby little hand and grabbed one of the rosaries. The wrong one.

Tsering tried again, with the rosaries in different positions. The baby chose one, pulling it down and attempting to chew on one of the beads. But it was still the wrong rosary.

Tsering took out the plain wooden bowl from which the late Dalai Lama had eaten his meals and held it in his left hand over the baby. In his right hand he held one of the metal bowls belonging to the *drogpa* chief. The infant's eyes darted from one bowl to the other. Then he stretched out his hand and grasped the metal bowl.

'This is the only new-born boy in your tribe?' Tsering said.

The nomad chief nodded. 'He is not the one?'

'No, he is not the one.'

The chief looked crestfallen. A *tulku* in the tribe would have been a real cause for celebration.

'You are sure?'

'I'm sure.'

The chief gave a dismissive wave to the child's mother. She wrapped the shawl back around her baby and hurried out of the tent before they could change their minds. Tsering thanked the chief for his help, then asked him if there was a blue mountain nearby.

'A blue mountain?' the chief repeated, perplexed. 'What do you mean?'

'I'm not sure. Some blue rocks, maybe a lake.'

'There is a lake higher up, over the ridge. Half a day's walk.'

'Are there people up there? Villages?'

'No villages,' the chief said. 'Maybe *drogpa*.'

Tsering packed the rosary and bowl away in the silk cloth and returned them to his bag.

'We have travelled a long way,' he said. 'Can we rest here for a few hours?'

'You can stay as long as you wish.'

'Just till dusk,' Tsering said. 'Then we must be on our way.'

There was a full moon that night, a glowing silver hole punched into the dark fabric of the sky. They walked for four hours in the pale ethereal light until they came over a ridge and saw the dark shadow of the lake below them. They pitched their tents by the water's edge, drank black tea to warm themselves through and crawled beneath their blankets for a few hours' sleep.

It was daybreak when Maggie awoke. Tsering was no longer beside her. She threw back the flap of the tent and wriggled out. Tsering was sitting meditating a few metres away. He was clad only in his *chuba*, but he didn't seem to notice the penetrating cold. The lake was a greyish-black smudge half hidden by a drifting fog which wasn't mist but low cloud, they were so high up. Maggie had slept badly. Even lying down doing nothing she'd been conscious of her heart pounding, struggling to pump enough oxygen around her body. She was aware of it now too, throbbing inside her skull.

277

She filled the pan with water from the lake and set it on the kerosene stove to boil, huddling close to the flames in a vain attempt to keep warm. The damp air seemed to cut through her flesh like a rusty hacksaw.

She caught a movement out of the corner of her eye. Tsering was standing up, walking to the lake and splashing some of the icy water over his face, wiping himself dry with the sleeve of his *chuba*.

'Why are we here?' Maggie asked. 'There are no people living this high.'

'There is the lake,' Tsering said, walking over to the stove.

'So? You're looking for a child, not a lake.'

'Pasang Rinpoche saw a blue mountain in his vision. He said it looked as if a piece of the sky had fallen to earth.'

'A piece of the sky? That inky lake?'

'Wait until the clouds lift. Then we'll see.'

But as the sun rose, the waters maintained their blackness, as dark and opaque as liquid charcoal. The clouds disappeared from the top of Mount Gebur, leaving behind a vault of clear azure sky above the deserted landscape.

'Where now?' Maggie said.

Tsering shrugged. 'North, I suppose.'

They walked on, ascending a glacial valley that ran up the western side of Mount Gebur. No one spoke. They didn't have the breath, but neither did they have the inclination. A gloomy despondency had seeped inside them all. None of them, Tsering included, truly believed they would find the chosen one in this harsh, empty terrain.

For two hours they climbed. Maggie guessed they were above seventeen thousand feet now. They could walk only at a shuffle, each step a labour as though their feet had turned to lead. Even the monks were struggling with the altitude, but Maggie felt as if a steel hoop had been wrapped around her chest and was being slowly tightened.

Then the moment came.

It was a moment that all four of them would remember with absolute clarity until the end of their days.

They walked over a rise and there in front of them, on the far slope of a hollow, was a swathe of vivid blue which did indeed look as if a piece of the sky had fallen to earth. The whole hillside was smothered with a dazzling, vibrant carpet of blue poppies.

'Dear God,' Maggie breathed.

Next to her, Jigme let out an exclamation of wonder. 'The third sign,' he whispered. 'It is a miracle.'

There was no other word for it. The Himalayan blue poppy flowered in summer and it was now very nearly winter. It flowered only once, after several years, and then died. For a whole hillside to be simultaneously in bloom in October was nothing short of miraculous.

For a long while they gazed in awe at the expanse of poppies, the flowers rippling like water in the breeze. Maggie took out her camcorder and captured the scene on tape. Then in the bottom of the hollow they noticed a single black nomad tent, a herd of yaks grazing nearby. A small girl, maybe five or six years old, came out of the tent and saw them looking down at her. She gave a startled cry and scurried back inside the tent, re-emerging moments later with her mother and younger brother in tow.

Tsering walked down the incline towards the tent. His stomach was like a nest of writhing snakes, twisting and coiling in a knot of nausea, but his spirits were soaring. They had seen three of the signs. The Lord Buddha's hand was guiding them inexorably to their goal. The omens could not have been more auspicious. If there was a child here of the right age . . .

The *drogpa* woman looked at them warily as they came to a halt before her.

'*Tashi delek*,' Tsering said.

'*Tashi delek*.' She watched them with her big, dark eyes, then said something to her daughter. The little girl raced away up the side of the hollow and disappeared from sight.

The woman seemed reluctant to invite them inside so Tsering exerted some subtle pressure.

'We are tired and thirsty. Could we perhaps have a drink of water?'

The woman didn't reply. She kept glancing anxiously in the direction her daughter had taken.

'You are alone up here?' Tsering said.

'My husband . . .'

'Ah, we are waiting for him?'

A figure appeared on the rim of the hollow: a man in a sheepskin *chuba* and fur hat, a rifle dangling from one shoulder. The little girl was trotting along on one side of him, and on the other side was a huge *dogkhyi*, a Tibetan mastiff. The man strode down the slope to the tent and scrutinised the visitors, the dog slavering eagerly beside him as if awaiting the order to pounce.

'Who are you?' the man asked. 'Officials?'

'We are monks,' Tsering replied.

'Monks?' The *drogpa* didn't conceal his surprise. His manner became a little less hostile. 'What are monks doing up here?'

'We seek a *tulku*. The holy signs have led us here. May we rest a while in your home?'

The *drogpa* gave the request some consideration, then shrugged and pulled aside the door flap of the tent. Inside there were yak-hair rugs on the floor, a fire glowing brightly in a hearth constructed from a few stone slabs. The *drogpa* owned nothing that couldn't be packed away in a matter of hours and loaded on to a yak. Tsering looked around, noting the altar at one side of the tent, the bowls of water and the butter lamp set out before it. These people were obviously practising Buddhists.

The two children came in after them. The little girl squatted down next to Maggie, fascinated by her European features, her pale skin and fine hair. Maggie smiled at her. The girl smiled back shyly, then her face broke into a broad grin.

Tsering felt his heart, beating until now with an uplifting excitement, suddenly plummet into despair. He could see no other children in the tent.

'You have just the one son and daughter?' he said.

'It is all the Chinese allow us,' the nomad replied.

The woman poured them tea and passed round a plate of dried yak meat. The monks and Maggie took a strip each and chewed on the lean salty flesh. The yak was the key to life in Tibet, particularly up here in the mountains where no crops could grow. It provided milk to drink, cheese and butter and meat to eat – the people given dispensation from the normal Buddhist prohibition on eating animals because there was no choice if they were to survive. The yak gave hair to be woven into clothes and rugs and tents, skins for boots and hats, dung for cooking and a broad back for transporting both people and baggage over the rugged country.

'Are there more *drogpa* up here?' Tsering asked. 'Other families?'

'Some, but not close,' the man answered.

'We are looking for a new-born child, just a few weeks old.' Tsering tried to control his mounting sense of desperation. He'd been so sure that this was the place where he would find the child. 'Do you know of any near here?'

The man's eyes darted to his wife, then he looked away. To Tsering there was something shifty about the glance. He was beginning to sense undercurrents here.

'Are there any?' he asked again.

'The Chinese allow us nomads only two children. Any more and they punish us. They come round. They cut the mothers.' The *drogpa* made a slashing motion across his belly. 'Some of them die.'

Tsering knew what he meant. The Chinese had a policy of enforced abortions and sterilisation for the Tibetans. Even here in the remote interior, there were teams of doctors roaming the land, operating on women to keep the birth rate down.

'We are not Chinese,' Tsering said.

'I can see that. But not all Tibetans are true to their people.'

'We are monks. We are not informers. We have nothing to do with the Chinese authorities. You have to believe that. We are seeking only a new baby, nothing more. Do you know of any near here?'

As if in answer to the question, there was a sudden cry from behind a curtain in the corner of the tent. Tsering went rigid, a pulse like electricity shooting down his spine. The cry came again, the unmistakable mewl of a baby. The nomad woman glanced uncomfortably at the curtain, but stayed where she was. Its call unheeded, the infant began to bawl; a full-throated yell that filled the tent with its unsettling noise.

The woman got to her feet and pulled aside the curtain, bending down to pick up the baby from its basket.

'He is yours?' Tsering said, certain the baby was a boy.

The *drogpa* looked sheepish, embarrassed and maybe a little ashamed to be caught out in the deception. 'We thought you might report us to the Chinese,' he said guiltily.

'We understand,' Tsering said, his eyes never leaving the howling bundle in the woman's arms.

The mother laid the child down on a rug and peeled off the swaddling. Maggie moved in closer with her camcorder. The mother unwrapped a cotton handkerchief that covered the baby's backside and groin, and the ripe, pungent smell of soiled nappy spread across the tent. The inside of the handkerchief was lined with moss, now soaked with urine and excrement. The woman tipped the nappy's contents on to the fire before wiping the child clean with more dry moss and replacing the handkerchief, newly lined with fresh moss.

Tsering leaned closer, examining the baby's features, its plump naked limbs. It had the large ears and curving eyebrows they were looking for, and on its legs were a number of pale bands like stripes. Tsering took the baby's hands gently in his own and turned them over. On the left palm was a peculiar spiral mark like the imprint of a sea shell.

But it was as the mother was refastening the handkerchief around the baby's waist that Tsering saw the other mark. He craned forward quickly.

'Stop! Let me see.'

On the child's back, just above the waist, was a strawberry pink birthmark in the shape of a lotus flower. Tsering stared at it, then reached out and touched the baby's skin. He felt sick with anticipation. It was the fourth sign: a lotus flower, a special symbol in the Buddhist faith, for the lotus had roots in the filth and mud of the pond and swamp yet grew into a beautiful flower – a metaphor for the human spirit developing and blossoming, no matter how unfavourable the conditions.

'When was the child born?' Tsering asked.

'Since the last moon,' the mother replied. Up here days and weeks had little meaning. The moon and sun were the only calendars they needed.

'How many days is that?' Tsering could barely contain his impatience.

The woman shrugged. 'Is it important?'

'Yes, it's important.'

She did some simple arithmetic on her fingers. 'Twenty, perhaps twenty-one days.'

The monks exchanged tentative, anxious glances. The signs, the dates were right. That left only the tests.

'May I show him some things we have brought with us?' Tsering said. 'Things which belonged to the departed lama.'

'If you wish.'

Jigme opened the yellow silk parcel again and passed the contents – the rosary, the bowl, the spectacles, the silver pen and the small hand drum – to Tsering.

Tsering knelt over the baby. The child had stopped crying and was looking up at him, his gaze somehow clearer, more focused than it should have been in an infant of his age. Tsering took out his own *mala* and accepted a second from Lobsang, then dangled the three rosaries over the boy's face. The child looked at each in turn, then reached up without hesitation and grasped the late Dalai Lama's string of carved ivory beads.

Five times more, Tsering showed the child the rosaries, mixing their positions each time. Unerringly, the child chose the right one.

Tsering moved on to the other items, showing different eating bowls, then offering a series of different objects – a scarf, keys, a pocket knife, a coin, a woollen cap, mixed in with the Dalai Lama's genuine possessions. The child showed no interest in the false items, but selected only the spectacles, silver pen and hand drum.

Maggie taped every moment, feeling privileged to be there. This was history in the making, the first time in six hundred years of reincarnations that the discovery of a new Dalai Lama had been witnessed by an outsider and recorded for posterity.

Tsering too felt the weight of history on his shoulders. His responsibility was huge. There were no high lamas to consult, no senior ministers from the Government in exile. It was just he and Lobsang and Jigme; they had to make the decision. He thought back over the previous few weeks: the predictions of the Nechung Oracle, Pasang Rinpoche's vision at Lhamo Latso, the signs that had guided them to this child, and now the tests which the boy had passed with a certainty that seemed divinely inspired. Everything had fallen into place. There was absolutely no doubt in Tsering's mind. This was the one. This was His Holiness the Fifteenth Dalai Lama of Tibet.

Tsering drew back from the child, trying to clear his mind, to decide what to do next. He looked at Lobsang and Jigme and nodded. The three of them went outside and stood in the open air by the tent, looking across the hollow to the wash of blue poppies.

'Is there any doubt?' Tsering said.

'Not one iota,' Lobsang replied firmly.

'Jigme?'

'We have seen it with our own eyes. I feel blessed to be here.'

'Let us give thanks to the Lord Buddha,' Tsering said.

They knelt down on the stony ground and prayed together, offering up their devotions for the benefit of all sentient beings. When they had finished, Tsering felt as if the burden on his shoulders had lifted. He was tranquil, serene, his responsibility shared now with a greater power who would lead them on the next stage of their journey just as he had guided them this far.

'What next?' Lobsang asked.

'We must tell them,' Tsering said. 'They are his parents. We must give them time for the news to sink in. Give them time to recover from the shock.'

They went back inside the tent. The mother was holding the baby in her arms, rocking him to sleep. The monks sat back down by the hearth. The mother and her husband looked at Tsering expectantly, knowing he had something to say.

'I must tell you who we are,' Tsering began. 'We said we were monks. That is true. But I did not say where we were from. We come from Dharamsala. From the Tibetan Government in exile.'

The mother stopped rocking her baby. Maggie sensed what was about to happen and kept her camcorder on the faces of the *drogpa* couple.

Tsering continued: 'We said we were looking for a reincarnate lama. That also is true. What we didn't say is that the rebirth we are seeking is that of Gyalwa Rinpoche.'

At the mention of the Tibetan name for the Dalai Lama, the nomads gasped, then froze, their mouths gaping open in astonishment.

'Gyalwa Rinpoche,' the mother stammered when she had recovered the power of speech.

'Yes. The Lord Buddha has brought us here. He has revealed your son to us. From the signs, the tests we have undertaken, there is no doubt whatsoever. Your son is the new Gyalwa Rinpoche.'

The mother stared at him. 'How can that be? We are poor, uneducated *drogpa*, living simply in the mountains. How can our son be Him?'

'Gyalwa Rinpoche shows his strength, his infinite wisdom and compassion by choosing this humble place for his rebirth.'

The mother looked at her husband, numb with shock. They had been blessed in the greatest way imaginable for a Tibetan. For them, the Dalai Lama encapsulated everything that was sacred and special about their land: the beauty of the scenery, the purity of its rivers and lakes, the sanctity of its skies, the solidity of its mountains and the strength of its people. He was the human embodiment of their country and their profound faith, their hopes, aspirations, their very identity itself.

The silence seemed to last for ever. Then the mother's face crumpled and she began to weep: tears of joy, not sorrow. Her husband put an arm around her shoulders and held her as the unrestrained emotion flooded forth. Throughout it all, the child lay in its mother's arms, blissfully asleep.

In the evening, they sat together around the hearth and ate a stew of yak meat and turnips which Pema – the *drogpa* mother – had made in a huge sooty iron cauldron. Afterwards, the father took out a pipe as long as his arm, the bowl embossed with silver, and began to smoke. His wife produced a dusty bottle of *arak*, a whisky distilled from barley pulp, and passed it around the group. The monks declined, but Maggie had a drop in a metal tumbler. The *arak* was fierce and potent; Maggie could feel the line of fire it left all the way from her mouth to her stomach.

The two older children were given a drink of melted butter and honey mixed with a thimbleful of the whisky to help them sleep. Then they were sent away to their beds in the corner of the tent. They lay on their rugs beneath their yak-hair blankets, wide awake and curious, watching the adults by the fire. Pema suckled the baby through the open front of her *chuba*, then winded him and settled him down in his basket.

Tsering had given the couple several hours to absorb the revelation about their new-born son, to come to terms with what it might mean. Now he judged the moment right to move on to the next stage.

'I do not expect you to make a decision immediately,' he began. 'And I emphasise now that you have complete freedom in what you choose to do. The child is yours. There will be no coercion whatsoever from us. Do you understand that?'

Pema nodded. 'We understand.'

'We are monks, not soldiers or policemen or anything else. Our task was to find the chosen child and that – with the Lord Buddha's guidance – we have done. What comes next is up to you.' Tsering paused. The *drogpa* couple were gazing at him intently. 'You are devout, religious people. I can see that from your altar, I can sense it from your demeanour. You know the significance of Gyalwa Rinpoche, his importance in our faith and our culture. You will be feeling the burden that his rebirth as your son has placed on you. You are probably feeling bewildered, apprehensive, scared. That is only to be expected. But you are not alone. We are here to support you.'

'You're going to take him away, aren't you?' Pema said, her voice quavering.

'We are going to do nothing without your consent. You have my word on that,' Tsering reassured her. 'Whatever we do must have your agreement. But you know the position in Tibet. You know how much the Chinese hate and fear our faith, our beliefs which they do not understand and cannot control. Gyalwa Rinpoche encapsulates that faith, and our aspirations for independence. To the Chinese, Gyalwa Rinpoche is a dangerous threat because he keeps alive our hopes and our determination to be one day free of the Han yoke.'

'Our son is in danger,' Pema said. It was a statement, not a question.

'Yes, he is in danger. If the Chinese identify him, they will certainly take him away. Who knows what they will do after that. I'm not trying to alarm you, but Tibet is not a safe place for him. We must get him out to India, put him under the protection of the Tibetan Government in exile.'

'I will not hand him over to anyone,' Pema said, a glint of steel in her eyes.

'We do not ask you to. The child will go nowhere without you. You are his mother. He is just a baby. He needs you.'

'I will go with him?'

'Of course.'

'And my husband, my other children?'

Tsering hesitated. 'We will get them out of Tibet too. But they may have to wait a few months. To take all of you now – two adults and three children – would be risky. It would make our chances of being caught all the greater.'

Pema's husband removed the pipe from his mouth and said stoically: 'The child is more important than we are. I will look after the other children until the time is right to join you.'

Tsering nodded his thanks. He'd feared the father might raise objections to the whole plan, but he seemed to have accepted without reservation that his son would have to leave Tibet.

'We will keep your identity and location a secret,' Tsering promised. 'Once your wife and baby are in India, we will send someone – it may even be me or one of my brothers here – to bring you and your other children out.'

'We will wait,' the father replied phlegmatically and Tsering wondered at his composure. But then he was a nomad. His whole life was spent wandering the mountains, uprooting every few months and moving on. Relocating to India was not such a daunting step to people who had no fixed home.

'Sleep on it,' Tsering said. 'Discuss it together. This is not a decision that should be taken lightly. Let me know in the morning.'

He said goodnight and went outside. The monks had pitched their own tents next to the *drogpa's ba*, preferring to leave the nomads their privacy. Maggie followed Tsering out. A flock of Saurus cranes was flying in a V formation across the face of the setting sun, their flapping wings and extended necks silhouetted against the burning orb. It was a good omen.

'Your search is at an end,' Maggie said. 'You must feel elated.'

'No,' Tsering replied reflectively. 'I fear the hard part is yet to come.'

The morning was fragrant with the scent of damp earth and yak-dung smoke from the chimney of the *drogpa* tent. Maggie took a deep breath and looked around. There was a barely visible bluish haze over the hollow, as if the Himalayan poppies were emitting their own soft luminescence. A few metres away a large shaggy yak took a mouthful of grass and lifted his head lethargically. His heavy eyes stared at Maggie through a curtain of matted dreadlocks, then he turned away and continued his slow, thoughtful ruminations.

Inside the tent, Pema was making butter tea in the *dhongmo*. Maggie refused a bowl, but took some plain boiled water from the kettle. She was sipping it, smiling awkwardly at Pema when Tsering, Lobsang and Jigme came in. They ate their breakfast in silence. Pema was preoccupied with her children, changing the baby's nappy and feeding the older boy and girl. Her husband was somewhere out on the mountain with his fearsome mastiff, tending to his animals.

Only when the baby was fed and nestled comfortably in his mother's arms did Pema address Tsering directly.

'We talked about everything last night,' she said almost casually. 'My husband and I. We are agreed. If it is the Buddha's wish, then the child and I will go with you. My husband will stay here with the other children until someone comes for them. Someone *will* come, won't they?'

'Yes, they will come,' Tsering replied.

'When do we leave?'

'The sooner the better,' Tsering said. 'You will need to pack a few things, for both yourself and the child. We can help you carry them. We will leave this morning.'

The monks went outside to strike their tents. Pema went to the family altar and replenished the seven bowls with fresh water. Lighting the butter lamp in front of the image of Chenresig, the Buddha of Compassion who, in his reincarnated form, lay snugly against her breast, she knelt down and began to pray.

Maggie left her to her devotions and went out into the fresh air, watching the monks folding the tents and packing them away in their bags.

'She and the child are coming with us?' she asked Tsering, having been unable to follow the conversation in Tibetan.

'Yes.'

'You know how you're going to get them out?'

'Not in detail, no. Why?'

Maggie shook her head. 'Your naivety amazes me. What are you going to do, trust in the Buddha?'

'He has brought us this far. He will protect us on our return journey too.'

'Forgive me if I don't have the same faith in him as you do. I'm just a cynical Western heathen. But have you forgotten that the Chinese are searching for you?'

'So?'

'They're thorough, and they don't give up easily. They'll be checking the whole area around here. People talk. People can be made to talk. How long do you think it will be before the Chinese get word that three monks have been asking about a *tulku*?'

'What are you suggesting?'

'That we should work on the assumption that the Chinese know why you're here, and know roughly where you are, and make a few plans accordingly.'

Tsering straightened up from his pack and looked at her. 'What do you mean?'

'Get me the map and I'll show you.'

Shen Tzu was in his quarters at the PSB barracks on the outskirts of Lhasa, preparing for bed, when a signals orderly, despatched by the night duty officer, came to tell him he was wanted on the telephone.

'Is it Beijing?' Shen asked with a mounting sense of dread.

'It is Major Chang, in Chamdo,' the orderly replied.

Shen's relief was palpable. He felt his stomach relax, the tightness in his chest ease a little. Chang he could handle.

He put his colonel's tunic back on and followed the orderly across the parade ground to the communications room.

'This had better be important,' he said to Chang over the telephone.

'It is, Comrade Colonel. I've just had word from the field. I posted a squad of officers to one of the villages in the mountains, to keep watch. They've just radioed in with the news.'

'What news?' Shen said tetchily. 'Get to the point, Major.'

'We have them, Comrade Colonel. We have the monks.' Chang paused, savouring the moment. 'And what's more, we have the child and its mother too.'

EIGHTEEN

Chang snapped open the metal hatch and peered through the slit into the detention cell. A man and a woman were sitting next to each other on a wooden bench, the woman cradling a swaddled baby in her arms. The man looked calm, composed. The woman was rocking backwards and forwards, but whether from nerves or simply to comfort the child it was hard to say.

Chang closed the hatch and stepped back from the door.

'What happened to the other monks, and the Western woman?' he said to Lieutenant Chou who was standing beside him.

'I don't know, Comrade Major,' Chou replied. 'The prisoners have not been very forthcoming.'

'I was told you had apprehended all of them.'

'That was an error in the radio transmission. It was just the one man and woman.'

'But you're sure this is one of the monks?'

'Without a doubt. The peasants in the village by the lake confirmed that he was one of the three who passed through two days ago.'

'The others didn't slip past you unnoticed?'

'That would have been impossible,' Chou said stiffly. 'I posted men all round the village and lookouts on the surrounding hills. We saw the monk and the woman come over the ridge and observed them all the way down to the village. There were just the two of them, and the baby.'

'They've said nothing at all?'

'We have not pressed them, Comrade Major. I thought you would probably want to carry out the interrogations yourself. We simply detained them overnight in the village and the helicopter picked us up this morning. I hope that was the correct thing to do.'

'Yes, Lieutenant, it was. I'll take the woman first. She will be easier to break than the monk.'

Chang went down the corridor into a room furnished with a desk and four chairs. The walls were bare, unplastered concrete, the only light a single unshaded bulb dangling from a wire in the ceiling. The interpreter was already there, waiting for him. He stood up and bowed obsequiously as the major entered. Chang ignored him. The interpreter was a Tibetan, a civilian with no more status than the other Tibetan menials who cleaned the floors and lavatories of the PSB's district headquarters. He was hardly worth noticing.

Chang sat down at the desk and waited for the woman to be brought in. Chou stayed for the interview, perching on a chair a respectful distance behind the major. Chang studied the woman. She was just a peasant girl; coarse, uneducated, probably stupid like most of the Tibetans he encountered. She was looking down at her baby, unable to meet the major's probing gaze.

'What's your name?' Chang asked. He was an experienced interrogator. He was confident he would get the information he required out of this ignorant bumpkin.

The interpreter relayed the question.

'Dolma Tashi,' the girl replied.

'Dolma Tashi.' Chang repeated the name, struggling a little with the Tibetan syllables. He'd been in Tibet for more than four years, but could speak barely a word of the language. He'd made the decision not to learn it out of principle. Wasting time on such a primitive tongue was beneath him. 'How old are you?'

'Eighteen,' came the reply through the interpreter.

'This is your first child?'

'Yes.'

'You registered the birth?'

'Of course. That is the law.'

'You are married?'

'Yes.'

'Where is your husband?'

'With the tribe. We are nomads.'

Chang's lip curled with distaste. Nomads. They were even more backward than the rest of the Tibetans.

'You love your child, I can see that. You wouldn't want anything to happen to him, would you?'

As the interpreter translated the question, the girl's head jerked up in alarm. She hugged the baby closer, her eyes widening with fear.

'What do you mean?' she asked tremulously.

Chang smiled at her, softening his tone. 'I mean that if you cooperate with us, we will treat you leniently. If you do not, things will be very hard for both you and the child.'

The girl was bewildered. 'What have I done? Why have I been brought here? I don't understand.'

'You were caught with the man in the cell along the corridor. The monk. Do you deny that?'

'No. But I have done nothing wrong.'

'The monk is a criminal.'

The girl started. 'I did not know that. I swear I didn't know.'

'Where was he taking you?'

'I don't know.'

'Don't lie. I don't like people who lie to me.'

'I *don't* know. I was told to go with him by my tribal chief.'

Chang watched her carefully. Perhaps she was telling the truth.

'Why?' he asked.

'I wasn't told. It was just an order. To go with him with my son.'

'Was the monk alone?'

'This time, yes.'

Chang frowned. 'This time? You mean there was another time?'

294

The girl nodded. 'The first time there were three of them. They came to our tents.'

'For what reason?'

'To look for a *tulku.*'

Chang licked his thin lips, leaning over the desk. This was what he wanted. 'Tell me what they did.'

'They asked questions. Did some tests on my son. Then they went away.'

'Where?'

'I don't know. Then one of them came back. That's all I know.'

'Your son is the *tulku*?'

'No.'

'What do you mean, no? He must be. Why else is the monk taking you away?'

'They said he wasn't the *tulku.*'

'He must be,' Chang repeated forcefully. 'Don't try to deceive me. Tell me the truth or the child will be taken from you and sent to a state orphanage. And you will be imprisoned for aiding these criminals.'

Chang's words were translated by the interpreter. Dolma Tashi listened closely. Her face sagged in disbelief, then horror. She burst into tears, murmuring the same phrase over and over in between sobs.

'What's she saying?' Chang snapped at the interpreter.

'She's saying, "I *am* telling the truth. I *am* telling the truth."'

Chang turned to Chou. 'I can't get any sense out of this stupid girl. Take her away and have her papers checked. Then bring the monk in.'

Jigme's hands were cuffed behind his back. Lieutenant Chou pushed him roughly on to a chair and resumed his place behind the major. Jigme stared straight ahead, focusing on the far wall of the room.

'I know who you are,' Chang said. 'And I know why you're here. Where are your two colleagues, your fellow monks?'

The interpreter translated, but Jigme gave no sign that he'd heard. His eyes were fixed on the wall, his expression vacant as if his mind were elsewhere.

'Where are they?' Chang asked again.

The room might have been empty for all the response Jigme gave. His eyes never left the wall. He appeared to be in a trance. Chang reached over the desk and slapped the monk hard across the face. Blood trickled from Jigme's lip but he didn't move.

Chang slapped him again. To release his pent-up anger rather than because he expected a reaction. The major leaned back in his chair, panting with fury. He'd known the monk would be stubborn. Every Tibetan monk was stubborn. But in the end most of them cracked. Faith was no match for suffering.

'Take him to the basement,' Chang said.

Chang returned to the office he'd commandeered for the duration of his stay in Chamdo and sat down at the desk. He clicked on the intercom and ordered the secretary he'd been allocated to bring him a bowl of black tea. He was in no hurry to continue his interrogation of the monk. An intermission to allow the prisoner to be prepared for the next stage was an essential part of the softening up process. Keep the monk waiting. Allow him to dwell for a time on what was to come. Chang had always found that people became more cooperative when they'd been allowed to reflect on their fate; when their imaginations and fear had been given a chance to eat away at their resolution. It was basic human psychology.

Ten minutes later there was a knock at the door and Chou entered.

'The prisoner is ready for you, Comrade Major.'

Chang nodded indifferently. 'Lieutenant, I want you to do something. Contact my office in Lhasa. They have been collating a list of all male Tibetan children born and registered in the TAR over the past few weeks. Have them fax through the names and dates of all the births in this area, in

Chamdo, Riwoche, Tengchen and Bachen counties. Check the list for the prisoner Dolma Tashi's son. I want to know exactly when he was born.'

'This *tulku*, he must be very important,' Chou said.

'You run ahead of yourself, Lieutenant. Just carry out your orders. That will be all.'

Chang sipped his tea, thinking back over his interview with the nomad girl. She was clearly being used by the monks, kept in the dark about the true identity of her son. That was exactly the kind of devious stratagem he would have expected of the Tibetan Government in exile: mislead the mother, take advantage of her naivety and stupidity, and abduct her child in the cynical pursuit of their own pernicious interests. Well, it hadn't worked. Chang permitted himself a brief smile of satisfaction. He had the child, the mother and one of the monks. Now all he needed were the others. He glanced at his watch. He'd waited long enough. It was time to go back to work.

The room was a plain concrete box: no windows, no furniture, the harsh lighting recessed behind toughened glass panels in the walls. In the centre of the ceiling was a steel ring from which a chain was suspended. Dangling from the chain, his wrists still handcuffed together, was Jigme. He was naked, the tips of his toes just touching the concrete floor. The sinews of his arms and shoulders were stretched taut, the pain starting to show in his face.

Chang slipped on a pair of rubber boots and a plastic apron to protect his uniform and went into the room. The interpreter, similarly clad, was standing behind the door with another man, a PSB orderly with a blank, vacuous face. Chang held out his hand and the orderly passed him a stubby implement the size and shape of a sawn-off cricket bat with an insulated plastic handle, a calibrated dial and a metal tip – a *lok-gug*, an electric cattle prod.

Chang gripped the prod in his right hand, feeling its familiar, solid weight. Below the 'on/off' switch were printed, in English, the reassuring words, 'Made in England'. The British might be a washed-up world power, but they still made the finest torture equipment on the market.

'You know what this is?' Chang said.

Jigme didn't look at him. Hanging by his arms he was finding it hard to breathe. He gritted his teeth, trying to forget about the burning ache in his muscles.

'You're a monk. Of course you do,' Chang went on, pausing for the interpreter to translate his words.

'I don't want to use it, you know.' That was true. Chang wasn't a sadist, he was a pragmatist. He would do whatever was necessary, but it gave him no pleasure.

'Hose him down,' he instructed the orderly.

The orderly turned on a tap and directed the jet of water on to Jigme's body. The electricity was more effective when the skin was wet.

Chang approached Jigme. He looked up at the monk's dripping face. 'We can stop this now, if you agree to cooperate.'

Chang waited while the interpreter translated. Jigme said nothing. Chang sighed and switched on the electric-shock baton.

Maggie had never been so exhausted in her life. She'd walked in the tropical jungles of Indonesia and South America, in the deserts of southern Sudan, in the remote valleys of the Hindu Kush, but nothing had compared to the sheer physical grind of the climb around Mount Gebur. For five gruelling hours they'd wound their way slowly up the mountainside, the air getting thinner and thinner so that by the time they reached the pass on Gebur's western flank there seemed barely enough oxygen in the atmosphere to sustain life. Several times on the ascent Maggie had felt faint; so dizzy she thought she was going to pass out. Only her dogged determination kept her going.

On the pass, nineteen and a half thousand feet above sea level, the snow was thick on the ground. Maggie collapsed to the earth, gasping desperately for air, her skull aching so much that it felt as though it were going to explode. Above her, soaring into the clouds, the three peaks of Mount Gebur were ice-white in the sunlight. She stared at them in a daze, wondering if they were to be the last things she ever saw.

Tsering and Lobsang were adding a stone each to the cairn the Tibetans called *dgra-lha*, the castle of the warrior gods, and from somewhere finding the breath to shout out: 'The gods are victorious, the demons are vanquished, *ki-ki so-so*!' Nearby, apparently immune to the effects of altitude, Pema sat patiently on a boulder, her baby in a sling across her breast.

Tsering hauled Maggie to her feet and held her arm to support her as they descended the other side of the pass. She nodded her thanks, too drained to speak. They lost height quickly, almost sliding down the loose scree that covered the mountainside in a treacherous sheet. The pain behind Maggie's eyes decreased and in time she found she could walk unaided. She felt so much better she even hurried on ahead then stopped and took out her camcorder and taped Pema and the monks coming down behind her.

By nightfall, they were over the highest section of the walk, but there was still a long way to go. They paused to rest and cook a supper of noodles and some of the yak meat Pema had brought with her. Then they walked on until it was too dark and they were too weary to continue. Tsering and Lobsang shared one of the tents, Maggie and Pema the other, the baby wrapped in its blanket nestled between them.

At dawn, Tsering woke them from a heavy sleep and made them walk on, setting a punishing pace until Pema too began to flag.

'We need to rest,' Maggie said.

'We have no time,' Tsering replied bluntly.

'Think of the baby. He needs to feed. Pema needs food in order to support him.'

Tsering hesitated. The child's well-being was of paramount importance.

'Half an hour,' he said. 'No more.'

It was in the late afternoon, nearly thirty hours after they'd left Pema's tent, that ahead of them in the distance, twisting through the mountains like a meandering river, they saw the road.

'This is foolish,' Chang said wearily. 'Why not make things easy for yourself?'

Jigme was swaying on the end of the chain. His naked body was covered with burn marks from the electric-shock baton. There was a sheen of moisture on his skin, some of it water from the hose, some of it the sweat of agony.

Chang jabbed him again with the cattle prod. Jigme's face contorted, his whole body convulsing, but he emitted not a sound.

'Answer my questions,' Chang shouted. The monk's silence unnerved him. The major was used to screams, to sobs for mercy, not this unbelievable stoicism. There was something superhuman about the monk's unyielding strength.

'Where are they? Where are the others?' Chang asked again, turning away as the interpreter relayed the questions. Jigme's gaze never wavered. He stared at the bare walls of the cell, closing off his mind so that Chang couldn't reach him; so that the jarring torment of the electricity couldn't burn away his will to resist.

'Tell me how they are planning to get out of Tibet. Who is helping them? Give me names,' Chang said. He'd lost track of how many times he'd asked the same questions. 'Why not tell me? We have you. We have the child and its mother. Your mission has failed. Why prolong the pain? Just answer the questions and the pain will stop.' Chang looked up at Jigme, trying to understand what it was that made the monk so obdurate. 'Don't you want the pain to stop?'

Chang waited. He shook his head, his anger beginning to rise to the surface again. He lifted the cattle prod and sank it deep into the monk's flesh. Jigme shuddered, his face twisted into a silent scream. Then he passed out.

'Hose him down,' Chang said. 'We'll start again in an hour.'

*   *   *

The lorry was going from Chamdo to Lhasa via the northern route through Nagqu. The driver was Tibetan, a garrulous individual named Chuma who was desperate for company on the long journey. Tsering and Pema, posing as man and wife, travelled in the cab with the baby. Lobsang and Maggie were consigned to the back, squeezing in between the boxes of Chinese television sets Chuma was transporting to the capital.

It was an uncomfortable journey for all of them. The Dongfeng lorry was noisy and had a hard suspension that amplified every rut and bump of the road, transmitting the jolts through the chassis and up through the floor of the truck with boneshaking force. For Maggie and Lobsang it was particularly hard. They had no seats to cushion the impact and in addition had the bitter cold in the back to contend with. They huddled down out of the wind, lying on their bags with blankets wrapped around themselves, and tried to sleep.

In the cab, it was a little easier for Tsering and Pema. They were insulated from the elements, a padded seat beneath them, but their situation wasn't entirely without drawbacks. Chuma was a chain-smoker, his head permanently cocooned in a fug of acrid cigarette smoke which spread throughout the cab in a thick, choking cloud. And he was a compulsive talker. Starved of conversation during his long days on the road, he felt a seemingly irresistible need to chat.

'You waited long for a lift? Haven't seen a hitchhiker all day. Not since Chamdo. I gave a fellow a ride to Ratsaka. Odd chap, clerk going home to visit his mother. Didn't say much. Where are you headed? All the way to Lhasa? Good. It's a hell of a journey. From Chamdo, nearly twelve hundred kilometres. Usually takes me thirty, thirty-two hours. Depends if there are hold-ups. Landslides, you know. They can block the road for days. Or PSB. They put up checkpoints, ask a lot of damn fool questions. I hate the PSB.' He removed his cigarette from his mouth and spat on the floor of the cab.

Tsering murmured a response only occasionally, hoping

Chuma would get the message and shut up. But the driver just kept going, breaking off every few minutes to light a new cigarette before resuming his flow of verbal diarrhoea.

'That your first?' Chuma asked, nodding at the baby on Pema's lap. 'I've got two in Lhasa. Two girls. Drive me mad. I can't wait to get away. It's hard work, but I like driving. Well, it's better than working in a factory, isn't it? I picked up a fellow last year. You wouldn't believe what he told me went on in his work unit . . .'

'How long is it to Lhasa?' Tsering asked when he could get a word in.

'From here? Twenty hours. Something like that. Not including stops. I stop for food, to take a piss. But not often. I like to keep going. The time soon passes.'

Tsering suppressed a sigh. It was going to be a long night.

'We'll try again, shall we?' Chang said. He fiddled with the dial on the electric baton, musing on how high a charge he could risk administering. All prisoners were different. Some started singing on only a low voltage, others had a higher tolerance to pain. This monk was particularly tough, though he didn't look it. Chang increased the dial a fraction. It was important to get the balance right. High enough to really hurt, not so high the prisoner blacked out after every shock.

'Let's start at the beginning. Answer my questions and we can end this now. We can end the pain. Do you understand?'

Jigme was barely conscious of the major's words. Every muscle, every nerve end of his body was in agony. He knew he couldn't last much longer. He tried to estimate what time it was. It must be evening by now. Had he given the others long enough? That was the only thing that concerned him. He had to hold out long enough to give them time to get away.

He had never known pain like this. Compared to monks like Lobsang he had had a soft, easy existence. He hadn't been imprisoned, hadn't suffered the deprivations of the labour camps. Nothing in his life had prepared him for this. He was hurting; hurting more than seemed physically possible while still remaining conscious. And with each stab of the cattle prod it got worse. A few more hours, he thought. Just keep going for a few more hours. Then it will all be over.

'. . . just tell me where they went. Tell me how you intended to get out of the country. Give me the names of the people who have helped you . . .'

The major's rasping voice seemed to be a long way off. Then the interpreter's. Jigme had heard the same phrases, the same questions repeated so many times that he didn't need to listen to the translation. How could a Tibetan do this? Jigme wondered, diverting his brain away from what would inevitably come next. How could a Tibetan help the Han, stand by and watch while one of his fellow countrymen was tortured? It was incomprehensible to him.

Chang was looking up at him again, brandishing the cattle prod. Jigme was too exhausted to be frightened. He was past fear.

The pain came like a sudden explosion that pulsed out to every inch of his body, twisting and wracking his muscles and obliterating his vision in a searing blaze as if red-hot pokers had been jammed into his eyeballs. He swung on the chain, his limbs bursting from their sockets, and summoned up the image that had kept him going throughout the day. A vision of a tiny baby; a baby crying, now smiling, now sleeping, an aura of light around its face. He saw the child looking at him, felt the power, the benediction of its gaze, before the whole world went dark again.

Chou placed the sheet of paper on the desk in front of Chang and stepped back.

'The list of births you asked for, Comrade Major.'

'You've checked it?'

'The prisoner's child is here, Comrade Major.' Chou leaned over, pointing at a name he'd underlined in red ink. 'Pedor Jamang, born on September the sixteenth, his birth registered by his father in Tengchen county on September the twenty-fourth.'

Chang studied the sheet, a sudden chilly premonition touching the back of his neck. 'That can't be right,' he said.

'I've checked with the prefecture at Gyamotang,' Chou replied. 'The details are correct. They examined the register for me to make absolutely sure.'

'It can't be right,' Chang said again. 'There must be a mistake. There must be another child with the same name.'

'I also checked the details with the prisoner, Dolma Tashi,' Chou said. 'She confirmed them. The father's name, the place and date of birth, the child's name. They are all correct. This is the child. There is no doubt about it.'

Chang picked up his pen and scribbled a few numbers at the bottom of the sheet of paper. He'd already done the calculation in his head, but the answer was not what he wanted to find. It couldn't be right. It *couldn't*.

The dates didn't add up. The child was too old. He'd been born at least a week before the Dalai Lama died. Chang thought back to the meeting he'd witnessed in Shen's office, when the pedantic little academic from the University of Tibet had explained that it was possible for a new Dalai Lama to be born before the old one died. It had seemed a preposterous concept at the time. Now, in retrospect, it seemed no more credible. But there was another explanation. It was one that Chang did not really want to contemplate, but it was more likely. Likely? No, certain. It was the only logical, the only rational, conclusion to reach. Chang felt his anger returning, taking hold of him. Not a hot, boiling anger, but something much more controlled: a cold, clinical fury with a core of pure ice.

'Phone downstairs, Lieutenant,' he ordered. 'See if the monk has regained consciousness.'

Chou picked up the phone on the desk and called the basement, conversing briefly with someone at the other end.

'He is conscious, Comrade Major,' Chou said, replacing the receiver. 'But the custody officer says he is in no condition for more questions. He advises a longer break if you wish to progress further.'

'I'll be the judge of that,' Chang replied frostily.

Jigme was dangling limply from the chain. His wrists were rubbed raw and bleeding from the handcuffs and he could no longer feel any sensation in his arms. He half opened his eyes as Chang entered the room with the interpreter. He was surprised how indifferent he felt. What more could they do to him now?

As soon as Chang started speaking, Jigme could tell from the major's tone that something had changed.

'Where is the real child?' Chang said. 'Have you found him? Have you? Is that why you set up a decoy to fool us? Where is he? We will find him, you know. *Where is he?*'

So they knew. A wave of relief swept through Jigme. He'd done all he could. Now it was time to rest.

Chang reached up and grabbed Jigme's face, forcing him to look down. Jigme saw the major's pock-marked skin, the eyes shot through with a cruel, bitter hatred.

'You tricked us,' Chang screamed at him. 'Have you found the child? Where is he?'

A strange serenity settled over Jigme. His body seemed to hurt less. His nerve ends were numb, his mind clear but quite calm. He knew in his heart that the others had got away. Why else was Chang back here asking more questions?

The major was holding the cattle prod now. 'Where is he?' he shouted furiously.

Jigme's lips twitched. He opened his mouth. Even that slight movement took a monumental effort. He wondered if he had the strength to speak.

Chang waited for him. 'Just tell me,' he said softly.

Jigme's tongue touched his lips. Soon it would all be over.

'*Bo Rangtsen,*' he whispered. 'Freedom for Tibet.'

Even Chang knew those two words of Tibetan. They hit him like a blow, and for a moment he lost all reason as the anger erupted inside his head. He twisted the dial on the electric-shock baton to maximum and thrust it into Jigme's body, holding it there in a blind fury until the monk was still.

NINETEEN

There could be few more marked contrasts anywhere on earth, Maggie thought as she stepped out of the truck depot on to the teeming streets of Lhasa: from the remote untouched wilderness of northern Kham, a region with more yaks than humans, to the crowded Tibetan capital where the noise, the smells, the traffic and above all the hordes of people assaulted the senses from all directions. She had to pause to draw breath, to accustom herself once again to the chaos of the metropolis.

For Pema, the transition was even more of a shock. She'd spent her whole life in the open spaces of the mountains, living in a tent, roaming free over the high, deserted plateau with only a few other nomad families for company. She'd never seen a town before, let alone a city the size of Lhasa. She stood transfixed with terror at the edge of the road, watching the cars and lorries and bicycles whizzing by, the crowds of people making their way home at the end of the day. A bus roared past, its slipstream knocking her sideways, the exhaust fumes choking her with unfamiliar odours. Everywhere there seemed to be people. The activity, the noise, the ugly detritus of civilisation washed over her, making her reel.

Tsering put a reassuring hand on her arm. 'It's all right. I know it's a shock for you. Just stay close to me and you'll be safe.'

He guided her along the pavement. Pema kept both arms wrapped protectively around her baby who was fast asleep in the sling across her breast. Her eyes moved ceaselessly, taking in the strange sights all around her. She had heard of Lhasa, but had never imagined it would be like this.

Maggie had her dust mask tied over her face again, her Mao cap pulled down to shield her eyes. No one gave her a second glance. She followed Tsering and Pema across the road, Lobsang just behind her, and they headed east for the Tibetan Quarter. Maggie was stiff from the long journey in the truck, but she was amazed at how easy it was to walk in Lhasa. They were twelve thousand feet above sea level, but after Mount Gebur the air was rich in oxygen, the terrain just an easy afternoon stroll.

Half a kilometre from the Jokhang, Tsering suddenly stopped. Ahead of them a PSB truck had pulled in to the kerb and police officers were setting up a checkpoint across the road, stopping both vehicles and pedestrians.

'This way,' Tsering said, turning off down a side-street. There were more people here, mostly Chinese but some Tibetans. A couple of cyclists wove in and out of the throng, tinkling their bells. Tsering, taller than most of the people in front, looked ahead and stopped again so abruptly that Maggie almost walked into the back of him. She gave him an inquiring glance, not wanting to speak English in case they were overhead. Tsering inclined his head, his eyes directing her gaze up the street. Another PSB truck was blocking the thoroughfare. Uniformed officers were checking everyone's papers.

'Back,' Tsering said softly.

They retreated up the street. Two police officers came round the corner, heading straight for them. Tsering didn't hesitate. He took Pema's arm and turned into the entrance of a Chinese clothing store. Maggie and Lobsang went after them. A smiling female shop assistant came forward, pointing at the racks of drab workers' uniforms and jabbering at them in Chinese. Tsering ignored her and went straight out of the side entrance of the store. They were in an alley between buildings, a narrow passage full of piles of rubbish and rotting cardboard boxes.

Tsering went up the alley, emerging into a wider street. Directly in front of them was another uniformed police officer. He was standing stiffly outside a pair of iron gates set in a high stone wall. His knee-length boots were polished to a brilliant sheen, his tunic buttons gleaming, and on his hands he wore immaculate white gloves. Maggie noticed the brass plaque on the wall next to him. In Chinese, Tibetan and English it read, 'United Kingdom Consulate'.

Turning her back on the police officer, Maggie whispered to Tsering, 'You see the plaque?'

He saw where her thoughts were headed and shook his head. 'We must get to the Tibetan Quarter.'

'That's the last place we want to be. There are police everywhere. The Tibetan Quarter is the obvious place they'll look. Even assuming we can get there past all the checkpoints.'

'I'm not sure . . .'

'They're going to pick us up, Tsering. We have no papers. Every way we turn there are *Gong An Ju* waiting.'

Tsering hesitated. 'How?'

'We have to get rid of the guard.'

The police officer by the gates was watching them suspiciously. He called out to them, demanding to know what they were doing.

'Leave it to me,' Lobsang said quietly.

'What are you going to do?' Tsering asked.

'Don't worry about me. Just look after the child,' Lobsang growled in reply.

'Lobsang . . .'

But Lobsang was already moving away, walking down the street past the policeman. The officer told him to stop.

'Who, me?' Lobsang said in Chinese.

'Yes, you. Come here,' the officer ordered. 'Show me your papers.'

'I'll show you my arse, you Chinese nincompoop,' Lobsang said.

The policeman gaped at him in astonishment. Then his eyes narrowed. He reached for the truncheon on his belt.

'Son of a whore,' Lobsang shouted at him in Chinese, then hared away down the road, running awkwardly with his strange rolling gait. The officer flushed with anger and raced after him. Lobsang ducked into an alley and vanished from sight.

The gates to the consulate were unlocked. Maggie pushed them open and crossed the small enclosed courtyard to the main entrance of the building. She pressed the intercom buzzer by the door.

'Yes?' a voice crackled in English.

'I'm a British citizen,' Maggie said. 'Let me in.'

The consul was in a meeting so his secretary, Joan – an efficient, motherly woman in her mid-fifties – took care of them. Maggie explained to her why they were there and Joan – recovering quickly from her initial surprise – applied herself to making them welcome.

She found a quiet room in which Pema could feed her baby and from somewhere produced a pack of disposable nappies made in Hong Kong. Pema had no idea what they were.

'I'll show you, dear,' Joan said. 'They're very easy. So much simpler than the old terry ones. You can wash him in here.' Joan opened a door to reveal a small bathroom complete with Marks and Spencer towels, Palmolive soap and Andrex toilet tissue.

Pema had never seen a bathroom before in her life. Taps, running water, a flush toilet were all a mystery to her.

'Don't worry, I'll give you a hand,' Joan said kindly, continuing to chat away in English though it was clear Pema couldn't follow a word of the language.

'You must be hungry,' Joan said. She went to the kitchen and brought them tea – Twining's English Breakfast – and a plate of McVitie's digestive biscuits. 'I'll get you some proper food in a while. Make yourselves at home. I'll let you know when the consul is free.'

Joan hurried away. The outposts of the British Empire had always been run by women – by wives and nannies and governesses. In the diplomatic service, nothing much had changed in the intervening century and a half.

Maggie went into the bathroom and had a hot shower, her first in more than a fortnight. She found some shampoo in a cupboard and washed her hair, luxuriating in the consulate's opulent – for Tibet – facilities. She put on fresh clothes from her bag and looked at herself in the bathroom mirror. Her hair was shining, her face tanned to a golden brown. The skin was dried out by the altitude, but there was a pot of Nivea moisturising cream on a shelf above the wash basin. She slapped some on her face and chapped hands and rubbed it in, enjoying the feeling of cleanliness, of renewed vitality it gave her.

Tsering looked at her when she emerged – an appraising glance that for the first time since they'd met seemed to come from a man not a monk. Maggie pushed her damp hair back and let him stare.

'You should try it,' she said. 'These diplomats don't believe in hard living. Take advantage of it while you can.'

Tsering was looking distinctly grubby. He hadn't had a proper wash in days and the grime was beginning to show. He ran a hand over the dark stubble on his jaw.

'Is there a razor?' he asked.

'There's everything.'

'Perhaps I should.' He looked away distractedly.

'Something bothering you?' Maggie asked.

'Lobsang.'

'He's a wily old fox,' Maggie said. 'He'll be fine.'

'And Jigme?'

'He's tougher than he looks, you know.'

'Oh, I know that. He wouldn't have been chosen to come if he hadn't been up to it. I'm just wondering where he is now.'

'Have a shower. Take your mind off things.'

Tsering was still in the bathroom when Maggie was called into the consul's office. The room was furnished as though it were in Whitehall – leather-topped mahogany desk, brown leather gentleman's club sofa and a gaudy ormulu and crystal chandelier which would have looked more at home in the ballroom of some minor Home Counties stately home. The rug on the floor looked Tibetan, but had probably come via Harrods.

There was some artwork on the walls: bright vivid paintings of Africa which Maggie guessed were the legacy of a previous posting; and a few personal possessions on the desk – family photographs, some books on Tibetan language and culture.

The consul himself was younger than Maggie had expected, a smooth, inscrutable man in his early forties. He was in shirtsleeves, his jacket tossed casually over a chair beside the desk.

'Sit down, please, Miss Walsh,' he said, giving her a thin smile. 'My secretary has filled me in on the background. You seem to have a habit of creating problems for us.'

'Sorry?' Maggie said.

'You were here a few years ago, filming secretly. The Chinese were very upset by your documentary. We had to work very hard to re-establish good relations with them.'

'That was then, this is now,' Maggie said, not wanting to dwell on the incident.

'And now you're back,' the consul continued. 'In the country illegally again. You're not making things easier this time round either, are you?'

'What do you mean?'

The consul pushed back his chair and crossed his legs, fixing Maggie with a clear, unwavering gaze. 'I mean the child you brought with you. The one you claim is the new Dalai Lama?'

'It's not a claim. He is.'

'I find that difficult to believe. His reincarnation found already? It's only a few weeks since the previous one died.'

'They moved quickly. They had to.'

'I hope this isn't some elaborate hoax, Miss Walsh.'

'You have my word. I was there when they found him.'

'"They"?'

'The search party from Dharamsala. The monk outside is one of them. Ask him. Check with the Tibetan Government in exile.'

'You must understand why I'm sceptical. It seems quite incredible.'

'I witnessed the whole thing. Believe me, it *was* incredible. Please, we need your help. The child's in great danger. If the Chinese capture him, his life is as good as over. Will you give him and his mother political asylum?'

'If they ask for it, we will have to consider it.'

'And if it's granted?'

'The Chinese may not let them leave the consulate.'

'So they could remain trapped inside this building?'

'That is entirely possible.'

'Couldn't you just give them temporary British passports and get them out of the country now? Find us some transport to get us to the border?'

'It's not quite that simple.'

'But you could do it, couldn't you?'

'The British Government really can't get involved in Chinese internal affairs, you know.'

'You think the fate of the new Dalai Lama is a Chinese internal affair?'

The consul looked away, reluctant to answer. Maggie leaned forward over his desk.

'It's because the West hasn't wanted to get involved that one and a half million Tibetans have been exterminated by the Chinese since they occupied the country. That baby needs protection. Please, I urge you to do everything you can to help him.'

The consul lifted his hands defensively. 'This is well above my head, Miss Walsh. A matter as complex and sensitive as this will have to be discussed at the highest level. I will inform the embassy in Beijing of the situation and they will have to consult the Foreign Office in London.'

He forced another smile. 'You can rest assured that the

British Government will do everything in its power to resolve this matter. You may stay here for the time being. I'll inform you as soon as a decision is made.'

Joan fixed them up with places to sleep. Pema and the baby were given a bedroom in the small accommodation annexe adjoining the consulate. Maggie and Tsering had to make do with the sofa and floor in one of the ante-rooms.

'I'll take the floor,' Tsering said. 'The sofa is too short for me.'

He spread out a blanket on the wooden tiles and lay down on his back, gazing up at the plaster relief ceiling.

'How is Pema?' Maggie asked.

Tsering shrugged. 'She is tired, and overwhelmed by everything. Fortunately, she does not understand fully what is happening to her and her son. She does not understand the difficulties we face. That ignorance will protect her. She has her baby to look after. We will look after her.'

Maggie noted his use of the word 'we' and wondered whether he meant Lobsang or whether it was a tacit admission that he saw her now as an ally rather than an irritating encumbrance.

'Perhaps it was a mistake, coming here,' he went on.

'We had to get off the streets. It wasn't safe.'

'When will the consul know?'

'That's hard to say. The Foreign Office in London has to make the decision. They're not noted for their speed, and this is going to be a very tricky one for them. We've stirred up a hornet's nest by coming here.'

'I don't like relying on them,' Tsering said uneasily. 'If there's one thing we Tibetans have learnt since the Chinese invasion, it is not to rely on outside help. The British have done nothing for us over the last fifty years. Why should they do anything now?'

'Because we've presented them with a tangible problem,' Maggie replied. 'On *their* patch. They can wash their hands of the Tibetan Government in exile, pretend it doesn't exist.

They can ignore Chinese oppression in Tibet. But they can't ignore us. We're here, sitting in their consulate with the infant Dalai Lama. They've got to do something about us.'

'What are their options?'

'The best-case scenario is that they provide us with transport, a vehicle with diplomatic protection, to take us to the Indian border.'

'You think they'll do that?'

'It wouldn't be difficult. They can give us papers. I'm a British citizen. They could come up with some plausible cover story for you and Pema and the baby. They could quietly get us out of the country.'

'It would upset the Chinese if they found out.'

'Who's going to tell them? We're not. And the British Government is very good at being economical with the truth. It's one of their specialities.'

'And the worst-case scenario?'

'Let's not think about that. It'll give us nightmares.'

But Maggie thought about it anyway. It was impossible not to. Seeking sanctuary in the consulate had been an impulsive action, a spur-of-the-moment decision to get them away from the immediate danger of the PSB checkpoints. She still felt they'd had no choice, but she was beginning to wonder now whether it had been a wise move.

The British Government – like every other Western government – had long ago sacrificed the Tibetans on the altar of political expediency. They were irritants that wouldn't go away; a tiresome distraction from the important business of currying favour with the Chinese. With the death of the old Dalai Lama, Maggie had no doubt that the British Government would have felt an immense sense of relief. Their leader and inspiration gone, the Tibetans would surely now become even more of an irrelevance on the world stage, one more dispossessed people who could be safely consigned to the dustbin of history. The news that a new Dalai Lama had been found could only be unwelcome in the corridors of Westminster. That he had been found and was seeking sanctuary on British diplomatic territory was a disaster of unparallelled proportions.

Maggie didn't trust her government to act honourably or humanely – they were politicians, after all. Over the years, they'd betrayed millions of Tibetans with their compliant silence. What were a few more?

Maggie was well fed, clean and comfortable for the first time since she'd entered Tibet. She should have passed a peaceful night on the consulate sofa, but she didn't. She was too worried to sleep.

It was nine o'clock in the morning, and Shen Tzu had already been at his desk for more than two hours, when the call came through. His secretary transferred it immediately.

'It's Beijing, Comrade Colonel,' she said breathlessly. 'General Fang Lo himself.'

Shen's bowels turned to water. He noticed his hand on the receiver start to tremble. Fang Lo was the head of the *Gong An Ju* for all China. Shen had never spoken to him in his life. The call could mean only one thing.

'Colonel Shen here, Comrade General,' he said, amazed at how calm his voice sounded.

Fang Lo was short and to the point. The conversation – or rather monologue, for Shen said nothing throughout – lasted no more than twenty seconds. When Shen replaced the receiver, he realised he'd been holding his breath the whole time. He exhaled with relief and paused for a moment to allow his heartbeat to return to normal. But it continued to race – not out of fear now, but through excitement.

Shen pushed back his chair and almost ran out of the door and down the corridor. Chang was at his desk, reading through the overnight reports. He'd returned from Chamdo the previous evening, recalled by Shen the moment the colonel was told that the monk had died under interrogation. Shen had been livid with his deputy. Looking up now from his paperwork, Chang saw his boss's flushed face and prepared himself for more of the same.

'You've got a chance to redeem yourself, Major,' Shen barked urgently. 'I've just spoken to General Fang, in Beijing. The child we're seeking, his mother and a monk from Dharamsala are hiding in the British Consulate. Get some men and go over there at once.'

Chang stared at him, momentarily too stunned to speak. 'The British Consulate?' he repeated with a puzzled frown.

'Get a move on, Major,' Shen snapped. 'You're wasting time.'

'You want me to enter the British Consulate and seize them, Comrade Colonel?' Chang asked, his wits returning.

'Don't be stupid. Force will be unnecessary. The British are going to hand them over to us.'

TWENTY

Maggie sensed there was something wrong the moment Joan came into the room. The consul's secretary seemed hurried, almost flustered. Her face was tight, her movements nervous, urgent.

'He's turning you in to the Chinese,' she said, her voice little more than a whisper.

Maggie stared at her. The piece of toast she'd just buttered was frozen in mid-air, halfway to her mouth. '*What?*'

'The embassy in Beijing have told the Chinese authorities you're here. We've just had a fax through ordering the consul to hand you over. Get out now while you can. There's a side door. I've unlocked it for you. It leads directly into an alley. This way.'

Maggie threw down her toast and grabbed her bag. Tsering was in the bathroom down the corridor. Maggie banged on the door.

'It's me. Open up.'

'I'm washing,' came a muffled voice from inside.

'Open the bloody door, Tsering.'

The bolt clicked back. Tsering was stripped to the waist, water running down his chest.

'The Chinese are on the way,' Maggie said. 'Get your stuff.'

Tsering blinked. 'The Chinese . . .'

'*Now*, Tsering. I'll get Pema.'

Maggie ran down the corridor. Pema's room was at the back of the consulate. Maggie didn't bother to knock. She burst in abruptly. Pema was sitting on the bed feeding her baby. She looked up, stifling a cry of surprise.

'Gyami,' Maggie said. 'Chinese.'

'Gyami?' Pema's face turned pale. She pulled the baby off her breast. The child immediately started to howl.

Maggie beckoned her urgently. 'We have to go. Quickly!' She picked up a couple of items of clothing from the bed and stuffed them into Pema's bag, adding the rest of the packet of disposable nappies.

'Gyami,' Maggie repeated. 'Here.' She pointed out of the door.

Maggie took Pema's arm and pulled her to her feet. Tsering was coming down the corridor as they came out of the door.

'Follow me,' Joan said.

She led them round a corner and through a door into a storage area that was packed with boxes of stationery and other supplies. Joan pulled open a door on the far side and leaned out.

'It's all clear. Go!'

Maggie paused on the threshold, about to speak.

'Just go.' Joan pushed her out into the alley. 'That way. Good luck.'

Maggie ran. Pema was right behind her, running awkwardly with the baby clasped in her arms. Tsering brought up the rear. At the end of the alley they paused.

'Which way?' Maggie said.

'It doesn't matter,' Tsering replied. 'Just keep running.'

There was a shout behind them. Maggie spun round. Two uniformed Chinese police officers were racing down the alley towards them. She turned and sprinted away up the street. There were pedestrians in front of her, a dented van unloading outside a shop. Maggie dodged around them and veered off down another street, slowing a little to let Pema keep up. Emerging at another junction, Maggie stopped. A PSB truck was pulling in to her left, more armed police jumping down from the back. She went right. The pedestrians were edging to the sides of the street, instinctively moving out of the way, giving the police a clear view of the fugitives.

A second truck loomed up suddenly, screeching to a halt and blocking the road in front of Maggie. She ducked down a narrow passageway and kept going. Pema was struggling with the pace, burdened with her baby. There was more shouting, a piercing blast on a police whistle that was repeated over and over. Boots thudded on the ground behind them. Maggie glanced round. A line of police officers was snaking through the passageway, gaining on them. She erupted into a small square and stopped abruptly.

Every exit from the square was blocked by policemen.

Maggie stared around, not giving up hope yet. Then her shoulders slumped. There was no way out. Tsering came up beside her. Pema was between them, shaking with fear. Maggie put her arm around her shoulders. Tsering followed her lead, holding Pema tightly from the other side as they waited for the police to move in.

An officer with a pock-marked face and the insignia of a PSB major on the sleeves of his tunic stepped forward, a gleam of triumph in his eyes. He examined them in silence, his gaze coming to rest finally on the distressed baby who was crying inconsolably on Pema's breast.

'So this is him,' the major said with a sneer. 'The new saviour of the Tibetan people. Well, not any longer.'

Chang's lips curled into a sardonic smile and he turned to the officer behind him. 'Put them in the truck.'

They were sitting on a wooden bench in the back of the canvas-topped truck, sandwiched between two armed policemen. Across from them, perched watchfully on the other bench, were three more policemen. Maggie eyed them resignedly, furious with the betrayal by her own government but clear-headed enough to absorb fully the hopelessness of their position. There would be no escape from a PSB truck, and soon they'd be in a Chinese prison cell which would be even more secure.

The truck began to slow. The gears crunched as the driver changed down. The vehicle swung to the left. Maggie clutched at the edge of the bench to prevent herself sliding off it. It was impossible to work out where they were headed. The rear canvas flap was down over the tailboard so they couldn't see out and the truck had turned so many times that Maggie had lost all sense of direction.

The truck straightened up again and accelerated a little. Maggie could feel the vibrations buzzing through her feet and up her legs. Next to her, Pema was hunched over her crying baby, trying in vain to comfort him. Maggie glanced at Tsering. He was like a statue, sitting absolutely still, his face devoid of emotion.

Then suddenly the driver braked heavily. There was a loud bang, the noise of metal hitting metal. The front of the truck slewed sideways. Maggie was thrown violently off the bench. Pema too was flung forward, but managed to twist her body around to land on her shoulder, her arms cradling the baby in a protective embrace. The policemen on either side toppled off into a tangled heap on the floor.

Maggie rolled over, winded but unhurt, and heard gunshots outside. The truck had come to a halt. The back flap was pulled aside and a face peered in: Lobsang. Bolts were disengaged and the tailboard banged down. More faces appeared – Tibetan faces. Maggie recognised the plaited hair and wide-brimmed hat of the *Chushi Gangdruk* leader, Thondup.

'Quickly!' he yelled, reaching in to drag Maggie out.

Lobsang was clambering inside, helping Pema to her feet. The policemen were disentangling themselves, fumbling for the pistols on their belts. Thondup jerked his rifle up and shot two of the policemen at close range. Another Tibetan shot the remaining three officers. Tsering stared in horror at the bodies, the blood spattered everywhere.

'Move!' Thondup shouted at him. 'Hurry!'

Maggie jumped out of the back of the truck. There was more gunfire from the front. She caught a glimpse of young Tibetan men with rifles. They were running for cover, crouching down behind cars parked at the side of the street, firing blind at the Chinese who were hidden from sight. A huge Dongfen lorry, exiting from a side road, had smashed into the front wing of the PSB truck, sending it skidding across the carriageway. The Dongfen's radiator had punctured and steam was hissing out in a cloud. Flames were licking from under the bonnet of the PSB truck and there was a reek of diesel in the air.

Pedestrians were scurrying for cover. Someone was screaming. A burst of automatic gunfire raked the front of the Dongfen, the bullets pinging into the metal. Maggie ducked, twisting round, trying to see what was happening. The Tibetans were returning fire. One of them caught a bullet in the stomach and was hurled backwards by the impact, blood erupting from his *chuba*.

'Over here,' Thondup yelled. He grabbed hold of Maggie's arm and pulled her away from the truck. Lobsang and Tsering were helping Pema, shielding her with their bodies as they ran for shelter. They'd reached the buildings along the edge of the road when the PSB truck exploded. A searing ball of fire shot into the sky, the shock waves flattening the people nearby. Maggie was knocked to the ground, catching her thigh on the edge of the kerb. A cloud of acrid black smoke billowed across the street, smothering everything with thick, choking fumes. The two trucks were almost hidden by the smoke, only the dancing flames marking their position.

Thondup hauled Maggie to her feet. There were screams of fear, and of pain from somewhere close by, then more gunshots. Maggie noticed three more bloodstained bodies lying in the road. Thondup dragged her into a side-street where a white van was waiting, its engine idling, its rear doors swinging open.

'Get in,' Thondup ordered. His dark face was smeared with sweat and dirt. He'd lost his hat in the confusion and his red-tasselled plaits swung loose around his shoulders.

Pema was bundled into the van after Maggie, then Lobsang and Tsering scrambled in. Thondup turned away in time to see a Chinese policeman emerging from the gusting smoke, his sub-machine-gun blazing.

'Go!' Thondup shouted at the van driver, his rifle swinging up from his hip. Thondup fired, hurling himself across the open back of the van. The sub-machine-gun burst caught him full in the chest, shattering his flesh as though it were water melon pulp. Blood splattered on to the doors of the van, stippling the white paintwork like a pointillist canvas. Thondup went down, limbs flailing, his rifle clattering away across the tarmac. Lobsang and Tsering threw themselves over Pema and the baby to shield them as the policeman raced forward. The van was already moving, accelerating fast down the side-street. The policeman fired. Maggie felt a gust of air as a bullet hissed past her cheek. She looked back. The policeman was tumbling to the ground, gunned down by one of Thondup's men. She saw more armed police bursting out of the cloud of smoke. Then the van turned sharp right and she saw no more. The stench of the smoke was still harsh on her nostrils, her ears full of the sound of Pema sobbing and a small baby crying.

The back of the van was sealed off from the cab so they couldn't communicate with the driver. Nor could they see out. There were no windows and Tsering had pulled the rear doors shut only seconds after leaving the scene of the shoot-out. Since then they'd seen nothing. The van had kept going without a pause for more than four hours. None of them knew where they were going.

Finally, the vehicle slowed. Maggie felt it turn off the road, bouncing over ruts and potholes. Then it stopped completely and the engine was turned off. The rear doors clicked open and a Tibetan man looked in at them. Maggie had seen him before. It was one of Thondup's lieutenants, a thick-set, stocky man wearing sheepskin boots. He gestured at them to get out.

They were on a rough track behind a thicket of willow trees which was set in the bottom of a broad valley whose sides were bare and sandy coloured like enormous dunes.

'Where are we?' Tsering asked.

'Near Samye,' the driver replied. 'The Tsangpo is that way,

an hour's walk.' He pointed due south. 'I'll leave you here. Stay hidden in the trees. At nightfall I will return.'

'We have to get to the border. Why don't we drive on?'

'Impossible. You have to cross the Tsangpo. The only ferry is to the east near Tsetang. There's a *Gong An Ju* post there. It's too dangerous. I will arrange for a boat and come back to pick you up. Stay hidden until I signal you with a torch.'

He climbed back into the van and drove away down the track. Tsering waited until the noise of the engine had gone, then led the others into the thicket. They found a tiny clearing in the trees and sat down on the hard, parched ground. For the rest of the afternoon they stayed there, dozing a bit, talking intermittently, waiting.

At dusk, the driver did not return.

'What if he doesn't come?' Lobsang said.

'He'll come,' Tsering replied.

An hour later a vehicle came down the track from the main road and stopped. The headlights were extinguished. In the darkness, a torch flashed on and off three times.

'It's him,' Tsering said.

They picked their way out through the willows. The driver had brought food and water with him.

'Eat while we walk,' he said tersely. 'Stay close together, no talking and watch your feet.'

They followed him along the track, chewing on pieces of coarse brown bread and strips of dried yak meat. After half a kilometre, the track petered out and they walked across open land. The ground was rough underfoot, as barren as the surface of the moon.

They saw the dark ribbon of the Tsangpo River ahead of them. The driver told them to wait and continued on alone. When he returned, he gave a nod and said: 'The boat is there. Don't talk on the crossing. Sound travels a long way at night.'

'And once we reach the other side, what then?' Tsering asked.

'The boatman will show you where to hide. Someone will come for you in the morning.'

'Does the boatman know who we are?'

'No. He knows you're wanted by the police, that's all. He can be trusted. He has a brother who died in Drapchi. He is no friend of the Han.'

The boat – a small yak-skin coracle – was moored on the north bank of the river. They climbed down on to a narrow strip of sandy beach and the van driver helped Pema into the boat. Before he let go of her arm, he looked down at the baby asleep in the sling across her chest and touched the child's head gently with his fingertips.

'It has been an honour to help you,' he said softly.

Maggie joined Pema in the bow of the coracle, then Tsering and Lobsang clambered into the stern. The boatman picked up his oars and pushed off. There were no seats in the boat, just a narrow wooden plank lashed across the centre for the boatman to rest on as he rowed. It was a strange, tactile sensation, sitting in the bottom of the coracle. The yak-skin hull moulded itself to the buttocks so you could feel every movement of the water as the boat slipped out into the river. Further east, in the gorges of Kham, the Tsangpo became a raging torrent as it dropped down off the Tibetan plateau and made a wide loop round into India as the Brahmaputra, but here it was wide and sluggish, broken up by long sandbanks.

The boatman, a slight but wiry fellow with a face like carved walnut, manoeuvred the boat away from the bank and began to row across, his oars dipping smoothly into the water with hardly a splash. In the faint moonlight the ripples were threaded with filaments of silver. The boatman let the current do most of the work, simply steering the boat in a diagonal line downstream. The first sandbank was only fifty metres from the shore. The boatman let the coracle ground in the shallow water and jumped out, ordering the others to follow. With Tsering and Lobsang's assistance, the boatman pulled the coracle out of the water and they carried it between them to the far upstream side of the sandbank where they launched it again and floated across the channel to the next sandbank. Forty minutes later they were clambering out on the south shore of the river.

The boatman beached the coracle and led them along the bank to a dilapidated wooden hut. Planks were missing from its walls and there was a gaping hole in the roof where one of the rusting sheets of galvanished iron had fallen off.

'No one comes here,' the boatman said, pushing open the rotting wooden door.

There was a smell of decay and damp and old fish inside. Broken wooden boxes and the torn remains of discarded fishing nets were strewn around the bare earth floor. The boatman kicked aside a crumpled tarpaulin and there was a scuttling sound as rats scurried away and out through the gaps in the walls.

'You will be safe here,' the boatman said. 'No one will find you.'

He went away, pulling the door to behind him. Maggie had a pencil torch in her bag. She shone it carefully around the interior of the hut, making sure she shielded the beam so it couldn't be seen from outside.

'What are you doing?' Tsering asked.

'Looking for vermin. If there's one thing I hate it's rats.'

A pair of beady eyes gleamed at her from a corner. Maggie kicked a piece of wood towards them and the rat scampered away through a hole under the wall.

'Not exactly five-star accommodation,' Maggie remarked dryly. 'Still, I've slept in worse places.'

In Groszny, holed up in the city's cellars with the Chechen rebels, there'd been rats the size of chihuahuas; big, bold brutes feeding off the corpses that littered the streets. At night she'd felt them running over her feet and legs, woken once to find one entangled in her hair. She could cope with a few of the Tibetan variety. Rats preferred meals that didn't fight back.

They cleared away some of the debris and spread the tarpaulin out on the floor. Then they lay down, all five of them together, and tried to sleep.

*   *   *

325

It was getting light when Tsering awoke. He crawled to one of the gaps in the wall and peered out. The river was still as a lake, its surface smooth and grey like a tarnished mirror.

'What is it?' Lobsang murmured.

'Nothing,' Tsering replied. He crawled back to the tarpaulin and lay down. He was wide awake now. 'How far is it to the border?' he said.

'As the crow flies, probably no more than two hundred kilometres,' Lobsang answered.

'Can we do it?'

'Just the two of us, I'd say yes. We both walked further than that when we left last time. With the child and its mother, I'm not so sure.'

'She's a *drogpa* girl. She's tough. She's used to walking.'

'Maybe,' Lobsang conceded. 'But it's not just the walking. The Han are going to stop at nothing to find us. They lost some men yesterday. At least six dead that we saw. It could be more. When did that last happen? Six Chinese killed by Tibetans. The Han won't stand for that. Every policeman in Tibet will be looking for us. And not just the police. They'll mobilise the army too. How far do you think we'll get with the PLA on our tails?'

'We're not giving up.'

'I'm only pointing out the difficulties we face.'

'When you walked out before, how long did it take you?'

'Six weeks. But I started much further north. And I did the whole thing on foot. Whoever comes for us today will surely have a vehicle.'

'I don't know. With Thondup dead I'm not sure how organised they'll be.'

'*Chushi Gangdruk* isn't just one man. There are dozens of them. Committed brave men who have had enough of the Chinese. You saw how they fought in the ambush in Lhasa. I was with them when they planned how they were going to get you out of the consulate. They knew the British would betray you. We were watching the outside of the building all night, waiting for the right moment.'

'And the truck that crashed into us?'

'That was a piece of brilliant improvisation. We didn't expect the Chinese to show up, never mind capture you, but Thondup didn't lose his nerve. Nor did his men. They will fight on without Thondup. As long as the Han oppress us, there will be men willing to resist them.'

Daylight was creeping in through the walls and roof of the hut, playing over the sleeping forms of Pema and Maggie. The nomad girl was curled up on her side, the baby tucked into the open front of her *chuba* where he'd fallen asleep at her breast.

'We will make it,' Tsering said confidently.

'And Jigme?' Lobsang asked, his thoughts turning to their younger colleague. 'Will he make it?'

'That is out of our hands.'

'I should have gone, not Jigme.'

'He wanted to. He knew it would not be easy.'

'I think he's dead. I sense it.'

'Then he gave his life for a noble cause,' Tsering said with a philosophical calm. 'He will find a good rebirth.'

Tsering stood up and opened the door of the hut. He looked around cautiously. In the distance, on the southern edge of the Tsangpo flood plain, he could see the outline of houses, fingers of smoke trickling into the sky, but the area immediately adjacent to the river was deserted. He walked down to the water's edge and washed. The sun was bright, but there was a coolness in the air that reminded him that winter was close.

They still had the kerosene stove and pan in Tsering's bag so they boiled some river water and made tea, drinking it with the remains of the bread the driver had brought the previous evening. Pema fed the baby, then she and Maggie changed his nappy, using some of the warm water left over from the tea to wash him. Tsering watched the slick way Maggie handled the disposable nappies, showing Pema how to put them on and fasten the adhesive tags around the baby's waist.

'You've done this before, haven't you?' he said.

'My sister has three children,' Maggie replied. 'They're beyond nappies now, but I've watched her put them on a few times.'

'An older sister?'

'Yes.'

'Where is she?'

'She lives in Bristol. In the south-west of England.'

'You've never wanted them?'

'Children?' Maggie hesitated. 'Children aren't really compatible with the way I live my life.'

'You could change the way you live.'

'I don't think so.'

'And you've never been married?'

'No.'

'Never wanted to be?'

Maggie shrugged. Maybe she'd contemplated it once, before a sniper's bullet in Sarajevo had blown away her dreams. But Alex hadn't been the marrying kind. He hadn't been a family man either. She could never have envisaged Alex changing a nappy, putting up shelves, mowing the lawn at weekends. The thought made her shudder. Her sister was happy, but her way of life wasn't for Maggie. The school run, dinner parties, two weeks in Cornwall every summer – it was like a living death to Maggie.

She rummaged in her bag for a cigarette. She was down to her last packet of Marlboros. She lit one and looked at Tsering.

'How about you? Does marriage appeal?'

'Me?' He was surprised. 'I'm a monk.'

'I know. But monks have feelings. Don't you ever miss the companionship and affection that comes with a close relationship? The feeling that somebody cares about you, that somebody needs you and you need them.'

'I don't think about it. I have taken a vow of celibacy.'

There was something fascinating about men who renounced sex, Maggie thought. It gave them a mystique that other men didn't have. They'd forsworn something important in life, something fundamentally human, and most people could not comprehend why they'd done it. But it was celibacy that gave the Buddhist monk, or the Catholic priest, his strange allure.

'You think I'm peculiar, don't you?' Tsering said.

Maggie tapped the ash off her cigarette. 'No. Some people just aren't interested in sex.'

'What makes you think I'm not interested?'

'Are you?'

'If I didn't want it, my vow of celibacy would hardly be very onerous. That's the point. You have to sacrifice something that matters.'

She studied him quizzically. 'How do you cope?'

'We are taught to control desire through meditation,' Tsering said. 'To see that attraction and revulsion are transient states brought about by mental aberration.'

'Desire is an aberration?'

'To the pure mind, yes. If a woman were inherently attractive, then her body should still be attractive whether she was alive or dead. Yet a decaying corpse is revolting to us. As monks, we are taught to imagine a beautiful woman as a rotting corpse, the flesh slipping off her bones. To understand that beauty, and sexual desire, are ephemeral, conditioned states.'

'So if you fancy a woman, you imagine her dead?'

Tsering nodded. 'You would be amazed how it diminishes desire.'

'I don't want to diminish desire,' Maggie said. 'Why should I when it's natural and pleasurable?'

'Nagarjuna, the great Indian scholar, said: "When you have an itch, you scratch. But not to itch at all is better than any amount of scratching."'

'Well, personally,' Maggie said, 'I quite like scratching.'

'No one is coming for us,' Lobsang broke in suddenly. He was standing by the door, looking out across the valley.

'Give them time,' Tsering said.

'Someone should have been here by now. What if they don't come?'

'Sit down, Lobsang. They will come. Be patient.'

The large-scale map of the Tibet Autonomous Region was spread out across Shen's desk. A cigarette in his hand, the ash a centimetre long, the colonel was poring over the layout of his territory.

'Lhasa?' he said without lifting his head.

'Every exit sealed since yesterday afternoon,' Chang replied. 'All vehicles are being stopped and searched.'

'You think they're in the city?'

'It's possible. I'm having the Tibetan Quarter searched again. Just in case.'

'And if they got out yesterday?'

'There are checkpoints on all the roads south.' Chang leaned over the map with a pen, marking the locations.

'*Gong An Ju*?' Shen said.

'And some PLA. The army is very keen to get involved.'

'I know,' Shen said acidly. He'd had a meeting only that morning with the PLA divisional staff, an uncomfortable hour during which the army commanders had made plain their utter contempt for the Public Security Bureau and its handling of the shoot-out with the splittists. They'd cast doubt on whether the police were competent enough to catch the fugitive Tibetans and hinted at a PLA takeover of the whole operation if there were any more setbacks.

'This is still our show,' Shen said. 'The army will try to muscle their way in and take the credit for any results, but I want them kept in the background. We're in charge. I want the fugitives caught by us, not the PLA.'

'And Beijing?'

'So far they have agreed to a joint operation, coordinated by us. But they may get impatient if we don't produce the goods quickly.'

'If the fugitives are still in Lhasa, we'll find them soon,' Chang said.

'And if they're not?'

'It's a long way to the border.'

Shen scanned the frontier areas, the long, mountainous boundary with India, Nepal, Sikkim and Bhutan.

'Where do you think they'll try to cross?'

Chang pointed with his pen. 'The main roads all go south-west, to Nepal and Sikkim. They know we'll be watching those routes, so I think they'll head due south and try to cross into Bhutan or Arunachal Pradesh.'

'By road?'

'On foot. The border is several thousand kilometres long. They know we can't possibly guard it all.'

Shen traced the direct route south from Lhasa and stopped at the thin line of blue running east-west across the path.

'The Tsangpo. They have to cross the Tsangpo,' he said.

'The ferry stations for Dorje Drak and Samye are both being watched,' Chang replied.

Shen tapped the ash off his cigarette and took a long drag, filling his lungs with smoke. He was already on his third packet of the day, a sure sign of nerves.

'You are checking the river?'

'Not so far, Comrade Colonel.'

'Get a boat out from Tsetang. Check both banks of the river.' Shen leaned back in his chair, trying to remain calm. 'We lost eight men yesterday, Major. The splittist barbarians humiliated us. They have spilt Chinese blood, made fools of us. I feel the loss of face very deeply. I want revenge for those deaths.'

'So do I, Comrade Colonel.'

'Then find the child. He is the Tibetans' hope, their future. Without a leader they are nothing. If we have the child, they are finished.'

Lobsang heard the noise first. He moved to the door and opened it a fraction, peering out through the gap. A dirty green, long-snouted Jiefang truck was rattling down the track towards the hut. Lobsang watched it, trying to make out the nationality of the driver – Tibetan, or Chinese – but the sun was reflecting off the windscreen, turning it opaque. The truck slowed, its engine misfiring explosively, and came to a standstill by the hut. The driver climbed out and looked around. He was a Tibetan – a thin stick of a boy wearing baggy navy trousers, a zip-up jacket and a flat cap. Lobsang signalled to Pema and Maggie to keep back and stationed himself against the wall just beside the door.

As the door creaked open, Lobsang grabbed the boy around the neck.

'Who are you?' Lobsang demanded.

The boy clutched at Lobsang's arm, almost choking, trying to ease the pressure on his throat.

'*Chush* . . .' he began incoherently.

Tsering stepped in. 'Go easy on the boy.'

Lobsang loosened his grip. 'Who are you?'

'*Chushi . . . Gangdruk*,' the boy stammered, rubbing his neck and backing away uneasily.

'We expected you earlier,' Lobsang said accusingly. 'What happened?'

'Lobsang . . .' Tsering gave a shake of his head, then turned to the boy. 'We were told you'd come this morning. We were worried something had happened.'

'There are roadblocks everywhere,' the boy said. His voice was high-pitched, making him seem even younger than he looked. 'Lots of soldiers and police. It took me two hours to get across on the ferry. They were questioning everybody, searching all the cars and trucks from top to bottom.'

'They questioned you?' Lobsang asked tersely. 'What did you say?'

'That I was going to Gonggar to collect a consignment of freight from Chengdu. I have all the paperwork.'

Lobsang regarded him suspiciously. 'You're very young for this. Why did they send you?'

'The others have all been rounded up. The *Gong An Ju* are pulling in everyone they can lay hands on – detaining them, interrogating them. Our victory yesterday has really put the wind up them.'

'What were your instructions?'

'To come here and collect you. To take you wherever you wanted to go.'

'What else?'

'Nothing. That's all he told me.'

'Who is "he"?'

'One of Thondup's men. One of the Khampas.'

'Did he say who we were?'

'Just friends. That's how he put it.' The boy stared around at them, at Tsering and Maggie and Pema and the baby. 'Did I do wrong?' he asked anxiously.

Tsering clapped him reassuringly on the shoulders. 'No, you've done well. What's your name?'

'Dorje.'

'Well, Dorje, why don't we get on the truck? We've a long journey ahead of us.'

The police launch came slowly up the river, the harsh noise of its outboard motor shattering the tranquillity of the valley. There were five officers on board, one of them – the sergeant in charge – steering from the stern, his hand on the throttle, the others scanning both banks as the launch headed upstream between the sandbanks.

Several times they'd pulled in to the shore to search isolated patches of woodland or outcrops of rocks, but they'd found nothing. They were bored and tired, daydreaming about what they were going to do when they'd finished their shift. *If* they finished their shift. The divisional captain had cancelled all leave on orders from Lhasa and placed all his men on an emergency footing which, in theory, meant they were on duty twenty-four hours a day.

'Sergeant . . .'

The young officer on the port bow was pointing ahead to a ramshackle hut on the south bank of the river. The sergeant eased back on the throttle and steered the launch towards the shore. They cruised slowly past the hut, giving it a cursory inspection, then the sergeant manoeuvred the boat to the bank.

Two officers were dispatched to the hut. They trudged along the bank, grumbling under their breath. This was going to be another waste of time, they were sure. They could tell before they even got to the hut that there would be no one there. The place was falling down, a complete wreck of a building. It didn't look as if anyone had been near it for years.

They pushed open the broken door and stepped inside the hut. It was a warm evening and the interior was ripe with a combination of different odours – of damp and rotting wood and fish. And something else: a rank, fetid stench that turned the stomach. One of the officers flashed his torch around, picking out the shapes of the mouldy old wooden boxes, the tatty fishing nets gathering dust in the corners like giant spider's webs. Then the beam landed on another object that glistened white in the light. The officer walked across and bent down to examine the object, prodding it with the end of his torch. The smell was unbearable. He straightened up and went back to the open door.

'Sergeant!' he shouted. 'I think we've found something.'

TWENTY-ONE

The darkness was absolute. The sky, obliterated by thick cloud, was as black as the earth. The headlights of the truck drilled twin holes in the night, the beams illuminating only a narrow area in front so that it seemed as if they were heading through an endless tunnel.

The Jiefang was old, but it had been built to last, its wheels and chassis constructed to withstand the rigours of the Chinese road network. None of the highways in this remote part of Tibet was metalled. They were little more than broad tracks from which the larger boulders had been removed, leaving behind a covering of small rocks which rain and landslides soon washed away. There were potholes thirty centimetres deep, great hollows and depressions and cracks in the surface like fault lines, but the Jiefang coped with them all.

Tsering was in the cab, navigating while Dorje drove. Squeezed tightly between them were Pema and the baby. Maggie and Lobsang were once again in the back, clinging to the sides of the truck as it bounced violently along the road. It was cold and noisy and very uncomfortable.

They avoided villages whenever they could, skirting round them on side roads or farm tracks, and once or twice drove cross-country to keep away from a junction that looked like an obvious place for a police checkpoint.

For two hours their luck held. Then ahead of them, maybe two or three kilometres away, they saw lights at the side of the road.

'*Gong An Ju* for certain,' Dorje said agitatedly. 'What do

we do?' And when Tsering didn't reply, he repeated: 'What do we do?', his voice trembling.

'Slow down, but don't stop,' Tsering said, trying to stay calm. The boy was jumpy enough for both of them.

'Then what?'

'Just listen. Slow to a walking pace. We'll drop out and make our way round the checkpoint. Pick us up again a couple of kilometres down the road. Find a spot and wait for us. Do you understand?'

Dorje licked his lips and nodded. He eased on the brakes. Tsering swung open the door and leaned out, calling round the back of the cab to Lobsang and Maggie.

'We're getting off. Get ready to jump.'

Tsering took the baby from Pema. 'He'll be safe, don't worry. Just do as I say. Slower still,' he said to Dorje.

The truck slowed to a crawl. Tsering held the baby close and stood on the steps of the cab. He jumped. He hit the ground with a jolt, but stayed upright. Maggie and Lobsang were already over the side, leaping clear of the truck's wheels. Tsering jogged along beside the cab and held out his arm to Pema. She hesitated.

'Jump!' Tsering urged. 'Hurry!'

Pema closed her eyes, stretching out her hand. Tsering grasped her fingers and pulled, catching her in one arm as she stumbled to the ground. He steadied her, then ran on and slammed the cab door shut before the truck accelerated away.

They walked off the side of the road, looping round in a wide semicircle to avoid the checkpoint. The ground fell away into a deep gulley. They lost sight of the road, could no longer see the tail-lights of the truck or the lights at the roadblock. They moved cautiously, taking care on the slippery side of the gulley. Before they reached the bottom, they heard the sound of running water. A fast-flowing stream cut across their path, following the floor of the gulley for a while before disappearing through a narrow cleft. There was no way round the stream on this side, the bank was just a sheer cliff. They would have to ford it.

Tsering pulled off his boots and socks and rolled up his trousers above the knee. He stepped into the stream. The water was icy, freezing all sensation from his feet in seconds. He waded across into the middle to test the depth, swaying a little as the fierce current battered against his legs. The water came up to his knees but no higher. He picked his way back across the stony bed, lifted Pema and her baby into his arms and carried them across the stream. Maggie and Lobsang removed their footwear and followed them. They were drying their feet and replacing their boots when the baby began to cry. The sound echoed off the walls of the gulley, amplified by the close confines.

'Can't you quieten him?' Tsering said, fearing the noise might be audible at the PSB checkpoint.

'He's hungry,' Pema said. 'He needs feeding.'

'Can't he wait?'

'If you want him to stop crying . . .'

'Well, make it quick. Dorje might already be waiting for us.'

Pema sat down on a boulder and opened the front of her *chuba*, the baby lunging greedily for her breast. Tsering turned away, trying to contain his impatience, reminding himself that the child was the only thing that mattered.

The PSB sergeant shone his flashlight on the papers. After a while he looked up at the *mantze* – the Tibetan barbarian – who was standing by the side of his truck.

'Where are you going?'

Dorje squinted at him quizzically. 'Uh?' He understood enough Chinese to know what the sergeant had said, but he thought if he acted dumb they might just let him go.

'Where are you going?' the sergeant repeated. He pointed at the truck, then along the road, trying to communicate in sign language. Why did these peasants not learn Chinese?

Dorje made a face and grunted again.

'*Where?*' The sergeant increased his volume as though shouting would make his question easier to understand. But Dorje just shrugged and held out his arms in bewilderment.

'These papers are for Gonggar,' the sergeant persisted. 'What are you doing down here? What . . . are . . . you . . . doing . . . down . . . here?' He articulated each word slowly as if hoping the Tibetan might somehow be able to lip-read Chinese.

Dorje stared at him blankly. 'Chinese . . . no,' he said gormlessly, shaking his head and sticking his tongue out like an idiot.

The sergeant shone his torch into Dorje's face. What did you do with a half-wit like this? The *mantze* was clearly a simpleton. Stupid, but probably harmless. The sergeant was inclined to wave him through and go back to the warmth of the PSB Landcruiser which was parked at the side of the road. His orders had been clear. They were looking for two Tibetan men, a Tibetan woman and her baby, and a Western woman. This fellow was clearly nothing to do with that, he was just a clueless truck driver, but still the sergeant hesitated. No policeman was ever reprimanded for needlessly detaining an innocent Tibetan, but letting one go who turned out to be guilty – that was an unpardonable mistake. It was better to err on the side of caution; at least consult a higher authority before he made a decision.

'Wait here,' the sergeant said.

He walked across to the Landcruiser and reached inside for the radio.

They came back on the road a kilometre beyond the checkpoint. The detour, including the stop to feed the baby, had taken them three-quarters of an hour. Tsering stood on the verge and looked both ways. He could see no sign of the truck.

'He must be waiting for us further on,' he said.

They walked on along the road for another fifteen minutes without coming across the Jiefang. Tsering looked back. The checkpoint lights were just a dull glimmer on the horizon.

'Where is he?' Tsering said.

'They've detained him,' Lobsang replied grimly.

'Maybe he's being very cautious and is waiting further on,' Tsering ventured, but he could already feel his stomach starting to tense.

'He's not here,' Lobsang said after they'd walked another kilometre. 'They must be holding him.'

'We'll give him a while longer,' Tsering said with an optimism he didn't feel.

'Tsering . . .' Lobsang was looking at him intently. 'He's had enough time. If he were going to come, he'd be here by now. Something's gone wrong – his papers, his travel documents, something. If they question him . . . He's just a boy. How long do you think he'll last?'

'What do you suggest?'

'We get off the road. If he's talked, that's where they'll come looking.'

Even as Lobsang finished speaking, there was the sound of a truck engine starting back up the road at the checkpoint. The noise carried clearly through the still night air. Two beams of light lanced through the darkness. Headlights. Tsering watched them, rooted to the spot.

'Maybe it's Dorje,' he said. 'They've let him continue.'

'Or maybe it's the *Gong An Ju* coming to look for us,' Lobsang said.

But the headlights didn't come towards them. They veered across the road, sweeping out in an arc across the open land beside the carriageway.

'It's turning round,' Tsering said.

Another set of headlights burst into life. An engine turned over, smoother, less throaty than the first. Not a truck engine, but a Landcruiser. These headlights too swung round, the Landcruiser overtaking the truck and heading away north up the road. Tsering watched the two sets of red tail-lights receding into the distance.

'What are they doing?' Lobsang asked.

'Escorting him back the way he came,' Tsering said.

'Or he's in the police car in custody and someone else is driving the truck.'

'Either way, we've lost our transport. We'd better get going.' Tsering turned to Pema. 'How are you feeling? We have no choice but to walk now.'

'I will manage,' Pema said.

'And the child?'

'He is asleep.'

Tsering smiled ruefully. At least one of them had the right idea.

Five or six kilometres further on, they came to a village beside the road. It was in darkness, not a light to be seen. Tsering checked his watch. It was nearly one o'clock in the morning. The villagers would more than likely be asleep, but he didn't want to risk being spotted by a sleepless inhabitant who happened to look out of their front window.

'We'll go round,' he said.

They cut down the embankment at the side of the road and skirted around the village, keeping well away from the houses. The cloud cover had lifted and at the edge of the plateau to the south, only a few kilometres away, they could see clearly the jagged silhouette of the Himalayas.

The land around the village was cultivated. The barley fields were stubble, but there were patches of vegetables, of potatoes and turnips and radishes which were still growing. They found a narrow path between two strips of winter cabbage and were almost beyond the village when Tsering looked to the side and stopped.

'What is it?' Lobsang asked, coming to a halt behind him.

'Wait here,' Tsering said.

He walked out across the cabbages to a low stone wall that marked the boundary between fields and village. He leaned over the wall and lifted something up that had been propped on the other side. Then he lifted a second object. When he came back, the others saw that he was carrying a bicycle in each hand.

'Much quicker than walking,' he said softly.

He gave one of the bicycles to Lobsang and they carried

them until they were a safe distance past the village. Only when they were well out of earshot did they risk wheeling the bicycles up on to the road. Pema stared at these strange contraptions and Tsering realised she'd probably never ridden a bicycle before. In the *drogpa* communities of the high plateau they were hardly an essential appurtenance of life.

Tsering showed her how to sit on the seat. The baby, secure in the sling across Pema's chest, was still asleep. Pema wobbled a bit and clutched at the sides of the saddle.

'You can hold on to me,' Tsering said. 'It's quite safe.' Then in English he said to Maggie: 'You can ride a bicycle?'

'Of course. Two of us to each one? I haven't done that since I was a kid. Who's going to pedal?'

Lobsang shrugged. 'We take it in turns.'

'Okay, you first.'

Maggie slid on to the saddle. Lobsang grasped the handlebars and pushed off, standing up on the pedals. The bicycle rattled away down the road. Maggie gripped the saddle tight behind her, her feet swinging in mid-air on either side. With each turn of the pedals the mountains came closer.

'This had better be worth it,' Chang said ominously, doing up the last two buttons of his uniform tunic. He'd been asleep in the officers' quarters of the PSB barracks in Tsetang when the orderly came to tell him he was wanted by the duty captain. Sore-eyed, pale with fatigue, Chang was in no mood to be understanding.

'I thought you wouldn't want to wait until morning, Comrade Major,' the duty captain said. 'The urgency of the situation. You said when you arrived yesterday that . . .'

'Yes, yes,' Chang interrupted peevishly. 'Just tell me what you've got. Another nappy?'

'A prisoner, detained at a roadblock a hundred kilometres south of here. He was driving an empty truck. His travel papers said he was going to Gonggar to collect a shipment of freight, but he was nowhere near Gonggar.'

'He was alone?'

341

'Yes.'

'You've questioned him?'

'He claims he took a wrong turning and got lost.'

'Maybe he did. Why should this interest me? What relevance does it have to my operation?'

'He was behaving suspiciously. His manner is shifty, evasive.'

'You got me out of bed for this?'

'He was heading south. You told us to stop all vehicles heading towards the mountains.'

Chang sighed. He was used to the PSB's endemic culture of passing the buck, the reluctance of junior officers to make decisions or take action without the approval of their superiors, but sometimes it was an irritating nuisance.

'I thought you might want to question him yourself, Comrade Major,' the captain continued defensively. 'Particularly as we found this in the back of the truck.'

The captain held up a transparent evidence bag which on first sight appeared empty, but on closer inspection could be seen to contain a tiny white cylinder. Chang peered at it and realised it was a cigarette stub. Perhaps the duty captain wasn't so stupid after all.

'It's the same brand of American cigarette we found in the hut by the Tsangpo,' the captain said.

Chang's weariness ebbed away in an instant. 'Where is the prisoner?'

Dorje was being held in an interview room in the custody block, his hands cuffed in his lap, two police officers watching over him. Chang entered the room accompanied by the interpreter and sat down without a word. He studied Dorje impassively, deciding what course of action would be the most effective. The prisoner was young – eighteen or nineteen, Chang guessed – and from his face and manner, very scared. That was a good combination. Chang liked them young and scared.

'Get him up,' Chang said to the two officers.

They pulled Dorje to his feet and stepped back.

342

'Give me your truncheon,' Chang said to one of the policemen. Then he looked at Dorje who was eying him apprehensively. 'We can do this the hard way, or the easy way.'

Chang paused for the interpreter to translate, then swung the truncheon hard across Dorje's face. Dorje screamed, cupping his hands over his shattered nose, the blood pouring out between his fingers. Chang hit him three more times, then sat down again.

'I think we'd both prefer the easy way, wouldn't we?'

The road hit the foothills of the mountains, then began to climb steadily, winding its way up the empty valleys in long, twisting switchbacks, the peaks on either side growing ever higher. On the flat terrain of the plateau, the bicycles had been a boon. In two hours they'd covered twenty kilometres or more, two or three times the distance they could have managed on foot. But now, as the gradients got steeper, the bicycles became increasingly redundant. They were impossible to pedal and pushing them was an extra effort they could all do without. They were tired and hungry. Conserving their waning supplies of energy was their most important consideration. Tsering decided it made sense to ditch the bicycles.

On one of the bends in the road, they found a deep ravine through which a mountain stream was cascading. Tsering lifted the bicycles and hurled them over the edge, watching them crumple on the rocks and splash into the foaming water. Then he took out their map and studied it by the light of Maggie's pencil torch, calculating how far it was to the border. The road made a long detour to the west before resuming its path south towards India, a total distance of nearly a hundred kilometres. But he had no intention of taking the road. The walking would be easier, but the road was too obvious, too open. There would be police on the road, border guards where it crossed into Arunachal Pradesh. It was harder, but safer, to head cross-country. As the crow flew it was only forty kilometres to the frontier. *Only*, Tsering thought wryly. Forty kilometres across some of the toughest, harshest terrain on earth. They would do it. They *had* to do it. For the child's sake, for their people's sake, they had to succeed. Tsering picked up his bag and walked on.

'Get me Colonel Shen.'

'Colonel Shen is asleep,' the night duty switchboard operator said.

'I know he's asleep,' Chang fired back. 'Wake him up. This is Major Chang calling from the district office in Tsetang.'

Chang waited. It was the middle of the night, but he felt fresh and alert, a subdued excitement coursing through his veins.

'Shen,' the voice on the line said. No angry expostulations, no recriminations for waking him up. Shen knew there would be a good reason.

'We have the driver who took them south from the Tsangpo,' Chang said. 'We know exactly where he dropped them off.'

'What do you need?'

'It's a two-hour drive from here and we may have to search a wide area off-road. I need a helicopter and a squad of commandos.'

'You'll have them. How soon do you estimate apprehending them?'

Chang hesitated, knowing it was rash to make predictions. But he was feeling very sure of himself.

'A few hours,' he said. 'By noon today they'll be ours.'

TWENTY-TWO

They left the road shortly after dumping the bicycles and took a path up the valley side. The path wasn't marked on their map, but it was obviously well used, its surface worn away by countless feet into a stony track that was easy to follow even at night. It climbed relentlessly for several hundred metres, then levelled out and cut through a notch in the mountains. The gradient became less severe. For a time they walked almost on the flat, pine forests on either side. It was a welcome reprieve. They were all desperately tired, their limbs aching from the long bicycle ride and then the ascent from the road. They needed rest more than anything, but they didn't dare stop. The Chinese wouldn't be far behind.

Only when the baby awoke and started crying with hunger did they pause for a break. While Pema fed the infant, Tsering and Lobsang opened their bags and checked how much food they still had left. Of the supplies they'd brought with them from India, supplemented by the provisions Thondup had provided in the Toyota camper van, very little remained. The butter and *tsampa* had all gone. There was still half a bag of rice, some dried noodles and a quarter of a brick of tea, but these wouldn't feed four adults for very long. The kerosene in the stove too was getting dangerously low.

'How many days to the border?' Tsering asked.

'Three, if we're lucky,' Lobsang replied.

'We don't have enough food for three days.'

'Then we make do without.'

'We should have something now. We've eaten barely anything all day. Get the stove ready.'

Tsering filled a pan with water from the nearby stream and they had a meagre meal of boiled rice, passing the pan around between them and downing a few spoonfuls each. It did little to ease the gnawing hunger pains in their bellies, but it would give them energy for a few more hours.

The path became steeper again. Their pace slowed to an agonised shuffle, each step accompanied by the laboured gasps of their breathing as they struggled up the gruelling incline. Maggie kept her eyes fixed on the path, partly to watch her feet on the uneven surface, partly because to look up and see how far they had still to climb was enough to make her give up. Gradually the summit got nearer. Maggie could look down and take heart from the long drop, the evidence of how far they had already come. The path took one last hairpin twist and came out on to a bluff. In front of them was a broad tree-filled valley, its floor gashed by a rushing alpine stream. Dawn was breaking and in the distance, closer now than she'd expected, Maggie saw the long ridge of high peaks that marked the frontier with India.

'We're passing over the checkpoint now, Comrade Major.'

Chang looked down out of the window. The shadow of the helicopter was racing along the ground below them like a huge black locust. He could see the line of the road, the PSB truck parked beside it, a couple of policemen looking up.

'Keep following the road,' Chang said.

The pilot nodded, holding the helicopter on its southerly course. Chang scoured the horizon. He could see every contour of the land from up here, every fold and dip in the ground. The sheer emptiness of the country was breathtaking. For hundreds of kilometres in all directions there was nothing but a vast, virtually uninhabited plateau fringed with mountains that from the air looked like chipped teeth biting through the thin crust of the earth.

A village flashed past below, a tiny oasis in the endless desert, then minutes later the road began to climb into the foothills. Chang checked the pencil line he'd marked on his map, relating it to the terrain underneath him. If the fugitives were still on foot, there was no way they could have come this far south. Chang signalled to the pilot, speaking into the microphone by his mouth.

'Go back. We'll look again.'

The helicopter banked, circling round to head back north up the road. The sky was overcast, but the visibility was good. If the fugitives were on the road, or in a band on either side, Chang should have seen them. But there was nothing. The road was as deserted as the surrounding plain.

'Put us down by the village,' Chang said.

It seemed as if the whole settlement came out to watch as the helicopter landed in the fields. Men, women and children gawped in fascination as Chang and his commandos disembarked from the Sikorsky Blackhawk.

'Search the place,' Chang told his men.

The major strode into the centre of the village while the commandos dispersed. The houses were the usual Tibetan hovels, Chang noticed. These people lived like animals, only one step up from the goats and dogs that roamed the narrow dirt streets. Outside the teahouse, three elderly Tibetan men were sitting on a bench smoking clay pipes and drinking that disgusting butter tea the *mantze* liked so much. Chang glared at them. Why weren't they doing something useful with their time? The men were regarding him curiously as if he were some species they'd never encountered before. One of them pointed with the stem of his pipe and his two companions chuckled maliciously.

Chang turned away, suspecting he was the butt of a disrespectful joke, but deciding to ignore it. Three cackling old men were not something a PSB major needed to worry about. At the edge of the village, just by the main road, he saw a sign in Chinese – a garage and petrol station. That was as good a place as any to start. At least he'd be with his own kind: the sale of petrol was an exclusively Chinese occupation, too important to be trusted to the feckless Tibetans. Chang strolled across past the pumps and pushed open the door of the station. Inside, a Chinese man in a navy worker's suit was stacking shelves with the groceries that the garage also sold. He looked up and started with surprise when he saw Chang's uniform. He wiped his hands on his jacket and came forward, smiling and bowing his head obsequiously.

'You have come very quickly, Comrade,' he said. 'But then the *Gong An Ju* are renowned for their speed and efficiency. I know my complaint is but a trivial one compared to the great crimes you are used to investigating, but theft is theft and I am sure you will do all you can to catch the anti-social perpetrators.'

Chang squinted at him. 'What are you talking about?'

'My phone call, of course, Comrade. I discovered the theft early this morning, but I only found time to call you an hour ago. I am most impressed with the speed of your response.'

'Theft?' Chang said. 'We are not here to investigate a theft. We have better things to do with our time.'

The garage manager's face fell. 'With respect, Comrade, this is an important matter. We Han must stick together. We must show the Tibetan barbarians that they cannot steal our bicycles and get away with it. I know it was the *mantze*. No Han would ever steal from another Chinese.'

'This is nothing to do with us,' Chang said sharply. 'Who did you call?'

'Well, you. The *Gong An Ju*, in Lhuntze.'

'We are not from Lhuntze. We are from Tsetang. Were you on duty last night?'

'Until midnight, Comrade.'

'Did anyone come past on foot? Two Tibetan men, a Tibetan woman and her baby and a Western woman?'

'On foot? On the road, you mean? No, no one came past on foot.'

'What about vehicles? Did you notice any come past with . . .' Chang stopped in mid sentence. 'Did you say bicycles?'

348

'Yes, Comrade.' The manager perked up a little. Perhaps the police would investigate the loss after all. 'Two bicycles, in very good condition.'

'They were stolen from here? From the garage?'

'From my home, on the edge of the village. They were in the garden where we usually keep them. In the past there has been no problem. We always leave them outside. We are too trusting, I fear. The *mantze* have taken advantage of our good nature. I advise you to question them, Comrade. One of them has our bicycles, I am sure.'

'When were they taken?'

'Some time during the night.'

'Show me.'

The manager shook his head apologetically. 'I'm sorry, Comrade, but I am not permitted to leave the garage during my shift.'

'Lock up, and *show* me,' Chang said.

Tsering stopped, holding up a hand to halt the others. He sniffed the air. They could all smell it now: woodsmoke.

'Stay here,' Tsering said.

He climbed up the steep bank next to the path, dropping to his stomach as he neared the top, and peered cautiously over. Below him, around a bend in the track, was a tiny hamlet, maybe nine or ten houses grouped together on the banks of another gushing stream. They were square, flat-roofed stone buildings, coloured prayer flags fluttering atop their walls. Trickles of smoke seeped from the chimneys, drifting slowly across the valley in the breeze. Tsering watched the houses for a time, but saw no sign of life. He slithered back down the bank to the path and pulled out the map.

'It's a village,' he said. 'It must be this one.'

A settlement was marked on the map, but it was so small and insignificant it wasn't named.

'Can we avoid it?' Lobsang asked.

'Do we want to? They may have food we can buy.'

'It's too risky,' Lobsang said. 'There may be informers there. If Dorje has talked, the Chinese will know roughly where we are. Our only hope is to stay hidden in the mountains for as long as possible. The moment we show ourselves to anyone, we put ourselves in danger.'

'You're right. We can't afford to take that chance.' Tsering studied the map. The scale was too small to show all the footpaths. In any case, there weren't many. There were tracks between the isolated villages, a few packhorse routes over the high passes which smugglers still used, but most of the region had no links with the outside world.

Tsering shook his head. 'This map is next to useless up here. We'll just have to find a way round on the ground.'

He looked up, surveying the terrain in front of them. The path to the village turned to the left around a spur, following the easiest line up the mountain, but if they kept straight on, they could circle round the southern edge of the village by traversing the valley side higher up. It was a steeper route, with a tricky-looking escarpment to negotiate in the middle, but it didn't appear impossible. What worried Tsering more were the clouds – a greyish mass rolling in from the southeast, enveloping the higher peaks and obliterating the sun. Already he could feel the temperature dropping.

'The weather's going to change,' he said uneasily. 'We'd better get moving.'

Chang did the calculation in his head as the helicopter flew south towards the mountains. He was sure beyond any reasonable doubt that the monks had stolen the two bicycles. On the outskirts of the village he'd found tyre marks on the earth embankment leading up to the road, scuff marks and traces of boot prints in the soft soil. Who else could it have been? The discovery had forced him to revise his estimate of how far the fugitives might have travelled during the night. A bicycle could easily have doubled the distance, taking them well into the foothills.

He looked down out of the window. The only sign of

movement was a truck heading north along the road, leaving a trail of dust in its wake. The landscape was dark now. The shadow of the helicopter no longer kept pace with them on the ground. The sun had disappeared completely behind the clouds.

'At the first bend in the road,' Chang said to the pilot. 'Begin your grid search.'

The pilot nodded, glancing down through the window. As he saw the bend appear below, the road starting to climb from the plain, he changed course and began a narrow east–west sweep over the foothills. Chang covered his side of the cockpit, knowing that the twelve commandos behind him would also be scanning the ground. For close on an hour they flew to and fro without seeing any trace of people on the move. Once, they passed over a village, the only one in the area, and saw a few of the inhabitants gazing up at the helicopter, but otherwise the landscape was deserted. The fugitives seemed to have melted away into thin air.

Chang looked at his watch. It was gone eleven o'clock in the morning. He was beginning to regret the noon deadline he'd predicted to Shen. In retrospect, that had not been a wise move.

'What do you want me to do now, Comrade Major?' the pilot inquired.

Chang hesitated. He had to make a decision. *Any* decision. They couldn't simply keep flying backwards and forwards indefinitely.

'The village we saw,' Chang said. 'Put us down there.'

Maggie watched the Blackhawk come up the valley with a sickness in her belly, the sight taking her back to Afghanistan in '82 – her first time in the Panjsher with Alex and the *mujahideen*. She could still see the Soviet Mi24 gunships strafing the valley sides, the decoy flares bursting all around them to deflect heat-seeking missiles. There was something sinister about a helicopter, something alien. A fighter plane was over and out of range in a matter of seconds, but a helicopter came more slowly. It gave you time to see it, time to dwell on what it might do. She'd seen them elsewhere since, in every war zone she'd ever visited, but nothing compared to that first time in the Panjsher, that sheer, shit-scared terror she'd experienced.

And now another helicopter was coming for her: a big, black shape silhouetted against the skyline, the noise of its rotor blades reverberating across the valley. She was crouching in the trees, knew she couldn't possibly be seen, but was frightened nonetheless – of the helicopter, and of the men it contained. Up till now she'd put the Chinese out of her mind, thought of them as a real but distant threat. To see them a few hundred metres below her in the valley, climbing out of the Blackhawk with sub-machine-guns, was truly unnerving.

'Do they know we're here?' Tsering said, speaking softly as if his voice might carry down to the village.

Maggie shook her head. 'They're starting with the obvious – check the villages, search the houses, question the people. Find out if anyone has seen us. Thank God we kept well away from there.'

'And then?'

'They'll look again from the air. Maybe send out ground patrols to cover the paths.'

'Should we find somewhere to hide?'

'Not now,' Maggie said. 'Delay favours the Chinese, gives them time to tighten the noose on us. We're safest while the helicopter's on the ground. Let's get going before it takes off again.'

The wall of pine trees shielding them from view, they resumed their ascent of the valley side.

The search took only fifteen minutes, the village was so small.

'Nothing,' the commando sergeant reported back to Chang.

'You've rounded up all the inhabitants?'

'This is all of them,' the sergeant said, indicating the motley collection of people who'd been herded into what passed for the village square. Chang cast his eye over them. They were mostly old and decrepit, though there were a couple of middle-aged women among them. No young men. They would all have gone away to look for work in one of the towns. Up here in the mountains, apart from subsistence-level animal husbandry, there was nothing for them to do.

'Do any of you speak Chinese?' Chang asked, wishing now he'd brought an interpreter. He hadn't expected to need one.

The villagers stared at him blankly. Then an old man said something in Tibetan.

'What was that?' Chang said. 'Speak Chinese.'

'He asked what we wanted here,' the sergeant translated.

'You speak Tibetan?'

'Some.'

'Ask them if any strangers have passed through in the last twelve hours.'

The sergeant conveyed the question in halting Tibetan and listened carefully to the answer.

'No, Comrade Major. They have seen no strangers.'

'You believe him?'

'I'd say he was telling the truth.'

'Tell them they can go back to their homes.'

As the villagers dispersed, Chang took out a map from his tunic pocket and unfolded it. This was the only village for miles around, and it was the closest settlement to the main road. If Chang had been attempting to reach the border on foot, this was the way he would have come. It was the shortest, most direct route.

'I want you to split your men up,' Chang said to the sergeant. 'Leave half of them here. Two to watch the village itself, the other four searching the area between here and the road.'

'And the other half?'

'Will come on the helicopter with me. We will resume the air search. If we see nothing, then we get the pilot to drop us here, to the south, covering the Kangri-La Pass. To reach the frontier, they'll have to cross the pass. When they do, we'll be there waiting for them.'

They were still in the forest, hidden by the trees, when the helicopter flew past overhead. Tsering looked up, watching the dark shape through the pine branches.

'What now?' he asked, turning automatically to Maggie. She had experience of these kinds of things, worldly things a Buddhist monk knew nothing about.

'We keep walking,' Maggie said.

'And when we leave the shelter of the forest? What then?'

'We pray,' Maggie said.

As they came out above the treeline, it began to snow; not heavily, but enough to coat the mountainside with a dusting of white. The temperature dropped markedly and the clouds thickened into a dense bank that began to creep down into the valleys, smothering the upper slopes with a fine mist.

Maggie followed Tsering up the incline, a flurry of snowflakes gusting in her face. The weather worried her. The snow in particular was bad news – they weren't equipped for winter mountaineering. But if it brought with it a covering of cloud to hamper the helicopter, then that could only be a blessing. Just so long as the snow didn't get worse. She lowered her head against the wind and struggled on wearily up the mountainside.

'One more sweep,' Chang said.

The pilot shook his head. 'The mist is getting too thick. It's too dangerous to continue.'

'Then put us down somewhere.'

'It's risky. The visibility is very bad.'

'Do it.'

The pilot glared at him, but he put the helicopter into a shallow dive, dropping down through the drifting mist. Snow was starting to collect on the Blackhawk's windscreen. The wipers were working full out to keep the glass clear.

'There's nowhere to land,' the pilot said. 'We'll have to abort.'

'Keep looking.'

'The terrain's too rough. The wind will push us into the mountain.'

'There!' Chang pointed.

'Too small,' the pilot said. 'I'm sorry, we have to get out now while we can.'

Chang twisted round in his seat. 'Prepare to rappel.'

'Comrade Major, there's no time,' the pilot said.

'Hold your position. That's an order.'

Chang unfastened his harness and scrambled out of his seat. The commandos had the side doors open, the ropes already dangling into space.

'Go!' Chang shouted over the noise of the rotorblades.

The commandos went out one after the other, abseiling down the ropes to the ground. Chang looked out, holding on to the rail next to the door. The wind was buffeting the helicopter, rocking it from side to side. Clouds of snow were blowing in and melting on the floor of the fuselage.

'I can't hold her much longer,' the pilot yelled.

Chang grabbed one of the ropes. It was years since he'd done this. Could he still remember the technique?

'Time's up,' the pilot shouted.

Chang went over the side, paying the rope out behind him, dropping like a stone. The rope started to sway. He felt it cutting into his skin through his uniform. The ground raced up to meet him. He was going too fast. The impact would break his legs for certain. He swung his arm across his chest. The rope dug in harder, the friction burning the material of his tunic. But he slowed; hit the earth with a jarring thump, remembered to bend his knees. Then the sergeant was disentangling him from the rope. Just in time, for the Blackhawk was already climbing, turning to starboard. Its nose dipped and it burrowed away into the mist, the throb of the rotors dying away until only the muted howl of the wind remained.

* * *

Maggie wondered if she'd imagined it. If the snow and the wind were playing tricks with her hearing. But Tsering had also stopped, one ear cocked as if he were listening.

'Did you hear that?' he said.

Maggie nodded. 'A bell.'

The sound came again, a distant, very faint tinkle.

'It's over there,' Tsering said.

He changed direction, striding over the top of a snow-covered hillock. He noticed a movement in the mist, a shape emerging, becoming gradually clearer. It was a goat, a lean, bony creature with a bell around its neck. It saw Tsering approaching and trotted away up the hill. Tsering followed. There were a couple of other goats in the distance, then further on an outline that was hard to make out. A shape that seemed too regular to be part of the mountain. A stone hut.

Tsering walked towards the hut. As he drew nearer, he saw smoke coming out of the chimney, a dim glow in the window. He edged cautiously up to the door and pushed it open. A boy was kneeling on the floor inside, adding dried turf and goat dung to the small fire that was burning in the hearth. The boy looked round and started as he saw Tsering, then he leapt to his feet, reaching for the knife he carried at his belt. Tsering held out his hands in a gesture of peace.

'We are friends. We mean you no harm.'

The boy eyed him warily, his hand still on the hilt of his knife.

'We seek shelter from the snow, that's all,' Tsering said. He moved aside to let Pema in behind him. She was wearing the sheepskin jacket she'd brought with her, the baby tucked inside it. Seeing a woman, the boy relaxed a little. His hands dropped to his side, then moved back to his knife as Lobsang and Maggie walked in.

'How many of you are there?' he said.

'Just four. And the baby.'

'Baby?' The boy noticed the bulge beneath Pema's jacket. 'Oh.'

'The snow is getting heavier,' Tsering said. 'Can we stay here a while? We are tired.'

The boy shrugged, glancing apologetically around the Spartan hut. 'It is not much.'

'It's dry and warm. That's an improvement on outside. May we?' Tsering indicated the fire. The boy stepped to the side, letting them draw near the hearth. He was watching them with bright, inquisitive eyes.

Tsering warmed his hands over the flames. 'You are all alone up here?' he said. The boy nodded. 'It's late in the year.'

'I'm taking the animals down soon,' the boy replied. 'The snow has come early.'

Tsering nodded and smiled at the goatherd. He looked about thirteen or fourteen years old, a skinny kid with a dirty face and hands. But then there was no mother around to make him wash. He'd live up here by himself all summer, tending the goats and making butter and cheese from their milk which he'd take back down to his village at intervals during the season. There was a wooden butter churn and a cheese vat at one side of the hut, a couple of bulging goatskins stored on a shelf above them.

'You have butter here?' Tsering asked, pointing at the skins.

'There's just those two left. I'll take them down with the goats.'

'Can we buy some from you?'

'Buy?'

'I'll give you a good price. We're hungry.'

Tsering took out a leather purse and offered the goatherd some notes. The boy stared at them uncertainly, then snatched them quickly and hid them away in the folds of his *chuba*.

'Do you have *tsampa*?' Tsering asked.

'A little.' The boy indicated a small, half-empty sack on the shelf.

'I'll buy some of that too.'

The boy made them goat's-butter tea, pouring it into their bowls and offering them the sack of *tsampa*. When it came to Maggie's turn, she hesitated, unsure how much to take.

357

'Here, let me,' Tsering said.

He added a handful of the roasted barley flour to her tea and mixed it in with the liquid, rolling the resulting dough into small balls for Maggie to eat. She nibbled one of the balls. They tasted worse than the yak's-butter mixture, if such a thing were possible, but she was too ravenous to care.

'You are acquiring a taste for butter tea?' Tsering said, watching her.

'I think that would take several lifetimes,' Maggie said.

'In your next rebirth then. Perhaps you'll come back a Tibetan.'

'I think I'd prefer oblivion to a diet of this stuff.'

Tsering grinned at her. 'It is most nutritious.'

'I'm sure. It just tastes so bloody awful.'

Tsering rolled a *tsampa* ball for himself and held it up. *'Bon appétit.'*

The snow continued throughout the day, the wind blowing it into thick drifts against the walls of the hut. They kept the door closed, the wooden shutters fastened over the window, and took the opportunity to catch up on their lost sleep. It made no sense to attempt to continue their journey. Walking through the blizzard across such treacherous, unknown country would have been suicidal. It was better to sit tight and wait for the weather to clear. The delay was frustrating, but at least they could be sure the Chinese weren't closing in on them. With visibility down to only a few metres, conditions were too dangerous for either air or ground searches to continue.

Towards evening, the snow stopped. The goatherd went outside in his thick sheepskin coat to make sure his animals were safe. He had a rifle slung over his shoulder. There were wolves up here and hungry brown bears looking for an easy meal. Tsering stepped out of the door for a moment. A blanket of snow covered everything in sight, smoothing out the contours of the hillside, concealing the rough edges, the rugged blemishes of the terrain. The clouds hung low and dense so that it was difficult to work out where the ground ended and the sky began. It was tempting to walk on, to get a few kilometres nearer the frontier, but Tsering resisted the idea. In a couple of hours it would be dark. They would have to find shelter for the night and he knew there would be nothing as warm and secure as this hut. They had to be patient; stay put for the time being and continue their journey in the morning.

They settled down around the hearth. The boy had a large basket of dried goat dung which he used to stoke the fire, heaping it on top in a thick layer which would slowly smoulder all night. But even with the fire it was cold. Maggie slept only fitfully, shivering beneath her blankets, listening to the others shifting around as they too tried to sleep. Only the baby was really warm, tucked inside his mother's *chuba*, the sheepskin jacket wrapped around them both.

At first light the goatherd went outside again to check his animals, returning with a kettle of snow which he melted over the fire to make more tea. The weather had improved a little, though Tsering was glad to see the cloud cover remained. No helicopters would be flying today.

After breakfast they got ready to leave. Tsering consulted the map.

'Which is the best route to the border?' he asked the goatherd.

The boy pointed. 'Down the other side of the mountain.'

'Is the way easy to follow?'

'In the snow it may be difficult.' The boy went to the shelf and took down a coiled rope. 'Take this. You may need it. I will show you where to go.'

He took them up the hill to a ridge. The snow was five or six inches deep, more in places.

'Follow the line of the ridge, keeping just below the escarpment,' the goatherd said. 'There is a track beneath the snow. When you get to the bottom go left. You see the valley over there, between the two peaks? That will take you to the Kangri-La Pass. The border is another day's walk beyond that.'

Tsering thanked him and gave him some more money. 'For the rope, and your hospitality,' he said. 'How much longer will you stay up here?'

'Another day perhaps. I may even take the goats down later today. I feel the winter coming on.'

'Don't mention to anyone that you've seen us. It's important,' Tsering said. 'Do you understand?' The boy nodded. 'There are Chinese in the area. Police. They are looking for us. Keep away from them.'

'I always keep away from the Chinese,' the boy said.

They edged their way cautiously down the ridge, Tsering at the front, Pema, Maggie and Lobsang in a line behind him. The snow was light and fluffy, easy enough to walk through, particularly as the ground underneath was stony, providing a solid footing for their descent. They took their time, conscious of the risks they were taking. The snow had drifted across the hillside and it was impossible to tell what hazards it concealed, what hidden hollows or sudden drops.

In places, where the route seemed exceptionally hazardous, Tsering tied the rope around his waist and went on alone, Lobsang holding the other end in case he fell. Then they stretched the rope out between them like a handrail for Pema and Maggie to grip as they clambered down the slope. Maggie knew what she was doing, but Pema worried Tsering. She had the baby in the sling around her chest. One awkward fall and the child might be seriously injured.

It was a relief when they finally reached the bottom of the hill and the ground levelled out. For a time the walking was relatively easy, then they began the long ascent towards the pass. The snow was deep, but it was still possible to discern the line of the path as it snaked its way up the valley. Maggie started to feel the effects of the altitude again. The combination of the thin air, the cold and the exertion left her breathless and panting. The others too were struggling. Every few hundred metres they had to pause for a few minutes to recover. Maggie tried not to think about the pain in her chest and legs. She blanked out everything from her mind and plodded up the mountain like a zombie, concentrating on one step at a time, one breath at a time.

She was lost in a daze of almost punch-drunk exhaustion when she looked up and saw that Tsering had stopped. There was a slight dip in the track by a small outcrop of rock whose vertical face was free of snow. At the foot of the outcrop was a spring, a trickle of water seeping out under the base of the rock to form a tiny pool.

But Tsering wasn't looking at the pool. He was looking at the footprints around it.

There were several – big, heavy indentations in the snow, the marks exhibiting the distinctive treads of climbing boots. Or army boots. The prints came down the hill from the pass, then back up the same way as if someone had come to fetch water from the spring.

'Stay here,' Tsering said.

He slipped his bag off his shoulders and followed the boot-prints up the slope. After half a kilometre the trail disappeared around a high, rocky spur. Tsering climbed on to the top of the spur and peered over. Fifty metres below him, half hidden in snowholes beside the path, were two men in dark green PSB combat fatigues. There were two more further up the path, similarly concealed, and beyond them – close to the highest point of the pass – four tents dug into the snow. Three men were huddled around a kerosene stove, eating from billycans. One was wearing the field uniform of a PSB major. Tsering recognised the hard, bony face of the officer who'd arrested them in Lhasa.

Tsering didn't linger. He scrambled off the spur and back down the hill to the spring.

'You find anything?' Maggie said.

'Public Security Bureau,' Tsering replied. 'Seven of them waiting beside the path.'

'Is there any way round?'

Tsering shook his head. 'They're completely blocking the pass.'

TWENTY-THREE

Tsering glanced at Pema – she was watching him with big, frightened eyes – and kept talking in English, not wanting to alarm her.

'We'll have to go back,' he said.

Maggie looked down into the valley, her heart sinking. They'd come so far. She couldn't face a retreat, then another punishing climb up to some other pass. Assuming there *was* another pass.

'Back to where?' she said.

'I don't know. But we'll never get over this way.'

'Show me the map.'

She studied the contour markings, working out the heights. The Kangri-La was five thousand three hundred metres above sea level, about seventeen and a half thousand feet. There was another pass to the west, the Ngü-La, but that was close on nineteen thousand feet high and from the steepness of the contours looked virtually impassable to a group without any climbing equipment.

'This is the only other pass near us,' Maggie said. 'It's too high. In this weather it's going to be blocked with snow. We'd need crampons, ice axes, proper gear to get over it.'

'Are you sure?'

'I've done some snow and ice climbing. Believe me, we wouldn't have a chance. Especially with the baby. It's too dangerous.'

'So what do we do? Where else can we cross the range?'

'Here, to the east, is the nearest pass that looks suitable.

The Kangtshup-La. But it's at least two, three days' walk from here. We don't have that kind of time.'

Tsering frowned at her. 'That doesn't leave us any options.'

Maggie was looking up the mountain. The Kangri-La pass was on the eastern side, a deep V-shaped gash between two peaks. But higher up the mountainside, a few hundred metres above the pass, was a wide shelf, a horizontal cut into the flank of the mountain with a sheer escarpment overlooking it.

'If we can get up there where it's flat,' Maggie said.

'You're not serious?'

'I think we can do it. We have a rope.'

'It's too risky. We have to think of the child.'

'You want to wait here for the Chinese to pick us up? We don't have a choice, Tsering.'

They took no chances on the treacherous slope. Tsering, the strongest of the group, went first, the rope fastened around his waist. He climbed in a diagonal line to reduce the gradient, his legs sinking to the ankles in the soft snow. Every twenty metres or so, he stopped and turned, making sure his footing was secure. Then the other end of the rope was tied around Pema and Tsering reeled her in, holding her tight as she climbed up to join him. Maggie and Lobsang followed in similar fashion and they repeated the move, working their way gradually up the mountain. They made slow progress, but it was the only safe way of tackling the steep, slippery ascent.

After two hours of arduous climbing they reached the shelf. They kept to the inner edge, at the base of the rock escarpment, to avoid being seen by anyone looking up from the pass. They were all near to dropping, but they didn't dare stop to rest. It was bitingly cold. Their feet and hands were half frozen, their trousers and calves soaked from the snow. Maggie could no longer feel her toes and was worried that frostbite was setting in.

On the far side of the shelf they came out of the shelter of the escarpment and the wind hit them like a punch in the face, almost knocking them off their feet. They roped themselves together and inched cautiously out on to the exposed southern slope of the mountain. Only it was not a slope. It was a sheer drop.

Tsering waved the others back. He looked over the edge. It wasn't a long drop – maybe only twenty-five metres from top to bottom – but it was as smooth and perpendicular as a brick wall. A gust of wind caught him off guard. He lost his balance, tried to recover and slipped. He felt himself toppling out into space. Then the rope around his waist went suddenly taut. Lobsang grabbed his arm and dragged him back from the edge. Tsering nodded his thanks, too shocked to speak.

'What now?' Lobsang said. 'We're trapped.'

Maggie dropped to her stomach and peered over the cliff. There was no way they were going to climb down it, but perhaps there was an alternative. She wriggled backwards and stood up, surveying the shelf behind them, then checking the rope, estimating how long it was.

'We can do it,' she said.

Tsering and Lobsang turned to stare at her. 'How?'

'Untie the rope from your waists.'

There was a large boulder a few metres back from the edge. Maggie tied one end of the rope securely around it and threw the other end over the cliff. It was just long enough to reach the bottom.

'Have you abseiled before?' Maggie asked.

'Abseil? What is that?' Tsering said.

'I didn't think it likely. Never mind. We'll have to lower you down.'

She explained what they were going to do. Lobsang and Tsering regarded her sceptically.

'It sounds risky,' Tsering said.

'It's the only way. Unless you want to go back down the route we came up?'

Lobsang was first over the edge. Maggie had tied the rope

under his armpits with a bowline, then Tsering lowered him down the cliff, paying the rope out slowly. Pema, the next to go, was less straightforward. She was clearly terrified of the descent and had a long, agitated discussion with Tsering about it before she allowed Maggie to tie the rope around her.

'My son,' Pema said, almost in tears.

'He will be fine,' Tsering reassured her. 'Just hold on to the rope. Lobsang will catch you at the bottom.'

Tsering lowered her down. Pema's face was crumpled with fear, her knuckles white as she hung on tight to the rope. Tsering took it easy, trying to eliminate any sideways movement as Pema dangled in space. When she neared the base of the cliff, Lobsang reached up and grabbed her, helping her down the last few feet and untying the rope. Tsering hauled the rope back up and looked round to see Maggie taping him with her camcorder.

'You can think of that now?' he said incredulously.

'I said I'd keep a record,' Maggie replied. 'Smile, you're going to be on television.'

She'd got the whole of Pema's descent, even managed a close-up of the baby's pudgy face gazing up at her as he went down. She considered going back along the shelf to see if she could get a shot of the PSB camp below in the pass, but thought better of it. The chances of being spotted were far too high.

'Are you still sure you want to go last?' Tsering said. 'I could lower you.'

'That's not necessary. You know what you're doing?'

'I'll manage.'

Tsering grasped the rope and slithered backwards over the edge, going down hand over hand, his feet keeping him from swinging into the cliff face. Maggie followed a few minutes later. It was a while since she'd done any abseiling, and she'd always used a harness and karabiner in the past, but it wasn't a long drop. She wrapped the rope around her waist and swung out, bouncing down the precipice in just a few bold leaps. Tsering caught her arm to steady her as she touched the ground next to him. Maggie detached herself from the rope. She'd have felt happier taking the line with them, but they had no choice but to leave it behind. She tucked the trailing end behind a rock and nodded at the others. With Tsering taking the lead once again, they headed carefully down the other side of the mountain.

The young commando slid the last few feet down the hill to the spring and tossed the expandable plastic water container he was carrying down into the snow. He took out a packet of cigarettes and a lighter from the inside pocket of his jacket and sat down on a nearby rock for a quiet smoke. He was glad to be away from the camp. The intelligence major from Lhasa was getting on everyone's nerves. He really was an insufferable little jerk. Constantly giving orders, telling them what to do, yet what did *he* know about anything? He was a desk man, a paper pusher. He should never have been out in the field.

The commando inhaled, then blew the smoke out, watching it melt away into the mist. He was equipped for the mountains, but still he was cold. The dampness cut through his layers of clothing and settled on his skin like a clammy rag. All the waiting around only made things worse. What were they playing at? They should do something, or get out, but at the moment there seemed little prospect of either. There was no sign of the fugitives they were seeking and unless the weather improved, no possibility of the chopper coming back to pick them up. They just had to sit tight and wait for their bollocks to freeze.

He finished his cigarette and tossed the butt away. It hissed as it touched the snow, burning a tiny hole in the glistening crystals. Did he have time for another? That sod of a major probably had a stopwatch on him, counting the minutes till he came back. Reluctantly, the commando bent down to pick up the water canister.

It was then that he saw the footprints on the far side of the spring.

*   *   *

Chang looked at the line of marks coming up the side of the mountain. The mist had closed in, reducing visibility so that the valley floor was completely invisible, but he could see the zig-zag pattern quite clearly for at least a couple of hundred metres. The commandos themselves had come up that route, but there had been a heavy fall of snow since then. These were fresh prints.

'Who fetched the water last?' Chang demanded.

'I did, Comrade Major.' The young commando was standing by the spring, stiff and attentive as if he were on the parade ground.

'When?'

'This morning, Comrade Major.'

'Did you see any footprints then?'

'No, Comrade Major.'

'You are sure?'

'I would have noticed them for certain, Comrade Major.'

Chang scanned the slopes above them. From where he stood, the snow appeared smooth and untouched. Yet whoever had left the footprints must have gone somewhere. They hadn't continued on over the pass. That left two other possibilities: they had found another route over, or they had gone back down the way they'd come.

Chang walked a short distance down the hill, studying the prints. They were smudged and merged together so it was impossible to make out the individual feet that had left them, but in places he discerned that they were going in both directions. So they *had* gone back down. He walked on for a few metres more. The prints now seemed to have become much clearer, all of them coming up the hill. He saw why. Above the path another line of footprints branched off, heading diagonally up the slope. Chang looked up. Visibility above was even worse than it was below. The mountain's summit had vanished into the mist and the sides were just a blur of hazy white into which the line of footprints faded and finally disappeared.

The young commando, and the sergeant who'd come down

from the camp with him, watched Chang walk back up to the spring.

'It's them,' Chang said. 'It has to be. Strike the tents and get the men down here. They can only be a few hours ahead of us.'

As dusk approached, it started to snow again, a heavy fall so thick the flakes seemed to blend together in a translucent white sheet. In the fading light it was impossible to make out anything except the shifting drifts, the surging wind sculpting them into amorphous shapes that changed with every sweeping gust.

Walking was getting harder. The wind was fierce, like sandpaper on the skin, and with each step their legs sank into the snow almost to the knee. It was like hiking through quicksand. For Pema, the smallest of them, it was particularly tough. Lifting her feet high enough to take a proper step was difficult so she was forced to plough her way ahead using her legs to batter a path through the deep layers of snow. It was exhausting work – and potentially dangerous. Her thin cotton trousers, her felt boots were soaked. Her toes were numb, the flesh starting to freeze. If they didn't find shelter soon, she would be too crippled to continue.

'We have to stop, Tsering,' Maggie shouted. 'Tsering!'

Tsering turned his head, trying to catch her words through the seething gale.

'Pema can't go on. Look at her.'

Tsering shifted his gaze to the young nomad woman. She could barely lift her head, never mind her legs. She was swaying unsteadily, too tired even to stand up straight.

'Help me, Lobsang.'

The two monks, worn out and drenched themselves, took an arm each, pulling Pema along between them.

'We have to stop,' Maggie repeated, yelling at the top of her voice.

Tsering ignored her. From somewhere Maggie found the energy to overtake him, planting herself firmly in his path.

'We're all exhausted,' she said. 'Can you feel your toes, your fingers? We're getting frostbite. You know what that means?'

'Better frostbite than a Chinese labour camp,' Tsering retorted. 'We have to keep going.'

'Much more of this and we won't be able to walk.'

'The Chinese are right behind us. We cannot afford to stop.'

'And the baby? What's the point in getting to India if the child dies on the way?'

That gave him a jolt. Tsering pulled open the lapels of Pema's sheepskin jacket and glanced in at the baby. His eyes were closed, his skin had an unnatural pallor that shocked Tsering. He touched the infant's cheek. It was cold and damp. He leaned closer, trying to feel the baby's breath. It was there, but coming in shallow, disquieting bursts.

'She's right,' Tsering said to Lobsang. 'We have to rest, warm ourselves up. Get the tent out. Lobsang, are you listening?'

Lobsang wasn't looking at them. He was staring ahead through the blizzard. 'You see it?'

'See what?'

'Look.'

In the distance, flickering through the veil of snow, was a light.

'Chinese?' Tsering said in alarm.

'I don't think so.'

A sudden gust of wind parted the veil and they saw not one light, but several. Several faint orange beacons glowing in a strange pattern, some in a line next to one another, others higher up. They walked on, screwing up their eyes against the raging snowstorm. The lights seemed to be above them now, suspended in mid-air. It was only as they drew nearer that the bulk of the mountain behind the lights emerged from the snow and mist. There was a building on the lower slopes, or rather a series of buildings arranged in tiers, their windows illuminated by burning lanterns.

'What is it?' Maggie said.

'It's a monastery,' Tsering replied.

*   *   *

It was the commando sergeant who found the rope. Most of it was buried beneath the fresh fall of snow, but the loop tied around the boulder was just visible.

'Comrade Major.'

The sergeant tugged on the rope, ripping it up from the snow, then following it to where it disappeared over the edge of the cliff. Chang stepped cautiously up to the sergeant's shoulder and looked down. The rope had frozen stiff in the sub-zero temperature. It hung in a rigid line down the precipice like a long, slender icicle. Any footprints there might once have been at the base of the cliff had been obliterated by the new covering of snow.

'We go down?' the sergeant said.

Chang gave a nod and the sergeant barked an order. One by one, the commandos went over the edge.

Maggie massaged her toes, kneading the flesh with her fingers until some kind of sensation began to return. Then she stretched out her legs towards the stove, feeling the heat on the soles of her feet. She had one blanket around her shoulders, another draped over her waist and knees. On the top of the stove her damp clothes hissed and steamed.

Pema was next to her, her frozen feet soaking in a bowl of warm water. The baby was cradled in her arms, a yak-hair rug wrapped around him. Pema rocked him gently, murmuring softly to him. When he opened his eyes, she guided her breast to his mouth and he suckled half-heartedly, pulling away after just a few mouthfuls. Pema stroked his head and he fell asleep again. There was colour in his cheeks now. He looked warm and peaceful.

A young monk was making black tea, filling a pot with boiling water from a huge copper urn which stood at one end of the kitchen range. He brought two bowls over to Maggie and Pema and offered them with a polite bow. They sipped the tea gratefully. The monk came back with a loaf of coarse brown bread that had been warming in the oven. He broke off a chunk and gave them each a piece, saying something in Tibetan that Maggie didn't understand. She smiled at him and he bowed again, withdrawing to the range from where he watched them attentively like a conscientious waiter.

Tsering and Lobsang did not appear until Maggie and Pema had finished their tea. Accompanying them was a thin, elderly man with a shaven head and a face like a gnarled piece of oak. He was introduced as the *kenpo*, the abbot of the monastery. He instructed the young monk to leave and waited until the kitchen door had closed before he approached Pema. He stood before her and gave a low, respectful bow.

'You are most welcome,' he said in a quiet but sonorous voice. 'I am deeply honoured to have the pleasure of serving the mother of Gyalwa Rinpoche.'

Pema shifted uncomfortably on the wooden bench. She was awkward, nervous. She didn't know what to say.

The abbot stepped closer, looking down at the sleeping baby.

'Is this His Holiness?'

'Well . . . he is my son,' Pema stammered.

'May I ask something?' the abbot began. Then he too seemed at a loss for words. 'No, perhaps I am presumptuous. And yet . . . this is a moment of the most serene happiness for me. I feel the privilege of my position most keenly. May I . . . may I be allowed to touch him?'

Pema seemed bemused. 'Touch him? Of course you may touch him. To have the blessing of a holy man like you, the abbot of a monastery, well it is . . .' Her voice trailed off.

The abbot smiled benevolently at her. 'It is I who will be blessed.'

He knelt down on the stone flags, steadying himself with a hand on the bench. Pema gestured at him to stand up, aware of his age, his position, feeling unworthy of his respect. But his eyes were fixed on the child. He stretched out his hand, hesitating for an instant before touching his fingers to the baby's forehead. He left them there for a moment, his eyes closed. He shuddered as if some unseen current were passing through him. Then a smile of pure joy lit up his wrinkled face. He opened his eyes. They glistened with tears and an expression of such transcendental beatitude that they seemed to blaze with an incandescent light. No one moved. The room seemed filled with a holy spirit, a divine aura that touched everyone present. Then the abbot withdrew his fingers and the moment passed. He stood up, bowing again to the child and his mother.

When he spoke, his voice seemed an intrusion on the tranquil silence.

'You will be safe here for the night,' he said. 'In the morning I will send someone to show you the way to the border. Meanwhile, make yourselves comfortable. If you need anything, just ask.'

The abbot bowed to each of them in turn and left the kitchen. Tsering crouched down next to Pema and lifted one of her feet from the bowl of warm water.

'How are they?' he asked.

'I can feel them again,' Pema replied.

'That's good.'

Tsering rubbed her toes, examining the skin. The blood had returned, he could see the pinkish hue beneath the surface.

'And your baby?'

'He has fed a little,' Pema said. 'He is warmer now.'

Tsering nodded. 'Get as much rest as you can. The abbot has provided us all with beds.'

'And the Chinese? The policemen?'

'Try not to think about the Chinese,' Tsering said.

They dined alone with the abbot in his quarters, attended only by the young monk, Yulu, who'd taken care of Maggie and Pema in the kitchen. The food was plentiful, but plain: yak-butter tea, bread, spiced potatoes and strips of dried goat meat. Throughout the meal, the abbot kept up an almost continuous conversation with Tsering and Lobsang.

'What are you talking about?' Maggie asked eventually, tired of listening to their incomprehensible Tibetan.

'He is telling us about the monastery,' Tsering answered. 'The struggle they are having to re-establish it, to rebuild it.'

Maggie nodded. She'd already noticed that the *gompa* was in ruins. The prayer hall, the kitchen and refectory and some of the monks' cells had been rebuilt, but most of the complex, which had once sprawled over a large area of the mountain, was still derelict, just a pile of shapeless rubble.

'Who did it?' she asked. 'The Red Guards?'

'They did their bit. But much of the monastery was destroyed in 1960, after the Dalai Lama fled to India. The PLA shelled the buildings, killed a lot of the monks. The abbot himself was wounded.'

'*This* abbot?' Maggie said. 'He was here then?'

'He was a young monk, one of the few who survived.'

'And he's been here ever since?'

Tsering shook his head. 'He spent twenty-eight years in Chinese labour camps.'

'Twenty-eight years?'

Maggie turned to look at the wizened little man sitting at the head of the table. The abbot glanced in her direction, but he seemed to be looking past her. He snapped something suddenly in Tibetan, an angry shout that was out of keeping with his hitherto calm demeanour. Maggie twisted round. The door had opened and standing just inside the threshold was a monk. Not Yulu, but an older monk with a weasel face. The man's beady, rat-like eyes were staring at Pema, then her baby which had been placed on a cushion in a wooden box on the floor. The abbot yelled again at the monk who gave him a slow, insolent look that was shot through with an arrogant contempt. His eyes flickered across the others in the room, then he walked out. The abbot pushed himself up from his chair and hobbled across the room to close the door, muttering something to Tsering and Lobsang by way of explanation.

'What was that all about?' Maggie said. 'Who was that monk?'

'The Chinese placeman,' Tsering replied. '*Gynipa*, the abbot called him, our word for a collaborator.'

'Collaborator? Here in the monastery?'

'There is at least one in every monastery. Everyone knows who they are, but they are untouchable. They keep an eye on the abbot, the other monks, and report back to the Chinese authorities. You don't think the Chinese would allow our monasteries to be re-established without having some control over what goes on inside them, do you? That is not their way. They make a show of permitting us a degree of religious freedom, but the freedom is only skin deep. Every aspect of it is controlled by the Chinese.'

'And the abbot has to live with that?'

'He has no choice. Not if he wants the monastery to continue. We compromise. It is the first rule of survival. Look around you. Every wall of this room, of this monastery, has been rebuilt stone by stone – much of it by the *kenpo* himself. The Chinese released him from prison in 1988. He'd been in six different Chinese prisons, some of them the gulag labour camps in the far north. You cannot imagine the deprivations of those places, Miss Walsh – what men can endure and survive. The *kenpo* came out of them alive, but he is one of the few who did. Most die of cold or starvation. Some commit suicide because they cannot bear the hardship any longer. That is a terrible thing for a Buddhist for suicide means they can have no more rebirths. For five of those years he was kept in solitary confinement, in a cell just a couple of metres square. When they let him out, he'd forgotten how to speak, forgotten his own name.

'He came back here with a few other monks and they started to reconstruct the *gompa*, mixing the mortar by hand, re-laying every stone, living in tents while they did it. There are thirty of them now, some young monks with the energy and the will to continue his work. But it is a shadow of what it was. In 1960 there were eight hundred monks living here. At their present rate it will be years before even half the monastery is rebuilt. Most of it probably never will be. After what the *kenpo* has been through, a Chinese informer is the least of his problems.'

Maggie looked again at the abbot and a phrase came into her head, something that Samdrup, the old *Chushi Gangdruk* guerrilla had said to her in Nyingchi: 'I am a leftover of death.' The abbot was the same. So too was Lobsang. So were thousands of others. Tibet was a country awash with the leftovers of death.

The major from Lhasa was a gritty little bastard all right, the commando sergeant had to concede. In his experience the desk officers at *Gong An Ju* headquarters were all gutless, flabby creatures, but Chang was different. He was only small, but he had the physical strength of a man twice his size and the determination of a whole platoon put together. The sergeant didn't like him, but over the past few hours the major had more than earned his grudging respect.

The conditions were appalling. The snow on the ground was two feet deep and more was falling every minute. Most police commanders, never mind one with a cushy office posting, would long ago have called a halt to the march and set up camp to wait out the weather. But not Chang. He'd driven the commandos on relentlessly through the blizzard, taking his turn in the vanguard where the swirling snowflakes, propelled by the wind, hit the face with the force of flying needles.

Only when night fell and the temperature plummeted even lower did the major allow them to stop, aware that to continue would be sheer folly. They pitched their tents and slid thankfully inside, out of the biting cold. They boiled water for tea and rice on their kerosene stoves. The sergeant shared his tent with Chang who took out his detailed military map from inside his sodden uniform and studied it by the light of a torch.

'Where do you reckon we are, Sergeant?' Chang asked.

The sergeant peered at the map and gave a noncommittal shrug. 'In this weather, Comrade Major, it's impossible to be sure.'

'But somewhere around here, wouldn't you agree?' Chang persisted, placing his finger on the map.

'Perhaps. If the snow stops and the mist lifts, we might be able to see a landmark to gauge our position.'

'And over here – three, maybe four kilometres south-east of us – we have a monastery,' Chang continued. 'The Se-po Thorang Gompa.'

'You think that's where they are, Comrade Major?'

'They're monks. What better place for them to seek shelter?' Chang folded the map and slid it away. 'Before dawn, Sergeant, I think we should find out.'

A wood fire was burning in the hearth, the flames casting flickering shadows over the stone flags, the fingers of light creeping out and fading to nothing before they reached the dark recesses of the room. Maggie was conscious of the special treatment she was receiving. The monks' cells were unheated, most of the monastery had the chill damp atmosphere of a tomb, yet she had a blazing fire all to herself. Wood was precious up here above the treeline. Every log would have had to be carried up by hand or on the back of a yak.

She felt her clothes, which were draped over a chair in front of the fire. They'd almost dried on the kitchen stove but she wanted to finish them off before she put them back on. There was a bowl of warm water on the table, a towel folded next to it. Maggie slid the blanket from her shoulders and washed herself, the scent of saffron from the water clinging to her skin. Then she knelt down on the rug by the hearth and let the heat of the fire dry her.

It was the slight draught, a movement across the room, that made her glance up. Tsering had come in. He stepped forward into the light.

'I'm sorry, I didn't know you were . . .' He didn't finish the sentence. He looked at her. Maggie made no move to cover herself up.

'Why don't you come nearer the fire?' she said.

She watched him emerge from the shadows. He was still looking at her, his eyes straying.

'Are you imagining me as a rotting corpse?' she asked.

His brow furrowed momentarily. Then he gave a nod of understanding. 'No, I'm not imagining anything. I'm seeing.'

'You've seen a naked woman before?'

'Yes.'

'Have you?' When he didn't reply, Maggie went on: 'Who was she?'

'A girl. It was a long time ago.'

'You didn't just see her, did you?'

'No.'

'You broke your vows?'

'I was a *getsul*, a novice, at the time. It was before I took my final vows.'

'Nothing since?'

'No.'

'Why?'

'My vows are important to me.'

'I mean, why the first time?'

Tsering shrugged. 'She offered. I didn't want to go through life not knowing what it was like.'

'And what was it like?'

'Disappointing.'

Maggie smiled at him. 'That's normal. Everyone finds it disappointing first time. You should have practised more.'

'It would have brought only turmoil.'

'It brings peace too.'

'A transient peace. I was seeking something more lasting.'

'And have you found it?'

He looked away. Maggie picked up her blanket and wrapped it around herself. Why were women such a threat to these men? she wondered. Why was desire such a threat? That pervasive misogyny was there in all religions. Tibetan Buddhists believed that Man originated from the union of a monkey and an ogress. The monkey was the incarnation of Chenresig, the Buddha of Compassion, a gentle, contemplative creature who wanted only

377

to be left alone to meditate. But the ogress was wild and lustful, desperate for congress. So out of pity the monkey mated with her and their offspring were born without tails and walked upright. All human nature could be traced back to these two creatures: gentleness and love and compassion to the monkey; wilfulness, aggression and greed to the ogress, the wily female who had seduced the male and thereby corrupted him. Like Eve and the apple, woman was temptress, the source of all negative human traits. Yet most of the evil Maggie had seen in the world had been caused by men and their aggression.

'Denying what makes you human doesn't make you a better man, you know,' Maggie said. 'Enforced celibacy is a sign of weakness, not strength. What have you to be frightened of?'

'You think I'm frightened? Of what?'

'I don't know. Of your own desires, of being in thrall to a woman. What are you doing with your life, Tsering? Shutting yourself away and meditating. It's such a waste.'

'What would you have me do? Wander the world like you do? You are filling the vessel of your life with activity, but that doesn't mean it is not still empty.'

'That sounds like something out of a Christmas cracker,' Maggie said.

'A Christmas cracker? What's that?'

'The fount of all Western philosophy. You think my life is empty?'

'It is not for me to judge. But just because you spend your time travelling doesn't mean you know where you're going.'

'It's the journey that counts.'

'That's where we differ. For me, the destination is what counts.'

'And when you get there, what then?'

'It is arrogant to assume I will. Enlightenment takes countless lifetimes to achieve.'

'What about the tantric path?'

Tsering raised an eyebrow in surprise. 'You know of the tantric path? Yes, it will get you to Buddhahood more quickly.

But it is a dangerous path, only suitable for certain individuals. Others must follow the slower path of Mahayana.'

Maggie gave him a sly look. 'If you took the way of tantra you could have sex and still be a monk, couldn't you?'

'You Westerners are obsessed with sex,' Tsering replied irritably.

'Well, as obsessions go it's one of the best.'

'You enjoy trying to provoke me, don't you, Miss Walsh.'

'Maggie. Do I? I'm just interested. I'm right, aren't I? Tantric practitioners are allowed to have sex.'

'At the highest level of tantric practice, yes, sex is part of meditation. In orgasm the coarser levels of the mind drop away, but of course, most people don't see the potential meditative benefits of the experience.'

'So let me get this right,' Maggie said. 'When these old gurus are sleeping with their disciples – all coincidentally young, attractive and very gullible women – they're really participating in some sublime form of meditation? You expect me to believe that?'

'It is part of the tantric road to enlightenment.'

'Isn't that a bit insulting to women? Using them as a vessel for the enlightenment of a man?'

'I'm not going to rise, Miss Walsh.'

'Maggie. Go on, give it a shot.'

'Sexual union is only for highly advanced tantric practitioners. It takes years to get to that level.'

'Well, I suppose that's a bit better. By the time you get to that stage you're too old to get it up. Meditation is probably about all you're up to in bed.'

'Can you not be respectful about my faith for once?'

'It wouldn't be the same,' Maggie said. She pulled the blanket tight around her shoulders and gazed into the fire. The flames were dying down, the cold creeping in from the edges of the room, but she didn't want to waste more wood on stoking the fire back to life. 'Did you have a reason for coming in?'

'A reason?' Tsering gave it some thought. 'To see how you

were. To say that before dawn we must be on our way. The abbot says we have a glacier to cross before the pass over the frontier. The ice can be treacherous. It's best to tackle it before the sun warms it up.'

'And once we're over, what then?'

'What do you mean?'

'What happens to Pema and the child?'

'They will go to McLeod Ganj and he will be installed as the new Dalai Lama, of course.'

'It will be a terrible shock for Pema. A young nomad woman thrust into the international limelight.'

'She will not have to cope on her own.'

'Don't you think it's cruel? Taking that child from his home, his family, and condemning him to a life as a figurehead in exile?'

'It is his destiny. Tibetans see it as a great honour.'

'And you? Who were taken from your mother and shut away in a monastery at the age of nine. How do you see it?'

Tsering turned away without replying. 'Get some sleep, Miss Walsh. Tomorrow will be a very long day.'

It was still dark when she was awoken by the door banging open. Tsering came into the room, a butter lantern glowing in his hand.

'The Chinese are here,' he said with quiet urgency.

Maggie sat up in bed, throwing off her blanket. 'Where?'

'Outside the front door. Quickly, we have very little time.'

TWENTY-FOUR

The young monk, Yulu, took them along a narrow corridor and down a flight of stone steps at the back of the monastery. Faintly, in the distance, the sound of someone hammering on the main doors was just audible.

'This way,' Yulu said.

He passed through an archway, moving swiftly along another dark passageway, his butter lantern only just bright enough to light the way. It was icy cold and through one of the high windows Maggie caught a fleeting glimpse of the snow on the mountainside above the *gompa* glistening in the moonlight.

Yulu unlocked a heavy wooden door. Beyond it was another flight of steps going deep into the cellars beneath the monastery. They followed Yulu down, their footsteps echoing off the massive stone blocks of the stairwell, and came out into a long subterranean chamber.

'Be careful here,' Yulu warned them.

The walls and floor of the chamber were coated with a thin film of ice as if the stone had been painted with translucent gloss varnish. They picked their way cautiously across the flags to the far end of the cellar where a pile of rubble was heaped against the wall. Yulu scrambled up the rubble and leaned his shoulder against one of the stone blocks near the top of the wall. It swung outwards with a sharp scraping sound, like nails on slate. He beckoned to them, holding up his lantern to illuminate the hole.

'Quickly, go inside. You will be safe here. This chamber is

known only to the *kenpo*, the senior lama and me. Hurry!'

Tsering ducked his head and crawled through the opening. On the other side was a crude staircase made of rough-hewn boulders. He climbed down them into another chamber, much smaller than the first, whose walls were not dressed stone but the bare bedrock of the mountain itself. Pema came down after him, then Maggie and Lobsang with the lantern Yulu had given him. The stone hatch scraped shut and the darkness closed in around them with the cold, clammy touch of a sarcophagus.

The abbot stood in the vaulted entrance hall of the monastery, his hands folded together at his waist, the cloak around his shoulders flapping as a gust of wind blew in through the open door. He watched the Han come in, stamping the snow off their boots, their breath rising in a mist of fine vapour. There were seven of them. They looked cold and tired and belligerent. Their leader, a slight figure with a pock-marked face, stepped forward. The abbot had seen enough policemen to recognise the insignia of a *Gong An Ju* major. The abbot bowed and murmured a greeting in Tibetan.

'You speak Chinese?' Chang demanded, glancing around the hall. Painted *thangkas* of Buddhist deities and strings of coloured prayer flags were suspended from the walls.

'I spent twenty-eight years in your prisons,' the abbot replied in fluent Mandarin. 'Yes, I speak your language.'

Chang's gaze came back and settled on the inscrutable face of the *kenpo*.

'We are looking for four fugitives. Two men and two women. One of the women has a baby with her.'

'It is early, Major,' the abbot said. 'Let me offer you and your men some tea.' The abbot gestured with a bony hand. 'This way, please. The kitchen is much warmer than here.'

'We don't want tea,' Chang snapped. 'Have you seen the fugitives?'

The abbot took his time replying. He'd learned to counter the aggression of the Han with a slow, exaggerated politeness.

It seemed to annoy the Chinese much more than outright hostility.

'Two men, and two women, you say?'

'Yes,' Chang said impatiently.

'You think they are here? In the monastery?'

'Don't mess with me, old man. Have you seen them?'

The abbot pulled his cloak across his chest to keep out the cold air.

'No, we have seen no fugitives,' he said calmly.

Chang regarded him with a cool detachment. The Tibetans were all liars; and monks, for all their vows, were the worst of the lot. Chang didn't know whether the abbot was telling the truth, but it was wise to assume he wasn't. If he'd spent twenty-eight years in jail, he was obviously a troublemaker of the first order.

The major lifted his arm to call the commando sergeant forward.

'Search the place.'

The rock chamber was larger than it had first appeared. It stretched back ten or fifteen metres into the mountain, but most of the space was taken up by dusty wooden chests and stone sculptures. Tsering took the butter lantern and had a closer look at some of the artefacts. There were beautifully carved pillars and stone plinths, ornate mirrors and silver candelabra and, beneath a cotton sheet, a gilt statue of the Buddha encrusted with precious jewels. They must have been hidden away decades earlier, Tsering guessed. The Red Guards were notorious for their excesses, but the desecration of the monasteries had begun long before the Cultural Revolution. From the moment the Chinese invaded, they'd instigated a concerted campaign of looting, stripping the monasteries of their treasures and shipping them back to China to be melted down or sold to wealthy collectors on the international market. That the monks here had managed to save so much was a wonder.

'Tsering.'

It was Lobsang who'd spoken. Tsering turned round.

'I can hear something.'

Tsering listened. At first there was nothing. Then he heard it: a faint shout that sounded a long way off until he realised it was closer, but muffled by the thick stone wall. Someone was in the cellars.

Tsering snuffed out the butter lantern. The chamber seemed solid enough, but light had a tendency to find and escape through even the tiniest chink. The darkness was overwhelming. Tsering could see nothing, not even the shadow of his hand as he passed it in front of his face. But his other senses were keener now. He could smell the musty air, the atmosphere of damp and decay. And he could hear more acutely than before.

There were voices on the other side of the wall, the occasional scuff of a boot. They seemed terrifyingly close. Tsering couldn't make out any of the words, but they had the harsh, sing-song intonation of Chinese. Another sound intruded. A sound much nearer. The whimper of a baby. Tsering turned towards the noise.

'Stop him,' he hissed under his breath.

He heard a rustle of clothing, guessed that Pema was unfastening her *chuba*, pressing the baby to her breast. The whimpering stopped.

They waited. The voices seemed to have gone. Unless they too were waiting, listening. Tsering could feel his breath dry in his mouth, hear every exhalation. He counted to sixty, trying to calm his throbbing heart. Then another sixty. As he began a third minute, he heard the voices again. A long way off this time, down at the other end of the cellars. He waited a further five minutes before rummaging in his bag for some matches and relighting the butter lantern.

Chang waited alone for his men in the kitchen. As the abbot had said, it was warmer there than elsewhere in the monastery. He stood by the stove, letting the heat dry off his wet boots and trousers. He'd found a loaf of bread on the table and was chewing a piece of it pensively. How long did it take to search a place this size? The commandos were taking their time. Chang suspected they were dragging it out to avoid having to go back outside into the snow.

He heard the door open and turned round, expecting it to be his sergeant coming back to report. But it wasn't the sergeant. It was a weasel-faced monk with a shifty, yet somehow ingratiating manner. Chang told him to get out, but the monk remained where he was.

'Major,' he began, 'there's something you should know.'

The monks filed slowly into the *dukhang* – the prayer hall – of the monastery. The high, pillared chamber was in darkness except for a row of butter lamps which were burning dimly in front of a statue of the Buddha. Sticks of incense smouldered in two silver chalices on either side of the altar, filling the chapel with their perfume.

The abbot stood at the front, watching the monks come in, their faces puzzled, a little anxious as they saw the *Gong An Ju* commandos lined up by the door. The abbot caught Yulu's eye as he walked past and nodded discreetly. Yulu acknowledged the signal without moving his head. When he reached the far side of the chamber and the monks in front of him began to snake back to take up their places on the floor, Yulu slipped behind one of the massive stone columns. He stood there until there was a wall of monks to shield his movements, then eased back a thick brocade curtain covering a hidden archway and slid behind it. Even the abbot, watching out of the corner of his eye, didn't notice him go.

Chang waited until the monks were all assembled, sitting cross-legged on the floor now, before he stepped out to the front and placed himself next to the abbot. He let his gaze rove over the rows of upturned faces, giving the monks a moment to reflect on why they might have been dragged from their beds in the middle of the night.

'You are sheltering fugitives here,' he said. 'Enemies of the people. That is a serious offence. A capital offence. I know they are here. I will give you exactly one minute to tell me where they are.' Chang snapped open the leather holster on his belt and withdrew his pistol. 'If you refuse to cooperate, I will shoot the abbot.'

They heard someone scramble up the pile of rubble on the other side of the wall, then the stone block scraped open and Yulu's head appeared. He held up a butter lantern near his face, looking down at them with wide, fearful eyes.

'Quickly,' he said. 'We must go.'

Chang watched the second hand of his watch tick round, then looked up at the assembly of monks. They were staring intently towards the front of the prayer hall, not at him, but at the abbot standing a few feet away. It was at that moment that Chang realised they were going to call his bluff. Something in their manner, the set of their faces, told him that they would take their lead from the abbot and the abbot was not a man who was going to break. Chang admired discipline and obedience. They were very Chinese virtues. But in the Tibetans he regarded them not as virtues, but as acts of rebellion.

The second hand ticked round towards the minute. Chang had not made his threat lightly, nor without due consideration of its consequences. A strong man never made threats unless he was prepared to carry them out. But that didn't mean he didn't wish it otherwise.

'Your time is up,' he said. He turned to the abbot. 'Well?'

'You have your answer,' the abbot replied impassively.

Chang looked at him curiously, trying to gain some insight into the old man's mind.

'Why?' he said.

'You are a stranger in our land,' the abbot said. 'You will never understand.'

'I do what needs to be done. You may resist all you like, but in the end we will crush you.'

'Will you?'

The abbot's quiet defiance angered Chang. 'Kneel down,' he ordered.

The abbot shook his head. 'Never again will I kneel before the Han.'

Chang shot a glance at his men. Two of the commandos stepped forward and forced the abbot to his knees.

'For the last time, where are the fugitives?' Chang said.

The abbot turned his head to look at the statue of the Buddha. His lips were moving in a silent mantra, his fingers counting off the beads of the rosary he held in his hands. There was no fear in his face, just the serenity of a man at peace with his conscience.

Chang waited a second. Then raised his pistol.

They were outside at the back of the monastery, making their way through the maze of ruined buildings, when they heard the shot. Yulu froze and looked back towards the chapel. He listened, waiting for more shots, but none came.

Tsering touched his arm. 'We should go,' he said.

Yulu roused himself from his trance and nodded at Tsering. 'This way.'

The abbot's body lay curled up on the floor of the prayer hall as if he were sleeping. A pool of blood, dark and viscous like oil, glistened on the stone flags by his head. The pungent smell of cordite mingled with the scent of incense.

'I will kill one monk at a time until someone tells me where the fugitives are,' Chang said. 'Who's going to be first?'

The silence was so intense that the flickering of the flames of the butter lamps was audible. Then, as if their minds were all one, the monks stood up simultaneously. They came forward in a solid mass, heads up, proud and defiant, awaiting their turn.

Chang stepped back involuntarily, his fingers tightening around his pistol. His face felt as if it were burning under the glare of the monks' unswerving gazes. He turned away angrily, searching for his sergeant.

'Go over the place again,' he shouted. 'Check the walls, the floors, everything.'

He jammed his pistol back in its holster and strode quickly out of the hall.

Where the shattered remains of the monastery's perimeter walls lay buried in the deep drifts of snow, Yulu led them down off the slope of the mountain and south-west up the valley. After half an hour's strenuous walking they came to the mouth of a gorge which branched off the main valley. They turned into it. The steep, rocky sides closed in around them almost immediately. There were caves high up in the cliffs and a stream below them whose surface was glassy with a crust of thick ice.

The gorge ran deep into the mountain, becoming progressively narrower until it ended in a sheer wall of rock. A waterfall which flowed down the wall had frozen solid, forming an opaque curtain of ice a few metres across. Tsering looked around. On three sides they were surrounded by vertical cliffs. Unclimbable cliffs.

'This is a dead end,' he said. 'What are we doing?'

Without replying, Yulu clambered up on to a low rock shelf at the base of the gorge and disappeared behind the frozen waterfall. The others followed and found themselves in a small, wintry cave. There was a sheen of ice on the sides and gleaming icicles hanging from the roof like shark's teeth.

Maggie fumbled in her bag and produced her torch. She clicked it on. Yulu squinted in the sudden light, turning away and heading deeper into the cave.

'Follow me,' he said.

A narrow opening had been hacked into the back wall of the cave. They squeezed through it, emerging into a tiny chamber only just big enough to accommodate them all. Yulu pointed upwards. Maggie's torch flickered over the roof, picking out a vertical cleft in the rock. Embedded in one side of the cleft was a series of rusty iron rungs like a ladder.

'The monks built these back in the Fifties,' Yulu said. 'In

case they needed an escape route to the frontier. They bring you out at the top of the waterfall. But be careful. They may be slippery.'

'How far is the frontier now?' Tsering asked.

'A day's walk. When the sun comes up you will see the Dong-dre La pass in the distance.'

'You're not coming with us?'

'I must return to the monastery. I am needed there. May the Lord Buddha be with you.'

Tsering grasped the lowest rung of the ladder and started to climb.

Chang pulled open the heavy wooden front door of the monastery and watched the sun come up over the mountains. The *gompa* faced due east – that was the origin of its name, Se-po Thorang, Golden Dawn – and the first rays were already beginning to glow on the top of the high frontage, warming the stones with their muted grey light. Chang studied the horizon, noting the mist beginning to lift, a tiny patch of clear sky seeping through. It was still cold, but it had stopped snowing. The landscape before him was white and smooth and silent, not a mark or a blemish to be seen. There was nothing aesthetic about the major's gaze. The beauty of the sunrise was of no interest to him. He was looking to see if the weather was going to be good enough to get a helicopter into the air.

He pushed the door shut and walked back across the entrance hall. The sergeant was coming towards him down the corridor from the kitchen.

'Well?' Chang demanded impatiently.

'Nothing so far, Comrade Major. We've searched most of the rooms again. I've sent two men to check outside in the ruins.'

'Where's the radio operator?'

'In the cellars.'

'Get him up here. I want to contact Lhasa.'

The sergeant turned, but before he'd gone two metres, one of his men came running into the hall.

'At the back, Comrade Major,' he said breathlessly. 'We've found footprints in the snow.'

They emerged through another cave at the top of the waterfall, a natural opening which tool marks in the rock showed to have been enlarged by man. They were in a broader valley hanging above the gorge they'd just left. The sides were less steep, less oppressive. The valley was open to the sky which was turning pale blue in the hazy dawn.

They followed the course of the frozen stream for a kilometre or more, then began to climb gradually around the flank of the mountain on the western side of the valley. They looked ahead and, as Yulu had predicted, could see the notch in the range that was the Dong-dre La, the Devil's Pass.

Tsering paused, breathing heavily, his eyes lifted to the line of ice-capped peaks that filled the horizon. On the other side, just a few hours' walk away, was India.

The footprints turned off into a narrow gorge. Chang stopped, studying the escarpments high above them. Once they entered the gorge, he knew that the radio reception, already poor, would disappear entirely.

'Try Lhasa again,' he said.

The radio operator swung the transmitter off his back and set it up on the ground. He slipped headphones on to his ears and fiddled with the dials on the radio. It was several minutes before he said: 'I have them, Comrade Major. Do you wish to speak to them yourself?'

'Give them our position. Tell them I want a helicopter down here immediately.'

The radio operator relayed the message, then listened for a moment before turning back to Chang.

'There is mist over Lhasa. All helicopters are grounded.'

'Give it here.'

Chang snatched the headphones and microphone from the radio operator.

'This is Major Chang,' he barked. 'Grounded until when?

What's the forecast for later? What about Gonggar? What's the weather like there? Well, find out. I need a helicopter down here now. I have Colonel Shen's full authority, check with his office. This is important, you understand? Yes, do that.'

Chang ripped the headphones off and tossed them back to the radio operator.

'Stay tuned in. They'll come back to us later.'

Chang turned into the gorge, following the footprints in the snow. On the cliff above them, crouching behind a boulder, Yulu watched them go.

Slowly, the Dong-dre La came nearer. From a distance, the pass had looked like just another break in the mountains. But now they were close enough to see the high jagged pillars of rock that stood guard like sentinels on its eastern flank, their walls descending precipitously into the deep corrie below. Only the western flank was passable. The path climbed steeply up it, no more than a narrow line cut into the slope of the mountain which rose in snow-covered tiers until its top was chopped off by the clouds.

A few hundred metres below the highest point of the pass was the Chinese border post, a small, vulnerable concrete block built precariously next to the path. There was snow on its sheet-iron roof and deep drifts piled against its walls so that only its windows were visible, a pair of dark holes that glared out over the valley like gun barrels.

Tsering led the way, trudging wearily through the soft snow, glancing round at intervals to make sure the others were still with him. It was warming up. The sun was just peeping over the peaks to the east, though most of the ground was still in shadow. Ahead of them, oozing out from the mouth of the corrie in a broad mottled river of ice, was the glacier they had to cross.

Chang looked around with a puzzled frown. The rock walls were smooth and sheer. Experienced mountaineers with the right equipment could have climbed them, but surely not a couple of monks and two women, one of them with a babe in arms. So where had they gone? The frozen waterfall he dismissed with a brief glance. There was no way anyone, mountaineer or not, was going to climb up that. So if they hadn't retraced their steps back down the gorge – and their footprints indicated they hadn't – then they must have found some other way out of the dead end.

There was a rock ledge at one side of the waterfall. Chang noticed the snow had been brushed off the top of it. He scrambled up and saw the gap behind the waterfall.

'Up here,' he said to the sergeant. 'Give me a flashlight.'

The cave was small, easy to explore. In a matter of minutes Chang had found the opening in the back wall, the chamber beyond. There appeared to be no way out. Then Chang shone the flashlight upwards and saw the iron rungs in the rock.

The wind picked up as they climbed higher, whipping the snow up into clouds that blasted their faces with icy particles. They narrowed their eyes to protect them, cupping their hands around their faces in an effort to fend off the stinging spray.

The path became harder to see. They slowed to a cautious shuffle. Below them, the slope dropped away a thousand feet to the valley floor – not a sheer drop, but if you fell it wouldn't make much difference. They came to a rock spur that jutted out from the mountainside. The path went round the spur on a narrow ledge. Tsering hesitated. This was a perilous traverse. Common sense dictated that they shouldn't even begin to attempt it. But they had no choice if they wanted to reach the pass.

'Watch your step,' he shouted at Pema who was just behind him. 'Let me go first to test the path. Only follow me when I say it's safe. Do you understand?'

Pema gave an anxious nod, her gaze fixed intently on Tsering. She'd let herself be led by these men, these monks. The only way she could cope with the terrors of the journey was to trust them implicitly, to abrogate all responsibility for her own safety and leave it to them to take care of her.

Tsering inched out along the edge, moving sideways now with his back pressed to the rock wall. He could feel the ledge slippery beneath his feet, the wind swirling up past him. He wished they still had the rope with them.

He covered a few feet and stopped, holding out his hand to Pema.

'Take it,' he said.

Pema swallowed, but didn't move.

'Take it! I'll hold you. Pema, take my hand.'

The young woman stretched out her arm and grasped Tsering's hand.

'Now move towards me. Slowly. Make sure one foot is secure before you move the other.'

Very carefully, Tsering drew her to him. He could feel her trembling.

'That was all right, wasn't it?' he said reassuringly. 'The rest is no harder. Just do as I say.'

Together they crept out along the ledge, taking it just a few feet at a time. Then they rounded the spur and the path disappeared.

For a distance of about a metre there was nothing. A section of rock had broken away and in front of them was a drop into thin air.

Tsering stopped. He was short of breath. His heart was thumping like a hammer. He looked down into the gap. There was only space between him and the valley floor.

'I'm going across,' he said to Pema, trying to keep his own fear out of his voice. 'It's not far.'

He twisted round until he was facing the wall, then he moved along to the edge of the gap. Reaching across with an arm, he ran his fingers over the rock, feeling for a crack, a handhold of some sort. His fingers slipped into a narrow opening and held. The rock was icy. He could feel his skin sticking to the surface. He spreadeagled himself against the wall and stretched out his right foot, his body forming a cross over the gap in the ledge. His foot found the other side, slid a little, then got a better grip. He tested the purchase. It seemed secure enough. It *had* to be secure enough. He didn't dwell on the risks of what he was doing. He just went for it. His right hand digging into the crack in the wall, his right leg braced, he hauled himself across. His left foot fumbled for the other side of the gap, his left hand skittered across, slipping a little on the icy rock. Then he was over.

He took a moment to recover his breath before turning to look back at Pema.

'I can't do it,' she said.

'You can.'

'It's too far.'

'I'm here to help. Take my hand.'

'No.'

'Take my hand. Just like before. I'll pull you across.'

'I'll fall.'

'You won't fall.'

'No.'

'Pema, do as I say.'

Tsering reached back across the gap. Pema's gaze wavered.

'Don't look down,' Tsering shouted. 'Keep your eyes on me.'

Pema stretched out her arm. Her fingers entwined with Tsering's. He squeezed them and forced a smile.

'It's easy. Trust me, Pema. Now move to the edge.'

Pema shuffled along the ledge until she was standing right by the gap.

'Now step across.'

She shook her head. 'I can't. I can't.' Her voice cracked in terror.

'You can. Step across.'

'Please, no. My baby.'

'Your baby comes with you. Listen to me, Pema. You can do it. Do you hear me? You *can*. Now, after three. One . . .'

Pema shuddered. Her fingers dug into the back of Tsering's hand like talons.

'Two . . .'

She closed her eyes, held her breath.

'Three . . .'

She stepped out, felt Tsering pulling her across. Her foot touched solid ground. Then her other foot. Suddenly her boots slipped. She started to fall. She screamed. An arm came around her waist. A hard, muscular arm. She opened her eyes and saw Tsering's face a few inches away. His other arm came around her waist and she realised that both her feet were on the ledge.

Tsering was holding her tight. Pema looked down between them and saw her baby's face gazing up at them. She clung on to Tsering and began to sob.

Chang panned across the horizon with the field glasses, moving backwards and forwards until he found them. There they were. Four distinct figures, the monks at the front and back, the two women in between. They were only a couple of kilometres away, moving very slowly as if they were exhausted. Chang could see their faces, their breath steaming in the cold air, even make out the bulge in the Tibetan woman's jacket where the baby was hidden.

He adjusted the angle of the field glasses, tilting them up to find the border post hut on the Dong-dre La pass.

'Get on the radio,' Chang said, lowering the field glasses and walking on at a breakneck pace. 'Get me through to the border post. I want to speak to the officer in charge.'

The radio operator fumbled with his set, searching for the right frequency and listening through his headphones while trying to keep up with the major.

'We should stop . . . it would make it easier, Comrade Major,' the operator pleaded.

'Do it on the move. They're only just in front of us.'

Chang marched on relentlessly, the commandos strung out in a line behind him. The gradient and the altitude were hurting, but he was determined not to slow up for anyone. They were moving faster than the fugitives, gaining on them rapidly. But not fast enough, Chang estimated. Unless he did something, the fugitives would be over the frontier before the commandos caught up with them.

'I have the border post, Comrade Major.'

Chang came to a halt and took the headphones and microphone. The frontier guards in Tibet were PLA, but most of them were conscripts, not career soldiers. In theory, Chang had no direct authority over them, but he knew that he could intimidate them into cooperating with him.

The officer in charge was a lieutenant. He sounded uncertain, reluctant to take orders from a mere policeman like Chang, even a major.

'This is a joint PLA, *Gong An Ju* operation,' Chang told him. 'It is vital these fugitives are caught. They're just below you, nearing the glacier. I want them stopped before they reach the pass.'

'I'll have to check with the PLA regional command . . .' the lieutenant began.

'You'll check with no one,' Chang interrupted. 'Unless you want a spell in an army jail for gross dereliction of duty. Get some men down to cut them off immediately. You hear me, Lieutenant? *Now!*'

The glacier stretched out in front of them, a vast stream of ice that began at the head of the corrie and flowed slowly down between the steep rock sides, curving in an arc around a high buttress before sweeping out into the valley in a huge frozen cataract.

Tsering surveyed it, looking for the safest route across, then clambered down on to the surface. There was a covering of snow over most of the area, but in places the wind had blown it aside to reveal the ice beneath. He reached up and helped Pema down behind him, then Maggie.

'Be very careful,' he said to Pema. 'Try to keep to my footprints if you can. And watch for exposed ice. That's where it will be most dangerous.'

They went across in a line. The surface of the glacier was

anything but smooth. The ice was pitted with hollows and ridges and great crevasses several metres deep which they had to manoeuvre their way around. The sun was getting higher now, burning down through a clear sky. The ice was starting to melt a little, making it even more treacherous. Tsering stepped on a glistening patch and his feet shot out from under him. He fell heavily to the ground, the impact juddering through his body. Maggie was the first to reach him.

'You okay?' she asked, kneeling down beside him.

Tsering nodded, winded by the fall. He sat up, whooping for air, then slowly dragged himself to his feet, relieved that it had not been Pema who had slipped. If the young woman had an accident . . . the consequences didn't bear thinking about.

For close on an hour they edged tentatively across the glacier. As they reached the far side, Maggie glanced up and caught a glimpse of a line of soldiers disappearing behind the upper end of the buttress that partially concealed the path to the pass.

'Border guards,' she said to Tsering.

He looked up quickly, but they'd vanished from sight.

'Did they see us?'

'It's hard to tell. The buttress may have shielded us. But they'll be out the other side any second.'

Maggie gazed around desperately. 'Over here!'

She squatted down by a crevasse which cut in from the edge of the glacier. The ice river had split in two to form a crack about half a metre wide and two metres deep.

'In here.'

Maggie went over the edge, hanging by her hands and dropping into the crevasse. Tsering lowered Pema down to her, then he and Lobsang clambered in. They crouched down, the ice arching over their heads. There was moraine under their feet, sharp icicles against their backs. From somewhere came the steady drip of meltwater.

Maggie ducked under an ice overhang and crawled along

the crevasse to where it opened out at the edge of the glacier. Lying on her belly, she peered out warily. Six soldiers were crossing the narrow, snow-filled gulley that ran next to the glacier. They paused momentarily, then climbed up on to the ice.

Chang saw what was happening through his field glasses, but was powerless to stop it.

'Get the border post on the radio,' he said urgently.

'There's no reply, Comrade Major.'

'The imbeciles. They've left it unmanned.'

Chang increased his pace. He was going recklessly fast over the hazardous terrain, but he didn't care. He hadn't lost hope. He was fit, determined. He was sure he could catch up with the fugitives before they reached the frontier.

Pema was close to collapsing. She was used to the altitude, acclimatised to the thin air at nearly eighteen thousand feet above sea level. But she wasn't used to walking so far, in such arduous conditions. Physically, she was drained, but there was also the mental strain that was taking its toll on her body, sapping her strength.

Tsering and Lobsang had to help her up the last few hundred metres to the border post, supporting her as she staggered up the steep, gruelling incline. The monks, too, were exhausted, fatalistic about what lay ahead. There was no way round the border post, and no way back. They just had to hope that the guards had all left, that there was no one there. If there was . . . then that was their destiny.

Tsering pushed open the door of the hut and stepped inside. It was the warmth he noticed first, the heat emanating from the big bottled-gas fire which the border guards had left burning at one side of the room. The PLA didn't waste money on its border posts, at least not one as remote and insignificant as this. The walls and floor were bare concrete, the ceiling sheets of old, stained plywood, broken away in places to reveal the roof insulation. It was basically just a single room: a kitchen and dining area at one end, eight shabby bunk beds at the other. A more depressing, cheerless environment would have been hard to imagine.

Lobsang remained in the doorway, looking back down the mountain. The Chinese were coming up the path at a ferocious speed, the *Gong An Ju* major in the lead.

Without turning round, Lobsang said: 'How far is it to the frontier?'

'I don't know,' Tsering said. 'It's at the top of the pass.'

'A kilometre?'

'Maybe.'

'And all uphill. We'll never make it.'

Tsering stepped up to his side and followed his gaze down the mountain. The Chinese would be here in minutes. Tsering's shoulders slumped.

'So, they win after all.'

Lobsang swung round to look at him. His eyes had a steely fire in them.

'Not now. We're not giving up now.'

Lobsang pushed past him and gazed around the room. There was a wooden cupboard on one wall. It was locked. Lobsang picked up a steel-framed chair and smashed it against the cupboard doors. The timber around the lock splintered and Lobsang wrenched open the doors. Inside was a rack for weapons. Most of the slots were empty, but one rifle remained. Lobsang pulled it out and weighed it in his hands. He'd never touched a gun before.

'You know how to use one of these?' he said to Maggie.

She nodded. It was a Chinese Type 56 assault rifle, an exact copy of the Kalashnikov AK-47. How many AK-47s had she seen over the years? The guerrilla's favourite weapon, a rifle you could teach even the dimmest child to use in five minutes.

'Show me,' Lobsang said.

'What're you doing?' Tsering said incredulously.

'Take the girl and her child and go, Tsering.'

'And you?'

'I will deal with the Chinese.'

'With a gun?'

'What else can I use?'

'Your vows, Lobsang. What of your vows?'

'What do my vows matter at a time like this?'

'You are a monk.'

'It is permitted for us to fight for the right cause. No cause is more right than this. Now go.' Lobsang turned back to Maggie. 'Show me.'

Maggie took the rifle from his hands and checked the magazine. It was fully loaded. She showed Lobsang the lever on the right-hand side of the receiver.

'This is the selector lever. In the top position it's on safety, you can't fire it. The centre position is for automatic fire, but you don't want that. There are only thirty rounds in the magazine; you'd use them all in one burst.' She depressed the lever fully. 'It's on single shot now. Just point and squeeze the trigger. It's as simple as that.'

'It's ready now?'

'Yes.'

'Then get out. Take the girl and baby.'

'Lobsang . . .' Tsering began.

'Go, Tsering. Go!'

Lobsang went to the window and smashed the glass with the butt of the rifle. The Chinese were fifty metres away. Lobsang fired a shot, the recoil throwing him backwards. The Chinese came to an abrupt halt and scuttled for cover. Lobsang loosed off a few more rounds, not trying to hit the Han, just to keep them at bay.

'Lobsang . . .'

'Get out, Tsering.'

Lobsang turned. For a moment their eyes locked. They clasped hands. Tsering gave a nod. The words not coming. No words needed. Then Tsering broke away, heading for the back door of the hut where Pema and Maggie were waiting.

'Anyone hit?' Chang called.

'No, Comrade Major.'

They were grouped together behind a rock outcrop next to the path. Chang looked them over. There were six *Gong An Ju* commandos, highly trained professionals, and six PLA border guards including the lieutenant in command. The soldiers were callow raw recruits, poorly equipped and inexperienced. Most of them weren't even wearing boots. Their feet were clad in the thin canvas plimsolls the PLA issued to conscripts in warmer regions of China. A hopeless bunch. Chang could expect no help from that quarter.

'How many guns were left in the hut?' Chang asked the lieutenant.

'One, I think.'

'You're not sure?'

'No, Comrade Major.'

Chang shook his head in disgust. Who made this incompetent idiot an officer?

'Sergeant,' Chang said, 'I want blanket fire. When I give the word, we storm the place.'

'Yes, Comrade Major.'

It was rash, but they had no choice. While they were waiting there, the woman and the child would be getting away. Chang drew his revolver.

'Now!' he shouted.

The sudden fusillade took Lobsang by surprise. Unfamiliar with firearms, careless, he allowed himself to stray too far in front of the window. The bullet hit him in the shoulder, the force of the impact hurling him backwards on to the floor of the hut. His rifle clattered away under the table. He rolled over and stared at his shattered flesh, the blood soaking through his *chuba*, the pain so intense he was close to passing out. He knew he wouldn't be able to lift the rifle again, much less fire it. He sat up, taking his weight on his good arm. His vision blurred for a second, then cleared. He looked around the room, saw the gas fire still burning. Very slowly, he dragged himself across to it. There was a rubber hose connecting the fire to a cylinder of propane. Lobsang twisted round, his shoulder in agony, and wriggled closer. He paused, trying to stay conscious. He thought of the years he'd spent in Chinese prisons. He saw the faces of his friends who had not survived. He was tired of being a leftover. It was time to rest. He waited for the first Han to appear in the doorway, then kicked the hose off the blazing fire.

Tsering stopped dead as he heard the explosion. Then he whirled round and looked back down the slope. The border hut was in flames, the walls and roof blown apart, tongues of fire licking over the shattered remains.

'Lobsang?'

Tsering stared at the inferno, trying to locate his friend through the billowing clouds of smoke. Then, automatically, he started to run back down the path. He had to see, had to make sure.

'Tsering . . . leave it,' Maggie called, but he took no notice. He plunged down the hill, taking huge leaps through the snow, sliding most of the way. He was thirty metres from the flaming hut when the avalanche hit him.

An overhang above the hut, loosened by the force of the explosion, broke away suddenly and a torrent of snow and ice came sweeping down the mountain. Tsering was on the fringes, away from the full impact of the deluge, but he was still knocked off his feet and carried off the path. Over and over he tumbled, drowning in the barrage of foaming snow. He dug in his hands and feet, trying to slow his descent. He couldn't breathe, couldn't see, his ears were deafened by the roar of the cascade.

Then he felt himself slowing, managed to find an outcrop of solid rock to grab on to. The snow rolled over his back, but he stayed where he was, struggling desperately for air. He was crushed under an enormous weight. His lungs felt as if they'd imploded. He was going under, suffocating. His vision started to blur. He felt himself start to black out and with his final, waning breath heaved himself up from the ground, twisting round and punching his clenched fist upwards. His knuckles stung, the bones cracking as if they were broken, but his hand burst out through the snow and he felt the breeze on his skin. He scooped aside more snow, his head and shoulders breaking free. He rolled out from the icy debris and lay on his back, gulping in the blessed mountain air.

It was the explosion that saved Chang's life. Thrown backwards by the force of the border hut blowing up, he was out of the path of the avalanche when it tore down the mountain. He felt the ground shift beneath him, the vibrations shudder through his body, but the wall of snow and ice passed by, leaving him unscathed. His men were not so lucky. Those not killed directly by the hut exploding were engulfed by the avalanche and buried alive. When Chang finally hauled himself to his feet and looked around, he saw the bodies of two of the PLA border guards sprawled nearby, their necks and limbs twisted unnaturally. Of the others there was no sign. The border hut had disappeared completely beneath a mound of snow. Chang searched the ground for his pistol, flung from his hand when he was knocked over, but it was nowhere in evidence. It didn't matter. He didn't need a weapon. Summoning every last remaining shred of his strength, he started up the mountain.

Tsering didn't know how long he lay there in the snow. Five minutes, ten minutes, longer, he had no real recollection. He wasn't even sure he was conscious all the time. He was in a daze, his body bruised, his mind still reeling from the impact of the avalanche.

Then gradually, as if emerging from a dream, he became aware of a distant sound. A scream. A woman's scream. A cry for help. He sat up and glanced around, trying to clear his fuzzy head. The scream came again, from higher up the mountain. Tsering stood up weakly and paused for a second, swaying unsteadily. His *chuba* was caked in snow. He was shivering with cold and shock. He wanted to lie down again, to go to sleep, but he could hear the scream reverberating inside his skull. A distress call he had to answer. Sinking thigh deep into the loose snow, he clambered up the steep slope.

He found them near the top of the pass, where the path ran close to a sheer drop off the mountain. Pema was cowering in terror, her baby clutched to her chest, while Maggie attempted to fend off the aggressive assault of the *Gong An Ju* major. She was kicking out at Chang, her feet chopping at him. He took a blow to the side of the thigh but shrugged it off. Maggie backed away. Chang charged her, his fists swinging. A right hook caught Maggie on the chin and she fell over, but she wasn't finished. One of her feet scythed up, hooking Chang behind the knee and pulling him to the ground. By the time the major scrambled to his feet, Tsering was there in front of him.

The two men eyed each other warily. Tsering glanced fleetingly at Maggie.

'Are you hurt?'

'No.'

'And Pema and the baby?'

'Both okay.'

Tsering turned to look at Maggie, holding her gaze. 'Get them over the pass. Whatever happens to me, get them to Dharamsala. I'm relying on you, Maggie.'

'I'll do it.'

Tsering smiled at her. 'Go!'

He looked back at Chang. The major's pock-marked face was angry, determined. Tsering waited. It was up to Chang to make a move. Maggie and Pema were walking away up the hill. Chang glanced at them. They were slipping from his grasp. He had to act. He lunged at Tsering, grabbing him around the waist, trying to butt him in the face. Tsering toppled over backwards, taking Chang with him. They rolled a few metres off the path, down the incline towards the precipitous drop. The deep snow slowed their descent. Chang twisted away and stood up. Tsering was slower. He was on his knees when Chang's boot swung round, aiming for his head. Tsering threw himself out of the way, but the boot caught him a glancing blow on the temple. He tumbled over again and, sensing Chang moving in, rolled quickly down the hill. He felt the draught as Chang's boot knifed past only a couple of inches from his face.

Tsering dragged himself into a sitting position. Chang kicked out viciously. Tsering threw up his arms to protect his head, shuddering as Chang's foot thudded into his flesh. Tsering twisted away and scrambled to his feet, turning to face Chang. The major was breathing heavily, his lips pulled back from his teeth in a feral grimace. The cliff edge was only a couple of metres away now. They could feel the wind dragging them nearer to the drop.

Tsering kept his eyes locked on Chang. The major made a feint with his left fist, then swung his right. Tsering blocked it and punched Chang hard in the stomach. The major coughed and stumbled backwards, collapsing to his knees. Tsering kept his distance.

'You can walk away now,' he said in Chinese. 'Leave us to cross the frontier.'

Chang shook his head. 'Never.'

'Don't be a fool. Walk away down the hill. Let's end this now.'

Chang straightened up. Tsering saw pride and arrogance and hatred in the major's eyes and knew he had no choice. When Chang charged him, Tsering was ready. He dropped to one knee, ducking under the major's outstretched arms, then rising up quickly, lifting Chang off the ground. Tsering spun round and with all his strength hurled Chang out over the cliff. Chang screamed, his limbs flailing, then he was gone, a crumpled figure fading to nothing in the silent void.

Tsering turned away, seeing his own damnation in that one terrible action, feeling something inside him dying too. He walked slowly back up to the path. Maggie and Pema were up the hill, waiting for him. Tsering could not speak, but held out his arms and the three of them embraced. Then they walked on higher. At the top of the pass, they paused. They looked back one last time, absorbing the mountains, the air, the memories. Then arm in arm, the snow beneath their feet glistening like crushed diamonds, they walked down the hill into India.

EPILOGUE

McLeod Ganj, India

The sun was on the mountains. A white-bellied vulture soared on a thermal high above the valley. From the inside of the Tsuglagkhang Temple came the sound of monks chanting.

Tsering was standing in the courtyard. Maggie smiled at him. He was wearing a layman's *chuba,* his colourful woven bag slung over one shoulder. His hair was longer. He didn't look like a monk any more.

'So you're going back,' she said.

'Yes.'

'To Pangor?'

'Yes.'

'That's a brave decision.'

'I broke my vows. I killed a man. I am no longer fit to be a monk.'

'What will you do?'

'I will work my family's fields. Look after my mother. I can teach. I can do my bit to make sure our culture survives. You were right. What use is a life of contemplation and service in Dharamsala when my people are in desperate need of men like me?'

'And the Chinese? What will they do?'

'They will welcome me back with open arms. An exile returning to the glorious People's Paradise.'

'You're not afraid? After all the publicity?'

'What publicity? I have given no interviews, had no photographs taken. Tsering is a common Tibetan name. My face is on your tape, but one shaven-headed monk looks very much like another. No one will recognise me.'

'What of the child?'

'He will be well looked after. There are plenty of wise men here to guide him. I have done my bit.'

'It will be twenty years before he's old enough to lead. What will happen to the Tibetans in the interim?'

'We will survive. Our will is strong enough. We are a nation of survivors.'

Maggie looked into his eyes for a moment. 'I hope you'll be happy. I'll come back in a few years' time and film you again. You, your wife and children.'

Tsering gave a start. 'What makes you think I'll have a wife and children?'

Maggie smiled, thinking of a bright-eyed girl called Nyima whose name meant 'sun' in Tibetan.

'Call it female intuition,' she said.

'And you?' Tsering asked. 'When are you going to stop? To slow down and taste the air.'

'When they put me in a box.'

'You're famous now. Your face has been in papers all around the world, your tape of our search on television everywhere. What do you do after that?'

'One thing I know, I'll never run out of wars to cover. Maybe I'll write a book about it. I've had offers.'

'If you can sit still long enough.'

'Yeah, there is that. When are you going?'

'My bus leaves Dharamsala this afternoon.'

'You're walking down?'

He nodded. 'They offered me a car, but I prefer to walk.'

'I'll come some of the way with you.'

They walked across the courtyard. At the edge, Tsering paused, listening for the last time to the sound of drums and cymbals, of his brothers praying. Then they went down the hill into the forest. The path was shady, the air sweet with the scent of pine. They walked in silence until the temple was far behind them up the hill. Then Maggie stopped.

'I'll leave you here,' she said. 'I've got something for you.'
She handed him an envelope.

'What's this?'

Tsering opened the envelope. Inside was a thick wad of dollar bills.

'I can't take this.'

'I made a lot of money from the syndication of my tape,' Maggie said. 'You're entitled to some of it.'

'No, this isn't right. It's yours. You need it.'

'Life wouldn't be the same without an overdraft.'

He tried to give her back the envelope, but she pushed it away.

'Take it. For your mother.'

'My mother?'

'She isn't blind, you know. She has cataracts.'

Tsering's face lightened. 'She has?'

'Get her to a surgeon. Pay for an operation. I think your mother deserves to see her son again, in every sense. Don't you?'

There were tears in his eyes. 'Thank you.'

He opened his arms and they embraced, holding each other tight.

'Goodbye, Maggie.'

'Goodbye, Tsering. Good luck.'

She watched him walk away down the hill. A tall figure, upright, graceful. As he receded into the distance he got smaller. He looked now not like a man, but a young boy. A young boy making his way home.

Maggie waited until he disappeared from sight in the trees. Then she turned and hurried back up the hill. She had a plane to catch.

mL   2/07